INSPECTOR OVERBOARD!

Freeman Wills Crofts (1879–1957), the son of an army doctor who died before he was born, was raised in Northern Ireland and became a civil engineer on the railways. His first book, *The Cask*, written in 1919 during a long illness, was published in the summer of 1920, immediately establishing him as a new master of detective fiction. Regularly outselling Agatha Christie, it was with his fifth book that Crofts introduced his iconic Scotland Yard detective, Inspector Joseph French, who would feature in no less than thirty books over the next three decades. He was a founder member of the Detection Club and was elected a Fellow of the Royal Society of Arts in 1939. Continually praised for his ingenious plotting and meticulous attention to detail—including the intricacies of railway timetables—Crofts was once dubbed 'The King of Detective Story Writers' and described by Raymond Chandler as 'the soundest builder of them all'.

Also in this series

Inspector French's Greatest Case
Inspector French and the Cheyne Mystery
Inspector French and the Starvel Hollow Tragedy
Inspector French and the Sea Mystery
Inspector French and the Box Office Murders
Inspector French and Sir John Magill's Last Journey
Inspector French: Sudden Death
Inspector French: Death on the Way
Inspector French and the Mystery on
Southampton Water
Inspector French and the Crime at Guildford
Inspector French and the Loss of the 'Jane Vosper'
Inspector French: Man Overboard!

By the same author

The Cask
The Ponson Case
The Pit-Prop Syndicate
The Groote Park Murder
*Six Against the Yard**
*The Anatomy of Murder**

*with other Detection Club authors

FREEMAN WILLS CROFTS

Inspector French: Man Overboard!

COLLINS
CRIME
CLUB

COLLINS CRIME CLUB
An imprint of HarperCollins*Publishers*
1 London Bridge Street
London SE1 9GF
www.harpercollins.co.uk

This paperback edition 2020

First published in Great Britain for the Crime Club
by Wm Collins Sons & Co. Ltd 1936

A catalogue record for this book is
available from the British Library

ISBN 978-0-00-839315-1

Set in Sabon Lt Std by Palimpsest Book Production Ltd, Falkirk, Stirlingshire

Printed and bound in Great Britain
by CPI Group (UK) Ltd, Croydon CR0 4YY

Contents

CONTENTS

While in no sense a sequel, this book might be called a companion to my *Sir John Magill's Last Journey*. It dealt with one approach to Northern Ireland, this with another.

F. W. C.

1

As Pamela Grey Saw It

From the drive outside Pam's window there came a sudden crunching of car wheels on gravel, the squeak of a too forcibly applied brake, and a toot—in code—on the horn.

Pam started up, called 'Coming!' through the open window, glanced hastily at herself in the crooked little wooden mirror, hurriedly smoothed an errant curl, and ran down the steep winding stairs and through the narrow hall to the car standing in front of the door.

Though her expression had not indicated what she thought of her reflection, she had every reason to be satisfied with it. Pam was not exactly pretty, and she was not beautiful at all. All the same she was a sight to gladden tired eyes. The overwhelming impression she gave was of what used to be called wholesome. She was young, little more than twenty, with a small, finely formed body and movements graceful as a faun's. In her face there was character; intelligence in the broad forehead and the grey eyes which looked so steadfastly out on the world, a fastidious humour in the small mouth with its delicately

1

twisted lips, strength in the firmly rounded chin. The glow of health shone in her creamy complexion and her expression radiated good humour and the joy of life.

At that moment indeed Pam was looking her best. An eager excitement had brought colour to her cheeks and a flash to her eyes. It was evident that something thrilling as well as delightful was about to happen.

One cause, though by no means the chief, was that waiting for her in the car was her fiancé, Jack Penrose. For a year or more they had been engaged. At first it had looked as if marriage was very far off. Jack was not yet earning anything like enough to set up house on, and Pam's people were poor and could allow her nothing. But Jack's prospects were good and the couple had perforce to wait.

Jack Penrose, tall, fair and typically Nordic, was a budding solicitor. At present he was a clerk in his father's office in the neighbouring town of Lisburn, but he was soon to be taken into partnership and then a marriage would be arranged. Old Mr Penrose's business was prosperous enough, and there would be sufficient for the moderate establishment the two young people wanted.

All this had been the idea at the time of the engagement, but recently a wonderful vista had opened out before them, a vista so marvellous that at first it seemed wholly incredible. Indeed even now it still appeared infinitely too good to be true. Suddenly and unexpectedly there had come a promise of money. Not a little money—not even a competence. What was dazzling their bewildered gaze was the prospect of a vast fortune: wealth almost infinite: utterly beyond ordinary limits: staggering in its magnitude. And now the journey they were about to take would bring that wealth appreciably nearer.

Pam climbed into the rather elderly Vauxhall. 'When did you hear?' she asked as Primrose let in his clutch.

'Rang up half an hour ago. Said he was ready any time, but I couldn't get away before.'

'What did he sound like?'

'Oh, I don't know. Can't tell much about a chap from half a dozen words on the telephone.'

'Oh, yes, you can! What did he say?'

'Why just that: he'd done his other business and could come down when I was ready.'

'Sounds all right if that was the way he put it.' She paused, and then gave an ecstatic little wriggle. 'Oh, Jack, I'm so excited! I shall simply faint when I see him!'

'Nice way for an engaged young woman to talk about a strange man.'

'I'll just throw myself at him. I'll make love to him without stopping, all the time he's here.'

'If I see you as much as throw an eye in his direction I'll cut both your throats.'

'To think of all that's happened in the last six months! Isn't it just incredible? There we were and not a bean anywhere. And now! I can't believe it even now.'

'Haven't got it yet.'

'Fancy enough money to do anything we want! Just fancy! *Anything*!'

'Only money? What about a spot of matrimony?'

'Money of course! You don't imagine you matter, do you?'

Pam was intoxicated with the amazing prospect of wealth. But Pam could not foresee the future. She didn't realise that very often Fate offers her benefactions with her tongue in her cheek. They come as promised, but not alone. Some ingredient is added which robs them of their value. Pam didn't know that a day was coming—was even then on them—when she would have given everything she had if only she had never heard of the fortune or of any person or thing connected with it. She didn't know that instead of bringing joy and freedom to herself and Jack, the whole affair should grow into a ghastly horror whose memories threatened to stay with them during every remaining moment of their lives.

Jack Penrose and Pamela Grey lived in the little town of Hillsborough in the County of Down, that county which forms the south-eastern corner of Northern Ireland. It is scarcely a town as the word is understood in England, being little more than a collection of grey slate-covered houses fronting both sides of a single steeply falling street, with the church in the middle and the castle at the top. But though small, it is a town of honour in the province, for in the castle lives no less a personage than the Governor—or lived, till a recent fire necessitated his removal. Its street moreover is no mere village street; it is part of the main highway from Belfast to Dublin, and though the unhappy division of the country has reduced the flow of traffic between the two cities, Hillsborough still rumbles by day and night with cars and buses and great lorries grinding their way north or south.

Hillsborough is some dozen miles from Belfast, to which city Jack and Pam were now bound. The road is good, comparatively straight and level, broad and with an excellent surface. At that time, five o'clock in the afternoon, traffic was not heavy, the evening homeward rush having scarcely started. Jack made good speed and they expected to pick up their visitor and be back at Hillsborough well within the hour.

It was early in September and had been a day of gorgeous sunshine: if anything too hot. Now as they drove swiftly along Pam subconsciously feasted her eyes on the colours of the great trees beneath which they passed, dark with the full maturity of summer, but not yet beginning to turn to the reds and browns of autumn. The air through the open roof blew cool and pleasant on her face as she thought over the coming meeting or exchanged a word, half chaff, half earnest, with her companion.

How well she remembered that marvellous evening when 'the affair' had begun! As Jack threaded through the traffic of the Lisburn Road she pictured again the scene.

It was almost exactly six months earlier, at the end of February. She was sitting with her father and mother after supper, her father reading the paper, her mother knitting silently and herself with a book. She could remember every detail of the scene, her father sitting crosswise in his chair to get the light more directly on his page, the rubbed patches on the old brown velvet jacket he wore in the evenings, his two sticks placed within easy reach of his hand. She could see again the steel grey of the wool her mother was using, the dancing blue flames from the beech log on the fire, the luxurious abandon with which the large tabby lay extended on the hearthrug. And she remembered her own feelings of unrest and expectancy, of disappointment and of hope—not that she would have admitted these to any living soul.

Her worry was that Jack was overdue. He had promised to come in about eight, and it was now getting on towards nine and there was still no sign of him. Some question of amateur theatricals was to be talked over. They were doing *The Yeomen of the Guard* in aid of local charities, and she and Jack were taking part. The affair required a lot of discussion. Almost every night some point arose which had to be thrashed out. And until now Jack had never failed to turn up to do it.

Nine came and half-past nine, and then Mr Grey went to bed. He had been in the linen business, owning his own mill and being at one time quite well off. But he had met with an accident. His car had been run into by a lorry and he had been left crippled and an invalid. He had had to retire, and as the depression was then beginning, he had not sold his business to much advantage. The slump had played havoc with his investments, and now the family was tightly pressed for money. Had it not been for Mrs Grey they would have fared badly indeed. She took their financial cares on her shoulders and her unfailing cheerfulness made things run comparatively smoothly. She went to help her husband to bed and Pam was left alone.

Annoyed as Pam was by Jack's defection, she could not refrain from putting down her book and letting her thoughts centre on him. How splendid he really was, so straight and decent, and in spite of his being late tonight, how utterly dependable! Not too brilliantly clever perhaps, but such a dear! He was like a great dog, strong and brave as a lion, though perhaps none the worse for a little gentle suggestion as to the direction his energies should take. Pam smiled dreamily as she told herself that in future she should be the person to provide that suggestion. She could indeed make him do anything she liked, except where his 'not done' code was involved: then he could be as pigheaded as anyone. Never mind! She loved him the better for it.

Then at last at nearly ten o'clock came the quick step on the gravel and the ring on the front door bell. Pam had an urge to rush out, snatch open the door and fling her arms round Jack. But she restrained herself, deliberately even sat for a few moments before going to the hall. Jack must not be spoiled. He must make proper explanations and apologies before he could be received into full favour.

But Jack, when at last the door opened, was evidently thinking of neither of the one nor the other. Without ceremony he caught her in his arms and squeezed her to him, then planted a rather hasty kiss on her lips, put her down, and pushed his way in as if taking her joy at seeing him for granted.

'I thought you were coming at eight o'clock,' Pam said rather primly.

He brushed the suggestion airily aside. 'I know. Couldn't get away. Look here, Pam, I've something to tell you. Come out for a walk, will you? I can't talk here in the hall.'

She looked at him more critically. He was unduly excited. Something had certainly happened.

'You can come into the sitting room, I suppose?' she suggested coolly. The apology she considered inadequate.

He looked in and saw it was empty. 'Yes, I suppose so. Your father gone to bed?'

'Yes. Is it the costumes? Have they not turned up?'

He made a gesture relegating costumes to the limbo of the forgotten. 'Of course it's not the costumes,' he declared. 'Costumes!' he repeated in a voice of ineffable scorn. 'I've got something more interesting to talk about.'

'You're very mysterious,' she said thawing.

'It's nothing now,' he returned as he dropped into Mr Grey's arm chair and pulled out his cigarette case. 'But it's what it might become.' He held out the case. 'There seems to be no end to the possibilities.'

'Incidentally you might mention what you're talking about.'

'Isn't that what I'm doing? I don't think I told you, but two or three days ago I met M'Morris. As a rule, you know, I haven't much use for M'Morris, but this time he stopped and began to talk. Said he'd just been coming to see me to know whether he could interest me in a scheme that he was pretty much interested in himself and that he wanted some help with. He said if the thing was a success there would be pretty big money in it for all concerned.'

Pam looked doubtful. 'I never cared much for Ned M'Morris,' she declared. 'What's the scheme?'

'Something chemical: I haven't got the details yet. They think they've made some discovery that'll simply ooze money. But they want to do some more working out first to make sure everything's O.K.'

'They?'

'Yes, M'Morris and his friend Ferris. I've just been seeing them. That's what kept me.'

'And what do they want you to do?'

'Us.'

'Us?'

'Yes, it's you they want particularly. I'm only a cog: you're the mainspring that everything depends on.'

Pam was getting annoyed. 'For pity's sake will you explain the thing so that I'll know what you're talking about. What under the sun have I to do with it?'

'Well, you're a chemist, aren't you?'

'I've done some chemistry at Queen's, if that's what you mean.'

'They want a chemist to help with the experiments.'

'And what are you going to do? You're no chemist.'

'I'm to look after the legal side and the correspondence and so on. And I can give a hand with the experiments too if I'm shown what to do.'

Pam gurgled happily. 'A fat lot of use you'd be. "What's this muck in this jug? Well, let's shove in some of this bottle and see what happens," and the whole thing goes up in the air. I can just see you in a lab.'

'My legal advice is what is really wanted,' Jack said with dignity.

This time Pam fairly hooted. 'They may be fools, but they couldn't be as bad as that. Go on; tell me some more.'

'I don't consider your conversation at all seemly. It'll have to be dealt with.'

The discussion was interrupted while Jack took his tribute with kisses and Pam retaliated by boxing his ears.

'You were saying?' Pam suggested when the interlude was past.

'They want us to lunch with them tomorrow. At the Station Hotel. They're doing the thing in style. At this lunch they'll tell us the whole story. You'll come, Pam, won't you? Do be a sport and come.'

'Of course I'll come.'

So the fateful meeting was arranged.

Next day shortly after one o'clock Jack called with the car and drove Pam into Belfast to the L.M.S. Station. In the lounge of the hotel two young men awaited them with an air of subdued excitement.

Edward M'Morris and his friend, whom he introduced as Fred Ferris from the city of Newry, were contrasts in almost every particular. M'Morris was tall and thin, taciturn and of gloomy disposition: Ferris was short, stout and jolly. M'Morris was pale with long lank yellow hair and normal though undistinguished features: Ferris was swarthy of skin with thick dark hair and unusual ears, which had small well-formed upper portions and quite disproportionately long lobes. M'Morris if anything looked rather stupid and was evidently considerably under his friend's influence: in Ferris's little black eyes the sharp twinkle indicated a particularly wide awake and dominating mind. Both seemed a trifle ill at ease and were obviously on their best behaviour.

Though M'Morris had never been a special friend of Pam or Jack, they had known him for years. He lived about a mile from Hillsborough in the direction of Glenavy. He was, like them, a member of several of the local organisations, the tennis and badminton clubs and the dramatic society, and they had met at the houses of mutual friends. He was a technical assistant on the staff of Messrs Currie & M'Master, the analytical chemists, of Howard Street, Belfast. So much Pam knew, and after what Jack had told her, she was not greatly surprised when Ferris was introduced as another technical assistant in the same firm. He, it came out in the course of conversation, was unmarried and lived in rooms in Belfast.

After cocktails they went in to lunch. The brunt of the conversation fell on Ferris and Jack. M'Morris had not much to say, and what he did say had rather the effect of bringing the efforts of the others to a standstill. Pam was not quite at her ease. She felt a little distrustful of the whole affair, and she feared she might be let in for something she would dislike.

The business of the meeting was not mentioned till lunch was over and they were sitting over coffee in a corner of the deserted upstairs writing room. Then M'Morris opened the ball.

'I told Penrose last night, Miss Grey, that Ferris had made a chemical discovery and we think it is one of the most important made in this century. But I think he could tell you about it better himself, so I suggest he does so.'

'Lazy pig,' said Ferris with a slightly deprecating smile and his black eyes snapped with excitement, 'you might occasionally do something for your keep.' Then to Pam. 'Well, if he won't tell you, Miss Grey, I will. But that's right, what he says. We've made a discovery and we think it's a very big thing. For the matter of that, we know it's a very big thing. I don't want you to think it's complete, for it isn't, but if we could complete it, it would be one of the biggest things ever anyone got hold of.'

He paused, watching them shrewdly. Then as neither spoke, he went on.

'You'll be thinking I'm putting it on the high side. Well, I'm not, as you'll see when I tell you what it is. If we could get it properly completed there'd be more money in it than all the lot of us together could handle. More money than we could estimate. A fortune for everyone connected with it. Now see, here's what we want.'

Again he paused and again neither Jack nor Pam spoke.

'What we want,' he continued, 'is to work at the thing and see if we can't get it completed. But as things are, we can't, and you'll see why easily enough. We're not millionaires and we've got to live on what we earn. We'd like to get some help. We wondered if you, Miss Grey, and Penrose would come into the thing and help us on a share the profits basis?'

'How could we help you if we did?' Pam asked.

Ferris looked at M'Morris as if for inspiration. 'We thought if we could raise the necessary cash that M'Morris and I would devote our whole time to the thing,' he went on. 'There would be too much for two, and so we wondered if you would agree to work with us. We know of course you've done chemistry.'

'Not enough for that, I'm afraid.'

'Oh, yes, quite enough. I would fix up a programme of work.'

'And what about the spot of cash?' Jack put in.

Again Ferris looked as for help to his silent friend. 'We think that might be met. We think there might be someone found who would finance us, of course on the share the profits basis. However, let's leave that for the moment. Might I—eh—ask if you would feel disposed to come in?'

Pam looked at Jack. 'We couldn't say, could we, without knowing something more about it?'

'Ah, sure that has answered my question,' Ferris interposed swiftly, 'or anyway I hope it has. Certainly you'd want all details, and it was to give these we suggested this meeting.'

He paused while a waiter came in, glanced about him, and then disappeared with the coffee cups. It was very silent in the room, which they still had to themselves. The bulk of the hotel lay between them and the trains, and on a Saturday afternoon there was little more than an occasional tram passing outside the windows in Whitla Street. Pam glanced at the three men's expressions; Jack stolidly expectant, M'Morris anxious rather than sanguine, Ferris, master of himself and the situation and with his eyes twinkling more shrewdly than ever.

Whatever the result of the afternoon's deliberations, Pam

12

was enjoying herself. Whatever she was to hear, it couldn't fail to be interesting. And the prospect held out was alluring. She was fond of chemical work, particularly of research, and there was nothing she would have liked better than to join in perfecting some process, particularly if there was a chance of money at the end of it. She hesitated because—she didn't like to admit it even to herself, but she wondered whether she entirely trusted those two? Ferris's eye was very sharp, and he was very polite. Almost oily. Was he too polite to be quite wholesome? Then his voice interrupted her thoughts.

'There's just one preliminary,' he was saying with some slight appearance of embarrassment. 'You'll understand that the story is confidential. If a whisper got about as to what we're after, chemists over all the world would be tumbling over each other to forestall us. We're not wanting to risk that. I'm afraid I'll have to ask you to keep what I'm telling you to your two selves.'

'I promise, of course.'

'Thanks. And you, Penrose?'

'Wouldn't think of mentioning it.'

'Sure I know I needn't have asked. Still maybe it was as well. Right then, I can go ahead.'

He settled himself more comfortably in his chair and began his story, speaking with a certain amount of gesture and in a way that compelled interest and attention.

2

As Pamela Grey Saw It

'It was six months or more ago,' Ferris went on, 'that Currie, one of our respected principals, was reading a paper before some society and he asked me to do some experiments to illustrate his remarks. It was on polymorphism and he had—'

'Sorry to interrupt,' Pam broke in, 'but if you're going to be understood, you must translate. Jack knows nothing of chemistry.'

'I'm not a chemistry fiend,' Penrose admitted judicially, 'but if you can talk English, I'll understand it.'

'Right-o. I'll talk in words of one syllable. Polymorphism means that certain substances can exist in more than one form. We have, for example, water, steam and ice. Speaking roughly, all three forms are composed of the same elements in the same proportions, but some people think that the atoms of each have a different arrangement.'

'I can understand that,' said Jack.

'I wish I could,' Ferris answered. 'Anyway, several substances besides water occur in different forms, having

14

different properties. Many of these are due to different crystalline arrangement, when they are called allotropic modifications. I needn't go into it. There's red and yellow sulphur, for example, and many others.

'Going back to water, there's a fourth form, besides water as we know it, steam and ice. There's what has been called heavy water: water of the same elements as ordinary water, but with some of the elements in their heavy form. This liquid is heavier than ordinary water bulk for bulk. Its properties are different in other ways from ordinary water. Again I needn't go into it?'

'We'll take it as read,' said Jack.

'All I'm trying to make clear is that polymorphism or this change in the form of a substance is a common thing in nature and every year they're finding out more instances of it.'

'I did a little of that in my chemistry course,' said Pam.

'That's great. Then you won't have any difficulty in following what I'm going to tell you. Well, Currie had a theory about heavy water that he wanted to put up in his paper, and I was working on it. I needn't describe my experiments, but they were connected with passing various radiations through the water. I was working with a small quantity of water, about a tablespoonful, I should say. Ordinary water, I mean: not heavy water. I had the water in a test tube before I went for lunch, ready for me to begin work on it when I got back.

'It happened that day M'Morris had met some friends for lunch and they had got a bit jolly. You wouldn't think it to look at M'Morris, but it did happen. When he got back to the lab the idiot side of him was uppermost: and there's a good deal of it, though again you mightn't think it.'

'Shut up, you silly ass,' M'Morris grunted. 'Don't mind him, Miss Grey. There's not a word of truth in it.'

'All right, you were perfectly normal and serious in what you did. Not through any joke but in perfect seriousness, as he now tells you, it occurred to him that it would be a wise and intelligent act to remove the water from my test tube and substitute petrol, which he happened to be using to fill a lighter. You wouldn't believe it, but that's what he did. Might have blown the whole place sky high.'

'Rot! It couldn't have done any harm at all, that little quantity. I'm not saying it was a very high type of humour, but some of us thought it would be interesting to see what Ferris would do when he didn't get his reaction. Great new discovery in physical science made by Mr Fred Ferris and all that. Besides, see what the result has been.'

'No thanks to you that any of us are alive. However, we needn't pursue that side of it.'

'Take it as read too,' put in Jack.

'Well, I don't mind telling you that I was altogether done down by it. I got back from lunch and started on what I thought was water. And then I got the shock of my life.

'It didn't react as water should, but a pretty queer thing did happen. When the rays passed through it began to shrink. The volume decreased. It decreased till it was about two-thirds its former size.

'I couldn't make head nor tail of it. I kept the radiation on till all the shrinking seemed to be done. I thought I had somehow vaporised part of the water, but I hadn't seen any steam. Then I wondered if I'd got some new form of heavy water. You understand I'd never carried out the experiment in quite the same way before. Certain unusual features were present which I needn't go into. I can tell you I was fairly excited, but I decided to keep the thing to myself till I would find out more about it.

'I next took the liquid from the apparatus and began to test it to see whether it really was heavy water. I found it extraordinarily inert. It had neither smell, taste nor colour, nor could I get any reaction from it of any kind or sort. It was clearly not ordinary water, nor the usual form of heavy water, and I thought I had come on still another polymorphic form.

'Then I tried to repeat the experiment, and I was bothered worse than ever. I couldn't repeat it. I couldn't get the new liquid again.

'I puzzled and puzzled, but couldn't get any light. Then M'Morris's questions made me suspicious. He seemed to know too much. I pressed him till he admitted what he'd done.'

This story was quite unlike anything Pam had expected to hear. She was listening with immense interest, but still she couldn't see what was coming or where the tale was leading. Jack was obviously interested, too. The others were clearly delighted with the way the tale was going.

'You can imagine my next step. I tried again with the petrol and I got the same result as before. I was able to turn petrol into a new form, a new liquid I might say, a heavier liquid of smaller bulk, and so far as I could find, completely inert. Certainly it had lost all the properties of ordinary petrol.

'Though I didn't see then what this might involve, I swore M'Morris to silence, and when we could, both of us worked at the affair. We learnt a good deal about the stuff, its atomic weight, and things like that, but nothing more of real interest. Except this—that I was able to prove that what I had was a dimorphic modification and not a new chemical form.'

'By which,' Pam added for Jack's benefit, 'I presume you mean that what you had was still petrol, though in another form, and not some other chemical compound?'

'That's putting it absolutely correctly. Well, by this time I had begun to look at the thing from the practical side instead of considering it a mere scientific curiosity. And I soon saw, as I expect you've seen by now, that there might be simply tremendous consequences in it. The great objection to petrol was its danger. Petrol in the new form was inert and therefore safe. It could be carried and handled and taken up in aeroplanes in complete safety. Being smaller in bulk, it could be transported more cheaply.

'But obviously all these advantages could not be obtained if petrol proved to be monotropic. I mean'—he glanced at Jack—'if the modification could only be made in one direction. Ordinary petrol could be changed into this inert liquid, but that was no use practically unless the inert liquid could be changed back again into ordinary petrol. If it could, and if it could be done simply and cheaply, I seemed to see cars and planes filled with safe, inert liquid, which just as it reached the motor was changed into the power stuff we know. You follow me?'

Pam certainly followed him. She sat motionless, trying to take in the vastness of the idea, and rather overwhelmed by it all. Why, if what Ferris was hinting at proved possible, there would simply be no end to the profits. *Everyone* would use the new stuff. Probably it would be made illegal to take the old explosive variety on to a public road or to fly with it. A safe petrol was one of *the* things the world most wanted. She almost gasped as she envisaged the possibilities.

'Jolly fine notion, what?' Jack pronounced, obviously also impressed.

'Go on,' Pam murmured to Ferris.

Ferris was clearly having the time of his life. His face was wreathed in smiles and his black eyes snapped with delight. He had probably been looking forward to this moment for weeks past. He settled himself in his chair and continued in a slightly more consequential manner.

'You can imagine my next step. I again swore M'Morris to secrecy, and we began going back to the lab in the evenings and working at the problem. Then I thought that if we were found at this, my results might be claimed by the firm, so we scraped up some money and took a room and worked there instead.

'I needn't tell you what we did, the hundreds, the thousands of attempts we made to solve the problem. For five months we spent practically every evening and weekend in that cursed room, trying one idea after another till both of us were sick and tired of the sight of the place, and were getting badly knocked up. I don't mind admitting that I was considering giving up the job and getting what kudos I could out of reading a paper on what I had already done. And then, just a week ago, I solved it.'

'Solved it?' Pam repeated.

'Solved it!'

'You mean you turned the inert stuff back into ordinary petrol?'

Ferris grinned delightedly. 'That's just what I do mean. I've proved the stuff's dimorphic; I can turn it backwards and forward from one form to the other just as I want to.'

19

Pam gave a great sigh while Jack murmured disjointed congratulations. Ferris sat smiling and rubbing his hands, the embodiment of delighted self-satisfaction. Already he was beginning to taste the triumph for which he had worked so long. Even M'Morris looked happy.

'Go on,' Pam said again. 'Let's hear more details.'

Ferris's face changed. 'That's the best side of it I've told you,' he continued. 'That was the great difficulty, and it's been overcome. But I don't mean that the whole problem has been solved. Not by any means. There's a whole lot still to be done. If I tell you two further points, it'll let you know just how the affair stands.'

'It seems to me utterly wonderful,' Pam interjected. 'It's so big and far reaching. It looks like a glimpse into a new world. There's simply *no* end to what it may involve.'

'That's what M'Morris and I think. I'm glad you agree— gladder than you'd believe. Well, let me tell you.

'There are two further points, and one of them is as much for us as the other is against us. The first is that if you start the stuff changing, it'll go on doing it till it is all used up. I mean, suppose you have a litre of petrol. Well, if by radiation under special conditions you can start a cubic centimetre to change, you can cut off your radiation. The change will creep over the whole litre. It's like several other cases which you know. Take chlorate of potassium and picric acid powders. A drop of sulphuric acid will explode any amount of the mixture—not only the place where the drop falls, but the whole of it. The chemical change seems to creep from the point it starts at over the whole mass. It's the same with this. The point is that with a tiny initial expenditure of power, an infinitely great quantity of the stuff can be changed. That means cheapness.'

'I should say so,' agreed Pam. 'Do you mean in both directions?'

'Yes, in both directions. Once ordinary petrol is started to change, the whole volume will turn. And the same is true of turning inert into ordinary.'

'It's—it's overwhelming. I simply can't take it in.'

'Now,' went on Ferris, 'for the bad point—the snag. Once you start changing the stuff, you can't stop it—not till the whole volume is changed. It goes on in spite of you. I mean you can't change half of a litre. If you start with the litre at all the whole thing will go.'

Pam thought. 'But I don't see that that matters. Why should you want to stop?'

Ferris drew back and shook his head knowingly. 'As far as I see, it matters quite a lot. In fact, it matters so much that unless we can get over it we can't get very far with our scheme. You see, take an aeroplane. You change your petrol into inert stuff to carry in your tanks, so that if there's an accident there'd be no fire. Now, to use it in your motor you must change it back again. But you only want to change just enough for one stroke. You see? You don't want to change back all you're carrying. If you do, the whole advantage of the inert stuff is gone. But that's just what you can't do—so far. If you change enough for one stroke of the motor, say, in the carburettor, it'll creep back through the feed pipes and change all that's in the tanks.'

'And if that happened you might as well not have started in to do anything?' Jack interrupted. 'Yes, I've got that. Then what do you propose?'

Ferris moved uneasily. His self-satisfaction grew less in evidence. This was clearly not so congenial a part of the interview.

21

'Well, it's like this,' he said with a sharp glance at M'Morris. 'Suppose we represent the total work that's wanted to make this affair a gold mine by a hundred per cent, we've already done ninety or ninety-five. What I mean is that so much has been done, that comparatively little more should finish it up. M'Morris and I have worked at it on and off for nearly six months. If we could only get at it for a bit longer, particularly if we had Miss Grey's help, I believe a short time would do the trick.'

'Then why not do it?'

Ferris laughed. 'Food,' he said shortly. 'Food and lodging and a spot of clothes. I mean we can't carry on two jobs any longer—it's too much for us. And we can't afford to give up the one we're paid for. You can be pretty sure, Penrose, that if we could have worked the thing alone, we should not have invited anyone into it with us, not even you and Miss Grey. But we can't go on without help.'

Jack looked over doubtfully. 'I dare say Pam would agree to help,' he said; 'and I certainly would if I was any use. But I mean help with our hands. Neither of us can put up any cash. At least I can't.'

'I would help,' Pam declared. 'I'd love it. But, as Jack says, it could only be with my hands. I couldn't put up any cash. I haven't got any to put.'

Ferris made a gesture of understanding. 'You're very good, Miss Grey,' he said with some warmth. 'And you, too, Penrose. You're already giving us as much as we could expect: encouragement and an offer of technical assistance. But there was something else we had in mind; and, to tell you the honest truth, I'm not particularly wanting to mention it.'

Jack lit another cigarette. 'Get along,' he invited. 'We're here to hear the whole story, aren't we?'

Once again Ferris changed his position. Then he looked at M'Morris with a crooked grin. 'Your turn, old man,' he declared. 'I've been talking too much.'

'Just do your own dirty work,' M'Morris returned indignantly. 'You'll want the lion's share in the square-up. Just go ahead and earn it.'

The others laughed and Ferris, with some show of embarrassment, returned to the subject.

'We were thinking, M'Morris and I, that if we could find some wealthy man who was interested in inventions and so on, he might care to come in on this. There would be a certain risk, of course. He might lose every penny he put in. But, on the other hand, he might make a hundred per cent, perhaps a thousand per cent. And he wouldn't lose much if we did fail. Not enough to make any difference to him. Much less than many a man would put on a horse at one race. Far from doing us a favour, we should be giving him a chance that nine men out of ten would jump at.'

Jack grinned. 'But could he be made to see that?'

'I think so. After all, M'Morris and I are not altogether fools in the way of chemistry, and we'd be showing our belief in the thing by giving up our jobs—the only thing we have to live by. I think a reasonable man could be convinced easily enough.'

Jack shook his head. 'He'd be darned suspicious that you wanted some of his money for nothing, I'm afraid. Anyway, where would we find such a man?'

'That's the point—you've got to it now.' Ferris glanced quickly up, and his eyes almost crackled. 'We think we've found him.'

23

'You've found him? Who is he?' from Jack.

'Do we know him, Mr Ferris?' from Pam.

Ferris bent forward and spoke much more seriously. 'Yes, you know him, both of you. You know him very well, Miss Grey. You mustn't mind what I'm going to say. It's Mr Whiteside.'

'Oh,' said Pam, and relapsed into silence.

Instantly she felt a wave of disappointment sweep over her. She had at first and unwillingly suspected an ulterior motive—and here it was. It was not her chemical knowledge and help these two wanted, still less was it Jack's legal knowledge. It was George Whiteside's money. She saw now the true inwardness of the whole manœuvre. Jack was approached only because they wanted to get hold of her, and she was wanted simply that she might act as a channel to George Whiteside, so that they might get money out of him. Interested as she had been, she had never wholly trusted either Ferris or M'Morris. Now she saw that she had been justified.

William Grey, Pam's father, and George Whiteside were first cousins. Old Mr Whiteside had occupied a high position in one of the Belfast shipyards, though he had retired some years earlier. He was now far advanced in the seventies, though he was still hale and hearty. He was a rich man and certainly could do what Ferris suggested without feeling it. He and Pam were close allies. Indeed Pam was treated as one of the family.

The Whitesides, father and two daughters, lived at Carnalea, near Bangor, on the Co. Down shore of Belfast Lough, and Pam spent a good deal of time with them. Mrs Whiteside had been dead for some years, and the girls ran the house for their father.

For a moment annoyance and a slight disgust filled Pam's mind, then there came a reaction. She wondered whether she was not misjudging Ferris. After all, Cousin George was just the man to be interested in a thing of the kind. He had himself taken out many patents, and he liked nothing better than to be in the forefront of discovery and invention. And the amount of money Ferris wanted would be the merest bagatelle to him; he simply would not notice it. Even if he lost it all, Pam believed he would willingly pay it for the interest which the scheme might give him. And his life since his retirement was dull enough. It might indeed be worth putting the thing up to him. Besides, he was very far indeed from being a fool, and he knew something about chemistry. If these two hadn't a really genuine proposition, he would pretty soon find it out.

Pam was also impressed by Ferris's own argument that he and M'Morris believed enough in their idea to give up their own job for it. In these times of unemployment that was, after all, a fairly severe test. No, perhaps she had been wrong in jumping too quickly to a conclusion.

'And you want me to ask him?' she said at length.

'We wondered would you?' Ferris answered. 'You may think, Miss Grey, that our taking you and Penrose into our confidence was just a trick to get an approach to Mr Whiteside. Well, maybe it was. But you can judge of the proposition we want to put up. If you think it isn't a suitable one, then don't go further with it. We want to leave the decision entirely to yourself.'

This was straightforward and direct enough. She had judged too quickly. There was a lot to be said for the case Ferris had made out. But he was speaking again.

'Perhaps I should tell you what was in our minds about

25

dividing up any moneys we may get out of it. I thought—
M'Morris agrees with me—that if you and Penrose and
Mr Whiteside come in we ought to divide our profits into
seven parts. Two parts each to M'Morris and myself, and
one part to you other three. That would be subject to Mr
Whiteside being first paid back what he advanced. We
think it's fair to ask double shares for ourselves, as the
idea is ours, and because of all the work we've already
put in. But,' he smiled crookedly, 'we would be open to
reconsidering this if it be thought desirable.'

'It could only be reconsidered to give you and Mr
M'Morris a larger share,' Pam returned. 'No, I think that's
a very handsome suggestion. What do you say, Jack?'

'Quite all right. And I think they're right about Mr
Whiteside, too. He'd love it. You go down tomorrow and
ask him, Pam. Or I'll drive you down now.'

Keen delight shone in Ferris's eyes at this sturdy support
for his proposal. Obviously nothing could have pleased
either him or M'Morris better. 'That would be splendid if
Miss Grey would agree,' he said tentatively. 'If Mr Whiteside
could be sounded, we would be available to put up our
case at any time that he might arrange.'

'If he goes into it at all, he'll want to go into it at once.
I'd suggest your coming, too, but it might look as if we
were trying to rush him. Better stay near a telephone, so
that we can get you if you're wanted. Do you agree,
Pam?'

Pam thought the arrangement was admirable, and they
proceeded forthwith to put it into practice. She and Jack
left at once for Carnalea, while the others remained in the
hotel, so as to be in reach of the telephone. Whatever was

26

arranged with Mr Whiteside, Jack was to let them know without delay.

The Penrose car bore two excited people from the station out into Whitla Street.

3

As Pamela Grey Saw It

The short February day was already drawing to a close as Jack and Pam drove out along the Bangor road. It was fine with a clear sky, but a bite in the air suggested frost. There was but little traffic, and Jack drove quickly. They soon passed through the rather drab streets on the east side of the Lagan and out into the comparative country of Sydenham. Then came Holywood and the rich, well-timbered estates leading up to Craigavad. An occasional glimpse of the Lough, the tiny village of Crawfordsburn, and finally Carnalea and the turn to the sea.

They passed the railway at Carnalea Station and went on down the road to the shore. The Whitesides lived in a red brick house of many gables standing in its own ground, one boundary being the beach itself. The space between the house and the beach had been levelled and turfed, making a lawn with a couple of tennis courts in the centre. Low evergreen shrubs where the ground sloped down to the shingle made the place private, but left the view open to the sea. In summer the outlook over the Lough was

28

charming, with the ever changing colours of the water and the undulating line of the Antrim coast stretching from the dark square tower of Carrickfergus Castle to the bluff cliffs of Black Head and the Gobbins. On specially clear days the faintest trace of the far off Mull of Kintyre showed to the right of the Gobbins, an ethereal blue band above the hard black line of the sea. But in winter the view had to be paid for, when wild nor'-westers snorted in over a Lough of lead flecked with white, and masses of spindrift were carried across the grass and up to the windows of the house itself. Pam loved the sea in all its moods, whether it roared in its fury or, as it was now, dark and silent, though with a faint reflection from the still luminous western sky.

As they approached the door it opened, and a young woman appeared. She waved her arm.

'Hallo!' she cried. 'Good business! We're all alone, and were hoping someone would turn up. Tea's just coming in, and after it we might try the new ping-pong table.'

This was Dorothy Whiteside, commonly called Dot. Between her and her sister Daphne there was the same contrast as between Ferris and M'Morris. Dot was short, dark, energetic, and inclined to be stout; Daphne was tall, fair, thin and languid. As they invariably went about together, it was perhaps inevitable that the 'p' of Daphne's name should be turned into an 's', and that she should be called Dash. Dot and Dash made a formidable combination socially, and were in constant request by hostesses. Wherever games or dancing were to be found, there usually were the sisters.

'We'd love some tea,' Pam answered, 'but I'm afraid we can't stop to play. We really just dropped in for a minute to ask Cousin George a question. Some technical thing Jack's interested in.'

'Oh, rot. What's the hurry? Dad's in his room. Go and ask your question and then come back and have tea and a game.'

With the first part of the programme Pam was in full agreement. She murmured a reply and then moved on towards the library.

George Whiteside was seated in a deep armchair before the fire with a technical shipping journal open on his knees. Though retired, he liked to keep himself up to date in his former profession. He was a long-faced old man with a spikey nose and a clever, whimsical mouth. He loved a joke and the last word in an argument, and for relaxation read three detective novels a week. He greeted Pam and Jack jovially, but pointed out that they had come to the wrong room, as he didn't suppose it was to see him that they were there.

'Oh, but that's just where you're wrong, Cousin George,' Pam retorted. 'It's you and nobody else we came down to see.'

He pretended to be overwhelmed by the honour, adding darkly that he expected there was a reason.

'Of course there's a reason. Jack's legal mind, you know. You won't catch him doing things from impulse.'

For a few minutes they sparred amicably in accordance with the old man's mood, then Pam came to business.

'We've got rather an interesting thing to tell you,' she began with guile. 'It interested us, who are not scientific, but it'll simply thrill you. The very latest and most wonderful discovery, and we know the man who made it.'

Whiteside allowed himself a little sceptical chaff, but

30

Pam could see he was interested, and when she went on to say that she and Jack had been sworn to silence, and that he must pass his word before she could go on, she saw that she had him properly hooked.

'If you're sworn to silence, why are you telling me?' he asked.

'Because we're going to make you an offer. We're going to let you in on it—if you want to come, of course—and, of course, on terms. You'll find it the most fascinating thing you ever took up—far more interesting than that old stuff.' She indicated the shipping journal with a disparaging gesture.

The old man chuckled. He liked Pam and was pleased to have her come and talk to him. 'Ah,' he said, 'terms! What a weight of meaning there is in the word! You remind me of poor old Magee. You could see the point of his funny stories about an hour before he got there himself. And what is it I'm to have the privilege of paying for?'

'You won't get anything at all if you don't treat it more seriously,' Pam said severely. 'I can tell you you've no idea how important this is.'

'Absolutely correct. How did you know?'

'I'm afraid he's in an unpleasant frame of mind. Come, Jack, we won't waste our time on him. We'll go elsewhere with our offer.'

'Not if I know you,' Whiteside shrugged. 'Come on,' he added, resigned, 'let's hear the worst.'

Pam grew serious. 'Really, Cousin George, it's *the* most wonderful thing. There's simply no limit to the possibilities. There may be a dozen fortunes in it, besides the extraordinary benefit to the world. I just don't know how to begin to tell you.'

31

'Perhaps I can help you,' the old man jeered. 'What was the first you heard of it? Begin with that.'

'It was through a man called M'Morris, who lives at Hillsborough, that we heard of it. He met Jack,' and Pam told of M'Morris's tentative inquiry and invitation to lunch, the meeting with Ferris, the story of Ferris's discovery, and finally the suggestion that Whiteside might care to finance the remainder of the research.

The old man listened with an interest which grew keener as the story progressed. When Pam had finished he didn't speak for some moments, evidently thinking over what he had heard.

'Either of you know anything about these two fellows?' he asked at last.

'M'Morris and his people have been living at Hillsborough all the time we've been there,' answered Pam. 'I've met him at games and so on, but I don't know very much about him, really. Ferris I never saw before.'

'M'Morris has been there for ages,' Jack added. 'So far as I know, he's all right.'

'I note your overwhelming enthusiasm. Well, I'll tell you what I'll do. I'll go in to these fellows' room where they do their experiments, and they can show me the petrol changing. If it really does what they say, I'll finance them. What could be fairer than that?'

'Nothing, Cousin George. You are a dear.' She got up and impulsively brushed his cheek with her lips. 'When will you come?'

'Practical beneath the sentiment,' he informed a non-existent audience, though obviously delighted with his payment. 'I'll go now—at least after tea. Is that soon enough?'

'For that you'll get another kiss. Will you come with us?'

'No, there's a contributory negligence clause in my life insurance. I'll have M'Dowell and the Daimler. I suppose I can get back in time for dinner?'

They reassured him—on somewhat inadequate grounds, as they had no idea how long a demonstration might take. But Pam believed in striking before the iron began to cool.

While old Mr Whiteside was getting ready, Jack passed on the splendid news and obtained the address of the 'room'. Ferris and M'Morris would return there immediately and prepare for the experiment.

An hour later the inhabitants of Warren Street, a rather sordid backwater running from the Lisburn Road down towards the Great Northern Railway, were thrilled by the unwonted spectacle of the arrival at No. 46 of two large motors, one a scintillating Daimler with a real chauffeur in livery. Such an event had never before been known in the street, and the passing of the travellers from the vehicles to the house was watched from the pavement by an admiring circle of infants and from adjoining windows by their seniors.

Ferris was a good host and did the honours creditably. He was respectful to Whiteside without obsequiousness, and his politeness to Pam was tempered with just the right amount of familiarity due to a prospective partner. M'Morris silently seconded him.

The room proved to be a large attic at the back of the house, which was inhabited, so Ferris explained, by a railway guard. It was so full of chemical and electrical apparatus that there was little space for anything else, but by dint of piling a lot of their stuff into a corner, the two men had made room for three chairs, which they had borrowed from the guard's wife. The visitors sat down.

'What we have to show you, sir,' went on Ferris, 'can be done very easily, but you'll forgive us if at this stage we don't explain the whole of our method. If we are lucky enough to have you join us, we can then give full explanations. At present we want simply to show you what we can do.'

Whiteside nodded, and the others could see he approved the caution and the direct way in which it was admitted.

'We're also wanting to give you every safeguard against possible misunderstanding or'—Ferris smiled twistedly—'fraud on our part. I hope we're going to ask you to put money into this thing, so it's only your due. No feeling, of course; it's a matter of business. We propose, therefore, to ask you to supply the sample of petrol that we use. Here is a glass syringe, which you can see is empty. Maybe you'd ask your chauffeur to fill it from the tank of your car.'

This was quickly arranged, and when Whiteside had examined the filled syringe, he passed it on to Ferris.

'I now pour the petrol into this graduated dish,' Ferris explained, suiting the action to the word. 'You'll see that it's standing on one pan of a scales. I now get the scales balancing, see.' He manipulated. 'Now, I want you to please note the volume of the petrol; you can read it off on the scale.' He paused. 'Got a note of it? Good. Then I put into it what I call my plus converter, that is the converter that changes from ordinary or active petrol to inert. This is it.'

He took down from a shelf an apparatus of horseshoe shape from the curved portion of which an electric flex stretched away to a wooden box on a side table. A second flex connected the box with a wall plug. At the end of each leg of the horse shoe was a small square metal box. There was a space of about quarter of an inch between the boxes.

'In here,' Ferris demonstrated, laying his hand on the large wooden box, 'is a transformer which gives me the current I require. This current is carried down to the converter'—he touched the U-shaped apparatus—'and there I produce a certain radiation. This radiation passes between the poles,' he pointed to the metal boxes.

'I may tell you that there's more than the radiation in these poles. However, we needn't bother about that now. For the present it's enough that you should see what happens. Now please watch.'

He lowered the plus converter into the dish of petrol, supporting it by a lazytongs bracket, so that it did not touch the glass, but was suspended in the liquid.

'That's put the scales off, but never mind. You'll see it's all right later. I now switch on the current and see what happens.'

He snapped down the switch at the plug. Immediately a few faint bubbles appeared between the poles of the apparatus. But it was not upon them that the watchers' gaze rested. The petrol was shrinking! They watched it go down the graduated scale on the side of the dish until it occupied only about two-thirds its previous volume!

Ferris switched off the current, then raised his plus converter from the liquid. 'Steady,' he said. 'Watch the scales.'

On the removal of the converter the pans once again exactly balanced. Though the petrol had shrunk, its weight, as Ferris had said, remained constant.

Ferris then picked up the dish and handed it to Whiteside, asking him to smell it. The old man did so.

'Bless my soul!' he exclaimed. 'It has no smell!'

'No smell, no taste, no chemical power, no nothing!' Ferris declared in triumph. 'Look here!'

He lit a match and held the flame to the liquid. Nothing happened. Then he put the match into the liquid. It was immediately extinguished.

'You could pour that form of petrol over red-hot metal, as M'Morris and I have done, and nothing happens. It doesn't even vaporise. With it in one's tank there'd be no danger of explosion or fire if one's car or one's plane crashed. Would you like us to do the hot-iron test?'

'No,' Whiteside returned. 'I'll accept that. Carry on as you're going.'

'That's the first thing I have to show you,' Ferris went on. 'The second is to turn that lot of inert petrol back to the active stuff. The process is somewhat the same, but here heat is wanted, also. You may have noticed that that last conversion gave out heat? The dish was slightly warm after it.'

'Yes, I noticed that. And now you have to put back that heat as well as whatever else you do?'

'Yes, sir, that's right.'

As he spoke Ferris removed the U-shaped apparatus from the liquid and disconnected it from the wooden box. Then he took another horseshoe-shaped affair, not unlike the first, and connected it in its place, dropping the ends into the liquid as before. Beneath the pan of the scales he put a Bunsen burner, and in the liquid a thermometer.

'We'll have only to wait for a slight heat,' he explained, 'and there's a tiny loss from evaporation, which I'm ignoring. While we're waiting till it's warm enough I'd like to tell you just what still remains undone and what we should like to do about further research.'

He went on to point out what he had already told Pam and Jack—that the discovery was useless unless they could convert only a limited quantity of any given volume, that he believed this would be found possible, and that he wanted to concentrate on the problem. By the time the point had been discussed he announced that the petrol was warm enough for returning it to its original form.

Having put out the Bunsen, Ferris switched on the current. Immediately the liquid began to swell. It increased in volume till it reached that of the original amount, and when he removed the converter and the thermometer the scales again became balanced. Now again the liquid smelled of petrol, and when Ferris put a few drops on another dish and put a match to them, they flared up as petrol does.

The three watchers were convinced—utterly and absolutely convinced. Indeed, of all those present, Mr Whiteside had become the most enthusiastic. 'I'll finance you,' he declared warmly. 'I don't mind what it costs. Get ahead with it, the lot of you. If I was twenty years younger I'd help you with my own hands.'

The atmosphere grew slightly electrical. Ferris and M'Morris seemed overwhelmed with their good fortune, while Pam felt thrills of excitement passing down her spine. Even Jack fidgeted and grinned.

'What's the next step?' went on Whiteside. 'Let's hear you plans.'

Ferris and M'Morris exchanged glances, then Ferris answered. 'I'll tell you what M'Morris and I'd like, but of course you and the others may not agree. We'd like first to form a sort of small syndicate to develop the thing. We'd like to have proper deeds drawn up, and all sign them. We thought that we four would put in our labour and professional knowledge, and that you, sir, as you have so kindly promised, would put in the capital to keep us going during the research. For what we do in the future we thought we should all share the profits equally, but for supplying the idea, and for what M'Morris and I have already done, we suggest that we two are entitled to an extra share each. That is, divide our profits into seven parts, give two each to M'Morris and myself, and one each to you three.'

'That sounds fair. I agree. What about you two?' Whiteside looked at Pam and Jack.

'We agree,' Pam said promptly. 'If anything, it's too liberal towards Jack and me.'

'Very well. Suppose we instruct Penrose to get the necessary documents drawn up. That's to be his job, isn't it?'

'His principal job,' Ferris amended with a grin. 'There's no reason why he shouldn't help with the research when he has time.'

'Of course he'll help,' Whiteside returned seriously. He was enjoying himself now, taking the lead and giving directions as he had done in the shipyard before his retirement. 'Very well: that's our constitution dealt with. What are your detailed proposals for carrying on the research?'

'We've thought of that, too. There's a small cottage to be had by the week near Hillsborough. If we could get that I could live in one room and the remainder could be used for the work. It would be handy for the others, who all live close by. Water is laid on, but not electricity.

However, the distributing line passes the end of the lane, and a connection wouldn't cost much. Of course, electricity is absolutely essential.'

'Where is this cottage?' Jack asked.

'Near your gate. It's the first cottage in Sloan's Lane. That is,' he looked at Whiteside, 'it's on a lane off the Lisburn Road, about a mile from Hillsborough. It's a mile or a bit more from Miss Grey's and about the same from M'Morris's.'

'Is it a little cottage with four rooms and a porch and a holly tree just at the gate?' put in Pam.

'That's the place. I've been over it, and I think it would do all right, and it's not dear. In fact, it's the only place near Hillsborough that either of us have heard of.'

Pam nodded in approval. 'It would be convenient, because the buses pass the end of the lane a hundred yards away. And it's very secluded and private. We could work there without being overlooked or interrupted.'

Whiteside indicated with a gesture that the point had been sufficiently discussed. 'Well,' he said to Jack, 'you go and arrange its hire. Take it for six months. By that time you should know whether or not you're going to succeed?' He glanced at Ferris.

'I hope we'll succeed long before that, sir. However, nothing could be better from our point of view.' The others nodded their approval.

'Next item?' Whiteside persisted.

Again Ferris and M'Morris exchanged glances. For the first time Ferris hesitated and seemed ill at ease. 'Well, I'm afraid there are our personal expenses—mine and M'Morris's,' he said with a deprecating smile. 'What I mean is, we have to earn a salary to live on. If we do this

39

research we have to give up our jobs and our salaries stop. We shouldn't want very much, but we should want something.'

Whiteside waved this point away also. 'That's understood,' he declared. 'I shall make each of you an allowance equal to your present salaries, and any extra expenses that you may incur in the research.'

'That's very handsome of you indeed, Mr Whiteside,' Ferris declared, and M'Morris murmured his agreement.

'I think, then, that that finishes our business, and in a better way than we could have hoped. Unless any of you wish to bring up some other point.'

But this no one did, and the meeting terminated.

Jack then became immensely busy and important. He spent hours in looking up large and musty tomes in his father's office and in discussing with Pam draft clauses in which the words 'the said enterprise' figured largely. But from these fragments eventually evolved a formidable document tastefully typed in quintuplicate on vellum, to which, with a little ceremony in which a bottle of champagne figured, the partners of the said enterprise affixed their various signatures.

Jack also took Wayside, the cottage in Sloan's Lane, for a period of six months, obtaining immediate possession. Ferris and M'Morris left their firm and brought their Warren Street plant down to Hillsborough. There work on an intensive scale was begun. Ferris and M'Morris spent their full day and most of their spare time on the job. Pam helped nobly, putting in most of her day at the cottage, while Jack came in and did what he could in the evenings. Ferris had worked out a programme of systematic experiments, and these were carried out in regular order.

Occasionally Mr Whiteside drove down to give the activities his blessing.

At first Pam found it enthralling, but as time passed and no apparent headway was made, she grew tired of it. Ferris and M'Morris were also obviously feeling the strain. After two months they had a meeting, and decided that they were knocking themselves up. They fixed definite working hours which normally they would not exceed, and which gave time for reasonable relaxation and amusement.

After this things went better. They settled down to steady, persevering work, but dropped the killing effort to accomplish everything at once.

So passed another two months of intensive labour, but without registering the slightest advance. All still maintained a front of cheery confidence, but in Pam's mind horrid little whispers of doubt were now beginning to arise. They had nearly worked through Ferris's programme, and it he had made as comprehensive as he had known how. Suppose they completed it without having reached the goal at which they aimed? What would they do then? Had Ferris another string to his bow—a series of further tests as yet untouched? Or were they going to have to confess defeat?

And then one morning in the fifth month Ferris gave a cry of triumph. Pam and M'Morris left their benches and ran across the room. Ferris's excitement had grown so that he could scarcely speak. But a glance at his face was enough. It was clear that at last he had succeeded!

When he was able to talk coherently he explained that he had connected two vessels of inert petrol by a tube in which he had placed both his converters. He had found that switching on both produced the two petrol forms simultaneously, each in the vessel next its own converter. By this mean active petrol remained in one vessel and inert in the other, no matter what flow took place between the two.

This obviously solved the problem, as inert petrol in the tank of a car or plane could be kept inert, while that taken from the tank could be changed to active at the carburettor.

Though there was wild excitement and delight, including the drinking of another bottle of champagne with Mr Whiteside, all realised that they were as yet by no means out of the wood. The somewhat cumbersome apparatus had to be simplified and cheapened. The power required had to be reduced to what a car battery would easily supply. The plus and minus converters had to be combined in one small fitting.

However, success seemed to stimulate Ferris's brain. His ingenuity and resource grew even more impressive. One by one the difficulties were overcome, and by the middle of August the new apparatus was complete. It had shrunk to a small brass casting housing some not too intricate mechanism, which was inserted on the feed pipe just in front of the carburettor and which was supplied with current from the batteries.

Now Ferris metaphorically sat back and wiped his brow while Jack Penrose became the star turn. Directly success seemed assured, they had begun to consider the firm to which they would offer their invention. It had been realised that patenting would give away their ideas, and that manufacture could only be by secret process. Now Jack was entrusted with the preliminary negotiations. Communications passed, with the result that the firm of Wrenn Jefferson & Co. of Bristol and Avonmouth was provisionally selected as the most suitable. These people expressed themselves as interested, and Jack and Ferris then went over for an interview. The result was that the firm agreed to send their representative, Mr Reginald Platt, to Hillsborough to witness a demonstration of the new process. If he reported favourably the managing director and some of his staff would then come over, and if things still went well, a firm agreement to work the scheme under licence would be entered into.

It was to meet this Mr Platt that Jack and Pam were now driving to the Grand Central Hotel in Belfast.

4

As Pamela Grey Saw It

Belfast, more perhaps than most towns, has a well defined city centre. It is familiarly known as 'The Junction', and there its principal streets meet—Castle Street, Castle Place, Royal Avenue and Donegal Place, radiating respectively north, south, east and west. It was to The Junction that Jack headed, for the hotel was situated in Royal Avenue close by. He pulled in to the pavement opposite the door and asked Pam if she was coming in with him.

'No,' she said, 'I'll wait for you.'

Jack disappeared, and she got out of her seat in the front of the car and moved in behind, so as to let their visitor sit with Jack on the return journey. She felt thrilled and excited, though she told herself that this was absurd. Mr Platt was in all probability a perfectly ordinary individual. Except on grounds of common politeness, it didn't really matter whether or not he was pleased with his reception.

And yet did it not? He certainly had immense power. On his opinion, approving or condemning, might depend their whole future. If he approved, a sale of the process would almost certainly follow. If he condemned, no deal with Wrenn Jefferson would take place. Of course, in that case they would no doubt do business with some other firm. But even so, it would be a dreadful disappointment if this first deal were to fall through. Pam felt that she had been wrong. It was urgently necessary that this autocrat's first impression of themselves and the process should be favourable. She prepared herself, therefore, to be as nice to Platt as it was in her to be.

But Platt, when a moment later he appeared with Jack, did not look so very prepossessing. He was youngish, not more than twenty-seven or eight, short and rather stout, with a pasty complexion and a pair of sharp little eyes set close together, which did not squarely meet Pam's. His expression was rather unpleasant, and the hand he offered was soft and flabby. Pam instinctively resented the glance he gave her, and she instantly had a revulsion of feeling, a sense of disappointment, as if she saw that a pleasure to which she had been looking forward would be denied her. But she greeted him cordially, and in a moment the men got in and they started on their homeward journey.

Jack was never much of a conversationalist, and the burden of such talk as they had fell on Pam. She made the conventional remarks: Had Platt ever been in Belfast before? Had he had a good crossing? What did he think of the country? Platt replied pleasantly enough. She thought he improved on acquaintance. He had crossed the previous night, never having been in Ireland before. He had been greatly struck with the view coming up the Lough and with the kindliness he had already met with in the city. His firm had some business out at Cregagh—did they know it?—and he had taken it first so as to be entirely free to devote himself to their demonstration. He was looking forward to a pleasant stay and hoped their meeting would bear fruit. It was all very amicable and commonplace.

'We've engaged a room for you at the local hotel,' Jack broke in to this artless conversation. 'I'll take you there now and when you've had a meal I'll call and introduce M'Morris, our fourth member: Ferris you've met already. We hope that on a later occasion you'll dine with us.'

'Thanks, that'll suit me first rate. Where is your—is it lab or workshop?'

'Ah, you mustn't expect too much,' put in Pam. 'We've just a couple of rooms in a cottage, a quite temporary rig up. I expect you don't want to be bothered with business tonight. We'll show it to you tomorrow.'

Platt looked relieved. 'That's very kind,' he said, 'but I'm tremendously interested in what I'm going to see. Penrose and his friend certainly impressed my respected uncle when they came over.'

'Is Mr Jefferson your uncle?'

'Yes, luckily for me. I'm working through the business now, earnestly hoping to get a partnership later on.'

'Same here,' said Jack. 'I'm doing it too, only in a smaller business. My father's a solicitor. This now is Hillsborough we're coming to.'

'You've surprised me with one thing already,' Platt remarked, 'and that is your roads. They're wider and straighter than most of ours and just as good a surface.'

'Not so old as yours, I should think,' Jack suggested. 'Now, here's the hotel. We'll leave you for the present.' He took Platt in and then with a hearty, 'See you later,' returned to the car.

'I wonder how long he'll stay,' Pam said as they drove

away. She was dining with the Penroses that night, as she did fairly frequently.

'Probably till tomorrow night or Thursday at the latest. It won't take long, all we've got to show him.'

'And then you're going to London?'

'Oh, yes, I forgot to tell you. I had a letter from old Carling this morning. He'll see me on the day I proposed, Monday. Unfortunately he's only free in the early morning, so I'll have to cross on Saturday night.'

'Why not cross Monday night and see them on Tuesday? Save hanging about on Sunday.'

'Could scarcely put Carling and Hepworth off so long. They wanted me to go this week, but I thought if this chap Platt was kept at his other job he mightn't start with us till Thursday or Friday and I'd be better here.'

'I should think so. Oh, how I hope it'll all go well.'

'Oh course it'll go well. Why shouldn't it?'

'Oh, I don't know. He may want to see more than Ferris will show him.'

'You mean details of Ferris's plant? Not if I know it. No details till the agreement is signed.'

'But he mayn't sign till he does know.'

'He has nothing to do with the signing: simply to report to Jefferson.'

Pam was silent for a moment, then she went on. 'Has it occurred to you that we haven't seen the details of Ferris's plant ourselves? If I were asked tomorrow, I couldn't say how the thing is done.'

'So much the better, in case Platt tries to vamp you.'

'But it is funny. We've never been shown.'

'Could you understand it if you were?' Jack inquired solicitously.

Pam was in a serious mood and ignored this. 'And Cousin George doesn't know,' she went on. 'He's asked me, and I haven't been able to tell him.'

'All to the good,' Jack declared as he pulled up at the door. 'I'll leave the car here and we'll drive down later.'

The Penrose family consisted of four members, of whom only three lived at home. Mr Penrose, the solicitor, was a man of about sixty, though he looked younger. He was tall and strongly built like his son, and carried himself well. A shrewd man, he was a hard fighter in business, though at the same time kindly and scrupulously honest. In both his professional and private capacities he was universally respected. His hobby was cattle farming and he was always slipping across to England or the Continent to study the life history of cows in countries other than his own.

Mrs Penrose was a pleasant motherly woman who had taken Pam entirely to her heart. If she had been allowed to select her daughter-in-law, she would have chosen Pamela Grey. Pam already felt as if she had lived in the Penrose household all her life. She pretended to share secrets with Mr Penrose, much to his delight, and was adored by the tiny staff of the establishment, which latter Mrs Penrose said was 'a good sign.'

'Well, and has the great man arrived?' Mr Penrose asked as they began dinner. He took a keen interest in the scheme and closely followed its somewhat spasmodic evolution.

They discussed Platt and his mission and Jack mentioned that they were all going to the hotel for a chat later. Whereupon Pam declared unexpectedly, 'I'm not.'

'You're not?' Jack looked up in dismay. 'But you said you would.'

'I've changed my mind. It would be better for you four men to get together. After all you'll not discuss business tonight. I'll go to the cottage in the morning when the tests begin.'

Though Jack dutifully protested, he secretly felt that she was right. He promised to take her home on his way to the hotel and to call in after the meeting to tell her how it had gone.

But when about eleven he appeared, he had nothing of interest to report. They had had a perfectly normal evening, simply chatting to the accompaniment of drinks and smokes. Ferris was to call for Platt with his small car about nine-thirty in the morning, and on their arrival at the cottage the demonstration would commence. Jack was going to take two or three hours off in order to be present.

Next morning Pam reached Ferris's cottage to find only M'Morris there. Ferris had gone for Platt and Jack had not yet turned up.

Sloan's Lane was a narrow winding cartway connecting the diverging roads from Hillsborough to Lisburn and Glenavy respectively. Its hedges were overgrown and its surface was rough. Some hundred yards from the Lisburn Road end stood Wayside, as the cottage was called. It was not a structure of high architectural pretensions, consisting simply of a cube of whitewashed plaster covered stone surmounted by a perfectly plain roof of purple slates, with, in the centre of the front wall a porch of the size and shape of the average sentry box. The windows were small and evenly spaced, five in front and five behind. Inside, the door led into a narrow hall from which a single flight of steps, steep as a ladder, led to the rooms above. On each side of the hall was a room, one with a tiled floor fitted with an old fashioned American stove and sink, the other with a wooden floor and a small open fireplace. The two other rooms were overhead. The house was damp, dark, dirty and uncomfortable, but it had served its purpose. One of its great assets was its privacy. It was set well back from the lane, and the hedge and shrubs which separated it therefrom were so overgrown and ill-trimmed as to form a complete screen. Besides, there was practically no traffic along the lane, which was really a farm track to certain fields.

Ferris slept and lived upstairs, using the two lower rooms for the great work. What had been the sitting room was now reserved for the demonstration, the kitchen forming an annexe in which apparatus was made and stores kept.

Presently Jack arrived and on his heels the other two men. A few words of explanation as to what was to be done, a little good humoured chaff all round, and the great moment had arrived.

Ferris had shrouded the electrodes of his U-shaped apparatus in opaque screens so that nothing could be seen of their construction. Platt at once took exception to this.

'You mustn't mind,' he explained, 'but I've been sent over here with the special object of picking holes in your scheme: not of course that we don't wish it well, but simply to make sure that it stands criticism. If you begin by hiding all the essentials from me, I shall not be able to do my job.'

'What we want to show you,' Ferris returned, 'is that we can produce at will an inert form of petrol, and that we can at will turn that inert form back again into the ordinary active form, and that at a trifling cost in both cases. We do not propose at this stage to give the exact details of the process.'

'But that's just it,' Platt persisted, 'I don't see how you can convince me of the one without showing me the other.'

'Oh, yes we can. Just you look at what I'm going to show you and you'll be convinced right enough.'

'It's this way, Platt,' Jack added. 'You're a business man as well as a scientist. If you were in our position you wouldn't give away your assets until you had made an agreement with the other fellow. We'll show you what we can do. Then if you like it we'll ask you—or your people—to sign a conditional agreement saying that provided our claims as to method are established, you'll do this and that and the other.'

Platt shrugged good humouredly. 'I ask your lordships to note my objection,' he declared. 'Right. Carry on.'

But though Platt gave way in this pleasant manner, he soon showed he was taking nothing on trust. Ferris did his stunts as he had for Mr Whiteside and Platt admitted his surprise and admiration. But he did not leave it at that. Every step of the process, it appeared, was to be ruthlessly questioned and tested.

He began with the obvious difficulty. 'You won't let me see what's at the end of those things you stick in the petrol,' he pointed out. 'How am I to know they're not pumps which suck the petrol up into one leg and discharge an inert liquid from the other?'

'Observation will tell you that,' Ferris returned. 'The vessel is not emptied. If what you suggest were true, it would have first be emptied and then refilled.'

'I grant you that. What I mean is, how am I to know that you haven't there some clever conjuring trick which

51

creates an illusion?' He smiled so that there could be no offence in his words.

'We can't show you our process,' Ferris repeated, 'but apart from that you can put the thing to any tests you like.'

Platt then settled down to it. He was indeed so thorough and painstaking that he evoked the admiration of the others. First he insisted that he must analyse a sample of the petrol which was about to be used, to make sure that no secret ingredient had been introduced into it. Then he required the U-shaped apparatus to be suspended from a spring balance, so that if it took up any liquid the change in weight would show. He analysed—endlessly—the inert product, and again the recreated active petrol. In fact he went with great care and pains into every point that he could think of.

He was observant, too, Pam noticed, even about matters outside his own particular line. She could see his sharp little eyes passing over the room and its furnishings and following every movement made by the quartet. When Jack mislaid his matchbox, it was Platt who pointed it out on the chimney piece where Jack had put it down. Pam came to the conclusion that there was not much that happened that was not recorded in the man's brain.

All these experiments and testings took time. They had expected that lunch time would have finished the demonstration, but by lunch time Platt had scarcely got into his stride. By the evening he had only completed his test of the petrol, and before leaving off work he required a complex system of seals to be put on the work he had done.

'How long do you think it will take you?' Pam asked

as they stood outside the cottage prior to separating for the night.

'The firm gave me a week,' Platt replied, 'but I do not think it will take anything like that. This is Wednesday night and I thought of crossing back on Saturday night, as if I can get done here before that I should greatly like to see something of the country before I go.'

'We'll drive you round with great pleasure,' Pam assured him as they parted.

Pam was amused at the precautions upon which Ferris insisted. Not for a single moment might Platt be left alone, lest curiosity should tempt him to remove the sacred screens. And Ferris saw that the watch was kept.

All Thursday Platt tested and experimented without coming to a definite conclusion, though he admitted he was nearly convinced. A few hours more, he declared that evening, would complete his investigation.

Though by this time Pam felt that she definitely disliked him—there were indications that he was of an amorous disposition and she hated the way he sometimes looked at her—she was anxious that he should be given as good a time as possible. This was partly out of sheer good nature, but admittedly it was also to bias him as much as possible in their favour in the coming negotiations. With these objects in her mind she took a step on that Thursday evening which afterwards she bitterly regretted. In fact, if she could only have foreseen where it was to lead she would have cut off her hand rather than make such a move.

She rang up the Whitesides and asked them if they would have the party down for the next afternoon.

Mr Whiteside was anxious to meet Platt and the girls

were always on for any kind of party or game. The suggestion was therefore hailed as an inspiration.

'Come down and we can have tennis or golf, or go fishing,' Dot invited and Pam tentatively agreed.

Later she put the idea to the others. Jack, whom she rang up, was sorry he couldn't get away. 'I want to come to the cottage on Saturday morning when Platt's fixing up finally. Couldn't get both times,' he explained, and though she was sorry not to have him at Carnalea, she felt he was right. Ferris and M'Morris were both pleased with the idea, and Platt expressed himself as delighted.

'What would you rather do, Mr Platt?' Pam asked. 'We've been offered a choice of tennis, golf and sea fishing.'

Platt was all for fishing. Tennis he could get at any time, and he was a poor golfer, but sea fishing would be a rare treat. So it was arranged. Pam rang up Dot and told her.

They were in high spirits when on that Friday afternoon they set off. They squeezed into Ferris's Austin Seven, Platt in front with Ferris and Pam and M'Morris behind. All were wearing their most disreputable clothes, Ferris and M'Morris in blue jerseys and Platt in an old waterproof of Ferris's. The weather smiled on them. The sun was warm and bright, the atmosphere was clear and there was no wind. It was an ideal day for their purpose.

On reaching Loughside, the Whitesides' house, they were welcomed with wavings and vociferation by Dot and Dash. The girls then took Ferris and M'Morris down to the shore to get the boat out, while Pam and Platt went in to see Mr Whiteside. The old gentleman was in a particularly good humour and joked with Pam and pulled Platt's leg mercilessly.

'They're taking you out to drown you,' he told him solemnly. 'They think you've got their secret and they're not going to let you out of the country alive.' And when Platt gasped and looked at Pam for enlightenment, he chuckled wickedly and added that if he were in Platt's place, nothing would induce him to enter the boat.

'You mustn't mind him,' Pam explained as they presently followed the others down to the beach. 'He loves a joke and he thinks that sort of thing is funny.'

The boat was moored a little distance from the shore by an ingenious arrangement common in that neighbourhood—and doubtless elswhere. The painter was attached to an endless rope, the loop of which was passed through pulleys on the end of the slip and on a post some hundred feet farther out to sea. By pulling the rope the boat could be drawn in to the slip or out halfway to the post, where it could swing about in safety. M'Morris under the direction of Dot had untied the rope and was engaged in pulling in the boat. Dash with Ferris was at the boat house, where Ferris was grovelling for the key in a hole beneath the step, where it was kept hidden. The lines had been prepared and all that was necessary for the start was to get the oars from the boat house. 'We'll not take the sail,' Pam heard Dash's voice. 'There's no wind, and besides when there are so many of us the lines would get foul.'

It is not necessary to describe their afternoon. One sea fishing expedition is very like another: a joy to those who like it, an interminable misery to those who don't. It is enough to say that they had good sport and came in about six o'clock with a basket full of grey and silver trophies.

Except for one thing Pam enjoyed the excursion, and that was that Platt became rather too friendly on more than one occasion. It happened that they were together in the stern, Dot and M'Morris being in the bow and Dash and Ferris amidships. Platt was for ever swinging over so as to lean against Pam and continually touching her hands as he manœuvred his line. Once or twice she determined to exchange places with one of the others, then she thought Platt would be leaving the next day and it would be better to avoid unpleasantness. Of the others, she thought that only Ferris, who saw everything, had noticed it.

They all dined with the Penroses that evening, Platt behaving with exemplary discretion. All, even Pam, were pleased with his visit and with the hints he dropped that his report would be favourable. Afterwards Ferris and M'Morris drove him to the hotel, where, as Pam afterwards learnt, he insisted on their going in for drinks.

Next morning, Saturday, there was to be a final meeting at the cottage to agree on tentative details of an agreement for submission to Messrs Wrenn Jefferson. Jack had produced a rough draft and they were to discuss its various items with Platt.

It was at this meeting that an incident happened which, though trifling in itself, yet had terribly serious consequences. It occurred, Pam told herself, through her failure to take action during the fishing excursion on the previous day, and for a long time she was inconsolable about what she thought had been her fault.

She walked to the cottage rather more quickly than she had intended, arriving a few minutes before the appointed time. Platt and M'Morris had however already turned up, and were chatting with Ferris. Jack, who had gone into Lisburn to his office, had not yet returned.

When Ferris heard Pam's step he came out quickly

from the 'demonstration' room and met her in the porch. 'Want to talk to M'Morris,' he whispered. 'Keep Platt from being too inquisitive,' then went on in his usual loud cheery voice, 'Hallo, Pam. You're in good time. Any sign of Jack?'

Pam nodded and answered in her ordinary tones, 'I haven't seen him. I came straight from home.'

They joined the others and for a moment chatted in a somewhat forced and perfunctory way. Then Ferris beckoned M'Morris. 'Come and let's get those blessed notes fixed,' he said, adding with a touch of his usual sardonic humour. 'Miss Grey will do the honours while we're away.'

'I'm sorry to be leaving, Miss Grey,' Platt said when they were alone. 'I've had a pleasant time here.'

Pam thought this a graceful remark. 'I'm so pleased you've liked it, Mr Platt,' she said cordially. 'But if our agreement goes through you'll probably be over again before long.'

'I hope so, I'm sure. It's been such a pleasure meeting you.'

This wasn't at all what Pam wanted, but after all he was going in a few hours. 'I hope our agreement will go through,' she returned with the idea of changing the subject. But Platt did not take it as a change of subject.

'So that I may come back? Do you really mean that— Pam?'

Annoyed now in reality, she turned to annihilate him. But before she could speak it had happened: she never knew exactly how. Platt had been toying with his handkerchief and now he dropped it. He lunged forward to catch it as it fell and brushed against her. The next moment she found herself in his arms.

'Mr Platt: let me go!' she cried in a low tone as she struggled to get free. 'Let me go at once!'

If the affair had ended there, probably no harm would have been done. With Ferris and M'Morris within call, Platt would doubtless have let go as soon as he realised that he had made a mistake. But as evil chance would have it, at just that moment Jack walked into the room.

For a moment he stood speechless, gazing with a sort of incredulity at Platt. Platt had released Pam and was beginning a muttered apology. 'I'm sorry,' he said, but got no further.

With a hoarse roar Jack sprang forward and hit him on the point of the chin. It was not a savage blow, but Platt went down like a ninepin. He crashed back against the work table, knocking it over and sending the objects it bore flying. He brought up on the floor, where he sat nursing his wounded jaw and apparently very sorry for himself. Pam flung herself on Jack.

'Stop! stop!' she cried, twisting her arms round him. 'Don't make things worse!' As she spoke Ferris and M'Morris ran in crying out to know what had happened.

Jack struggled, but could not free himself from Pam's arms. 'Get up and get out of this before I kill you!' he shouted angrily to Platt, who still sat on the floor.

'No, no! Don't speak like that!' Pam insisted. 'There's no harm done.' Then with an appealing look at Ferris she added, 'Take him next door. It'll be all right.'

Ferris quickly took in the situation. 'Come into the next room, you,' he said roughly, catching Platt by the arm and helping him up. M'Morris took the other arm and they hustled him away. Jack tried to unclasp Pam's arms. 'Let me go, will you?' he cried. 'I'll soon settle him!'

'Not till you promise to be quiet. Oh, Jack, do control yourself. Fighting won't help anything. And—and—it was partly my fault. I tried to be decent to him and he misunderstood.'

Jack was of a passionate disposition. His anger flared up suddenly on small provocation, but it died down almost as quickly. He never harboured a grudge.

While Pam, almost sick with annoyance, struggled and reasoned with Jack, the scene seemed to be burnt in on her memory. There was a long table of planks on trestles on which the demonstration was set out, occupying one entire wall of the room. Before it were the three chairs on which she and Jack and Platt had sat while Ferris and M'Morris dealt with the apparatus. And there, on its side was a small table of accessories that had been at Ferris's hand. She noticed even the smallest details. Ferris's notebook, open and upside down, a small condenser that he sometimes used, with one wire torn off it, M'Morris's green pencil case on which someone had stepped, breaking off the clip and slightly flattening the top which carried the india-rubber, and three empty test tubes and a pipette, all broken. She saw the wide joints of the stained uneven floor, the patches of discolouration on the faded wallpaper and the broken tile at the back of the fireplace. Had she been playing the memory game, she would have won with flying colours.

M'Morris came back into the room. 'No harm done?' he asked, looking curiously at the others.

'Of course not,' Pam answered him. Then trying to speak lightly, she added: 'Except to your pencil and all that glass.'

Before he could answer, Ferris looked in. 'Look here, you two,' he said. 'The man wants to apologise. He's upset about what's happened. You've knocked him down, Jack, and that should square the thing. I suggest you cry quits and forget it.'

'Yes,' Pam cried eagerly, 'that's what I want too. You will, Jack? To please me?'

Jack, breathing threatenings and slaughter, was by no means out for conciliation. But at last he suffered himself to be persuaded, Platt muttered regrets, and the subject was dropped. The suggested agreement was discussed on a strictly business basis and as soon as might be Pam and Jack took their leave. Ferris went with them to the door.

'We'll look after him this afternoon,' he announced. 'We've promised to take him to the Mourne Mountains. And we'll put him on board the boat tonight. Don't you worry about him any more.'

'We're not going to,' Jack returned drily.

It was then that Pam remembered that Jack was crossing by the same steamer.

'He's going by Liverpool, isn't he?' she asked Ferris.

'Yes, by Liverpool.'

'So are you,' she turned to Jack.

'By Jove, so I am! I forgot that for the moment.'

'Oh?' said Ferris with a sharp glance. 'You're crossing tonight, are you?'

'Yes: I've a legal appointment in London on Monday morning.'

'Change your route and go by Heysham,' Pam suggested.

'Not I,' Jack answered. 'Do you think I'm going to have my plans upset by that wretched fish? Besides I've engaged my berth.'

'Well, you won't want to see him on the journey, I expect!'

'I'll not see him. I'll go in latish and go to bed when I get on board.'

Ferris nodded. 'Sorry about this. I suppose there's no use in my offering you a lift?'

'No,' said Pam. 'I'll drive him in. That is, Jack, if you'll let me have the car.'

'Will you? Good girl. You hear that?' he looked at Ferris.

'Right,' said Ferris as they parted.

The boat left at eleven on Saturdays, and Pam arranged to go round to the Penroses' after dinner, so that they might start when they felt inclined. 'About quarter to ten, I suggest,' Jack said. 'Then you'll be back about half-past. Not too late for you? Because you have to walk home.'

'Of course not: don't be silly.'

This programme they carried out, but not in its entirety. One unexpected factor slightly upset their plans. When at quarter to ten they went out to the car, they found that one of the tyres was flat.

'Curse it,' Jack growled. 'It's a back wheel and it's the very mischief to get a jack in under the axle with all this overhang of luggage carrier and so on behind. And there's no room to work here. We'll have to push it out and chance cutting the tube.'

'Will you have time? Would it not be better to ring up for a taxi?'

'Might be long enough before we'd get one at this time of night. No, we'll be all right if you'll lend a hand.'

It was a small job to change the wheel, but it took a good deal more time than they had expected. Pulling the car out of the garage and getting it jacked up by the light of torches proved no joke, and to make matters worse about ten o'clock it began to rain. Before they had finished

Jack wished he had taken Pam's advice and rung for a taxi. Then he found himself hot and dirty and he had to take further time to wash and change. Instead of getting away about quarter to ten, it was nearer half-past when they started.

As the day passed Pam had grown more and more to regret that Platt's visit had been marred by the morning's unfortunate little incident. Particularly she was sorry that the relations between Jack and Platt had become so strained. If the deal went through, as she now expected it would, they would have further dealings with the man, and it would be a thousand pities if there should be continued friction. Besides on general grounds she hated an atmosphere of ill feeling.

'Jack,' she said suddenly as they turned out of York Street towards the Liverpool berth, 'I want you to do something for me. Will you?'

'What is it, old thing?'

'No: you must promise first. It's a very little thing and you can do it easily. Will you—to please me?'

'It must be something rotten if you make such a song about it.'

'It's not, I assure you. If you don't, I'll be really hurt. Do promise, Jack.'

'Oh, all right. What is it?'

'You do promise?'

'I do promise.'

'I want you to make friends with Platt.'

Jack frowned. 'I never want to see the blighter again.'

'But that's just it. We've got to work with him and we don't want everything spoiled by friction. Besides, I don't like it. Go to him on board and ask him to have a drink.

62

You needn't say anything about what's happened and you needn't spend any time with him. It's just to show him that the thing's over and forgotten.'

'It's not forgotten so far as I'm concerned.'

'But it must be. As I said, if you won't do this for me, I'll be really hurt. Besides you've promised.'

'Oh, all right; I'll do it. But it seems to me you're making an unholy fuss about nothing.'

'I'm not. You know perfectly well I'm in the right.'

Further discussion was cut short by their arrival at the boat. They had cut it fine and there was only five minutes to spare. Pam set Jack down outside the Liverpool shed and drove quickly back.

She was glad Jack was going to make peace, even though the unpleasant little episode was such a trifle. The really great thing was that Platt had been convinced as to their claims about the inert petrol. The next step would undoubtedly be that the managing director and his technical experts would come over and a firm agreement would be signed. Then all their work and stress would be over. Money would soon begin to pour in, and what mattered more than anything else, her marriage could take place at once. Oh, how utterly glorious that would be! Pam pressed the accelerator in her eagerness.

The car bounded forward. Fortunately the road was straight and there was no traffic.

5

As Philip Jefferson Saw It

Precisely at 9.30 on the Monday morning following, Mr Philip Jefferson, senior partner of Messrs Wrenn Jefferson & Co., Ltd., of Carfax Street, Bristol, entered his private room at the works and sat down at his desk.

Jefferson was tall and well built, with a shrewd, thoughtful face and a quiet manner. He was a good business man and he was also a good employer. These terms in their strict meaning are synonymous, because the man who is considerate to his employees gets more out of them. But in the narrow sense they mean two distinct and often contrary policies. Jefferson was both keenly alive to the profits of his firm, and he treated his staff well.

Wrenn Jefferson dealt in oils, at least, mainly in oils. They imported and distributed paraffin and crude oils of various kinds. They did a certain amount of refining, producing lubricating oils of all types from thick green stuff for the sight feed lubricators of locomotives to the transparent, almost watery fluid used by watchmakers. They had a fair sized works at Carfax Street, and a larger depot on the Bristol Channel near Avonmouth. They were in a large way of business, outstanding even among Bristol firms. Their reputation was like that of their senior partner: keen but straight in business, prompt with their customers, just with their employees.

Jefferson began the working day by glancing over his mail, which had been removed from the envelopes by his secretary, Miss Beecher, and left on his desk with the relevant papers attached. On the top was a note in the girl's own hand to say that the Belfast Steamship Company's Liverpool office had been on the phone and wanted him to ring them up as soon as possible. 'That blessed oil,' thought Jefferson as he laid the memo aside. They had supplied the company with a large consignment of lubricating oil which had not proved up to specification, and negotiations for replacing it were in progress. A very annoying affair it had been and Jefferson feared it would end in a heavy loss. Then there was a letter from the secretary of the Bristol Harbour Board about crude oil for their Diesel engines. That was a satisfactory deal; there was money in it all right. An advice from their representative in New York: one of their tankers had been in collision. There was not much damage done, but she would be delayed in dock for a week or more. Harrison Stoker of Bath were ready for the next lot of petroleum. And so it went on.

Jefferson's interest quickened as he picked up another letter. Platt wrote from some God-forsaken place in Ireland that he would be back that morning. 'I have seen the demonstration these people put up,' he wrote, 'and I must admit it looks convincing. But until some kind of preliminary agreement was signed they wouldn't let me see the exact process. Unless there was some extraordinary clever jugglery or something of that kind they can do what they say. At all events they've got an inert liquid which undoubtedly has the chemical composition of petrol. I'll give you all particulars on seeing you on Monday morning, but my recommendation will be to go into the matter further.'

Jefferson sat back, and for a moment gave himself up to dreams. What an amazing story the whole thing was! Of course they had taken Platt in. It *couldn't* be true. It was too utterly unlikely. But if it were true . . . Jefferson swore below his breath. If it were . . . If it were true it would mean money beyond counting or estimating! These Irish people claimed that the stuff could be rendered inert for a farthing a gallon or less, because it appeared that once the change had been started in a large volume, it would creep on through the whole quantity without further application of power. And they claimed to be able to re-energise it for a little over three farthings a gallon—a halfpenny to cover the installation of the plant on each given car or plane, and a farthing for the current necessary to operate it. One penny a gallon extra for absolute immunity from the fear of fire! The air lines would all use it immediately. Most private drivers would use it. Probably it would become compulsory in buses: probably eventually in all vehicles using a public road. If only it were true! Well, he would get rid of these papers and then he would have Platt in and hear his story.

Jefferson touched his bell. 'Take these letters, Miss Beecher,' he said as his pretty secretary entered. He dictated quickly and without hesitating for words. The pile of papers decreased, vanished. Miss Beecher stood up to go.

'Get the Belfast Steamship Company for me, will you, and then send in Mr Platt.'

The girl withdrew, but reappeared in a few moments. 'The line's engaged, Mr Jefferson, and Mr Platt has not come in yet.'

Jefferson nodded. How like Platt! Always unsatisfactory. If he wasn't his wife's nephew, he, Jefferson, would have kicked the fellow out long ago. Enjoyed the pleasant air of Ireland, he supposed, and wanted another day or two's holiday. It was really too bad. After he had been given this specially pleasant and interesting job the man might have bucked up a bit. Jefferson decided there would be some plain speaking when Platt did condescend to put in an appearance.

Platt had always been rather a worry. Even at school he had had a bad reputation. But his mother was Jefferson's sister-in-law. She was also a widow, and in very poor circumstances, and Jefferson, at his wife's earnest plea and against his own better judgment, had taken the boy into the business. Platt had not done well. He had not done badly enough to sack, but not well enough to promote. There had, however, been a period in which Jefferson felt that he would have to sack him. The wretched youth had begun gambling at cards and had got badly into debt. But because of his wife and for the sake of the family Jefferson hadn't sacked him. Instead he had paid up. Platt had had a lesson and so far as Jefferson knew there had been no more high play. And now he had been given this important job, and here he was, disappointing again.

The strange thing was that the man had real ability. He was a thundering good chemist and as clever and ingenious as they are made. But so far his cleverness had not been put to the uses which Jefferson would have liked. He would invent a new method of doing something, if thereby he were saved trouble: but he would make no similar effort for the benefit of the firm.

Jefferson had nothing to reproach himself with in his treatment of the young man. He had offered him a home—again to please his wife and against his own desires. To Jefferson's secret satisfaction Platt had refused the offer. Not offensively, it was true: he had seemed really to appreciate the kindness and had spoken nicely about it, but he had obviously preferred the freedom of lodgings in Bristol. He was extraordinarily secretive: Jefferson never knew what he did in his free time or who were his friends. Jefferson's efforts to befriend him were always defeated by the man himself. Jefferson felt he could do no more, that—

His reverie was cut short by his telephone buzzer and Miss Beecher's voice, 'You're through now, Mr Jefferson.'

'The manager of the Liverpool office of the Belfast Steamship Company speaking,' came another voice. 'Is that Mr Phillip Jefferson?'

'Speaking,' Jefferson returned.

'I want to ask you if a Mr Reginald Platt is connected with your firm, and if he was crossing here from Belfast on Saturday night?'

'Yes, to both questions.'

'Might I ask if Mr Platt has returned to his home?'

'Not that I know of. He was expected here in the office this morning, but he hasn't turned up.'

'Then, Mr Jefferson, I'm afraid I have bad news for you. Mr Platt came on board our steamer at Belfast on Saturday night, but he was not seen at Liverpool.'

'Not seen?'

'No sir, I greatly regret to inform you that he is missing. In due course his cabin was opened and his luggage was found there, but there was no trace of himself. From examining the luggage we found your firm's address.'

This was wholly unexpected news. Jefferson was upset. Surely nothing serious could have happened to Platt?

But his surmisings were cut short by the manager's voice. 'We tried to get in touch with you yesterday, but were unable.'

'I was from home for the weekend and the house was closed.'

'That explains it. I'm sorry to say that we fear an accident and in duty bound we have informed the police.'

The police!

'What exactly do you fear,' Jefferson asked in a somewhat altered voice.

The manager seemed to hesitate. 'Well,' he said at last, 'in such cases there must be the obvious fear that through some accident he has fallen overboard.'

'Good God!'

'I wondered if you would be good enough to communicate with his people,' went on the voice. 'We couldn't find any reference to relatives in his papers. I would suggest that perhaps some of his relatives would care to come to Liverpool and see what is being done.'

'He's a connection of my own. His mother is my sister-in-law. I'll probably go myself. I'll let you know later.'

The manager murmured regrets. He would be glad to see Jefferson and meanwhile everything possible would be done.

As Jefferson replaced the receiver, he felt slightly stunned. Platt, whom he had been expecting to walk into the office any moment, whom he was intending to call over the coals for being late, Platt perhaps was dead! Dreadful!

If the news were true his wife and her sister would take it hard. Not though either of them had seen so much of the young man in the recent past. Still he was nephew to one and son to the other. If he were dead his faults would be forgotten, his good points remembered. And rightly so.

Jefferson reached for a Bradshaw. He would go to Liverpool. Even if he had not wished to do so for his own peace of mind, he would have had to for the sake of his wife and sister-in-law. He wondered if his sister-in-law would want to go too. Far better for her not to, if only she would be satisfied to remain at home. She lived at Gloucester and if necessary he could pick her up on his way.

Then he thought the best thing to do would be to tell his wife at once and let her go to Gloucester and stay with her sister. He would go to Liverpool and keep them advised by telephone of what was being done. Mrs Platt was not on the telephone, but his wife could stay at an hotel and so remain within call. By letting his wife break the news it would be easier for Margery Platt, and the question of her going to Liverpool would not arise.

As these thoughts passed through his mind, he was turning over the pages of Bradshaw. There was a train from Bristol at twelve-twenty, which got in at five twenty-three. That would suit. He rang for Miss Beecher and Lewis, his assistant manager.

'I've had rather disturbing news,' he said when they appeared, and he repeated what the steamship company's manager had said. 'I'm afraid I shall have to go to Liverpool at once. Will you just carry on. I think you'd better put off that shopmen's deputation, but you can handle every-thing else.'

Both were obviously thrilled, but though they expressed a dutiful sympathy, he could see that neither had cared for Platt. They were interested in the dramatic side of the affair, not in the man's possible fate.

'Well,' said Jefferson, 'I'll be off. I want to go home and tell my wife before getting the train.'

He broke the news to Mrs Jefferson and then drove on to Platt's rooms and saw the man's landlady. But Mrs Russell could tell him nothing. Platt had sent her a card from Ireland saying that he expected to be back on Sunday night, but he hadn't turned up. She could not think what had kept him.

After sending wires to the steamship company's manager in Liverpool and to Mrs Platt, Jefferson and his wife left Bristol. At Gloucester Mrs Jefferson got out and Jefferson went on alone.

He scarcely realised it himself, but he had come to believe that Platt was dead. Though he did not see how on a calm night anyone could fall overboard from a cross Channel boat unknown to others on board, he supposed that in some way the accident had happened. The only other alternative, suicide, was unthinkable. Platt had no motive. Though perhaps not a favourite at the works, he had a comfortable enough billet there and was decently treated. The man had quite a good time, and excellent prospects, if only he would make an effort to embrace his good fortune.

All the same Jefferson began to wonder whether he himself had been at all lacking in his duty towards his nephew by marriage. The youth had been irritating enough at times, and Jefferson had never hidden his opinion of him. On the other hand he had treated him better than would most employers. No he could not see that he had been in any way to blame. If he had come short in what he might have done, it was because Platt himself was too secretive and distant in his manner to permit of anything else.

In due course Jefferson reached Liverpool and a few minutes later was shown into the manager's office. Mr M'Kinstry was a tall raw-boned Ulsterman whose manner was forceful and direct, but behind whose shrewd expression a real kindliness peeped out. He wrung Jefferson's hand in a powerful grip and asked him to be seated.

'I was sorry for having to send you bad news, Mr Jefferson,' he began, 'but you were the only person whose name we could find. But we didn't know then that you were a relative of Mr Platt's. The letter we found was from you as head of the firm, not as his—uncle, I think you said?'

'Uncle by marriage.'

'Uncle by marriage, is it? Well I'll tell you just what we know and then you'll be able to judge the position.'

'Thank you; I wish you would.'

'Mr Platt left Belfast on Saturday night by our motor ship *Ulster Sovereign*. He was travelling on the return half of a third on rail and first on boat ticket. The purser records the numbers of all through tickets, so that our company may get its share of the fare. There was one for Bristol, and this may have been Mr Platt's. Mr Platt had written two days before to our Belfast office to reserve a single berth cabin for the Saturday. There was an excess on this, which he paid to the purser.

72

'In accordance with our custom Mr Platt was given the number of his cabin and he showed his ticket and berth card to his cabin steward. The steward remembers him well and says Mr Platt told him he did not require any tea in the morning, or to be specially called.'

Jefferson nodded.

'The check of our passengers,' continued Mr M'Kinstry, 'is not like that on the Southern lines to France. We make it on embarkation: that is, no one can go on board our ships without a ticket. There is no absolute check of travellers leaving the ship. At the same time, as you can guess,' a certain dryness crept into the manager's tones, 'it is usual for the cabin stewards to see those whom they have attended before they go ashore.

'Now when the boat berthed at Liverpool there was the usual watch over the passengers. Mr Platt was not seen. When it was nearly time for the bus to leave for the stations his cabin steward went to his cabin to remind him of the time. Mr Platt was not there. His berth had not been slept in. But his luggage was there, unpacked.'

'You surprise me. His berth had not been slept in?'

'No, and I'm afraid that's one of the worst features of the affair. If he wasn't in his berth during the night, where was he? I mean he'd certainly have been seen about the ship—if he had been on board. But no one saw him.'

'Could he have gone ashore at Belfast for some reason and been left behind?'

'I'm afraid not. As I said, a careful check on the passengers is made at Belfast. The man who was on the job has been questioned, and he states positively that everyone who went aboard the ship with a through ticket sailed.'

Jefferson nodded. The more he heard of the story, the worse it looked.

'It is of course possible, though unlikely, that he reached Liverpool and went ashore unnoticed. As I've said, there's not the same systematic check on disembarking. But in this case his berth surely would have been slept in, and his luggage would have disappeared.'

'It would seem so,' Jefferson answered unwillingly. 'Well, then, what did you do?'

'The cabin steward reported to the purser and a search was made of the ship. Then the captain was informed and a more complete search was made. At last I heard of it. They rang me up at my home. I came up and had a chat with the men, and decided I must inform the police. An inspector was sent over and he searched Mr Platt's luggage and found a letter to him on your firm's paper and signed by you. We then tried to get in touch with you, but failed till this morning.'

'I know. We were away and the servants had gone home. And that's all that is known?'

'That's all, I'm afraid. The thing was kept out of the papers this morning, but it'll be in the evening ones.'

For some time Jefferson continued discussing the the affair, but without learning anything fresh. If Platt had not gone ashore in Belfast and been left behind—and it was difficult to see either why he should have done so, or if he had, why he should not have wired the fact—it looked increasingly like as if in some unknown and mysterious way he had fallen overboard shortly after the start. But how such an accident could occur was very far from clear.

'I think I'll go to the police station and hear what they

have to say,' Jefferson decided, which course M'Kinstry warmly advocated.

But when a few minutes later he was sitting in the superintendent's office he soon found that the officer's object was to obtain information, not to impart it. Superintendent Shepherd was extremely polite, but as close as a clam. They were looking into the matter, yes, but unfortunately they had as yet nothing to report. Mr Jefferson might rest assured that every possible step would be taken to clear the affair up, but so far there had not been time to ascertain all the facts.

But in the meantime Mr Jefferson could help their efforts by answering a few questions. He, the superintendent, presumed that Mr Jefferson would have no objection to that?

Mr Jefferson, on the contrary, was only too anxious to assist.

Then would Mr Jefferson please tell him—and an interrogation of extraordinary completeness followed. Who was Platt? What relation was he to Jefferson? What was his history? Was he a member of the firm? What position did he hold? First came questions whose answers gave a sort of general Who's Who of all concerned.

Then followed others on more special points, and some of these Jefferson found extremely suggestive. Was Platt addicted to strong drink, or drugs? Was he happy in his life? Was he in any difficulties? Any financial tightness? Any betting or gambling? Any entanglement with a girl? Any unpleasantness at the works? Any unpopularity? What was behind the questions was pretty obvious.

Superintendent Shepherd then turned to Platt's mission to Ireland. What had he gone for? Jefferson gave him the outlines of the petrol affair, which seemed to interest him a good deal. It was a secret process and might be valuable? Immensely valuable, if genuine? Quite. And Mr Platt thought it was genuine? Quite.

The superintendent thought over this for some moments, then asked if Platt had a note of the process on him. Jefferson thought not. He wasn't sure? Jefferson wasn't sure, but suggested that if they rang up the people in Ireland they would tell them. The superintendent nodded and said he would do so. The interview seemed to be drawing to an end.

'Tell me,' Jefferson said, as Shepherd indicated that he had got all he required, 'what do you think about the thing? You must have a lot of experience of cases of this kind and I should like to know whether—whether you think the young man is alive or dead?'

But Jefferson might have saved himself the trouble of asking. Shepherd was not going to commit himself. He said there was scarcely sufficient evidence as yet to come to a conclusion on the matter. It certainly looked as if Platt might have fallen overboard in some way shortly after leaving Belfast, but this was by no means proved and it would be very unwise to make any assumption on the subject. Jefferson should wait till they made some further inquiries, the result of which would be immediately conveyed to him.

'I'll wait till you have an answer from Ireland at all events,' Jefferson replied, to which the superintendent agreed without enthusiasm.

From his hotel Jefferson rang up his wife saying that while there was no evidence of what had taken place, things did not look well. He was waiting over till the next day and would ring up again.

On the following morning he presented himself once again at police headquarters. Superintendent Shepherd saw him again and was slightly more communicative.

They had made inquiries, he said, through the police of Northern Ireland. An officer had gone down to Hillsborough and seen the Mr Ferris whom Jefferson had mentioned. He, Ferris, had stated that Platt had with him detailed proposals for an agreement between the Hillsborough party and Messrs Wrenn Jefferson. He had also superficial notes of the production of the inert petrol, but Ferris was satified he had none of the actual details of the process.

'There's not a great deal of help there,' Shepherd remarked. 'It may be difficult to get evidence of just what has happened. We shall continue to make inquiries and if and when we learn anything, we shall let you know.'

Shepherd stood up and his manner indicated polite dismissal so strongly that Jefferson could do no other than to take his leave.

Greatly worried about the whole affair, he took the next train back to Bristol.

6

As Chief Inspector French Saw It

On the same morning on which Jefferson left Liverpool on his return journey to Bristol, Tuesday, 10th September, Chief Inspector Joseph French was seated in his room at New Scotland Yard, laboriously going through reports on a smash-and-grab raid which had taken place in Bond Street on the previous night.

He was tired and slightly fed up with life in general, and his job in particular. He had had a nasty attack of influenza in the late spring which had left him feeling washed out. A wave of burglary cases about that time had prevented him from getting the few days' change he would have liked while recovering, and since that his annual holiday had had to be postponed no less than twice. And now that the crime wave seemed to have passed, there had been an outbreak of illness among his fellow officers; not any special epidemic, but a series of minor illnesses of various kinds, which had left them shorthanded at the Yard. French's holiday had been postponed again.

He completed his study of the smash-and-grab raid

78

reports, formulated his proposals as to the steps next to be taken in the matter, and went in to see Sir Mortimer Ellison, the Assistant Commissioner to whom he was responsible.

'Ah, French,' Sir Mortimer greeted him. 'I was just about to ring you up. More trouble. But what did you want to see me about?'

'The Bond Street raid, sir,' French answered. 'The car has been found abandoned.'

They discussed the matter in detail, and French's proposals were approved. 'But you may get Tanner or Willis to carry on with that. There's something else that would suit you better. What about a trip to the sea?'

Sir Mortimer, while he kept strict discipline, was yet very free and friendly in manner towards his subordinates. He joked with them and pulled their legs. No one had ever been known to take advantage of it, but it meant that routine was carried on more smoothly and with less friction than often obtains in large concerns.

'I'd like nothing better, sir, if you approve.'

'I expect you'd like it better still if I didn't,' Sir Mortimer returned. 'However, I'm afraid it's not very good sea—only Liverpool. You know it?'

'Fairly well, sir.'

'There's no knowing where the trail might lead—perhaps, after hours, even to Southport. I'm sorry about your holidays, but you can take this as a sort of unofficial instalment.'

This was, French thought, exactly like Sir Mortimer. If it were possible to do his men a good turn, Sir Mortimer did it. Without ever sacrificing the work, he would make any adjustments possible to meet the convenience of the workers. It was no wonder that he received the extraordinarily loyal service that he did.

'Thank you very much, sir. I'm very grateful. What is the case?'

'I have a letter here from the Chief Constable of Liverpool. A man disappeared from the Belfast-Liverpool steamer on Saturday night. It appears there's some suggestion of foul play, though I don't don't know how far this is justified.'

'Is it known where he disappeared?'

'Apparently not.'

'Then is it necessarily a matter for the Liverpool police? I suppose it's known he sailed?'

'Visits to Belfast and the North of Ireland? Well, perhaps it may even come to that. You never can tell.'

French smiled. 'I hope so, sir.'

'The Chief Constable seems so sure it's his business that he's trying to shove it over on to us. You better go down and see what they have to say. I'll phone them that you're going by the next train. What about that Southend affair?'

'I've finished the papers. I think the local men are right, and that it was Peters.'

'So do I,' the Assistant Commissioner agreed; and the talk turned to other channels.

An hour later French and Sergeant Carter left Euston for the Mersey. French's spirits had risen almost to normal, and he was looking forward, if not to a visit to the actual sea, at least to a change of scene and work. It was the first out of town case he had had for some months, and he hoped it would develop into a stay of at least a few days. He had worked with Superintendent Shepherd before, and he knew him for an efficient officer who would not allow jealousy or departmental narrowness to impede work on the case. And if by a stroke of luck he had to go to Belfast—well, he knew the men over there also, and he liked the country, and it would be a better change still.

The journey passed pleasantly, and, on reaching Lime Street, the two men set off for police headquarters. There French had a cordial greeting from Superintendent Shepherd.

'The chief was sorry he couldn't wait to see you,' Shepherd went on. 'He had some engagement. But he'll be here in the morning. Been busy lately?'

They chatted for some moments, recalling their last meeting and dealing briefly with the affairs of the nation in general, and of the police services in particular. Then the super turned to the matter in hand.

'It seemed to the chief that it was only technically a Liverpool case,' he explained. 'So far as we can understand it, inquiries will be wanted at Belfast and Bristol as well as here. That's why he thought it should be handled by the Yard. That is, if there really is any case for inquiry at all.'

'A man overboard case, isn't it?'

'It looks like it. It's a disappearance, at all events. The man in question, Reginald Platt, is believed to have left Belfast on last Saturday night by the Belfast-Liverpool boat *Ulster Sovereign*. He went to his cabin in due course, and was never seen again. His luggage was in his cabin, unpacked, but his berth had not been slept in. That seems to cover all the essential details.'

French grinned. 'If he left Belfast and didn't arrive at Liverpool, and is not now on the boat, it would certainly be suggestive.'

'Very,' Shepherd agreed dryly. 'And your "if" seems to

me to cover the whole of the factual side of the inquiry. As to his motive if he jumped overboard, or someone else's if he was thrown—well, that's a different matter?'

'Any suggestions on these latter points?'

'None. But the man was over in Ireland on unusual business.' And Shepherd repeated what Jefferson had told him about the inert petrol.

'That would be a pretty big thing, surely,' French commented. 'That is, if there's anything in it at all. It sounds a bit far-fetched to me.'

'I imagined it did to Jefferson also, but he said Platt appeared to have been convinced by what he saw.'

'Interesting business. If the process is genuine, that young man had a pretty valuable secret in his possession.'

'That's another doubtful point. The man in charge on the Irish side, a man named Ferris, said that Platt hadn't learnt the details of the process, but only its results. I'd better tell you, chief inspector, just what we did and what we've learnt, so that you can take over and go ahead on your own lines.'

Shepherd went into details, Carter taking copious short-hand notes, and French entering in his own book those items which he thought should receive special attention. Having discussed these, he turned to a further point.

'Now tell me, super,' he said in more confidential tones, 'why you people thought this required an investigation? Evidently you don't think it was accident or suicide?'

'We don't say that,' Shepherd returned. 'What we say is that neither of these appear to be very likely. Take accident. How in hades would a man fall overboard—unless he was trying monkey tricks on the rail? And why should he do such a thing? Consider the night. It was very wet and cold.

That would tend to keep people off the deck. Then it was calm; the boat was perfectly steady.'

'That sounds all right.'

'With regard to suicide, we've less to go on. But so far we've found no motive. In fact, it's all the other way round. Platt wrote to Jefferson, reporting that this petrol affair looked very promising, and said he would be in the office on Monday morning to discuss it. Now, if it was promising it would mean prosperity for the Wrenn Jefferson firm, and so indirectly for Platt. Then we're informed that there was nothing in Platt's manner either before going to Ireland or in Ireland to suggest he was tired of life. Rather he seemed excited about this petrol business and anxious to see it through. Not of course convincing, but worthy of consideration.'

French was impressed. The argument did seem pretty strong. He thought for a moment.

'And you say he hadn't the details of the process on him?' he asked.

'So this man Ferris says. He says that Platt simply knew that the inert petrol could be made. He didn't know how to make it.'

'It's quite a problem,' said French.

'That's what we thought. And we thought, as I've said, that it was rather outside our beat. If co-ordination is required between different police forces, you're the man to bring it about. At least,' he smiled slightly, 'that was what the chief thought.'

'An able man, your chief,' French declared, smiling as he put away his notebook and slowly rose to his feet. 'If he wants a problem solved, he knows where to apply. Right, then, super. I'll start with what happened on the ship and then go on from that to motives. And I'll call in in the morning to see the chief.'

At first sight French thought his new problem a simple one. It surely should not be difficult to find out the facts. The statements of the ship officers, added to those of persons who knew the details of Platt's life, should give the required solution.

But was it so very simple, after all? So far, while accident seemed out of the question, there did not appear to be a motive either for suicide or murder. And in the case of a death it must be one of the three.

French pulled himself up. Here he was theorising before he knew his facts, and that after all the warnings he had had of the danger of such a proceeding! Time enough for that later on. Let him get on with his immediate job. Let him find out first what was to be known. Then he could try to build a theory on the result.

The first item on his programme was a call at the offices of the Belfast Steamship Company. There he saw Mr M'Kinstry, and from him learned that the *Ulster Sovereign* was in Belfast, but would be crossing over that night.

'If you want to see what check there is on passengers leaving the ship,' went on M'Kinstry, 'I would suggest that you go aboard her when she berths, and you'll see how the thing's done.'

French said that this was good advice, and that he would take it.

'Then see M'Bratney, the purser. He'll give you all information about tickets, and so on, and put you on to the cabin steward who looked after Mr Platt. I personally know nothing about the affair, but if there is any question I can answer, I'll be glad to do it.'

M'Kinstry could not, however, tell a great deal. He repeated what he had told Jefferson, and added an account of his interview with that gentleman. There was nothing in this, however, that French had not already learnt from Shepherd.

'I should be obliged for a copy of the passenger list for the trip,' French concluded. M'Kinstry, explaining that it contained only the names of those who had booked berths, promised to send it in.

Next morning French and Carter were on the landing-stage when the *Ulster Sovereign* came slowly alongside. French, accustomed to the boats running between England and France, was astonished at her size and build. This was not his idea of a cross-Channel steamer: this was a small-scale ocean liner. Her sides rose smooth and sheer from the water to high above the landing stage, and there was no question of going aboard by a gangway stretching to her deck. As with ocean steamers, the gangway was to a door comparatively low down in her towering side. Above this door were two decks, with the end of the navigating bridge showing high above the upper.

Directly the gangway was in place, French and Carter pushed on board, French showing a note he had obtained from M'Kinstry to the men in charge. The door opened into a reception hall the full width of the ship and long enough to accommodate easily the crowd of travellers waiting to go ashore. From the hall led alleyways to the cabins and companions to the decks above and below, and in it was the purser's office, the luggage store, and the entrance to the dining room. It was simply but tastefully finished in polished woods, with a rubber floor. Among the crowd were sailors and porters handling luggage and several deck and cabin stewards.

At first sight there seemed to French to be no check whatever on those leaving. There was certainly no one taking tickets or landing slips. Then he began to notice that, while this remained true, there were few passengers who were not, as it were, seen off the premises by stewards. Most of the latter were concerned with their patrons' luggage, and most of them received a tip. At the same time some travellers, usually carrying their own suitcases, did seem to leave unnoticed by an official.

This was in accordance with what M'Kinstry had said about the company's methods of check, and it appeared to show that there could be no absolute certainty as to whether or not Platt had reached Liverpool. Obviously he might have slipped ashore unnoticed.

French waited till the passengers had left. Then he asked for Mr M'Bratney.

The purser proved to be a pleasant looking man of about fifty, with a downright though courteous manner and a humorous eye. French showed him his card and M'Kinstry's letter and explained what he wanted.

'Come on to my cabin,' M'Bratney suggested. 'I'll be pleased to do anything I can for you; but I think I've already told the local inspector all I know.'

'I like to get things first hand, Mr M'Bratney,' French explained. 'Again and again I've known a misunderstanding arise through taking second hand statements. I'm sorry to trouble you, but I won't keep you long.'

The purser made a gesture of comprehension. 'That's all right.' He moved to his desk and indicated the remaining chairs. 'Sit you down, gentlemen, and away you go. I'm through now the passengers have gone ashore.'

French opened his cigarette case. 'Do you smoke here?' he asked as he held it out.

''Deed do I. There's not many places I don't have a pull. But I think I'll stick to the pipe. Thank you all the same.'

'I'd rather have a pipe myself,' French returned, pulling it out. 'Try this mixture. I get it made for myself in a little shop up in Town.'

For a few moments they talked tobacco, French poking fun at Carter because he stuck so wholeheartedly to cigarettes. Then they turned to business.

'I want to ask three main questions,' said French. 'First, is there definite proof that Platt came on board and sailed from Belfast? Second, is there definite proof that he didn't go ashore here in Liverpool? And third, are there any facts of any kind whatever which might throw some light on the affair?'

M'Bratney nodded. 'Aye, I'd be thinking that would be what you'd want to know. Well, I'll tell you as far as I can.'

He paused to push the tobacco down in his pipe, took three or four experimental draws with a critical air, was apparently satisfied, and continued:

'To your first question the answer is yes. I'll tell you how I know. When the passengers are coming on board we have a man on the gangway. He stands at the shore end of the gangway, and no one is supposed to pass him without showing a ticket. I admit that he has discretion to pass people who are going to see their friends off. But he counts all such, and he counts them again when they leave the ship. If the numbers didn't tally, he would report it, and the thing would be gone into aboard. I was speaking of the first class gangway, but the third's exactly the same.'

'That means that no one could go aboard on the excuse of wanting see a friend off and go on to Liverpool without being spotted?'

'That's right.'

'And also it means that no one who had gone aboard with a ticket could go ashore again without being spotted?'

'That's right again. There'd be more go off the boat than were passed on. In this latter case we mightn't know who had gone ashore, but we'd know someone had.'

'Quite so. That covers my point. And was this check made on last Saturday night?'

For answer M'Bratney pressed a button. 'Send me in Gillan,' he directed to the steward who appeared, continuing to French: 'I'll let you see the man who was on the gangway that night. He'll tell you what he did.'

A moment later a tall, intelligent looking man in the uniform of a petty officer appeared. 'This is a gentleman from Scotland Yard, Gillan,' the purser explained. 'He wants to ask you some questions. Go ahead, chief inspector. Gillan'll tell you what he knows.'

The man proved an excellent witness. He spoke quietly, using a minimum of words, and his statements were crystal clear and very definite. He had done this: he had not done the other. Such a thing had happened: such another had not. There was no doubt about it. He was sure.

He had seen the tickets of all the passengers but nineteen. Nineteen had gone on board to see their friends off, and nineteen had come ashore again before the boat sailed. So much was certain.

In response to a question from M'Bratney, the man further stated that, while he didn't pay a great deal of attention to ticket holders, he always specially noted those who were not travelling. He believed that not one of the nineteen answered the description of Platt.

'Did you notice a ticket holder who answered his description?' French asked.

'I did not, sir, but, as I said, I wasn't looking specially at those.'

Gillan said also that in his job you got to know who were 'right enough' and who might be trying tricks. He was quite satisfied about the nineteen on Saturday night. All were obviously with parties. If Platt had been one of those nineteen and had gone ashore again, a number of other people on board would know.

'That means that anyone who came on board with a ticket remained on board,' commented French. 'And Platt had a ticket?'

'Platt had a ticket all right,' M'Bratney agreed. 'That'll do, thank you, Gillan.' The big man saluted and left, and M'Bratney went on: 'I examined his ticket myself and nipped it. He had written, reserving a single-berth cabin, and the reservation had been arranged. There was a fee due, and he paid it then. I returned him his travel ticket and the cabin ticket and called out the cabin number. The cabin steward came forward and showed him to his cabin. But maybe you'd like to see himself?'

'Yes, please, I should. But first I should like to know if you remember Platt personally?'

M'Bratney shook his head. 'I don't remember him at all,' he declared. 'I'm speaking simply because I did the same thing with all berth tickets.'

'I follow. Then might I see the cabin steward?'

James Thompson was a sharp-featured young fellow of about thirty. He did not give the same impression of utter reliability as did Gillan, but he also seemed sure of his facts, and was definite in his replies.

He remembered Platt, and believed he would recognise him again if he saw him. He had shown him to his cabin, an outside one on A Deck. He had asked if Platt would have tea in the morning, but Platt said not, that he never had anything before breakfast. Nor did he want to be called. He would, he said, be up early enough. Thompson had wished him goodnight and had withdrawn, closing the door.

In the morning Thompson had kept a good look out for Platt, but had not seen him. With a somewhat sheepish look at M'Bratney, he explained he was 'looking for a bob or two off him.' But there had been no sign of Platt, and when they were approaching the landing stage Thompson had knocked at the cabin door, lest Platt had, after all, overslept. There was no reply, and Thompson looked in. The room was empty. Platt's suitcase was open on its stand, and his night clothes and a book were lying on the bed, which had not been slept in. Thompson was surprised, but for the moment he could not move in the matter, as he was engaged with other passengers. But as soon as he had a chance he had a look round the decks for Platt. He could not see him anywhere.

'Had the ship reached the landing stage when you had this look round?' French asked.

'She had, sir. She was berthed, and the passengers were beginning to go ashore.'

'And what did you do?'

90

'I was sure Mr Platt wasn't ashore because of his luggage being still in the cabin. So I kept a watch on the cabin, and then when he didn't turn up I told Mr M'Bratney'.

'It seems to me, then,' said French when he had finished, 'that there is no absolute proof that Platt didn't go ashore at Liverpool?'

'That's right,' M'Bratney agreed. 'There's every probability against it, but there's no absolute proof.'

'Well,' French went on, 'that disposes of my two principal questions. There is just the third: whether you can give me any other facts that may throw light on the affair.'

The two *Ulster Sovereign* men exchanged glances. 'There was just one thing,' M'Bratney answered slowly. 'As a matter of fact, I may admit I forgot all about it when the local inspector was speaking to me, but Thompson has since called it to my mind. And that's this: There were two men asking for Mr Platt that night.'

'Oh?' said French. 'Tell me about that.'

'One of them came to the office window before we left and the other after we had started. They both asked if there was a Mr Platt aboard. I said there was, and I put them on to Thompson. Go ahead, Thompson.'

'They came to me, sir, both of them, and asked me the same question: Which was Mr Platt's cabin? I said he was in 57, and did they want to see him. The first said not, that he wouldn't disturb him that night, but he'd see him in the morning. He asked me if Mr Platt was a short, stout, pasty-faced man, and I said he was. That seemed to satisfy him, and he went away. The second man said he'd look in on him presently.'

'What were they like, these men?'

'The first was a tall, thin man, and dark. The second

was tall, too, but fair. But I didn't pay much attention to them.'

'Can you tell me any more, Mr M'Bratney?'

'I can not. I was busy, and I'm afraid I scarcely looked at either of them.'

With this French had to be content. He tried to find out from the other stewards where the cabins of these unknowns could have been, so as to learn their names, but without success. And neither M'Bratney nor Thompson had seen the men again.

French next interviewed the man who had been on the third class gangway, also without result. He stayed chatting for a few moments, then, believing there was nothing more to be learned on board, he went ashore and with Carter returned to police headquarters to see if the chief constable had yet come in.

7

As Chief Inspector French Saw It

The interview with Major Bond proved unproductive. The chief constable was friendly and pleasant, but he had nothing to add to French's knowledge and no suggestions as to where more information might be obtained. He seemed pleased to have got rid of the principal responsibility of the case, and, while promising any help possible from his men, let it be understood that this would be only at French's request.

'What do you propose to do, chief inspector?' he asked when the matter had been discussed. 'Or perhaps you haven't yet made up your mind?'

'I think I shall go down to Bristol,' French answered, 'and try if I can find any adequate motive for suicide. On the face of it, suicide seems to me the most likely solution. Of course, further inquiry may tend otherwise.'

The chief constable approved. He also had thought that suicide would prove the explanation of the affair, and it pleased him to find that French was of the same mind. 'Well,' he said, standing up to show that the interview was

over, 'let us know how you get on. We'll see you back before long?'

'I expect so, sir.'

There was just one matter remaining to be done in Liverpool. Platt's suitcase and its contents must be examined in detail. It had been removed to police headquarters, and was quickly shown to French.

But a thorough inspection of all the articles led to nothing. There were no papers except the letter from Jefferson and a few bills. From the clothes nothing could be learnt.

'When do these blessed trains start for Bristol?' French inquired of Carter, part of whose business it was to have such matters at his finger-ends.

On this occasion the sergeant maintained his reputation. Surreptitiously he had examined a Bradshaw while the chief constable was speaking. 'Twelve noon, sir,' he was therefore able to reply with an air of omniscience. 'If we hurry we'll get it.'

'Then we'll hurry,' said French.

They spent the afternoon moving down the west of England, and by six o'clock had reached Bristol and found police headquarters. There French saw the officer in charge and explained the object of his visit. He did not expect that the Bristol men would have any information that would help him, but he would be glad if they would keep their ears open about Platt and let him know if they learnt anything interesting.

To this the officer said that, acting on a request from Liverpool, they had already made some inquiries about Platt. They had not, however, obtained any suggestive results. With salutes the interview terminated.

'Now, Carter, what about an hotel and a snack?' French went on when they had left the police station.

'Snack' did not exactly express the conception which had for some time been uppermost in Carter's mind. However, knowing French's snacks, he gave the proposal his cordial approval, and when later they sat down to a meal of soup, steak and onions, apple tart and cheese, washed down by draught ale, he felt that his optimism had not been misplaced.

'Going to do any more tonight, sir?' he asked presently, with visions of a free evening exploring the delights of Bristol.

But here his hopes were dashed. 'If that Jefferson man can see us, we might as well save time by hearing what he has to say. I'll ring him up in a few minutes. Where exactly does he hang out?'

There was a large scale map of the city hanging in the bar, and a study of this soon gave them the lie of the land and the positions of Jefferson's works and private house.

'I've never seen this Gorge of the Avon and suspension bridge that you hear so much about,' French went on. 'Let's go and have a look before it gets quite dark.'

'There's a full moon, sir, or very nearly. We should see it all right.'

They took a bus down the river and went first under the great bridge, then climbed up the side of the valley and walked across it. Daylight had gone before they reached the top, but the night was clear and in the moonlight they could see dimly the abyss they were crossing. One side of the gorge was in shadow, black as jet. The rocks and patches of vegetation on the other hung faint and unreal below them. Far below the river lay dark and mysterious, lit only by the lights of a steamer coming up to the city.

'Fine place this, right enough,' French approved. 'I'd like to come back and see it by daylight if we can find the time.'

Strolling on the south side of the river, they presently came to a telephone kiosk.

'The very thing I was looking for,' said French, disappearing within.

He rang up Jefferson and made an appointment to call on him in fifteen minutes. The house was not far from the north end of the bridge, and by the end of the allotted time he and Carter were seated in the merchant's study.

'I didn't know Scotland Yard had been called in,' Jefferson began. 'That surely means that you suspect a crime, does it not?'

'Not necessarily, sir,' French answered. 'It usually does mean that, I grant you, but it may only mean, as in this case, that there is the possibility of a crime. Often also we are called in when an inquiry seems likely to include a number of separate police forces—again as in this case.'

Jefferson nodded. 'I see. Well, if there's anything I can do to help you to clear it up, I shall only be too glad. But I'm afraid I can tell you nothing more than I've already told the superintendent in Liverpool.'

French repeated his little homily on first-hand information. Then he began to ask questions. Though he was as exhaustive as he knew how, he had to admit when the interview was over that Jefferson had been right. He learned little that he had not already known. Some additional information he obtained about the gambling break that Platt had made some three years earlier, but not a great deal.

'You paid his debts on that occasion, Mr Jefferson?' French asked. 'Do you know whether he remained all square, or whether he since contracted others?'

'I never heard of further difficulties. Certainly he never asked for help again.'

'And you don't know of any other trouble that he might have been in?'

'None whatever.'

So it went on. The result of the interrogation was almost entirely negative. Finally, after obtaining from Jefferson a family group containing what the merchant stated was a good portrait of Platt, French took his leave, saying he would call at the office on the following morning to have a look over the missing man's papers.

'Not that we'll find anything,' he went on to Carter, as they stood waiting for the bus to take them back into Bristol. 'Platt seems to have been a pretty wide awake gentleman. If he was in trouble he'll not have left a record.'

In this once again French proved himself a true prophet. A search of the man's desk and inquiries from his fellow workers revealed nothing whatever. Except perhaps the fact, not put into words, but felt by French, that Platt had not been liked. He had evidently been selfish and lazy and out only for what he could get.

'I suppose we better see the landlady next,' French decided when they had left the works.

No. 12 Honiton Street proved to be a dilapidated house in a somewhat squalid neighbourhood, and Mrs Russell was untidy and down at heel. But Platt's two rooms were not uncomfortable, and the landlady improved on acquaintance. She seemed kindly and efficient enough, though overwhelmed with her job and three small children.

She said that Platt was a fairly satisfactory tenant. He was in the habit of getting behind with his rent, but usually paid up in the end, though at the present time he unhappily owed her for three weeks. This she was now beginning to wonder if she would ever see.

She could not tell much about her lodger, who was of a very close disposition. He had few friends, if one was to judge by the number that he brought home or who came to see him. On the other hand, he was out a great deal. He kept very late hours. Often he didn't come in till one in the morning or later. Only twice in the five years he had been with her had she seen him the worse for drink, though he smelt of it often enough. The only person whose name she knew of those who had visited him was a Mr Evan Morgan, whom she thought had some position in the Corporation. Platt had been away during the previous week, and she had had a card, which she produced, from Hillsborough, Ireland, saying he would be back on Sunday evening. That had been written on Friday. No, she had no objection to the gentlemen searching anywhere they liked. She would like the affair cleared up for her own sake, as, if Mr Platt was dead or had left, she would have to try and re-let her rooms. Here again French read into her manner that she had not liked her lodger.

He turned then to Platt's desk, which was strongly made and fastened with a stout lock. However, stout locks could not prevail against skeleton keys if these were wielded with French's skill. In two minutes the desk lay open.

And here for the first time he came on what really did seem relevant and important evidence. The papers in the desk revealed a highly unsatisfactory state of things.

Platt had been hard up, extremely hard up. Unpaid

bills were there going back for a considerable time. There was a bank book showing a slight overdraft—probably as large a one as he could get. There was more. There was evidence that the man had been gambling, and that he was in the hands of money lenders, who were pressing him for repayment.

It seemed to French that this discovery should prove the end of his labours. However, he could not stop just there. He would have to leave the affair tidy and shipshape. He therefore continued his inquiries.

There was a bottle of fountain pen ink in the desk, a largish bottle with smooth sides. As a matter of ordinary routine French examined it for fingerprints. He found it bore a number of clear impressions. These were obviously Platt's, and in view of possible developments he thought it might be as well to have them recorded. When he had checked that they were the same as a number of others on papers and on the inside of the desk, he packed the bottle carefully and sent it to the Yard for the necessary photographs to be taken.

Next he visited Platt's bank. The manager had not much to tell, except that his client had reached the limit of the overdraft allowed him. French saw one or two of the moneylenders, and some of those to whom accounts were owing, but these had little to say except that they hoped that they would get their money.

Mr Evan Morgan turned out to be a clerk in the rating department of the Corporation. He said he knew Platt was hard up and had himself lent him money. He immediately put into words what had been in French's mind since his discovery. 'So he's taken that way out of it,' he said, shaking his head. 'I shouldn't have believed it of him.'

But this view was scouted by Jefferson. 'Nonsense, chief inspector,' he said when French mentioned it. 'Platt would never commit suicide. He's not that kind of man. If he had felt himself up against it he would have come to me. I couldn't do otherwise than help him because of my wife and her sister, and he knows that perfectly well.'

French was impressed by the emphatic way he spoke. He made it his business to sound others who knew Platt, and every one of them scouted the idea of suicide. 'Hadn't the guts for it,' most of them said, in these or other words.

As he sat opposite Carter in the train that afternoon on their way back to Liverpool, French gave himself up to a consideration of the case so far as he knew it. It was a little early to theorise, but for the moment there was nothing else he could do, and there was always the chance of coming on an illuminating idea.

In the case of death by violence there were usually three possibilities to be considered: accident, suicide and murder. In the case of a disappearance there was a fourth. Disappearance might be voluntary. Of these four possibilities, which in the present instance was the most likely?

So far as accident was concerned, French did not think it was likely at all. The only accident that could have taken place was Platt's falling into the sea, as otherwise his body would have been found. But how could he fall into the sea? Every part of the decks used by passengers is well fenced. Only if Platt were climbing on the rail could he slip overboard. But why should he climb on the rail? On a pleasant afternoon among a group of friends—perhaps; alone on a wet night—never. No, accident might be ruled out.

Then what about suicide? French involuntarily shrugged

as he thought of the conflicting evidence he had obtained. Slowly and systematically he began to sift it, arranging it on two sides, for and against.

For suicide, there was the obvious point of Platt's finances; against, the equally clear suggestion of his character. Which of these was the most convincing?

At once French noticed a fundamental difference between the two. The financial position was fact. He had obtained evidence of its truth which would be accepted in any court. But that Platt would not commit suicide was mere opinion, entirely unsupported by proof.

But French reminded himself that because the evidence from character was less tangible, it was not therefore necessarily less dependable. Generally speaking, a man does not perform actions inconsistent with his character, and popular estimates of character are usually not far wrong. On the whole, French thought that so far he could not reach a conclusion for or against.

Were there, then, no further considerations bearing on the matter? French thought there were. Indeed no less than four occurred to him, and all of them tended in the same direction. There was first of all Platt's letter to Jefferson saying that he would be back on the Monday morning. If he didn't intend to return, why should he have written?

Secondly, there was his similar note to his landlady. This, French thought, should have even more weight. There could be no conceivable reason for the man's writing it other than for the purpose the card stated.

The third consideration was more convincing still. In his letter to Jefferson Platt had stated that he was much impressed by the demonstration of the inert petrol. Clearly he believed they were on to a genuine discovery. And he must have known that, if genuine, it would be immensely profitable. But an immensely profitable deal for his firm would undoubtedly lead to more money for himself. Even if all employees did not get an increase, he, the nephew by marriage of the senior partner and the man who had been sent to Ireland on this very business, was certain to make out of it. When he was leaving Ireland, therefore, he had reason to be in a more optimistic mood than for weeks before. Was it likely, then, that he should choose this moment in which to commit suicide? French did not believe it.

The last point was of less importance, but it still weighed. According to the report the Liverpool police had received from Belfast, Platt's manner had been quite normal all that Saturday; scarcely a possibility if he meditated taking his life.

On the whole, French thought, the balance of probability was against suicide. There was not enough evidence to be sure, but there was enough to call for further investigation.

Was the case, then, one of murder? For some time French concentrated on this idea. For murder there must be motive. What possible motive could there have been?

French could think of one only. If Platt had obtained the secret of the petrol process, and if someone else on board knew it and could use it himself, then there would be an entirely adequate motive.

Against this theory there were two facts. The first was that Ferris had stated that to the best of his knowledge and belief Platt did not know the secret. Of course, in this Ferris might be wrong. Platt was an able chemist and he might, unknown to Ferris, have discovered the essentials of the process. Only an investigation at Hillsborough could settle the point. French noted that such an investigation might become necessary.

The second fact was that so far there was no suggestion that any outsider knew of the process or of Platt's business in Ireland. It was unlikely that either Platt or the Northern Ireland group should have talked, and, if not, there was no apparent way in which the information could have leaked out. Here again inquiry would probably be required.

Then French remembered the mysterious individuals who had inquired for Platt from the purser and steward. That Platt was crossing by that boat was therefore known. And, if so, why not the additional facts about the process? Yes, this was a suggestive inquiry. French believed that this was another matter into which he would have to go.

Murder of Platt for the secret was, then, by no means out of the question.

But there was a fourth possibility. Suppose Platt were not dead? Suppose he had managed to slip ashore at Liverpool unnoticed? Suppose he had left the luggage and the made up berth as a blind to suggest suicide?

The more French thought over this idea, the more likely it seemed to grow. There might be a very adequate motive. Suppose Platt had, unknown to Ferris and his friends, stolen the secret? Suppose he meant to sell it as his own to some other firm, probably himself disappearing and starting a new life in some other country. This firm could purchase safely, as they could always argue that their own chemists had made the discovery.

Such an action on Platt's part would not only get him out of all his financial difficulties at Bristol, but would enable him to restart life elsewhere and with a fortune.

The risk would be comparatively small, the reward enormous.

It seemed clear to French that a search for Platt would have to be made. If the matter were one of theft, and if for family reasons Jefferson proved loath to prosecute, Ferris and his friends would have no such hesitation.

But whether theft or not, it was clear that the affair could not be dismissed as a case of suicide. A great deal more investigation would have to be carried out before any conclusion could be reached.

With a little sigh French then and there set to work. From the information he had obtained at Bristol he drafted a description of Platt, and with the photograph posted it to the Yard from the next station. In a couple of days every policeman in the country would see the notice in the *Police Gazette* and would become French's helper in the search. From the same station French wired to Superintendent Shepherd, asking him to see him on his arrival at Liverpool.

It was just after 9.0 when the travellers reached Lime Street. They hurried to police headquarters and there saw Shepherd. French briefly reported what he had done and asked if anything further had turned up at Liverpool. Nothing had.

'Then I'll go over to Belfast tonight,' French went on. 'I think some inquiries on the spot are desirable.'

Shepherd agreed with warmth. Evidently the removal of the investigation from Liverpool was entirely to his mind. French then asked for the use of the telephone and made two calls. One was to Chief of Police of the Royal Ulster Constabulary in Belfast, saying he was going over in reference to the Platt case and asking for an interview in the morning. The other was a routine 'report progress' message to the Yard.

The Belfast boat left at 10.0 and, by jumping into a taxi and telling the man to hurry, they caught it with a margin of five minutes.

8

As Chief Inspector French Saw It

French was sorry that the ship was not the *Ulster Sovereign*, as on the vessel from which Platt had disappeared there was always the chance of picking up some useful information. This was the *Ulster Monarch*, a sister ship, identical in all respects save for the personnel of the crew. There was little that he could do on board. He did, however, walk round with Carter all the decks and areas to which passengers had access, only to be more than ever convinced that, whatever had happened to Platt, he hadn't accidentally fallen overboard.

Luckily for them, the ship was not full, and they were able to obtain berths. French fell asleep at once, but he rose early and went on deck. He wanted to see the approach to Belfast Lough. Last time he had visited Northern Ireland it had been by the Stranraer route. This was quite different. They drew in from the south-west towards the coast of County Down near the Copeland Islands, on one of which is the Mew Lighthouse, controlling the southern entrance to the Lough.

At 5.30, when French looked out, the dawn was coming and the land well in sight. A low line of coast dotted with houses, grouped here and there into tiny towns. Then came the Islands, flattish and not very interesting, and after them the ship swung round to port and headed along the coast towards Grey Point. French engaged a sailor in a somewhat one-sided conversation, learning from him the names of the places they passed. That cluster of houses was Groomsport, and the large town a little farther on was Bangor. After Bangor the land rose slightly and became more broken and interesting, as well as being better wooded. There was Carnalea, and though French didn't know it, he glanced at the house, some two or three miles away, in which at that moment Dot and Dash Whiteside were sleeping, and where old Mr Whiteside was lying wakeful, puzzling over the fate of Platt. Next to Carnalea was Helen's Bay, and then they rounded Grey Point and headed straight for the city.

Turning to starboard, French was able to recognise several of the places he had passed through on his previous visit. That massive square tower belonged to Carrickfergus Castle, that high ground farther down the Lough was Whitehead, and farther along that precipitous cliff at the end of the land was the Gobbins. A bolder coast, that of Antrim, though bleaker and less well wooded.

At length they reached the head of the Lough, and passing between the Twin Islands—which are now not islands at all—entered the River Lagan. The speed was strictly limited to 5 knots, and they crawled slowly up into the heart of the city, past the shipyards and commercial basins. Trade seemed to have revived well here, and on the slips were the skeletons of great ships, cradled between towering

107

gantries on the tops of which cranes pointed their jibs out over the work. Huge liners lay along the finishing wharfs in various later stages of development, some still red in their priming coats of paint and without funnels or masts, others nearing completion and decked in brilliant colours. One vast hull looked ready for sea, painted in dazzling white with blue linings, with a cruiser stern and tier after tier of portholes and decks. She was for tropical work, evidently, while her neighbour, in sombre black, was destined for more temperate zones. A short distance above the shipyards the *Ulster Monarch* came to a stop, swung round with her bow pointing seawards, and sidled gently alongside the wharf.

It was still only a few minutes past seven, and French and Carter, going ashore, found an hotel and had breakfast. Then about nine they went down to police headquarters in Chichester Street.

'Chief Inspector French of Scotland Yard,' French told the doorkeeper. 'I think* Superintendent Rainey is expecting me.'

They had not to wait long. The messenger soon showed them into a small but comfortably furnished and well lit room. At a table desk sat a thick-set man of medium height, whose rather stern face lit up and became attractive as he smiled at French. He rose and advanced with outstretched hand.

'I'm delighted to see you again, chief inspector,' he said warmly, and he really did seem pleased. 'And I'm delighted

* There is no such rank as superintendent in the Royal Ulster Constabulary. I have used it in order to avoid referring to an existing officer.—F.W.C.

to be able to call you by that title, too. I can only say that it was long overdue.' He turned to Carter and shook hands.

'Extremely good of you, super. I'm glad to be in Belfast again. This is Sergeant Carter from our headquarters.'

'Sit down, won't you?' Rainey indicated chairs and held out his cigarette case. 'Let's see—how long is it since you were here before? Six years, I think?'

French took a cigarette. 'A little under six years, yes. I was just counting up on the way across. I've not forgotten our evening on the Cave Hill.'*

'Lord, no! That was a wild night. I've never been out a worse. But we got our men.' He turned to Carter. 'You missed that, sergeant.'

'I've heard about it, sir,' Carter answered, greatly pleased at being included in so friendly a way in the conversation.

'What about my old friend Sergeant M'Clung?' went on French.

'You'll be seeing him directly. It was he who went down to Hillsborough on your case.'

'Still sergeant?'

'Senior sergeant now. Gone up a grade.'

'I'm glad to hear it. He's a good man.'

Superintendent Rainey admitted it with a subtle suggestion in his manner that a mere Englishman would naturally be impressed by the standard in Northern Ireland. Then the talk became general. They went over old ground in the Sir John Magill case, and French asked after some of the

---

* French's first meeting with Rainey was in 1929 when he was investigating the fate of Sir John Magill, described under the title *Sir John Magill's Last Journey.*—F.W.C.

people he had then met. They touched on the depression and how Belfast and Northern Ireland as a whole had weathered it. Briefly they compared notes on recent police developments in the two countries, and then Rainey came to business.

'You'll probably wish to go down to Hillsborough, will you?' he asked as he pressed a button on his desk.

'Yes, I think I should, now I've come so far.'

'Well, I've rung for M'Clung. He'll take you down.'

Before French could reply, the door opened and Sergeant M'Clung entered. His strong rugged face lit up with a smile when he saw French. French turned to him with outstretched hand.

'Well, sergeant, here I am to worry you again,' he greeted him.

M'Clung's enormous paw closed like a vice on French's. 'You're welcome back to Belfast, sir. Many a time I think of the job we had over that Magill case.'

The man was looking older. His powerful frame was still spare and he was obviously in excellent training, but his face was more lined and the hair on his temples had gone grey. "Probably he's thinking the same about me," French thought. "However, there's plenty of life left in both of us still."

'Sit down, sergeant,' Rainey invited, 'and listen to what the chief inspector wants you to do.' He looked at French.

'I'm a bit in your hands,' French returned. 'The point is this: There's a certain doubt as to what happened to this man Platt. Some of the facts point to suicide, but there are considerable difficulties in that theory. I'm afraid we have to admit the possibility both of murder and of deliberate disappearance.'

110

'I think that's quite clear,' Rainey declared. 'What about motive?'

'If this petrol business is genuine, and if Platt had got hold of the process, the motive would be there all right. One of the things I want to try and find out is whether he did get hold of it.'

'The parties at Hillsborough say not, sir,' M'Clung put in. 'But you can see them for yourself.'

'I should like to do so,' French agreed. 'Then there's the question of the men who asked for Platt on board.'

Rainey looked up with an expression of interest. 'I didn't hear about that,' he said.

French explained, and then it was Rainey's turn to enlighten French. 'Did you know that one of the members of the syndicate crossed in the boat with Platt—a man called Penrose? We got on to it through the passenger list.'

'No, I hadn't heard that. What does he say?'

'He's not home yet from London. I was going to suggest that we wire him to call at the Yard, and maybe you could see him on your return?'

'I'll do so,' French agreed; and they entered into a detailed discussion of the affair. Finally it was arranged that French, Carter and M'Clung should go down to Hillsborough and have an interview with the members of the syndicate.

The early promise of the day had been maintained. The sun was bright and the sky blue as M'Clung drove his visitors out along the Lisburn Road. He had telegraphed to Ferris to collect the party at his cottage, but he was not sanguine as to the result. 'Dear knows if he'll get it in time,' he explained. 'Some of them'll maybe be from home. If we'd 'a' known to wire last night, we 'a' had a better chance.'

111

'Never mind,' said French. 'We'll see some of them.'

They reached the cottage as Ferris arrived with M'Morris, and while Ferris brought them in M'Morris ran round for Pam.

M'Clung began by introducing French and Carter. The others were obviously impressed, and said with one consent that they were glad the affair was being handled so energetically, and that they would be only too glad to help in every way they could. French thanked them in his easy, pleasant way. Then he got to work.

First he asked each one of the three for a detailed statement of his or her connection with the affair. Then inquiring about the other two members, he obtained Jack's address in London and was informed that Mr Whiteside was at Carnalea, where he could be interviewed at any time.

He then had a look round the cottage, with the object, as it were, of providing illustration of what he had heard. He was shown the inert petrol and the apparatus for producing it, and though an actual experiment was not performed, the process was broadly and non-technically described. Its enormous value if genuine became obvious to him, and he was convinced that it provided a completely adequate motive for any crime.

'Now tell me,' he said, 'did Mr Platt know the details of the process? I mean, sufficiently for him to have had a plant made for producing the stuff?'

Ferris shook his head. 'He did not,' he answered emphatically. 'He saw our results, but he didn't see the way they were brought about. Sure that was what we're wanting to sell, and if we'd have given him the information he wouldn't have bought it.'

'Quite. I follow that. You didn't explain the details, but could he not have found them out for himself?'

'He could not—not that I can see, anyway.'

French changed his position as if, defeated, he was withdrawing and returning by another route to the attack.

'Now, don't think I am suggesting anything against Mr Platt. It's simply that we have to consider all the possibilities. Could he,' he lowered his voice and moved his head forward, 'have stolen it?'

Ferris in his turn moved uneasily. 'I know what you're after well enough,' he admitted; 'but I don't believe you're right. I don't believe he could have got hold of it. Could he, Mac?'

M'Morris shook his head. 'Not at all. He was smart, but he wasn't smart enough for that.'

'Probably you're right,' French said smoothly. 'At the same time, you might please let me know the circumstances. Was this process written down?'

'It was and it wasn't,' Ferris answered. 'There wasn't any complete account of it that a man could make the apparatus from. But there were formulæ that had to be put on paper. The composition of parts of the converters, for instance. Unless these were correct, the thing wouldn't work. And they couldn't be left to memory.'

'Suppose,' went on French, 'Mr Platt had in some way obtained those sheets. With his chemical knowledge, coupled to what he had seen at your demonstration, could he have reconstructed the process?'

Ferris hesitated and looked for inspiration at M'Morris. 'I believe he might,' he said at length. 'But he couldn't have got them.'

'Where did you keep your notes, Mr Ferris?'

'In there.' Ferris pointed across the room to a small safe on which was stacked some chemical apparatus. They were seated in what had been the kitchen, the demonstration room being full of apparatus. 'We had to have some place to keep our stuff. I picked that up second hand in Belfast.'

'No copies of your notes outside?'

'One set at the bank only.'

'Did you take out either set while Mr Platt was here?'

'I did not. They'd only be wanted if you were constructing the apparatus in the new.'

'Your keys? Could Platt have got his hands on them for a moment?'

'He could not. I never left them in his way.'

'Any duplicates?'

'One, but it's in the bank.'

French paused to consider his next line of questions, and Ferris went on: 'There's another thing against what you're trying to prove, chief inspector,' he declared. 'It wouldn't matter about the keys, because Platt wouldn't have had any opportunity to get at the safe. He was never left alone here. I'm sure of that, because if he'd had a chance he could have taken off the screens covering the pole pieces, and someone was always here to see that he didn't. So he couldn't have got at the safe either.'

'At night?'

'No, nor at night. First, he hadn't any key to the cottage, and next, I sleep upstairs. If he had tried to break in I would have heard him.'

'Are you a heavy sleeper?'

'I am not. I'm easy enough wakened.'

Again French thought for a moment, and again he presently started on another line.

'Now, who knew about this affair besides yourselves?'

'How do you mean, knew about it?' Ferris returned. 'If you mean the process, there was no one. If you mean knew we were working at something, everyone in the district knew. To satisfy curiosity we let on that we were working at a new motor to burn paraffin.'

'No one knew the process, except you three, Mr Whiteside and Mr Penrose?'

Ferris smiled crookedly across at Pam. 'No one, only Mac and me. What do you say, Pam? Would you say you and Jack knew it?'

Pam looked at French and shook her head. 'Mr Ferris is right,' she declared. 'Only he and Mr M'Morris knew it really—I mean in detail. I've never seen those shields off, and I've never seen the sheets of formulæ you spoke of.'

French nodded. 'I follow. Now, I wonder can any of you help me here? Two men asked on the steamer for Platt. Both were tall, but one was dark and one was fair. Who could they have been?'

Pam and Ferris exchanged glances. 'One of them might have been Mr Penrose,' said Pam. 'He crossed by the same boat, and he's tall and fair. But, of course, I don't know that it was he.'

'I thought one might turn out to be Mr Penrose,' French admitted. 'Now, what about the other, the dark one?'

Ferris shook his head. 'I don't know who that could have been. No idea at all.' French glanced at the others, who also shook their heads.

'You don't know if Platt made any friends while he was over?'

'Not that I know of.' Ferris looked at the other two, who once again shook their heads. 'Of course,' he went

115

on, 'he may have met someone that we wouldn't know anything about. Maybe at the hotel, or maybe when he went out walking. He wasn't in our company all the time.'

'Which hotel are you speaking of?'

'The hotel here in Hillsborough. Platt stayed there during his visit.'

French looked at M'Clung. 'We might call there presently, sergeant, and make some inquiries,' he said, and M'Clung nodded his agreement.

For some little time French sat with the trio, discussing various other aspects of the case. Then, taking a polite leave, the three police officers went on to the hotel.

They had a chat with the proprietor, but without learning anything valuable. Platt had stayed there from the Tuesday night till the Saturday evening. He had been pleasant enough in his manner, and had passed the time of day with any of the other guests he came across. But, as far as the proprietor knew, he had not made a friend of any of them.

French was a little worried as they drove back to Belfast. So far his visit had not been an outstanding success. In fact, he had learnt very little that he didn't know before he came. He had met the people concerned and seen the location in question and got the facts more clearly in his mind, but he had obtained nothing which pointed towards a solution of the problem.

He wondered whether he should remain in Northern Ireland for a day or two longer in the hope of picking up some fresh information. On the whole, he thought he had better not. In the first place, he didn't exactly see where he should look for it, and secondly, he was here, as it were, on sufferance: he could not take on himself inquiries which normally would be made by the local force.

He called, therefore, at Chichester Street for a final conference with Rainey, and it was presently decided that while he, French, was trying to get news of Platt having left the steamer at Liverpool, Rainey should have inquiries made as to the identity of the tall dark questioner on the *Ulster Sovereign.*

The wind had risen during the afternoon, and when French's boat got out of the shelter of Belfast Lough it began to roll. He wasn't ill, but he couldn't sleep, so to pass the time he set himself to clarify and register in his mind the impressions he had formed during his visit.

Pam he took first. A nice girl, he thought. Decent and straight and dependable, he felt sure. Good looking, too, in a mild sort of way. But not remarkable. Would make a good wife for someone, but wouldn't set the Lagan on fire.

And yet there was one thing that he had noticed with surprise: The girl was uneasy—very uneasy indeed. She had something on her mind, and from her manner French could not but think it was connected with his visit. She gave him the impression of knowing something which she wanted to keep from him, and which she was afraid he would find out. It was a state of mind which French was well accustomed to meet, and he recognised the symptoms. Yet he was a pretty good judge of character, and he found it hard to believe that this knowledge should be of a guilty kind.

Ferris, he had seen at once, was a sharp one. The man's little twinkling eyes were brimming over with intelligence. Ferris, he thought, might be too sharp to be entirely wholesome. Ferris he could imagine working a very pretty fraud if he thought it would pay him to do so. No, French felt he wouldn't trust Ferris further than he could see him.

And yet the man had been straightforward enough in

his statement. He had told a simple and convincing story, and he had told it simply and convincingly. There was no reason whatever to suspect that it was not the exact truth. French believed it was the exact truth. At the same time, Ferris was the kind of man who was always worth while watching.

M'Morris, he felt, was a more ordinary individual. Not so clever as Ferris, not so kindly and decent as Pam. Unlikely to do anything very good—or very bad, either. If he did anything out of the ordinary, it would probably be under the influence of some stronger personality. M'Morris, he thought, might be dismissed from serious consideration.

Then there was Jack Penrose. Well, he would see him in London. But this sort of speculation was not going to help him in his case. French turned to his next stop. He would intensify the search for Platt, and if after a reasonable time he heard nothing of him, he would accept what would then have become the obvious solution and conclude that the man had committed suicide.

Having reached this decision, French found himself growing sleepy, and presently he was no longer conscious of the straining of the *Ulster Monarch* as she rolled her way across the uneasy waters of the Irish Sea.

9

As Pamela Grey Saw It

When Pamela Grey opened her eyes on the Sunday morning following Jack Penrose's departure for London she was conscious of a weight on her mind. For a moment she could not account for the feeling. But as she struggled into more complete wakefulness the cause recurred to her. That scene with Platt in the cottage had left an unpleasant memory.

She liked to be on friendly terms with those around her, and for that reason alone regretted what had happened. But apart from that and from her physical revulsion at the incident itself, she was a little worried about Jack. For a moment his anger had been so great that he had seemed scarcely sane. Had she not been there to restrain him, she did not like to think what the consequences might have been. Of course it was marvellous and wholly delightful that he should feel like that about her and be so ready to protect her. But there was reason in everything; he had completely lost his self-control. She decided she must talk to him seriously when he came back.

Dear Jack! He was so good! She smiled dreamily as once again she compared him to some great dog. He would dash without a thought into trouble or danger, if only he thought his doing so would be to her benefit. Oh, if only they were married . . .

She got up presently and dressed. Rather like a fish out of water she would feel for these next few days. Work at the cottage had been so heavy and continuous that it had filled all her spare time and most of her thoughts. And now it was over. There would be nothing more to be done until the Wrenn Jefferson principals came over—if they ever did.

She remembered that she was due to lunch that day with the Whitesides. This had been arranged on the Friday afternoon after the fishing excursion. They had asked her for two reasons. In the first place she had mentioned that Jack was crossing to London on the Saturday night and Dot had immediately said, 'Then you won't know what to do with yourself at Hillsborough. Come down to us. The Smiths of Brookvale are coming and we can have some tennis.' This invitation the others had seconded. Then Mr Whiteside had added, 'I shall want to hear how your discussion about the agreement went off. You can tell me at the same time.' She had promised to turn up for lunch and stay for the afternoon.

Pam had no car, so she went by bus, first into Belfast, and then, changing, by the Bangor service. At the end of the Carnalea road she got out and walked down to the house. The rain, which had come on while she and Jack were changing the punctured wheel on the previous evening, had continued all night and during the morning, but now the clouds were breaking and it looked as if fine weather were coming. There would, however, be no tennis. Pam was not altogether sorry. She was not nearly as good as the others and when playing with them always felt a little out of it.

Dot, however, was loud in her regrets. 'I haven't had a game since Thursday,' she declared as if announcing some serious dereliction of fate. 'Friday we were out fishing with you and yesterday the M'Laughlins came in and insisted on golf. We were on the links the whole afternoon: two till after seven.'

'Too much of a good thing,' said Pam.

'So I think,' Dot agreed. 'Just as well the Smiths can't come anyway. They've just rung up.' She was in a very companionable mood and had Pam up in her own sanctum to discuss confidentially matters of high import. It appeared that Dot was daily expecting a proposal. She was doubtful as to whether or not to accept it, and put the pros and cons to Pam as one having authority.

On Monday Pam had an engagement in Belfast, but on Tuesday morning she really did feel herself at a loose end. She had grown so accustomed to starting off after breakfast to begin her day's work at the cottage, that now, when there was no longer anything to be done there, the day appeared stretching out rather interminably. She would, she decided, have a round of golf. Someone would be sure to join her on the links, and if not, she could go round by herself.

She changed, took her clubs and set out. But she had not gone more than a hundred yards when she saw Ferris's Austin Seven. It drew up beside her. M'Morris was driving. He leant out and Pam saw that his face was grave.

'I was just coming for you, Pam. There's been rather bad news. Come back to the cottage and let's talk it over.'

Her heart leapt. Jack! . . . Could anything have happened to him? . . .

121

'What is it?' she returned urgently. 'Tell me at once!'

'It's Platt,' he said. 'Get in and I'll tell you.'

Platt! A deep wave of relief swept over Pam. Then Jack was all right! A fierce anger burned for a moment against M'Morris. Why couldn't he have told her at once and saved her that fright? And what a fright! It seemed as if a hand had gripped her heart so that it could scarcely beat. Gasping slightly, she walked round the front of the car and got in beside M'Morris.

'What is it?' she repeated.

'Platt has disappeared.'

She stared at him. 'Disappeared? How? When?'

'On Saturday night. Off the boat. He left Belfast, but he never got to Liverpool.'

Slowly Pam turned a dead white. What was this? She felt slightly sick. She surely wasn't going to faint? No, she was all right.

She licked her lips, which had suddenly gone dry.

'Overboard?' she whispered hoarsely.

'Overboard; yes, that's what they think?'

'They?'

'Yes, the police. A sergeant has just been down talking to Ferris. He'll tell you.'

The police? Once again that strange feeling swept over Pam. She clenched her hands. No, she wouldn't faint. It was ridiculous of her. There was nothing to be upset about. Platt—even if he had—gone overboard . . . It was nothing to her. Dreadful! But nothing to her. No, of course, nothing to her.

'What happened?' she asked, still in that hoarse whisper. She couldn't speak normally.

'They don't know. We imagined they suspected suicide.'

122

Suicide! Another sudden wave of relief swept over her. Suicide! Of course that was what had happened. But how dreadful! She touched her forehead. It was wet. Surreptitiously she wiped it.

'Oh, Mac, how horrible!' she said in more normal tones, albeit a trifle shakily. 'What did the police want to know?'

'All they could about him: what he'd been over for and so on. Ferris'll tell you. Here we are.'

But Ferris hadn't a great deal more to tell. He was just finishing breakfast when a car had come to the door. He had opened it to find three men waiting. One was their own Hillsborough sergeant. The others were in plain clothes, but the sergeant had introduced them as Detective-Sergeant M'Clung and Constable Brown of the Belfast headquarters staff. M'Clung had immediately said that he wanted all the information about Platt that Ferris could give him. He asked all sorts of questions covering everything connected with the man, and when Ferris asked what was wrong, he said he was believed to have gone overboard on the way over to Liverpool on the Saturday night.

'What did you tell him?' Pam asked still rather hoarsely.

'Whatever he asked I answered as fully as I could,' Ferris returned. 'I didn't volunteer anything. Not,' he added, 'that there was anything to volunteer.'

'What sort of questions did he ask?'

'Every blessed thing that you could think of; about when the man came and what he came for and all that. Then he went on about whether he was depressed or seemed to have anything on his mind. It was easy to see what he was after. He was thinking of suicide.'

'Did he say he suspected suicide?'

'He did not. It was I asked him the question. He said

123

that was what they were trying to find out. But sure that's only what you'd expect. The police'll never give anything away.'

'Was that all he asked?'

Ferris shook his head. 'Not by a long way,' he declared. 'He was on first about the process. Did Platt know the process? It was a secret, wasn't it? Very well, did Platt know the secret? I said he did not, but that didn't satisfy him. How did I know that Platt didn't know the secret? Could he not have found it out for himself? Had I notes of it? Where were they? Then have a look and make sure they're there still. And so on and so forth till all was no more. Then he started about the safe key. He wasn't missing much, I can tell you.'

'There's no doubt what was in his mind anyway,' M'Morris remarked.

'There is not,' agreed Ferris. 'He was wondering if anyone had murdered him for the secret.'

Pam shivered. This was the most *dreadful* affair.

'What else did you tell him?' she insisted.

'What did I tell him? He wanted to know who we all were. I told him that, and I told him how I came to be living here and about you and Jack and Mac and Mr Whiteside. Mac by the way had come in and he talked to him too. He asked me was Jack the Mr Penrose who had crossed that same night, and I said he was. He said he would like a statement from him and when would he be back? I told him I didn't know exactly. Then I said we could get you in a few minutes, but he said that was all right, he didn't want to see you.'

Pam felt horribly upset. She continued questioning Ferris, but he said he had told her everything. After a time, there being no more to be learnt, she went home. In the afternoon she wrote a long letter to Jack, asking him when he would be back.

That evening there was an account of the affair in the *Belfast Telegraph*, and next morning notices in the *Belfast Newsletter* and *Northern Whig*. But none of these were illuminating. They merely said that Platt, a representative of the firm of Wrenn Jefferson of Bristol, had disappeared from the motor ship *Ulster Sovereign* during a voyage from Belfast to Liverpool on the Saturday night, and that it was feared he had been lost overboard.

Next day, so far as the papers were concerned, the matter was at an end. No reference to the affair appeared. Pam would have given a great deal to have forgotten it in the same way.

After discussion it was arranged that Ferris should write to Wrenn Jefferson, expressing the profound regret of the party at what had happened, and asking what the firm proposed to do in connection with the petrol process.

Pam found the following few days almost interminable. There was a short note from Jack saying that his business had dragged out unexpectedly and that he wouldn't be home till Sunday morning. He made no reference to the Platt affair, except one short comment which read, 'Rotten thing about Platt. I expect Jefferson will come over himself now.' Even Pam thought it was a little callous.

Wednesday and Thursday dragged away without incident. But on Friday Pam had another shock. Once again during the forenoon M'Morris drove round for her in Ferris's car.

'There's another inquiry about this affair,' he explained. 'The same police officer's back from Belfast and he's got a new man with him, an Englishman, a big pot from Scotland Yard. He said if you were disengaged, he'd like to ask you a few questions. A sort of Royal command, I would think. Anyhow you are disengaged.'

Pam's heart sank and for a moment she faced sheer panic. Then she began to pull herself together and by the time they reached the cottage, she had herself well in hand.

The police officers proved to be less formidable than she had expected. The Belfast sergeant—M'Clung, he said his name was—seemed straight and was civil and not over-bearing, while she actually took to the London man. Chief Inspector French was not only polite and appeared to be straight, but she thought he looked kindly and decent. He it was who asked the questions, and while he did not allow any point to slide, she could not but realise his efforts to make the interrogation as little irksome as possible, particulary to herself. Before the interview was over she felt grateful to him for his consideration.

But what the police gained by their visit she could not imagine. So far as she could make out they simply asked the same questions as on the first occasion and received the same answers.

Ferris, however, broke fresh ground by asking directly what the police thought about the case. French answered with an air of charming candour, though even Pam wondered if he were quite as transparent as he seemed. He said they really did not know what had taken place. There was the chance that Platt had fallen overboard by accident, that he had committed suicide, or that, if he had the secret, that he had been murdered for it. They hadn't enough evidence to say which of these had occurred. That was what they were here for—to try to find some more evidence.

And he, French, might take that opportunity of thanking the party for what they had told him.

On the surface it was all very pleasantly done, though what might be beneath it only the policemen knew. Presently they left to carry their investigation a stage further at the Hillsborough Hotel. The others remained on in the cottage discussing the interview.

'They didn't make much by that,' Ferris declared presently. 'I don't believe they learned a single thing that they didn't know on Monday.'

'The London one likely wanted to get the dope at first hand,' M'Morris suggested.

'But don't you think,' Pam asked, 'that they must think it was serious? I mean, if they thought it was suicide, they would never go to all this trouble?'

'Is it murder you mean?' asked Ferris.

Pam shivered. 'I suppose so,' she admitted. 'Would they make such a fuss for anything else?'

Ferris shook his head. 'Ask me an easier one,' he begged.

'They seemed satisfied with what we told them anyway,' M'Morris pointed out.

'Well, and why shouldn't they be? We told them everything. There was no more they could get from us.'

Pam controlled herself as best she could, but she was really terribly uneasy. Panic as to what the police might think assailed her, and it took all the strength she had to fight it back. While she was at the cottage she succeeded, but on her walk home it grew to almost overwhelming dimensions. How she wished that Jack was back! How she wished to see him and to hear him and to be comforted by what he would have to tell her!

Because that this would comfort her, she never for a

moment doubted. Never for a moment! And yet . . . Oh, how she wished he would come!

The remainder of Friday and Saturday dragged out as if each of them were a month. Each evening she walked over to the cottage to know if any news had come in, and each evening she was partly disappointed and partly relieved that none had. Both Ferris and M'Morris seemed to be feeling the strain also, though not to the extent she was herself.

At last Sunday morning dawned. Pam would have liked nothing better than to get up at half-past five and drive into Belfast to meet the boat when it came in about seven. But she could not admit her anxiety and she hadn't a car of her own. She decided she must just possess her soul in patience. Jack would come to her as soon as he could.

He did turn up—after breakfast. She supposed he could not very well have come earlier. When she heard the car she ran down, her heart throbbing painfully. Jack obviously was glad to see her, but he was just as casual and offhand as ever. 'Hallo, old thing,' he greeted her, and catching her in his arms, kissed her, though without any special warmth or significance. 'Got a letter that I think'll interest you. Look here!'

He drew a paper from his pocket, unfolded it, and handed it across. She glanced at the headlines, 'Wrenn Jefferson & Co., Ltd.' But for a moment she could not read it. She stood looking from the letter to Jack and from Jack to the letter, and her heart sang within her. What a fool she had been! What a *fool*! And a disloyal fool! If Jack were to throw her over, it would only be what she deserved. How could she have let that dreadful little doubt come into her mind and poison it and destroy her happiness? Well, it would be a lesson to her. She felt she could hardly look Jack in the face. Never again as long as she lived would she allow such a thought to enter her mind.

But he was staring at her in surprise. 'Well,' he said, 'aren't you going to read it? You haven't got a stroke or anything, I suppose?'

Then she surprised him further. Before he knew what she was going to do, she had thrown her arms round his neck and buried her face in his coat. When he lifted her in his arms she was sobbing.

'Good God!' he said.

For once in his life he showed tact. He sat down and took her on his knee, and when the weighty letter fell to the ground, he allowed it to lie there unheeded. She clung to him as if she would never let him go and he held her tight in his arms. But when presently he began to ask her what it was all about, she laughed through her tears and wanted to know how he dared treat her with so little respect.

'I thought you had a letter to show me?' she went on severely, trying to frown through her tears, but unable to do anything but smile.

'I gave it to you. It's here.'

'Then what did you take it away again for? Let me see it at once.'

He picked it up. 'I declare, Pam, I think you have gone off your nut. What have you been up to while I was away?'

But now she was reading the letter. 'Why, Jack, how splendid!' she cried. 'Mr Jefferson coming over this week! Then he believes in the thing?'

'Well, he's willing to see what we can do. I had a day and I thought I'd run down and see him. He'd had a letter

129

from Platt in which the chap said he was convinced, and recommending the thing be gone into further. Jefferson said he'd come over Wednesday or Thursday, according as he could work it in. Then I got this letter before leaving London, fixing Tuesday. So that looks like business.'

'Have you told the others?'

'No. Going to now.'

Jack was full of the coming interview. He said that Jefferson had seemed much more impressed about the affair than formerly. Platt's interview had evidently borne good fruit.

It was not till later that Pam was able to ask the question which had been so constantly in her mind. 'It was so dreadful about poor Mr Platt,' she said. 'It upset us all so much. You didn't see him on the boat, did you?'

'Never set eyes on the fellow. I did look for him because of what you said, but I couldn't find him.'

'Oh, Jack, isn't it dreadful? The poor man must be dead.'

'Best thing that ever happened to him,' he returned, at which she cried out till he withdrew the remark.

'The police were over here inquiring into it,' she went on. 'They asked for your address.'

'I know. A man called French, an inspector or something, called at the hotel in London.'

'What did you tell him?'

'What could I tell him? Nothing! He wanted to know had I seen the fellow? Well, I hadn't.'

'And did he seem satisfied with that?'

'Of course he seemed satisfied. Why wouldn't he? Do you think he took me for a liar?'

'Oh, Jack, don't be such an ass! Come and tell your news to the others.'

130

Ferris and M'Morris were hugely delighted with Wrenn Jefferson's letter. 'At last!' Ferris cried dramatically. 'It's looking like business at last!' And then he gave way to an unexpected outburst of feeling. It seemed that he had been bored and discouraged with the long tedious months of research to the extent almost, as he put it, 'of going off my chump,' and the sight of the end of his labours was more than he could bear quietly. M'Morris too was obviously much moved. Pam had not realised the intensity of their feelings, and a sudden wave of sympathy for them passed over her.

Monday passed for her in comparative ease of mind, and then on Tuesday came the great event. Jefferson and two technical experts arrived by Liverpool and were met by Jack, who after they had all breakfasted together in Belfast, brought them down to the cottage.

Pam at once took to Jefferson. He was gravely courteous to them all, spoke with evident feeling about Platt, and in a short speech before the demonstration said that he had had a favourable report from the missing man about the process. Provided the Hillsborough party were able to substantiate their claims—of which he had no doubt—his firm was prepared to enter into an agreement to work it. He believed that the affair would be profitable to all concerned. No one must mind if his experts were sceptical: he had warned them that they must be so. In order to give the process a real test, these men must be convinced in spite of themselves. And now, if Mr Ferris was ready, he suggested they made a start.

Ferris was ready. He made the demonstration to the obvious surprise and admiration of the visitors. Then tests began. These were just as searching as Platt's, but they were carried out in less than half the time. By that evening the two experts expressed themselves as satisfied.

Next morning came a discussion of the terms of the proposed agreement, an almost exact repetition of that which had taken place with Platt on that fateful morning some ten days earlier. The clauses agreed on with him were now provisionally accepted by Jefferson, and Jack was asked to get out fair copies. As soon as these were signed, Jack, Ferris and M'Morris would take the apparatus over to the Bristol works, and there a further demonstration would be made, this time with the screens off.

That evening Jefferson invited the entire party to a dinner in Belfast, at which the future prosperity of the venture was properly toasted. And when at nine o'clock he and his men left for home, it did really seem as if the end of the troubles of the Hillsborough party was in sight.

By the close of that week Pam was in a much happier frame of mind, though occasional little stabs of panic still fought their way into her consciousness. However, she fought against these, and with a good deal of success.

10

As Detective-Sergeant
M'Clung Saw It

At his usual hour on the Tuesday morning of the week
following Jefferson's visit to Hillsborough, Sergeant
M'Clung left his home in Cregagh for police headquarters.

He was looking forward to a busy day. There had been
a distressing child murder near Saintfield, in the investigation of which he had assisted. The inquiry had been
successful and, largely through his efforts, they had got
their man. Now he was at work on the preparation of the
case. He believed that with reasonable luck he would
complete it that evening.

He congratulated himself that he belonged to a first rate
department, and though he wouldn't perhaps have said it
in so many words, he was well aware that he was far from
being its least efficient member. Since they had cleared up
the murder of that Turk near Carrickfergus, the department
had gone steadily ahead. Not that he himself could claim
kudos over the Turk case: he had been on another job at
the time—which incidentally he had brought off with equal

success. But the Turk case had achieved almost world-wide fame, and he had shared in the reflected glory.

But this Platt business was of a very different type. It seemed to him an affair of much ado about nothing. The man had started off to England and had felt himself fed up with life and had gone over the side like many another before him, and that was all there was to it. And then instead of taking it as the obvious suicide that it was, the English police had gone and kicked up a quite unholy fuss, ending with French coming over from the Yard! Not that he had any objection to that. He liked French and was glad to see him again. But the thing was absurd, making this mountain out of a molehill. And it had lost him the halves of two good days!

His thoughts turned back to French. It certainly was pleasant to see him walking in again. It was like old times. They had had a long and a close association over that Sir John Magill case and French had stood the test well. A pleasant man to work with! M'Clung would not have minded another job carried out in the same company. And he was but little changed. A shade stouter perhaps and a little greyer about the temples, but otherwise unaltered. And just the same pleasant, easy manner. Yes, he liked French and no mistake.

He reached headquarters and settled down at his desk. Nothing had come in for him to attend to since the previous evening, and he could therefore get right ahead with the Saintfield murder papers. Well, he would be glad to be done with it. He was pretty sick of its gruesome details.

But his hopes were doomed to disappointment. Scarcely had he settled down to work when his bell rang. With a muttered curse he got up and went to Superintendent Rainey's room.

'See that,' Rainey greeted him, holding out a telephone message pad, though without looking up from his work. In silence M'Clung took it up and began to read.

It was from Sergeant Callaghan in charge of the Groomsport police barracks and read: 'Patrick M'Gonigle, master of smack *Sally Ann*, registered in Groomsport, reports finding body of man about five-thirty this morning in sea to west of Mew Island. He got it aboard and brought it in and I have it here at barracks. It is partly decomposed, but appears to answer description of Reginald Platt, who disappeared from *Ulster Sovereign* on seventh inst. Please instruct.'

'Well,' said Rainey, throwing down his pen, 'that'll probably settle that hash. You better go down and have a look round. These Englishmen are almighty feared of its being murder, so get hold of what evidence you can.'

'I've always thought it was suicide, sir, and this'll likely prove it.'

'I know: I think it was suicide myself. But don't take anything for granted. Get a doctor to make a proper examination, and if you think there's any doubt have a post mortem. We don't want to agree it's suicide and then have some other fact coming up to prove it was murder.'

'No, sir. I'll see to it.'

'And keep me advised of what you are doing,' Rainey counselled finally, as once again he bent over his work.

It did not take M'Clung long to make his arrangements. Fifteen minutes later he was in a car with Constable Brown and Dr Anderson, one of the police doctors, driving out over the same route through Holywood which Jack and

Pam took when going to visit the Whitesides. The day was fine and warm and it was a joy to be out of doors. The sun drew out the rich colours of the foliage and tiny clouds made of the landscape a patchwork of light and shade. Where they could see the sea it showed a steely blue, with beyond it the Antrim hills, dark and sharply outlined. Presently they reached Bangor, and passing down to the promenade and pier, they turned towards Ballyholme. Five minutes later they ran into the tiny little seaside village of Groomsport and drew up at the police barracks. Sergeant Callaghan, obviously filled with importance, hurried out to meet them.

'I have the body in behind, gentlemen,' he said saluting, 'and I have M'Gonigle, the man who found it, warned to be ready if so be you want to see him.'

'That's all right, sergeant,' M'Clung returned. 'You lead the way.'

In a whitewashed outhouse at the back of the building lay the remains. Even M'Clung's casehardened nerves were scarcely proof against the sight. The body had evidently been in the water for some time, and in addition to the horror of decomposition, fish or crabs had dreadfully mutilated the face. But in spite of this, M'Clung had little doubt as to whose it was. The size of the figure and the clothes were those of Platt.

For some minutes the three new arrivals stood looking down at the ghastly spectacle. Then with a shrug M'Clung made a move.

'I suppose, doctor, we'd better be getting on,' he said.

Dr Anderson nodded and routine operations ensued. Conquering their loathing with an effort, M'Clung and Constable Brown stripped off the clothes and took them to another room, while the doctor busied himself with the body.

It was not long before M'Clung came on the proof he was looking for. In the breast pocket of the undercoat there was a pocket book, sodden and spongy with the water. M'Clung, however, was able to open it, and there on the fly-leaf, faint and blotted but still legible was the name, Reginald Platt, with the Wrenn Jefferson address following. The cover contained a pretty considerable wad of papers. M'Clung did not attempt to take them out, but laid the book carefully on one side so that it might be dried before being handled further.

Except for this pocket book, there seemed nothing of interest about the clothes or the contents of the pockets. There was money, a knife, a bunch of keys and other objects, but all were ordinary and of the kind that a man like Platt might be expected to carry. M'Clung noted all of them and put them aside to be taken with the pocket-book to Belfast. When he had finished he went back to the doctor.

'I was just coming for you,' Anderson said, straightening himself up from his horrible occupation. 'As far as I can see the man was drowned, but I can't say for certain without an autopsy.'

'The super was saying he would like one,' M'Clung answered. 'He wants to be sure about the thing.'

M'Clung then made two calls. First he rang up Superintendent Rainey and made a brief report. Rainey listened, agreed that a post-mortem was desirable, and said he would send down the necessary authority. Meanwhile M'Clung was to assist the local sergeant about the inquest. 'What are you doing about identification?' went on Rainey.

'I was going to ring up those people at Hillsborough,' M'Clung replied, 'but none of them are on the phone, only Penrose: that's the one that was in London. But likely he's home by now.'

'Try, and if it's no good telegraph.'

M'Clung had Jack's business address among his notes and he got him at once. 'I'm wanting someone who knew Mr Platt to see the remains,' he went on. 'Maybe you or Mr Ferris or both of you would come on down here and have a look?'

The next business was to settle about the inquest, and here M'Clung let the local man make the arrangements. The coroner, Dr Purdy, was interviewed, and the inquiry was fixed for eleven o'clock the next morning. With the sergeant, M'Clung then interviewed Skipper M'Gonigle of the *Sally Ann* and his crew as well as the local coastguard. These he warned to be prepared to answer questions on the run of tides and currents. Subpoenas were issued to those whose attendance was required, and then M'Clung found himself back at the police barracks. There he found a message from Jack Penrose, saying that he and Ferris were then starting for Groomsport. He sat down to wait for them.

In a few minutes they turned up. 'I'm thinking the appearance of the remains will give you a shock,' M'Clung prepared them. 'But you needn't stay. See if you can identify the man without any doubt. That's all I want.'

Both men, and particularly Ferris, were greatly upset when they were ushered into the outhouse which was doing duty as a mortuary. Fortunately for them the doctors had not yet began to autopsy; at the same time what they saw turned Jack pale and made Ferris sick. But both were able without hesitation to give the identification.

'That's all right,' said M'Clung. 'I'm sorry I had to ask you to do it, but I couldn't help myself.'

In their turn they said that that was all right.

'The both of you will be wanted at the inquest,' he went on. 'You'll have to give formal evidence of identification and answer questions about the deceased's business over here. But you needn't mind. You won't have to see the body again.'

'Miss Grey won't be wanted at the inquest?' Jack asked anxiously.

'She will not,' M'Clung reassured him.

The two men, still looking very much upset, drove off. M'Clung settled a few further matters of detail and then left with Constable Brown for Belfast. There he arranged for the pocket book to be dried, and went in and reported to Rainey. 'The doctors are working this evening,' he concluded. 'We'll have a report from them first thing in the morning.'

'Did you advise French?' Rainey asked.

'Yes, sir. I wired him and Jefferson. I had a reply from Jefferson that he was coming over. He'll be here in the morning.'

'Good. Then in the morning you'd better go through those papers in Platt's pocket book. Will that be everything?'

'Yes, sir, I think so. Unless there's something unexpected from the doctors. But I don't believe there'll be that.'

'Nor I. Unless I'm very far wrong, the cause of death will be drowning. And if so, and there's no sign of violence, it seems to me the thing can only be suicide.'

M'Clung was in full agreement with his superior's opinion. If the cause of death were drowning, it would be the end of the case. If not, then the English suspicions would be justified and the trouble was only beginning. It was at least a blessing, M'Clung thought, that the issue should be so definite.

Next morning the pocket book was dry, and with the utmost care Sergeant M'Clung removed the bunch of papers it contained. In addition to this there were three items of interest. One was a number of Platt's business cards, another the return half of a third and saloon ticket from Euston to Belfast, dated September second, and nipped with a V-shaped cut, and the last, the ticket bearing the stateroom number, which M'Bratney had handed to the deceased on that fatal Saturday evening.

M'Clung then turned to the papers. They had been so sodden that they stuck together. He separated them as carefully as he could, to find that though they were largely illegible, he could make out fragments of the handwriting with which they were covered. They appeared to be notes of an agreement, presumably between Messrs Wrenn Jefferson and the party at Hillsborough. He soon saw that he could make little of the notes without help, and he rang up Jack, asking him to call with Ferris at headquarters on their way to the inquest.

The two men presently arrived and were shown the fragments. At once they recognised them as forming part of the suggested agreement between the parties which they had discussed with Platt.

'There's nothing here to suggest that the deceased had discovered the details of your process?' M'Clung asked.

Upon this point both men reassured him. The proposed paragraphs seemed to be all there in perfect order, but there was no suggestion of anything else.

'Sorry for bringing you gentlemen up,' M'Clung went on, 'but I had to get that information before the inquest. You'll be coming on to Groomsport now?'

Some forty minutes later they were all seated in the equivalent of the village hall in Groomsport. The affair had created a good deal of local interest, and the room was full to capacity. The coroner was sitting with a jury and those who had been called for that purpose were standing awkwardly round the walls. Seats at one side of the hall were being kept for them by a young constable with a worried expression. Amongst those at the table, at the end of which was the coroner's chair, were M'Clung, Dr Anderson, Penrose, M'Morris and Ferris, as well as Jefferson, who had just arrived from Bristol. In the background were other witnesses and members of the public. Sergeant Callaghan, looking more important than ever, was moving about, consulting a sheaf of papers in his hand, and speaking to various individuals. A second constable stood by the door.

On the stroke of eleven the coroner, Dr Adam Purdy, arrived and took his place, having bowed to those present. He spoke in a low tone to Sergeant Callaghan, and then turned to M'Clung.

'Are you headquarters people interested in this, sergeant?' he asked.

'There was a bit of doubt about what had really occurred, sir,' M'Clung replied, 'but I expect this inquiry will clear it up. I don't think we'll need to trouble more with it anyway.'

'But Callaghan's handling the thing?'

'Certainly he is, sir. We're only just watching.'

Dr Purdy nodded and looked at Callaghan. 'Now sergeant, if you're ready.'

The preliminaries were got through quickly enough. One by one the jurors were called, answered their names, and took their seats. Then they were sworn and the proceedings proper commenced.

The first witness was Patrick M'Gonigle, master of the smack *Sally Ann*. He deposed that with his crew of three hands he was out fishing on the night of Monday, September 9th. When they were returning about five-thirty on Tuesday morning he saw something in the water. They put about and found it was a body. They took it aboard and brought it into Groomsport and informed the police.

'Whereabouts did you find the body?' Callaghan asked.

'Just off Groomsport, about three or four miles out,' the skipper answered.

'Would that be near the path of the Liverpool boat?' the coroner queried.

'It would be farther out, sir. She would pass about a couple o' mile from the shore.'

'Then can you tell me how the current sets?'

This, it appeared, was a large question, opening many sidelines and providing much ground for interrogations. The currents altered with the tides. They varied from month to month and depended to some extent on the prevailing wind. But at last Purdy obtained the definite statement that the general set was north or north-easterly. That was to say, in fact, that an object dropped into the sea from the Liverpool boat on its passage down the Lough would probably sooner or later find itself in the position from which this body was taken. Finally, the evidence was brought back from the intricacies of tides and currents by Callaghan, who asked whether the body M'Gonigle had found was that now lying at the police barracks and upon which the inquest was being held. On giving the required assurance the skipper was told that that would do and with evident relief he stepped back from the witness chair.

Jefferson was then called and stated that he had inspected the body in question and it was that of his nephew by marriage, Reginald Wilcox Platt. He gave details of the unfortunate man's age, history and position, and explained the business which had brought him to Belfast. He, Jefferson, had received a letter from deceased from Hillsborough, saying that his work was complete and that he was returning by Saturday night's steamer.

Jefferson was questioned rather fully as to the possibility of the deceased having had a motive for suicide. The witness answered that he understood that there were debts, and that there had been debts and gambling at a previous period in the deceased's life. At the same time he pointed out that the process, in which Platt had obviously believed, was likely to prove a source of increased prosperity for his firm, in which prosperity Platt would have shared. Giving it as his opinion only, he, Jefferson, did not think there could have been any adequate motive for suicide. Deceased's manner the last time witness had seen him was normal. And the letter he had written a couple of days before his death was couched in quite normal terms. Besides, he was not, in the witness's judgment, the man to commit suicide under any circumstances.

Jack Penrose was the next witness. He described the negotiations which had taken place between the Wrenn Jefferson firm and the party at Hillsborough, together with the business which had been done with Platt during his visit. He said that he had crossed by the same boat, and that out of politeness he had looked for Platt on board to have a drink with him, but he could not find him. He had gone to his cabin, but it was empty, though the man's suitcase was partly unpacked. That must have been about a quarter-past eleven.

Ferris then told how he had driven Platt to the Liverpool boat on the Saturday night in question. He had not gone on board with him, but he had parked at the end of Corporation Square, opposite the Liverpool berth, and had accompanied him to the entrance to the sheds alongside the quay wall. Deceased had walked across the shed, and as witness turned away, he had seen him offering his ticket to the man at the gangway. Witness had then driven home. Deceased had appeared to be in a perfectly normal condition, and was neither excited nor depressed.

It had not been possible, Sergeant Callaghan explained at this point, to produce the officers of the *Ulster Sovereign* who had dealt with deceased, as they were in Liverpool. But statements had been obtained from them, which, if the coroner desired, he would put in.

Sworn statements from Purser Albert M'Bratney and Cabin Steward James Thomson were then handed in. These stated briefly what these two officers had already told to French. Deceased had written to the Belfast office asking that a single berth stateroom should be reserved for him and had handed M'Bratney the reply card sent him from the office. He had paid the excess and had been passed on to the cabin steward. The latter told about the conversation that he had had with the deceased and how in the morning he had found the stateroom empty and the bed undisturbed.

Both men referred in their statements to the two strangers who had inquired for Platt. One of these was a previous witness, Mr Penrose, the other they did not know. There being no further evidence on this point it was not followed up.

Dr Thomas Anderson deposed that he had examined the body of deceased, and with the help of Dr M'Gowan had made a post-mortem. Death in his opinion was due to drowning. All the symptoms of such were present, and there was no weakness of any of the organs which could possibly have proved fatal. Nor was there any wound or injury which might have suggested an alternative cause. In reply to the coroner, he was of the opinion that death had occurred about three weeks earlier. This, the coroner pointed out, would exactly work in with the presumption that deceased had been drowned on the Saturday night on which he left Belfast for Liverpool.

Dr Andrew M'Gowan, Groomsport, corroborated the testimony of the previous witness in every detail. This was the last witness and the coroner, after glancing through his notes, began his address to the jury. After the usual gambit about the importance of their office, he went on:

'Your first duty will be to state the actual physical cause of death, your second, to indicate what brought this cause into operation, and your third, to say if in your opinion any person was to blame for the death, and if so, whom.

'Now in answering the first of these, stating the actual physical cause of death, I do not think you will have much trouble. The doctors have told you the man was drowned. They have told you besides that there was no disease and that there were no injuries. And nothing was told you by anyone in any way inconsistent with this. You will therefore probably find in accordance with the medical evidence, that the deceased met his death through drowning.

'Now as regards your second duty, which will be to state how in your opinion the deceased came to be drowned, there are three obvious possibilities to be considered: accident, suicide and murder. Let us take these in turn.

'I think you will agree that we have had before us no evidence as to the possibility of accident, by which I presume we can only mean that the deceased fell accidentally into the sea while the boat was passing down Belfast Lough. But we are entitled to use our own knowledge and common sense, and I think these will tell us that such an accident is so unlikely as to be practically an impossibility. The decks of these ships—and indeed of all passenger ships—are well fenced, and only if a person climbed deliberately on to the rail and then lost his balance would there be danger of accident. Alone and on a wet night, it is not likely that the deceased would have been on deck at all, still less that he would have indulged in any such childish practice.

'With regard to the second possibility, that of suicide, there is more evidence. Whether it is convincing or not will be for you to say. But here we have the fact that this young man was in debt and that he was not very popular among his fellows. There is no evidence of further troubles, but of course he may have had some of which we do not know. Against the theory of suicide you have heard the statement of his employer, that this new enterprise which the firm was about to undertake would mean greater prosperity, and that such prosperity would have been shared in by the deceased. Also statements that the deceased was not a suicide type, that he was in normal health and spirits prior to the occurrence, and that he had written stating that he was returning to Bristol that night. These points you will take into consideration when framing your verdict.

'In connection with the third possibility, that of murder, I think you will agree that no evidence supporting this theory has been put before you. You may consider indeed that the evidence is against it. You will remember that the doctors have assured you that death occurred from drowning. Now it might be argued that if the case were one of murder, this could only be true if the deceased had been picked up from the deck by some powerful man, or a number of men, and thrown over the side. But, gentlemen, if this had occurred, do you imagine that the deceased would not have struggled, and if he had struggled, would not some sign remain on the body? Moreover, if he had been thrown over uninjured, would he not have cried out? And if he had cried out in his desperation would he not have been heard by the officer of the watch or some member of the passengers or crew? You will consider how far these suggestions are justified. But to your conclusion I think you must add the fact that no motive for the murder has been suggested, nor any other fact supporting the theory of murder has been brought forward. Speaking for myself alone I do not think that there should be much difficulty in rejecting this theory of murder. But of course, as I reminded you when I began these remarks, the decision is not one for me, but for you only.

'If there is no point on which you would like me to address you further, I will ask you to retire and consider your verdict.'

The jury whispered among themselves, then the foreman stood up and said they did not want to retire as they were agreed on their verdict. It was, he added on a question from the coroner, suicide while of unsound mind.

M'Clung was pleased. Once again his opinion had been vindicated. These Englishmen were barking up the wrong tree. He had known perfectly well that the thing was suicide, for the simple reason that it couldn't well have been anything else. Trust the boys of Northern Ireland! They knew their way round without any help from across the Channel! This was one up on Scotland Yard.

M'Clung was also pleased because he didn't want a fresh job. He had all the work he could very well handle. An hour or two in the morning would complete the records of the case required for the department's files and then he would be free to get that Saintfield affair finished.

Next day he sent a copy of the depositions to French, together with a few notes giving his and Rainey's views. Then with a sigh of relief he put the case out of his mind and went resolutely back to his former work.

11

As Philip Jefferson Saw It

If Sergeant M'Clung was satisfied with the result of the inquest on Reginald Platt, it was far otherwise with Philip Jefferson.

Ever since Platt's disappearance Jefferson had been worried. He had not known what to think. Accident had certainly seemed impossible, but so to Jefferson had suicide. Platt, he felt positive, was not the man to commit suicide. And the fact that everyone who had known him appeared to hold the same view, lent almost overwhelming weight to his own opinion. Jefferson had indeed slowly been coming round to the view that something more criminal had taken place. Platt, so he had imagined, had stolen the secret, and he had either been murdered for it, or had voluntarily disappeared with the intention of making what he could out of it for himself.

So strongly did Jefferson realise the possibility of this theft, that he had insisted on the inclusion of a clause in the agreement between his firm and the Hillsborough party, stating that should the process have been previously sold

149

to some other firm, his would be clear of any further liability in the matter.

In the process there would have certainly been ample motive. The more he thought over the process, the more impressed with the possibilities Jefferson had become. It was a big thing: almost incredibly big! There was in it not a fortune, but a dozen fortunes! His only fear was that his firm might not be strong enough to handle it. They must get ahead as soon as possible with arrangements to sell under licence to firms in other countries. And as for the English trade, they would have to extend their premises. They would bring petrol into their depot at Avonmouth, there make it inert, and from there send it by rail and road tanks to the distributors.

Then he had wondered whether the better plan would not be to install the converting plant at the sources of supply? The lesser bulk would then be hauled to Britain, besides giving the tankers the benefit of the safer cargo. But this would mean a world wide organisation. Jefferson wondered whether they would not have to go into one of the big combines.

But all of these tremendous possibilities were dependent on Platt not having stolen the process. How he wished he knew!

And now the matter had been brought a stage further. Poor Platt was not himself going to get any profit out of the process. But was someone else? Platt had either acted correctly all through and Jefferson's doubts of him were misplaced, or if he had really stolen the thing, someone else had discovered the theft and determined to reap the benefit. Again, how he wished he knew!

These thoughts had passed through his mind before

and during the inquest, but now he banished them in order to carry out the immediate necessities. The funeral had to be arranged, and his sister-in-law's wishes ascertained as to whether it should take place in Ireland or England. He sent off a long wire, then consulted the sergeant as to the local arrangements necessary.

In due course there was a reply from Mrs Jefferson. The sisters had decided the funeral should take place in Ireland, and they were coming over to attend it. Jefferson accordingly went ahead with the arrangements.

But that evening as he sat in a corner of the lounge of the Station Hotel in Belfast, his thoughts returned to the fate of Platt. Was it really suicide? Or was it murder? Was the process his firm's property, or was some other firm even then working on it.

Presently he decided that so far as he was concerned the affair could not be left where it was. Too much hung on the issue. He must make a further effort to reach certainty.

But what he should do was not so clear. At last he determined to see M'Clung once again, put his doubts before him, and ask whether the sergeant could suggest any suitable action.

Next morning he called at police headquarters and was at once shown into M'Clung. The sergeant received him courteously, but without enthusiasm, and Jefferson soon found that unless he could make a strong case, he would get but little sympathy.

'I don't want to keep you,' he said with guile. 'You're a busy man and you have no time to waste. But I'd like to put up these points to you and get your opinion. I don't know how far you have already considered them.'

M'Clung made a non-committal reply and looked bored.

'First,' went on Jefferson, 'there is the deceased's character. I knew him pretty well, and I simply cannot imagine his committing suicide,' and Jefferson went on to put his arguments as strongly as he knew how. He dilated on the character of Platt, the improbability that the man would kill himself because of financial difficulties without at least finding out whether he, his uncle by marriage, would help him, his belief in the process and knowledge that it would bring him in money, his writing the two letters to say he was returning to Bristol, and the normality of his manner on the day of his death. 'Then,' he concluded, 'there is my last point. A man asked for Platt after he had gone aboard the ship. Who was that man and what did he want? No one has yet answered those questions. Someone knew that Platt was crossing that night. Who? So far as we are aware, Platt was acquainted with no one in Ireland. Suppose I suggest that this unknown man murdered Platt, how are you going to disprove it?'

'No motive,' said M'Clung laconically.

'Ah,' Jefferson returned, settling down as it were to a fresh attack, 'but how do you know that? Suppose Platt had discovered the secret? Suppose this unknown knew of it. Suppose he wanted it for himself. There's plenty of motive there.'

'But that's only guesswork, sir,' M'Clung pointed out. 'You may suppose anything you like, but we can only act on evidence. You're very anxious to prove it was not suicide. May I ask just why?'

'Well there's not much mystery about that. I'm not anxious to prove it was not suicide, I only want to be sure what it was. You can see why easily enough. If it was suicide the secret is safe. If it was murder it has probably been stolen and is in the possession of some other firm. A difference of perhaps millions sterling.'

M'Clung shook his head. 'That's not right, sir. You've forgotten that Mr Platt was drowned. If what you're suggesting was true he'd have been knocked over the head or something first, to keep him quiet. But he wasn't. There weren't any signs of injury on the body and there wasn't any dope. No, sir, I can understand you would be anxious, but there isn't any call for you to suspect murder.'

From this position M'Clung wouldn't move, and his manner showed he was getting tired of the subject. Jefferson could do nothing but retire, particularly as he *had* forgotten that point about there being no wound on the body. Indeed, as he considered it, he began to think that the police must be right after all. They ought to be, of course. They had experience in dealing with these cases, and he hadn't. Yes, it was certainly pretty convincing.

All the same he was not convinced. Admittedly, M'Clung might be correct in his views. But that wasn't enough for Jefferson. He must be sure.

On that day he was at a loose end. All the arrangements about the funeral were made, but the funeral itself was not until the following morning, to give the ladies time to come across. He decided he would go down to Hillsborough and discuss the matter with the party there.

Accordingly he rang Jack Penrose up and asked him to arrange a meeting for three o'clock. He went to Hillsborough, lunched at the hotel, and at the hour in question knocked at the door of Ferris's cottage.

Jack had made the necessary arrangements and the whole party except Mr Whiteside was there waiting. After a brief greeting Jefferson got to business. 'This,' he said, 'is as much your concern as mine. If the secret has been stolen and sold, you'll lose as much as I will. In fact you'll lose more. You'll lose everything: your work as well as the money you've put into it. I shall lose only what I had hoped to gain.'

Jack, who took upon himself the rôle of spokesman, fully agreed. 'It's not a new point you're bring up, Mr Jefferson,' he declared. 'We've already discussed it pretty thoroughly. We think the whole question hinges on the one point: whether Platt had learnt the process or not. We don't believe he had.'

'But are you sure of that?'

'We'll hear what Ferris has to say.'

'What we looked at was this,' Ferris explained as Jefferson glanced at him. 'There were the two things to learn. The first was the construction of our pole pieces. We kept them screened and I think you'll agree the screens hid the things pretty well. Then there was the materials used. These and other essential details were on paper—they had to be—but the paper was locked up in that safe and I had the key.'

'That is to say, that while you were here no one could have taken off those screens or opened the safe without your knowledge?'

'We're all agreed on that.'

'Quite. But when you were not here?'

A long discussion ensued. Platt had never been left alone with the apparatus. He had been watched unobtrusively and those performing the task were sure that he could have made no secret investigation.

With regard to the safe, obviously he hadn't broken it open. Therefore if he had obtained access to its contents, it must have been by a key. But he had not had any chance of getting a key. Ferris was positive he had not left his keys about, nor had Platt borrowed them on any pretext. Besides, Ferris added, there would have been no opportunity to open the safe. During Platt's visits in the daytime some-one was always about the cottage and at night Ferris slept in the building. 'And I'm not by any means a sound sleeper,' Ferris concluded.

It certainly did look convincing. Jefferson, his mind prac-tically at rest, was about to leave. And then a chance remark of Pam's brought all his doubts back. Pam happened to mention that they were surprised that Platt had spent so long over his investigations and that they had been expecting him to return on the Wednesday or Thursday evening instead of the Saturday.

This was a point which had not occurred to Jefferson, and he at once went into it with them. How had Platt spent his time? Were all these elaborate tests necessary? Instead of spending a day analysing the petrol which was to be used, couldn't the man have gone out and bought a canful? Besides, that meeting on Saturday morning was surely unnecessary. Draft agreements had been prepared by both sides, and there was really nothing between them. Ten minutes talk would have settled everything, but Platt had spun out the discussion for a couple of hours.

Jefferson then asked for details of what had been done on each day. He questioned so searchingly that when it came to Saturday the party were hard put to it to keep secret the unfortunate incident which had happened on that morning. However, all concerned were determined that this should not become known. Platt, they explained, had reached the cottage about ten and had remained until nearly lunch time, talking principally about the agreement. Then he had gone to the hotel for lunch. About half-past two Ferris and M'Morris had called for him in Ferris's car, and the three of them had driven round the Mourne Mountains through Banbridge, Newry, Rostrevor, Newcastle and Ballynahinch, arriving back at the hotel about seven. Platt had invited the other two to stay for dinner, but as he had given them tea they had declined. Ferris and M'Morris had mealed together in the cottage and about nine had returned to the hotel. There, after a chat and a drink, they had all left. As they did so, Platt remembered that Ferris had not given him an address he had promised him, that of a mutual acquaintance in London. They had, therefore, stopped at the cottage to get it. M'Morris had left the others there, as it was the nearest point to his house that they touched. He had walked home and Ferris had driven Platt to the steamer, seeing him to the gangway.

In answer to a further question all concerned said that, so far as they knew, Platt had received no letters or telegrams or other messages during his stay.

All this was satisfactory so far as it went, and yet Jefferson remained vaguely suspicious. But he saw that nothing more was to be learnt from the party who, indeed, he suspected were becoming as bored with him as had M'Clung.

He went back to the hotel and ordered tea, and while waiting for it got once again into conversation with the manager. He explained his relationship to Platt, and said he was trying to find out about his last days, as his wife would be interested in such details. On this pretext he inquired about letters or other messages for Platt and went into his movements in and out of the hotel, so as to check up what Ferris and the others had told him.

Almost at once he learnt a fact which gave him a thrill of interest. Platt had not been at the hotel for lunch on the Saturday. He had gone out that morning shortly after breakfast and had returned just before half-past two. Asked if he would have lunch, he said no, that he had already had it. He drove out then with Ferris and M'Morris and returned for dinner about seven. About nine the two gentlemen had returned, and after half an hour or so all three had left.

This accurately corroborated Ferris's story, except on the single point that, according to Ferris, Platt had left the cottage between twelve and one to go to the hotel for lunch, while actually he had gone somewhere else. Was there anything of significance in this?

It was obvious that none of the party knew the fact. Why should Platt have made a secret of it?

After tea Jefferson lit a pipe and gave himself up to thought. Ferris had said he did not think Platt knew anyone in Hillsborough, and the others had agreed. It was therefore improbable that Platt had lunched in Hillsborough. Where else could he have had it?

Jefferson sent for a timetable. It was unlikely that the man had gone to Belfast: it was too far away. Only the two small adjoining towns seemed possible, Lisburn and Dromore. Ballynahinch was not far away, but the bus service would not have suited. It looked as if Platt had lunched in either Lisburn or Dromore.

If so, why? There was nothing to be had in either town that he could not have got equally well in Hillsborough, that was, of things that he was likely to want. It looked as if it must have been something secret, something which must be kept from the party. What could it have been?

Then another point struck Jefferson. This lunch hour on Saturday was the only period in Platt's last couple of days in Ireland when he was free from observation—at least during daylight hours. On Friday he was working at the cottage from nine in the morning till they started for the Whitesides at two o'clock. He had brought lunch from the hotel and he ate it with Ferris and M'Morris. On their return from Carnalea they had dined with the Penroses, and then Ferris and M'Morris had run Platt to the hotel, where they had stayed with him for a final drink. On Saturday he was with Ferris during the whole of the day except during lunch and dinner. Dinner he had had at the hotel, so that only this lunch period was left.

Jefferson continued wondering where Platt had spent it. There must have been something underhand about his movements, else why should he have lied about them to Ferris?

More uneasy than ever, Jefferson decided to try a plan which he had read of detectives adopting in similar cases. Could he make a reconstruction of Platt's possible movements?

Suppose the man had stolen the process, what would he do with it? Obviously, sell it to some other firm. He couldn't do anything with it himself. But when could he carry out such a sale? It would have to be at once, as, if he waited, he might not have another opportunity till it was too late. It would have been suspicious not to have turned up at the office on the Monday morning, and on the following weekend he might, for all he knew to the contrary, have been back in Ireland with him, Jefferson. Therefore, if he were to sell it, it could best have been done on the Sunday he reached England. But that would mean sending a message to his prospective purchaser. Could Platt have gone to Lisburn or Dromore on Saturday to send a message?

Still another point flashed into Jefferson's mind. French had told him in Bristol—and indeed he had learned it himself from Platt's landlady—that Platt had said in his postcard that he would be back late on Sunday evening. Now Jefferson knew that the Sunday morning train from Liverpool with which the Belfast boat connected, arrived in Bristol about 4.0 p.m. Was this not suggestive? Did it not mean that Platt did not intend to go to Bristol direct, but meant to pay a call somewhere on his way?

For some time Jefferson continued thinking, then at last he came to a decision. Taking the next bus to Belfast, he hurried down Chichester Street to police headquarters. By a stroke of luck Sergeant M'Clung had not gone home.

'I'm sorry to trouble you again,' Jefferson apologised, 'but I won't keep you a minute. I want to ask a favour.'

M'Clung was polite. Anything that he could do to help Mr Jefferson would assuredly be done. What did he require?

'I want you, if you will,' Jefferson said earnestly, 'to find out from the postal people at Lisburn and Dromore whether Platt sent any message between one and two o'clock on the Saturday of his death. I imagine it would be a telegram, but it might have been a phone call.'

M'Clung was clearly interested. 'Is this a secret?' he asked. 'Or would you tell me what's in your mind?'

'Of course I'll tell you, sergeant. I've found out that Platt disappeared between those hours, though he told Ferris he was lunching at the Hillsborough hotel. The timetable tells me he could only have gone to one or other of those towns. I wondered if it could have been to send a message.'

He could see that M'Clung was impressed, though he made no comment except to say that he would try to obtain the information. Thanking him, Jefferson took his departure.

Next day he met his wife and sister-in-law and all three attended the funeral. The good spell of weather had come to an end and the morning was wet and gloomy. The funeral was a dismal affair, made even more heartrending by Mrs Platt's face of stony despair. Jefferson was glad when shortly after midday they got back to the Station Hotel. There he found a message from M'Clung, asking him to call at his convenience, and after lunch he did so.

'I've got some information for you, Mr Jefferson,' M'Clung greeted him. 'Would you recognise that hand?'

He laid a telegraph form on the desk. Jefferson examined it with bulging eyes.

It was in Platt's handwriting and it had been handed in at the Lisburn post office at 1.11 p.m. on the Saturday in question. It was addressed to Mitchell, Willington, Coxon Road, Surbiton, and read: 'Got the goods. With you Sunday after lunch. Will hand over on conditions named.' It was signed Platt, and the address given on the back for official purposes, was another in Surbiton.

Jefferson stared at the sergeant. 'Got the goods!' What did that mean? What could it mean—except one thing? 'Good heavens, sergeant,' he said and his voice was hoarse, 'what meaning do you take out of that?'

For a moment M'Clung did not reply. Then he said slowly: 'I have more to tell you, Mr Jefferson. When I got that early this morning I rang up Scotland Yard to ask them to find out who Mitchell was. Their reply just came in about ten minutes ago. Mitchell is the head of Mitchell

Lovibound & Company of New Kent Road, London. Does that convey anything to you, sir?'

Jefferson gasped. Mitchell Lovibound! Yes, it conveyed something to him all right. This was his own firm's keenest rival! At one time they had worked in co-operation, but an unfortunate dispute about an Admiralty contract had occurred, and since then they had been in opposition. After his own, Mitchell Lovibound was just the firm to handle the inert petrol business.

With sinking heart Jefferson realised the truth. Platt had stolen the secret. He had negotiated with Mitchell for its sale. He had been going to Mitchell on Sunday to hand it over. Platt had been a crook and a thief. His wife's nephew!

But it was not on this aspect of the question that Jefferson's thought's lingered. If Platt had stolen the secret—and that 'Got the goods' made this certain—he hadn't delivered it. Platt hadn't lived to profit by his crime. Probably it was because of his crime that he had died.

But did this not make the whole affair still more inexplicable? If Platt were murdered for the secret, as it now seemed probable, who knew that he had it? The tall dark man who asked for him on board? If so, who was this man and how did he know? And if this man did know, and if he murdered Platt for the secret, how did he do it? How could he have overcome Platt sufficiently to get the papers from him without leaving some marks of violence on the body? How could he have prevented Platt from crying out when he was thrown into the sea?

Jefferson was completely puzzled. He put his speculations and doubts to M'Clung, and found that at last the sergeant was interested. At last the man believed in the possibility of foul play and showed an eagerness to go further into

161

the matter. He even complimented Jefferson on his achievement in deducing the message.

'I only thought there was a chance of it,' Jefferson pointed out deprecatingly.

'That's right enough, sir,' M'Clung returned, 'but it's the sort of thing that gets you there in our job.'

'Then what do you suggest should be our next step?' went on Jefferson.

M'Clung did not seem to appreciate the 'our' as he might. 'I doubt there's not much more you can do personally,' he declared judicially. 'You've done your share anyway. It's a job for the professionals now, sir. You leave it to us and I promise you it'll be gone into down to the very bone. And I wouldn't be saying anything about what you think to those people down at Hillsborough. We'll see to that.'

With this Jefferson had to be content. He extracted a promise that he would be kept advised of progress, and then M'Clung took a leave of him in which respect was a much more noticeable ingredient than formerly. In due course Jefferson returned to England with his womenfolk, settling down once again into the routine of his business.

12

As Chief Inspector French Saw It

Chief Inspector French had almost dismissed what he called 'The Petrol Mystery' from his mind, thinking firstly, that it was never likely to be completely solved, and secondly, that the solution was really a job for the police of Northern Ireland.

All the same when the news of the finding of the body and the inquest reached him, he was not surprised. It was what he had himself suspected. The man was in financial difficulties, he was unpopular, probably he was not very well—acute indigestion or some other depressing ailment, and he had been overcome by a sudden urge to end it all. French did not know what had occurred, but at all events this development definitely closed the case so far as he was concerned.

But though the news had not surprised him, he was genuinely astonished by M'Clung's second letter. So the affair was not closed after all! They had reopened it over there in Ireland with a very pretty theory of conspiracy, theft and murder! A bit far-fetched, surely, he thought.

Why choose a complicated explanation for a thing when a simple one would do equally well? In his experience the obvious and the likely solution had usually proved to be the truth.

However the Yard wasn't being consulted about theories of the crime. They were asked by the Royal Ulster Constabulary to find out—if they could—whether this Mitchell about whom they had previously inquired had either murdered Platt or had conspired with him to steal and market Ferris's process.

A direct and clear cut question, and yet not so simple and straightforward as it looked. A point of procedure arose. What *locus standi* had the police of Northern Ireland to demand help? The Yard had been asked to intervene by the Chief Constable of Liverpool, and now Liverpool interest in the affair appeared to have evaporated and the centre of gravity had shifted to Belfast.

French thought it was a matter for the Assistant Commisioner. He therefore went to his room and handed over the letter. Sir Mortimer Ellison, however, considered that the request was covered by the Liverpool application.

'They applied to us because they thought there was a chance of murder and they didn't want to be bothered with it themselves,' he pointed out. 'According to this letter it looks as if their idea had been correct. Very well, you're working on what they asked you to do. In my opinion you should go ahead—at their expense of course.'

So it happened that an hour later French and Carter left the tube at the Elephant and Castle and turned down the New Kent Road.

The Mitchell Lovibound premises occupied a complete block on the right side of the street. They were fronted by a massive wall of brick, originally red, but now almost black with age and grime. It was impossible to guess at the original colour of the doors and windows, so dirty were they. But the brass plate at the door was freshly polished and when the two men entered they found the offices clean and efficient looking.

They were kept waiting for nearly half an hour before being shown into Mitchell's room. Mitchell was a thick-set man with a heavy jowl and little eyes like a pig's. He had a shifty look and an overbearing manner. French saw that the interview was not going to be easy. However, he spoke as politely as was his custom.

'You, sir, are Mr Mitchell of Willington, Coxon Road, Surbiton, are you not?'

Mitchell fixed him with an impudent stare. 'Well what of it?' he asked.

'Merely that I want to be sure who I'm talking to. Scotland Yard has been asked by the police of Northern Ireland to make some inquiries from you, and I have been commissioned to act in the matter.'

'I know nothing about Northern Ireland.'

'I dare say not, sir,' French returned smoothly, 'but their question has an English bearing. It arises out of the engagement you had with the late Mr Reginald Platt for last Sunday three weeks.'

French believed he saw a sudden flash in the man's eyes. He could not be quite certain, but Mitchell's manner changed from mere rudeness to an aggressive opposition.

'What the hell are you talking about?' he said with a show of anger. 'I know no Reginald Platt.'

French made a warning gesture. 'Before we go any further I should explain that Sergeant Carter here will take down our conversation verbatim, and that should there be subsequent proceedings your statements may be given in evidence. And let me inform you that this is a case of murder, and remind you that in a murder case the police can call on anyone for help.'

Again French was sure that there was that fleeting look in Mitchell's eyes. 'Well, haven't I told you I know nothing about it?'

'I think, sir, we'll wash out that and start afresh. It has been stated that the murdered man, Reginald Platt, had an appointment with you at your home in Surbiton for the afternoon of last Sunday three weeks. I should explain,' French held up his hand as Mitchell would have spoken, 'that we're tracing Platt's movements during the last few days of his life. Now of course we know that he didn't go to Surbiton on that afternoon—his body was then floating in Belfast Lough. But we want to know what his appointment was about.'

'Hell!' said Mitchell aggressively. 'I told you there was no appointment and that I never heard of Platt!'

'Yes, but I'm afraid we can't accept that. The fact of the appointment is known.'

Mitchell's expression grew uglier. 'Oh, so I'm a liar, am I? Who sent you here? We'll see if it's your business to come and insult innocent people.'

French's tone grew a little harder. 'Well, we can put it to the test easily enough. Did you receive this wire?' He took a copy of Platt's telegram from his pocket and laid it on the desk.

Once again that gleam! But the man was not beaten yet. 'Damn your—insolence!' he exclaimed. 'I tell you I never saw the thing and I don't know what you're talking about.'

French thought it a moment for bluff. 'Oh, well, as you like,' he said. 'We produce the form left at the post office in Lisburn in Northern Ireland and prove that Platt wrote it and handed it in. We get evidence that the message was despatched from Lisburn and received at Surbiton. We produce the messenger who took it about four o'clock on Saturday afternoon from the Surbiton post office to your house. Your explanation will be required—in this murder case. Otherwise you may raise false suspicions. Is it that someone else received the message?'

Mitchell hesitated. Then once again he swore. 'Well,' he went on, 'suppose I did get it. What business of yours is it?'

'That's better,' French said easily. 'You now admit you got it, and I suppose, the fact of the appointment?'

Mitchell swung backwards and forwards in his chair. 'There's no admitting about it,' he declared roughly. 'It's none of your business who I meet or what I do.'

'Oh, yes it is,' French returned, feeling that as the bluff was working so well, he might as well try it again. 'Very much my business. I'll tell you, Mr Mitchell. We have received a communication stating that you and Mr Platt had conspired together to steal a secret chemical process belonging to a group of persons in Northern Ireland. Platt was to commit the actual theft, you were to receive the stolen goods. Platt did his part and was murdered for it. The question of the murderer arises. Now I am giving you a chance to make a statement on the subject to clear yourself, should you wish to do so. If you don't care to take the opportunity, you needn't. But if you don't, you see what suspicions may remain.'

'I suppose even you are not going to accuse me of the murder, seeing I was in Surbiton on Saturday and Sunday?'

French noted the changed tone with satisfaction. 'I haven't accused you of anything,' he said smoothly. 'I said that we have received a statement saying that you and the deceased did certain things. I'm giving you an opportunity to explain your actions in the matter.'

'The statement is a—lie.'

'Right,' French returned easily; 'that'll satisfy me—provided you prove it.'

'And if I don't?'

'If you don't we'll have to go to other sources for our information: that's all.'

'There aren't any.'

'Oh, aren't there? Has it not occurred to you that the party who gave us the statement must know where proof is to be found?'

This was evidently a blow. Mitchell seemed to cower beneath it. His aggressiveness began to melt away. For some moments he remained silent, obviously thinking hard. French did not interrupt him and at last he spoke.

'The party's a—liar,' he declared sulkily. 'However,' he shrugged, 'I've nothing to hide and I suppose I may as well tell you what happened. It'll be the quickest way of getting rid of you.'

French agreed. Mitchell grumbled and swore, but presently began a statement.

His firm, he said, had worked with Wrenn Jefferson at one time, and during this period he had become acquainted with Platt. Then through some disagreement the relationship was dropped and the firms became competitors. He lost sight of Platt and Jefferson and the rest of them.

He was therefore considerably surprised when on Saturday, first September—a week, French noted, before

Platt's death—Platt rang him up to say that he was on a good thing and could he, Mitchell, see him if he called next day at his house at Surbiton. Mitchell agreed. When Platt arrived in the afternoon he told him that some Irish friends of his own had discovered a way of making petrol inert at will, and through him had offered it to his firm, Wrenn Jefferson. Jefferson very foolishly as Platt thought, had turned the offer down, and now he, Platt, was prepared on behalf of his friends to offer the process to Mitchell.

Mitchell asked for details, but Platt would not give them, saying he must have an agreement first. Mitchell didn't for one moment believe that such a thing could be done, but at last he agreed to work any satisfactory process supplied through Platt and to pay Platt on behalf of his friends half the net profits. A provisional agreement was drawn up then and there and both parties signed it. Platt then admitted that he did not know the exact details of the process, but said that now that he had his agreement his friends would explain. He would go next day to Ireland for the information and would advise Mitchell when he had got it. The wire French had produced was his advice, and it meant that he had obtained the information and would hand it over to Mitchell on the following afternoon, that of Sunday, Mitchell had remained sceptical as to the value of the affair owing to the fact that Jefferson had turned it down, but he intended to examine the proposition with an open mind and act as he thought best. He declared he had never had the slightest suspicion that the process was stolen, or that Platt was not empowered by the Irishmen to act as their agent.

French could not but see that all this was quite possible. Mitchell might have acted innocently enough. On the other

hand his manner was suspicious, though this might only
have been due to a private doubt that the whole affair
was crooked.

Of the actual murder it was unlikely that Mitchell could
be guilty. He might of course have crossed from Belfast
on that Saturday night, but if so, he would almost certainly
have mentioned a matter which could be so easily checked
and the hiding of which would be so damaging. However,
a few inquiries would set the matter at rest.

It was also unlikely that a confederate had committed the
murder. Mitchell could only have arranged this to get
the process into his own hands. But he was going to do
that in any case, and he might as well share with Platt as
with his murderer accomplice. Besides, no one would commit
a murder if he could get what he wanted in a safer way.

But was Mitchell's story simply an ingenious lie, and
was he Platt's accomplice in the matter of the theft? This
French thought more likely. Mitchell's manner and the
whole circumstances of the case suggested it. But they did
not prove it. French had grave doubts about a charge of
conspiracy succeeding.

At the moment, however, nothing more could be done.
He must set Mitchell's mind at rest and then try elsewhere
for further information.

'I'm much obliged to you, sir, for that statement,' he said.
'Now if you will kindly sign it, that will complete my business. I'm sorry to have been a nuisance, but you must admit
it was your own fault. If you hadn't made a mystery out
of the thing we could have fixed it up in half the time.'

Mitchell seemed surprised at French's tone. However, he
signed the statement and was almost civil when the two
men left.

What he had learnt from Mitchell seemed to French definitely to confirm the theory of the Belfast police. And if Platt had stolen the process and been murdered for it, the question of the dark individual who had inquired for him immediately arose. This man was the only one yet suggested upon whom suspicion could possibly fall. He was not Mitchell: they were utterly unlike in appearance. Who was he?

For the remainder of that day French worried over the problem. Then dimly a theory began to shape itself in his mind. Suppose Mitchell knew that the tale about the process having been refused by Wrenn Jefferson was a myth? Suppose on that Sunday afternoon before Platt went to Ireland he and Mitchell had gone into partnership to steal the process: Platt to commit the actual theft, Mitchell to take over and work the stolen property. Suppose, however, Mitchell had not trusted Platt. He had known him before this affair and probably was well aware of his character. Suppose Mitchell had then evolved a scheme to ensure that he, Mitchell, would get the full benefit of the discovery. Suppose Mitchell himself—or the dark man as an emissary—went to Ireland, returned with Platt, committed the murder, stole the secret, and returned to London? Platt, a danger to Mitchell, would thus be eliminated, and possibly the accomplice could be put off with a great deal smaller share of the spoils than Platt had been promised.

Admittedly there were difficulties, such as that which had been raised about the absence of a wound or sign of a struggle on the body. Never mind, let him pursue his idea and see where it led.

The first thing was to find out whether Mitchell had

himself crossed to Ireland. French called Carter, and going to Surbiton, took a taxi to Willington. There he saw first the servant and secondly, Mrs Mitchell. Using an old trick which had invariably found to work, he said he was investigating a motor accident of which he had been informed Mr Mitchell had been a spectator. It had occurred on Saturday, 7th September, and he wanted to know if Mr Mitchell had been in Surbiton on that day, as if not, his information must have been erroneous and there would be no use in his troubling Mr Mitchell in town.

Both maid and mistress agreed unhesitatingly that Mitchell, had been at home on the day in question. 'I remember because that was the day we both went to call on some people in the next street,' Mrs Mitchell added. French felt instinctively that she was to be trusted, but he was the more certain that she was speaking the truth because he saw that she was anxious lest her husband should have to give evidence and would much rather have said he was from home.

Mitchell then, had not personally committed the murder. Had he sent an accomplice?

When previously considering this point French had decided that Mitchell would have been no more likely to put himself in the power of an accomplice in respect of the murder than in that of Platt in respect of the theft. Now he saw that he had been mistaken. Mitchell would not have put himself in his accomplice's power: no one could afterwards tell what had been arranged between them. But the accomplice would be absolutely in Mitchell's power—a very different thing. And if the accomplice bungled the job and was arrested, Mitchell had only to deny all knowledge of the affair, or at the worst, to say he had empowered his emissary to try to trick the secret out of Platt, but of course not to cause him bodily injury.

But would an accomplice act under such circumstances? French thought so. The man might already have been in Mitchell's power and been unable to refuse. Or he might have acted willingly on the promise of a share in the spoils. French was sure many persons would have been ready enough to undertake the job.

Suppose there had been such an accomplice. What then? French saw one thing.

If he had met Platt, he would have kept carefully off the subject of petrol. Under no circumstances would he let the man know that he was interested. Otherwise Platt might have become suspicious if he were urged to go to a lonely part of the deck of the *Ulster Sovereign* after leaving Belfast. And if he had become suspicious, it certainly would not have been possible to throw him overboard.

But if so, how would the accomplice know whether Platt had succeeded in stealing the secret, or even whether he was crossing that night? It would be a fool's game to murder the man for nothing. No. In some way the accomplice would have to be advised if he were to act.

Had he been so advised? Again if so, it could only have been by Mitchell. Now Mitchell knew Platt had stolen the secret. He also knew he was crossing that night. The wire from Lisburn told him. Had Mitchell on receipt of that wire sent a communication to an accomplice in Ireland?

French was pleased with his line of reasoning. If Mitchell had sent such a message there was an accomplice. If not, of course, the matter remained doubtful.

French decided to strike while the iron was hot. He went

173

at once to the postmaster at Surbiton and put his questions. First he obtained confirmation of the hour at which Platt's telegram from Lisburn was delivered to Mitchell. Then he asked whether after that there was a telegram from Mitchell to Northern Ireland.

It did not take long to look up the records, and then French experienced disappointment. There had been no such telegram.

French was turning away, when it occurred to him that the telegraph was not the most suitable means of communicating such a secret. Even if put in veiled language or in code, the mere fact of the existence of a message would be undesirable. What about the telephone?

A few minutes later French was at the telephone headquarters, in conversation with the supervisor. Once again there was a search among the records. And then French's heart gave a leap. From a street box there had been a call for Northern Ireland, as a matter of fact for Hillsborough!

For a moment French was filled with delight, thinking that he had proved his theory of the existence of the accomplice. Then he saw that there was no certainty that Mitchell had made the call, though he believed that under the circumstances any other explanation would involve too far-fetched a coincidence. But soon he began to wonder whether he really had got on so well. Hillsborough? Hillsborough was where Platt was staying. Was it not for Platt that this message had been intended?

If so, Platt had not got it, unless a verbal message for him had been taken by someone else. Platt at the time the telephone was used was somewhere in the Mourne Mountains. Well, it must be looked into in any case.

A job for M'Clung. M'Clung had managed to get him,

French, work to do. He would be glad to return the compliment. M'Clung could go and find out who had got the message and what it was. That night a letter to the Belfast police crossed the Irish Sea.

13

As Detective-Sergeant
M'Clung Saw It

In due course French's letter reached Chichester Street, was read by Superintendent Rainey, and was passed for action to M'Clung.

M'Clung was impressed by the rapidity with which French had done his work. Pretty smart too, getting those admissions from such an unwilling witness! Those Scotland Yard fellahs knew their job: there were no two ways about it. Good people right enough, though of course not like the men of Belfast.

After an interview with Superintendent Rainey, M'Clung called Constable Brown and they got out the small Ford and drove down to Hillsborough. On the way he thought out his plans, and on arrival he went to the local telephone exchange. The girl in charge was good looking, and as M'Clung was partial to pretty girls, his manner grew cordial and unofficial.

'I was wondering, miss,' he began, 'if you could give me a bit of a hand with a job I'm on?' and he went on to explain what he wanted.

The girl was flattered by this approach, though she took care to convey the opposite impression. 'Have you seen the supervisor?' she asked severely.

'I have not,' M'Clung admitted. 'But I thought I wouldn't need to be troubling any supervisor for a thing you could do all right yourself.'

She eyed him doubtfully. 'You only want to know if there was a call from London on Saturday afternoon, 7th September?'

'That's all: that and who it was for.'

'There are a good many calls from London come through here,' she declared coldly. 'I don't see how I could be expected to remember yours.'

'To the Castle? I suppose there are. Would there not be any kind of record that maybe you could look up?'

She shook her head. 'There's no record of inward calls,' she explained. 'If you'd wanted to know about a call to London, I might have helped you, but as it is—' She shrugged elegantly.

M'Clung was a little suspicious that she was playing with him, and in spite of her looks his temper began to rise. But he controlled it and went on pleasantly.

'That's too bad, miss, because I'm afraid I'll have to give you a bit of trouble. I'll have to ring up every number in the exchange and ask if it was them. If we start now we should get it done in a couple or three hours.'

As he had assumed, this was not at all the girl's idea of the best way to spend a morning which might otherwise allow breaks for the absorption of a particularly thrilling detective story. She suddenly found her memory was better than she had supposed.

'Did you say it was about four o'clock on that Saturday afternoon?' she asked.

'About that,' he answered. 'I can't say to a minute.'

'I have a sort of dim idea that I remember the call,' she said slowly. 'It was for the hotel, I think. But I'm not sure.'

'The hotel? That's great, miss: that's the very best. I'm sure I'm obliged to you.'

'I won't swear I'm right,' she insisted, 'but I think it was the hotel.'

M'Clung thought so too. He felt sure the message was for Platt, and if so, where but to the hotel would it be sent?

After a farewell which definitely stopped short of being affectionate, M'Clung went on with his constable to the hotel. There he asked for the manager.

'I don't know a thing about it,' Mr Agnew replied helpfully when M'Clung had put his question. 'But maybe Miss Quirk'll know. Come on, and we'll ask her.'

Miss Quirk, who intermittently inhabited the office, at first didn't know a thing about it either. But presently, after a heart-to-heart talk with the porter, she had an idea.

'Was that not the call that came for Mr Roberts?' she asked him. 'Do you not remember your going to the lounge for him?'

'I mind it rightly,' the porter corroborated. 'You're wanted on the phone,' I says, an' he says, 'Right,' he says, 'I'm coming,' he says. Aye, I mind it rightly.'

Further questions settled it. Soon no doubt whatever remained in M'Clung's mind that Mitchell's call from Surbiton had been received by 'Mr Roberts.'

'And who was Mr Roberts?' M'Clung proceeded.

Miss Quirk didn't know except that he was 'just Mr Roberts.' He had arrived on the previous Tuesday and had been going to stay, so he had said, a week. But on receipt of a message on Saturday—that very phone call that M'Clung was inquiring about—he had said he had just got word that he must return home at once, and that he would cross by the boat that night. And so he did, at least, he left by the bus in time to catch the boat.

'Then he was English?' said M'Clung.

'You wouldn't have had much doubt he was English if you'd heard him talk,' Miss Quirk declared.

'And what was he like to look at?' went on M'Clung.

'What would you say?' Miss Quirk again sought inspiration from the porter, who had remained, an interested spectator of the little scene.

'He was a well enough looking fellah,' the porter admitted with a faint air of surprise, presumably that such a thing could be true of anyone born outside the Province. 'At least,' he went on, anxious not to commit himself too deeply, 'I've seen worse.' Then lest this should be scarcely fair to the individual in question, he added firmly, 'many a time.'

'Was he tall or short?' asked M'Clung whose aim was definition.

'He was middling tall,' the porter considered. 'Wouldn't you say he was middling tall?' Politely he returned the compliment Miss Quirk had previously paid him.

Miss Quirk agreed that he was middling tall and her opinion was satisfactorily confirmed by Mr Agnew. Presently all three concurred that he was slight, and that his hair was dark, and then Miss Quirk added the decisive information that he had a small cut on his left cheek. This also the porter confirmed. 'Aye, now you mention it, I mind it rightly,' he declared, nodding his head.

Roberts, it further appeared, was a quiet and rather silent man who kept himself to himself and didn't mix much with the other guests. Not that he wasn't polite; he was quite the gentleman. But he was retiring. Yes, it was a coincidence that he had been there for just the same length of time as had the late Mr Platt. But he hadn't known Mr Platt. The last day or two they had begun to say good-morning, but no more than that. No, they never went out together. Mr Roberts was out a good deal, in fact he was seldom in, except at night and for breakfast and dinner. He was, so he had told Mr Agnew, a traveller from a big English multiple stores, and he was trying to fix up contracts for the supply of linen and other Northern Ireland products. His entry in the register was not illuminating: 'J. Roberts, Harrow, London. Nationality: English.'

The room he had occupied had since remained vacant, and with Constable Brown's help M'Clung now gave it a thorough examination. But he found nothing of interest, nor did his further inquiries from the hotel staff increase his knowledge.

One fact he learnt, however, which appeared to him significant. When he went to the police barracks to ask if anything was known about the man, it appeared that a patrol had seen him one night about ten o'clock standing in the lane outside Ferris's cottage, gazing earnestly at the house. On seeing the police he had at once lit a cigarette, obviously to account for his stoppage, and had strolled slowly on.

M'Clung spent a little time ringing up a dozen or more of the local linen manufacturers in order to try to trace Roberts' activities on behalf of his firm. Not one of them, however, had ever heard of Roberts or were in communication with any multiple stores in England on any subject whatever.

All this information considerably thrilled M'Clung. That he had got on the track of the tall dark man who had asked for Platt on the *Ulster Sovereign* seemed certain. Further, this man Roberts was clearly an emissary of Mitchell's. If so, it was surely obvious that Roberts had murdered Platt for the secret? And if so again, Platt had definitely stolen it.

Or was the converse of this the truth? What if Roberts had stolen the secret, perhaps on behalf of Mitchell, and Platt had somehow discovered the fact and been murdered for his knowledge? M'Clung didn't think this so likely, but he noted it as a possibility to be further gone into.

With Constable Brown, M'Clung returned to Wayside and once again interrogated Ferris and M'Morris. But neither knew anything of Roberts.

'Well,' declared M'Clung, 'he was taking a queer look at the cottage one night. Standing there in the lane staring in. You didn't see anyone in the lane?'

'I did not,' said Ferris. 'What time would that be?'

'Just on to ten.'

'Never saw a sign of him.'

'And no traces of anyone at the door or trying to break in?'

'Naht at all. Sure if there had been, wouldn't I have told you before now?'

M'Clung drove back to the police barracks and arranged with the local sergeant to make further inquiries in the district. Did Roberts travel by rail? Or bus? Or had he a car? Had he transactions at the bank? Or the post office?

Did he seem to know anyone in the place? Any information the sergeant could procure would, M'Clung indicated, be thankfully received.

On his return to Belfast, M'Clung called on the manager of the Belfast Steamship Company.

'It's this business of the death of Reginald Platt that I'm bothering you about again,' he began. 'There was a man crossed that same night by the name of Roberts. Can you tell me anything about him?'

'I can not,' the manager answered. 'What did you want to know?'

'If he booked under that name, and where to? Anything you can tell me.'

The manager telephoned for papers. 'Here's the passenger list for that night,' he explained. 'I suppose that's what you want?'

'It might be,' M'Clung admitted cautiously. 'Is the name Roberts on that?'

The manager glanced down the columns. 'It is, it's here.' He pointed. 'Cabin A 48.'

'Would that be reserved beforehand?'

'It likely would be. We'll soon see.'

He telephoned for further papers. 'It was reserved,' he announced after studying them, 'By telephone. On that Saturday afternoon.'

'No address nor nothing given?'

'There's nothing here.'

'I'd like to have found out where he came from,' M'Clung insisted.

'Couldn't you trace the call?'

'I know where the call was from: it was Hillsborough. I would have liked to know where the man came from.'

'Then he wasn't living there?'

'He was not. He was English.'

'Is that so? And had he just come over?'

'The Monday night before.'

'Man, why didn't you say so? Then he would have a cabin engaged that night too?'

'He likely would.'

'Well then, sure can't we get it from the Liverpool office? I'll ring them up if you like.'

'I wish you would, Mr Baxter.'

The manager asked for a Liverpool number, then sat back in his chair and eyed M'Clung quizzically.

'What's all the excitement about Roberts?' he asked in a dry tone.

M'Clung looked round, bent forward, and sank his voice. 'I maybe shouldn't be mentioning it, but you'll keep it to yourself?'

'I will so.'

'We're thinking it was murder.'

The manager's face changed. 'Holy Moses!' he exclaimed and whistled.

'You'll not let on,' M'Clung persisted anxiously. 'I maybe shouldn't have mentioned it, but I thought you'd be as interested as anyone.'

'Aye, it'll not be a good advertisement for our ships. What makes you think it's murder?'

'We don't know for sure,' M'Clung explained. 'It's a long story, but we think that this fellah Roberts might have had something to do with it.'

'But they said at the inquest it was suicide?'

M'Clung hedged, then thinking that the manager's good-will might be worth an indiscretion, he briefly sketched

183

the facts. They were still discussing them when the telephone rang.

'Baxter speaking,' said the manager. 'Is that you, M'Kinstry? Well, see here,' and he put his question.

There was some delay while records were being looked up, but presently all the available information was given.

It seemed that on the Monday afternoon on which Platt crossed to Belfast a wire was received at the Liverpool office from J. Roberts, asking that a single berth cabin should be reserved that evening for the sender. The returns showed that 'J. Roberts' had been allotted the cabin, which he had duly claimed.

M'Clung was well pleased with his progress. To obtain the man's address through the sending office would be simple. He decided to wire the Liverpool police requesting them to see to it. In the meantime he might make some further inquiries about the night of the murder. Possibly his new-found information would touch a chord in the memories of some of the staff.

'What boat's in today, Mr Baxter?' he asked.

'The *Sovereign*.'

'I'll go straight on down.'

Reaching the Liverpool berth, he went on board the motor-ship and once again sought out the long-suffering Mr M'Bratney. But here he received no help. If the records showed that Roberts had occupied single berth cabin No. A.48 on the fatal Saturday night, then M'Clung might take it that Roberts had done so. He, M'Bratney, didn't remember, and couldn't be expected to. There was nothing about the affair to fix it on his attention.

'Just one thing more, Mr M'Bratney,' M'Clung went on

when this stage had been reached. 'I'd like to see the cabin steward who attended Roberts.'

M'Bratney then sent for the man at once, but here again M'Clung obtained no fresh information. The steward couldn't at this time 'right call him to mind.' M'Clung saw it was hopeless, and went on to interview once again Thompson the steward who had attended to Platt, and from whom the unknown had made his inquiries.

Thompson was a much smarter and more intelligent man. M'Clung turned to him more hopefully, but he hadn't expected the really important piece of information he now received.

'You've described the man well enough,' M'Clung admitted, 'but I'm looking for something more about his appearance. Now, think, like a decent fellah. Was there nothing unusual about him?'

Thompson shook his head.

'No mark nor nothing?' M'Clung prompted.

This producing no result, M'Clung significantly rubbed his cheek. Thompson stared, then made a sudden gesture.

'By the hokey,' he exclaimed, 'I mind it now! He had his cheek cut. Just there where you pointed.'

A wave of satisfaction swept over M'Clung. Roberts then, the man to whom Mitchell had telephoned, was the man who looked for Platt on the *Ulster Sovereign*. He was the man, M'Clung would now have bet long odds, who found Platt, enticed him out on the deck and murdered him. Roberts was the man they wanted.

Impatiently M'Clung waited for a reply from the Liverpool police. Presently it arrived. The address on the back of the original telegraph form was 49 Maidon Road, Harrow.

With this information the finding of the man should be an easy matter. A visit to 49 Maidon Road, Harrow, should do the trick. M'Clung would have liked nothing better than to go over to London and make the call himself. But he was afraid there was no hope of this. It would be a matter for French.

Returning to headquarters, he drafted out a full report of what he had learnt, and after a consultation with Rainey, sent it to French at the Yard.

14

As Chief Inspector French Saw It

French received M'Clung's letter by the afternoon post on the following day. M'Clung on hearing from French had been impressed with the amount of work which the London police had done in a short time. Now it was French's turn to recognise the efficiency of the men of Northern Ireland. The finding of Roberts should materially advance the case. Indeed it might end it.

Though a holiday at the sea did not now seem to be materialising, French determined that as he had begun the case, he would carry it on. He would go himself to Harrow and interview Roberts. It would probably be best then to bring him in to the Yard, where he could be detained while his story was being tested, and where he would be available should a warrant for his arrest be decided on.

Before starting he rang up the police at Harrow to know where Maidon Road was and whether they knew anything about Roberts.

'Maidon Road?' returned the officer in charge. 'I'm afraid, chief inspector, there's some mistake there. I never

187

heard of it. Will you hold on a moment while I make inquiries?'

French experienced the sudden thrill of the hunter who comes on a lion's fresh spoor. If Roberts had given a false address, it surely meant that he was their man. If so, it was very satisfactory from his own point of view. It was due entirely to him that this line on Roberts had been discovered. Better than that, he had reached it by pure deductive reasoning. It was the sort of *coup* he loved to bring off: the highest form, he told himself, of the detective art.

But the Harrow officer was calling again. His first idea, he said, had been correct. There was no such road in or near Harrow, and neither he nor anyone in the station knew anyone of the name of Roberts.

Though this was entirely gratifying from one point of view, to French personally it had an obvious drawback. It meant that his work was by no means done. Roberts must be found, and that meant trouble and worry and possible disappointment. However, it was all in the day's work, and the sooner he got on with it, the sooner it would be done.

Fortunately there was an avenue of approach to the problem. Mitchell! If Mitchell had sent the man a message, he must know who he was. An immediate call on Mitchell seemed indicated.

With Carter, French set off once again to the New Kent Road. Mitchell was in his office and saw them after a short delay. His greeting was not effusive.

'Sorry to trouble you again, Mr Mitchell,' French began, 'but another question has arisen in this Platt case. I want you please to give me the correct name and address of the man calling himself Roberts, who crossed from Belfast on the same ship as Platt and who stayed for the few previous days at Hillsborough.'

Once again Mitchell bluffed. So French had got hold of another mare's nest, had he? Well, he, Mitchell, had something better to do than waste his time with such nonsense. He knew nothing about any Roberts.

'I didn't say his name was Roberts,' French returned. 'I said he called himself Roberts when he stayed in the hotel at Hillsborough.'

'What's that to me? If that's all you want, I'd be glad to get on with my business.'

'I'm afraid this is your business, sir,' French said sweetly. 'I have to get a written statement, signed by you. Do you wish it put on record that you don't know that a certain man was staying at the hotel in Hillsborough on the Saturday of Platt's death, and that he there called himself Roberts? Let me suggest,' he held up his hand as Mitchell would have spoken, 'that you consider before replying. Statements taken in this way can be put in evidence should a case go to court.'

'Go to hell! I've told you I know no Roberts and we'll leave it at that.'

'I'm afraid we can't. Look here, Mr Mitchell, I'm not threatening in any way, but I want you to realise this is a murder case, and that it's a risky thing to prevaricate in a murder case. There's such a thing as accessary after the fact, you know.'

Mitchell grew more indignant. What did French mean by saying he was not threatening? That was a deliberate lie. He *was* threatening. But he, Mitchell, would let him know that that sort of thing wouldn't work in England.

This wasn't Russia or Germany. His statement was that he knew no Roberts and French could either take it or leave it.

French bent forward. 'Then it's only fair to tell you that your telephone message to the hotel is known. You asked for Mr Roberts, so you can't pretend you didn't know the name. I don't say it was the man's real name and haven't yet. But if you can't explain the affair for me now, I shall take you to Scotland Yard, where you'll be detained till it's cleared up.'

Such straight talking was evidently quite unexpected. Mitchell considered in silence, then at last gave way.

'I've not said a word that's not the strictest truth,' he declared. 'I told you I didn't know any Roberts, and that's the fact. I do know a man who took the name temporarily for his own purposes, but I never said I didn't.'

French made an easy gesture. 'We're not going to quarrel over a split hair,' he pointed out. 'What I want is the truth. Perhaps I had better repeat my formal warning that what you say will be taken down and may be used in evidence, though I have already told you this. Now, if you please.'

Hate showed unmistakably in Mitchell's small close-set eyes as grudgingly he began to speak. But there was fear also. And the fear was the stronger. Whether his statement was true or false French didn't know, but it was certainly plausible.

'There doesn't seem to be a great deal that I can tell you,' he began unpleasantly: 'you appear to know it all already. You say I telephoned on that Saturday afternoon to Hillsborough. Well, I did. And I'm not ashamed of it. There was no harm in it, and even you can't make any.'

'That's all right, Mr Mitchell,' French declared. 'I'm not

out to make trouble. All I want is that the suspicious circumstances should be cleared up.'

'The man I telephoned to had gone to Ireland on my business and it was on my business I spoke to him. He is a man called Herd, one of my own clerks in the works here. He does any confidential work that I may require at a distance.'

'Full name and address, please.'

'Robert Herd, 76 Glamorgan Villas, Findown Road, Pinner.'

'Thank you. And why did he use a false name? Or don't answer that. Just tell me the story in your own way.'

Again Mitchell looked the personification of hate. 'It was about the petrol affair,' he went on with every appearance of resentment. 'When Platt came to me with his story about the inert petrol, I just didn't believe him. I knew Platt and I felt I couldn't trust him. I thought it was a put-up job to get money from me. All the same I could see that if the story was true, the process would be a very big thing. So I thought I couldn't afford to take chances. If Platt was trying on some swindle I wanted to keep myself clear of it. But if his story was true, I wanted to make a firm deal with him that he couldn't go back on. That clear?'

'Quite.'

'How was I to find out the truth? I thought of Herd. Herd was a good man who had served me well and whom I could trust. I would send Herd across to Ireland to keep an eye on Platt. He would just watch what went on and give me confidential reports. If the thing was genuine, he would get to know.

'I had a word with Herd about the affair and he told me he believed he could find out all I wanted to know. So

191

I sent him over to Ireland. He had a perfectly free hand to carry on as he thought best, and I was paying his salary and expenses and a bonus as well.'

'Quite,' said French again. 'Yes?'

'He went over on the same night as Platt, but of course Platt didn't know him. He stayed in the same hotel as Platt in Hillsborough and kept his eyes open. He reported that so far as he could see Platt's story was true.'

'And then?'

'Then I had the wire you know about from Platt, saying that he had got the goods, by which I understood he had made his deal with the inventors, and that he was returning to London that Saturday night. I naturally wanted to make sure that he did return, so I rang up Herd to tell him to come back too and to have an eye on Platt on the way. You seem to know all about it.'

'Did Herd do so?'

'Herd did so as far as he could. He traced him on board the boat at Belfast, but he never saw him there. He missed him at Liverpool and hung about till he heard Platt had disappeared on the passage. But he didn't believe it. He thought Platt had given him the slip. He waited about till the afternoon, then came to Surbiton and reported to me.'

'And what did you do?'

'What could I do? I did nothing. I supposed Platt had got some better offer elsewhere and had given Herd and his own people the slip. I was surprised when I read that the body had been found.'

The identity of Herd and the cause of his being sent to Ireland and recalled now seemed clear. But French was still profoundly sceptical as to the part Mitchell had played in the affair. That the man knew he was buying stolen property he had little doubt, though of course French was quite unable to prove it. That Herd had murdered Platt with or without Mitchell's connivance seemed also likely, but here again there was no proof. However his own next move was obvious. He had to reassure Mitchell and he had to interview Herd before Mitchell could communicate with him.

'Thank you, Mr Mitchell,' he said, 'that'll do as far as you're concerned. I must now see Herd. You said he was one of your clerks. Is he in the building at present?'

'I think so. I'll ring for him.'

'Better sir, if you didn't communicate with him direct. You'll see the advantage for yourself. If you let your secretary send for him, we could see him next door.'

"Pon my soul, you're not polite, chief inspector.'

'You can see for yourself that it would be better for both of you that no one should be able to say there had been collusion. I'm not suggesting there would be, of course. But it might be alleged.'

'Oh, all right. Have it your own way.'

Five minutes later French and Carter were seated with Herd in a waiting room. Herd exactly answered the description of Roberts, even to the slight scar on the cheek where the cut had been. He proved of a different calibre to Mitchell. Obviously panic-stricken when he learnt French's business, he put up no kind of bluff whatever, but agreed with the utmost readiness to tell everything he knew.

French realised that from this kind of witness an exhibition of stern officialism usually produced the best results. He therefore began by a harsh warning that Herd was not bound to answer any questions which might incriminate himself, and that what he said would be taken down and might be given in evidence. He made a good deal of Carter's notebook and the fact that the notes taken in it would have to be signed, and contrived to refer in passing to detention at the Yard as a preliminary to arrest. When he had finished Herd was as completely deflated as a burst rubber balloon.

'Now,' went on French, 'it's a matter for yourself, of course, and if you prefer it you can come to the Yard and wait to answer my questions till a lawyer is present; but subject to that allow me to advise you to be candid. Unless a man's guilty, the truth never hurt him. What do you say? Will you make your statement here or come to the Yard?'

Herd, as French expected, was pathetically anxious not to go to the Yard. He swore to tell the truth, the whole truth, and nothing but the truth. He was so much upset that French was inclined to believe him.

'Very well,' French went on. 'Now just start in and let me have your statement in your own words about this whole matter of going to Ireland to shadow Platt about the petrol business. I may tell you that Mr Mitchell has already told us his share of the matter, so you need not be afraid of giving him away.'

At that Herd seemed faintly relieved, but he evidently found it hard to begin. French therefore helped him.

'Well, now, let's get down to it,' he said in a pleasanter voice. 'What was the first you heard of the affair?'

A little prompting brought out the story. But it was very much what Mitchell had already stated.

On Monday morning, 2nd September, Mitchell called Herd into his office and said that he was considering going into a new line of business and that he wanted certain information as to the bona fides of the man with whom he would deal. Platt, whose description he gave Herd, had offered him a new process for producing inert petrol which was now the property of a syndicate in Northern Ireland. Platt had informed Mitchell that he was negotiating with this syndicate for the purchase of their product, and he had offered to resell to Mitchell. Mitchell was doubtful about the whole affair: whether such a process really existed and whether Platt was in a position to dispose of it. In fact, he didn't trust Platt. Herd was to follow Platt to Ireland and keep an eye on him, though without allowing Platt to suspect his mission. He was to keep Mitchell advised of what went on. This, Herd considered, was a reasonable and natural precaution for Mitchell to take and he had no objection whatever to doing the work for him.

That night Herd crossed to Belfast. He saw Platt leave the boat in the morning, but he had no skill as a shadower, and he soon lost his quarry. He then decided to go direct to Hillsborough, in the hope that he would find where Platt was staying. To his satisfaction Platt put up at the same hotel. He kept what observation he could on him and satisfied himself he did really spend his time with Ferris and the others. He so reported to Mitchell. He found nothing out about the process itself: that wasn't his job.

He had understood that Platt was likely to return about the end of the week, and by Mitchell's instructions he held himself in readiness to receive a message. It came on the Saturday afternoon: a telephone from Mitchell saying that Platt was crossing back to England that night and to keep him under observation. Herd accordingly went aboard the Liverpool boat and watched for Platt. But he hadn't seen him. He had therefore asked at the office if Platt were travelling, and was told he had come aboard. This he later confirmed by an inquiry from Platt's cabin steward. Platt presumably had embarked just at the moment when Herd was being shown to his cabin.

When he heard that Platt was in his cabin he, Herd, troubled no more about the matter, except to take up his position at the gangway and see that Platt didn't go ashore again. Next morning at Liverpool he was on deck before the ship berthed, and watched for Platt. He didn't see him and he hung about as long as he could—till the *Ulster Sovereign* left the Landing Stage for the dock. He waited till she got into the dock and then asked some of the stewards who came ashore if all the passengers were off her. They said they were, and then he, Herd, came to the conclusion that Platt must have given him the slip. He waited about the dock entrance for some considerable time, but soon realised he could do no more and returned to London and reported to Mitchell. It was not till later that he had seen in the papers that Platt was missing, and he had then supposed it to be a case of voluntary disappearance.

When later still he learnt from the same source that Platt's body had been found, he was not only horror-stricken, but completely puzzled. Platt had seemed to him to be in good spirits, and suicide was the last thing of which he had expected to hear.

In answer to further questions, Herd repeated very emphatically that he had not gone to Platt's cabin, nor had he seen him on board at all. Equally firmly he denied knowing the details of the process or having tried to find them out. He admitted having looked at Ferris's cottage one evening, but this was in the hope of seeing whether Platt was there, not of trying to learn his secret.

Questions on points of details were answered so promptly by Herd that French was inclined to believe in the general truth of the statement. He satisfied himself as far as it was possible, then turned to the crucial point still remaining.

'You remember the details of the crossing, I suppose, Mr Herd?'

'I think so, yes.'

'Very well, will you just give me an account of your actions between, say, eleven and twelve o'clock?'

The man hesitated. 'When the boat left I went to the smoking room and had a drink. Then I was asked to play a hand at bridge and I did so. We broke up and I went to bed shortly after twelve.'

French wondered if this statement were true. If it were, it looked very like an alibi for Herd. From the place in which Platt's body had been found, it was certain that the man had gone overboard before twelve, so that if it could be proved that Herd was in the smoking room till past that hour, he could not have been guilty of the murder. But could such proof be obtained?

'Who were you playing with,' went on French.

Herd shook his head. 'I have really no idea,' he declared. 'I didn't hear any of their names.'

'I don't suppose I could expect that,' French admitted. 'All the same describe them.'

Again the man paused in thought. 'One,' he said at last, 'was small and stout with a round, red face. A horsey looking man in checks with a loud voice and laugh. Another was tall and thin and stooped, with a pale face and a big domed forehead. Looked like a scientist or something of that kind. The third had a short toothbrush moustache

and horn-rimmed glasses. He might have been a professional man, I thought.'

'Tell me, did you leave the smoking room during that
hour from eleven to twelve?'

'For a moment only. Once while I was dummy I went
out just to stretch my legs and look at the night. I remember
it was cold and raining hard.'

'About what time was that?'

'I don't know exactly. Perhaps about half-past eleven.'

Just the time the murder must have taken place, French
thought. He wondered if he could get evidence as to the
length of time Herd was away from the others. It should
not be difficult. The chances were that all those who had
joined in the game had booked berths and their names
would therefore be on the passenger list.

He sent Herd to have a photograph taken, then got out
a circular to all the men on the list, asking if they had
played bridge. In due course there were three answers. One
was from London, from a Professor Brackenbury. Taking
some photographs, among which was Herd's, French set
off to the College of Science to interview the professor. He
was tall and thin and stooped, just as Herd had described.
French asked if he could remember any of the persons
with whom he had played bridge, and if so, were any of
them represented by these photographs?

The professor, it appeared, remembered the trio clearly.
There was a rather stupid little bounder who, as his partner,
had twice trumped his winning card, and a doctor who
played a good game. The third was a dark nondescript
individual who was neither good nor bad.

'Any of them among the photographs?' French persisted.

The professor slowly examined them. When he came to

Herd's he laid it aside and continued with the remainder. Then he handed the lot back.

'This is the dark nondescript individual,' he declared. 'I noticed a cut on his cheek and there you see the scar.'

So far, so extremely good. But the professor was not positive as to the answer to French's next question. The man had left the group between eleven and twelve but he could not say for how long.

'How long does it take you to play a hand of bridge after the bidding is complete?' he asked French. 'I never timed it, but from three to five minutes, I should think.'

Five minutes—three minutes indeed—would have been ample time in which to commit the murder, provided two things obtained: first, that Platt had been ready waiting at a deserted part of the deck, and second, that the crime had been committed by simply picking him up and hurling him overboard.

But under any other circumstances French did not believe the thing would have been possible. There certainly would not have been time to summon Platt to the place, nor to have made him unconscious with chloroform.

To French it was incredible that Platt should have been waiting for his enemy, for the simple reason that Herd could not possibly have known at what hour he would be dummy. And it was really next thing to incredible that anyone could have thrown Platt overboard without first rendering him unable to struggle or cry out.

This evidence was strongly—indeed he believed overwhelmingly—in Herd's favour. It tended to confirm his own opinion that the man was not of the stuff of which murderers were made, and he felt inclined to acquit him in his own mind. In any case it was clear that with the information he had obtained, a conviction would be out of the question. And subsequent application to the other two members of the bridge party only confirmed his opinion.

As he sat at his desk considering how he might reach complete certainty on the matter a quite fresh idea leaped suddenly into his mind. He gasped slightly as he took in its fundamental probability. Yes, he believed he had at last got the truth! What a pity it wasn't really his case! He could have made something spectacular out of it. But it looked like as if the advantage was to go to the police of Northern Ireland.

Suppose Platt had stolen the secret and the theft had been discovered, not by Herd, but by Ferris or M'Morris? Suppose Ferris or M'Morris were guilty of the murder?

Here would be motive, wholly satisfying and adequate! After all their precautions to keep the secret safe, they now find thay have lost it and lost it irrevocably. No agreement has been signed. They have no redress. A theft of the kind is almost impossible to prove, particularly where the pretence of independent discovery can be supported by manufactured evidence. They would see that if Platt were allowed to get out of the country alive their profits would be gone. The fortunes they had been building on would have vanished. Instead of wealth they would have debts. Yes, here was all the motive any prosecution could possibly want.

But neither Ferris nor M'Morris had crossed to Liverpool. French considered. Had they not? How was it known? Then he saw that it wasn't known. The movements of the party on that Saturday night had never been gone into. Penrose, of course, had crossed and it would be necessary to weigh the case against him. However, French did not think Penrose the kind of man to commit such a crime. Ferris or M'Morris was much more likely.

Satisfied that in his own mind he had at last reached the truth in this puzzling case, French went on to consider his own consequent action. One thing was clear. Further investigation on these lines was not for him. It would be a job for the police of Northern Ireland. To the formal statement of his discoveries which he was sending to Superintendent Rainey, he decided to add a personal note mentioning his idea. He would then leave it to Rainey to follow it up or not as he liked.

As he posted his letter he felt that at last he was rid—and satisfactorily rid—of the case.

15

As Pamela Grey Saw It

In the meantime Pamela Grey had been passing through a time of emotional stress, with alternating periods of elation and depression which she found very trying.

First there had been the shock of Platt's disappearance. This had profoundly moved her, particularly owing to the unpleasantness which she had had with him such a short time before. But the shock was as nothing compared with the dreadful fears and doubts which had immediately assailed her mind, fears and doubts so secret and so horrible that she scarcely allowed herself to put them into conscious thought. Happily her panic did not last. She was soon able to thank God that her fears had largely evaporated, while her shameful unworthy doubts had entirely vanished.

Next came an experience of a different kind—Jefferson's visit. This evoked her keenest interest, upon which was superimposed a magnificent crescendo of delight as Jefferson grew more and more impressed by the process, and finally signed the provisional agreement which bade fair to assure to the syndicate accomplishment and fortune. To Pam it meant a lot more than success in their undertaking. It was owing to her action that Mr Whiteside had put his money into the affair, and she was glad he was not going to lose it. But infinitely more important than anything else, Jefferson's action made possible her marriage with Jack. There would be money, more than enough, for everything they might want.

Then had come a fresh shock, the finding of Platt's body. Instantly all her fears had revived. But the verdict at the inquest had been a profound relief. As the death was now definitely known to have been suicide, she need no longer fear. The affair had been terrible; but it was over. A dreadful episode, but an episode past and done with.

She was therefore the more upset and distressed when Jefferson summoned the group to a meeting and she discovered that the matter was by no means over and done with. Jefferson's suggestion that Platt might have stolen the secret and been murdered for it was more horrible than ever. For a while panic again gripped her, then she gradually realised that the idea was Jefferson's alone, and that there was no proof of its truth. Her fears again subsided. Apparently Jefferson had frightened them unnecessarily and nothing would come of his theory.

But this optimism was soon dispelled. The police came back again. Not directly about the affair: they were making inquiries about someone called Roberts. Still, this suggestion of police activity behind the scenes was disquieting. She wondered what they were doing and if by any chance they could agree with Jefferson?

She was also worried about another matter, though it had been so overshadowed by her fears that it had grown relatively unimportant. The petrol affair was not progressing as it should. On the day after his arrival back at Bristol, Jefferson had met with an accident and he had put off the visit of Ferris and Jack. It was a temporary delay, of course, but still it was unfortunate.

Altogether the whole period since Platt's arrival had been pretty trying. It was true that the cloud was passing over, had passed over she might almost say, but while it had lasted it had been rather horrible. Pam, indeed, had almost begun to think that a fortune could be too dearly bought.

Now, however, she was cheered, this time by the preparations for her marriage. She and Jack had begun that fascinating though exasperating task of finding a suitable house. They had decided on having a quiet marriage and taking a cottage, a modest establishment, on a year or two's lease. Until the big money began to come in Jack proposed to keep on his job and their immediate expenses were to be met by a loan from Mr Penrose. When they were actually rich they would travel for a year or two, and then probably build. Excepting for the immediate future it was all delightfully vague and thrilling.

Then another blow fell which brought back with a rush all Pam's fears, and left her more anxious than ever.

It happened on a Tuesday afternoon, about a week after Sergeant M'Clung's visit to Ferris about Roberts. Work at the office was slack and Jack had decided to take a half-holiday to go with Pam to inspect a house at Knockmore, a district a short distance away from Hillsborough. As they were returning they met Ferris on the road. He held up his hand and Jack pulled the car over.

'I say,' Ferris began, 'this thing isn't over yet. That sergeant fellah has been down again from Belfast, M'Clung his name is. He started over the whole blessed affair again as if he hadn't heard a thing about it before.'

Jack looked startled, while Pam clenched her hands till the knuckles showed white.

'What affair are you talking about?' Jack asked. 'That Roberts man?'

'Not at all. The Platt business.'

'What about the Platt business? Hadn't he heard it all before?'

'Isn't that what I'm telling you? He wanted the whole story over again from the beginning; as if he had never heard a word about it. I don't know what he was after.'

Pam felt horror creeping like a fog over her mind. 'Oh, Fred,' she said tremulously, 'what was it all about? Did he not say what had started it again?'

'He did not. He said he was trying to collect some further information. But you'll see him for yourselves. He was asking when he could see the both of you.'

'It's about that Roberts,' Jack suggested. 'Did he not mention him?'

'He did not. Never mentioned the name.'

'Has he gone?'

'He has, but he'll be back.'

'You didn't tell him anything new?'

'Sure how could I when I had told him it all before?' Ferris returned with some irritation.

'You might have known from his questions what he was after.'

Ferris looked aggrieved. 'Well, so I did,' he admitted sarcastically. 'He asked about Platt and why he came over here and what he did while he was here and how he went away. I took it he was after what had happened to Platt.'

Jack continued asking questions as if he was somehow convinced that Ferris could have produced a full explanation of the whole affair, had he so desired. But in the end he desisted, and they drove on.

'Oh, Jack,' Pam moaned, 'what does it mean? Why can't they let it alone?' Her fears had swelled up like a great flood.

'Means nothing.' Jack took the news coolly. 'They have to fuss around a bit for their money.'

'But surely the thing was settled at the inquest. It was proved to be suicide. Why can't they let it be?'

'It wasn't proved to be suicide: the inquest doesn't matter two hoots. The police may think it was murder. Wouldn't be surprised myself. Platt didn't seem the man for suicide.'

'Oh, dreadful!'

'Jefferson thought it was murder: you could see that by what he said at that meeting. Maybe he's got the police convinced.'

Though Pam once again felt utterly terrified, she took some comfort from Jack's attitude. He was so obviously unimpressed. Clearly no idea of the nature of her fears had entered his mind. Well, that was all to the good. If he was so sure, perhaps there really was no danger. She knew she was imaginative, and perhaps it was simply that her imagination had run away with her.

But later on that evening her terror was renewed, and even Jack began to seem a little upset.

She had dined with the Penroses, and was beginning to feel happier as she and Jack sat chatting in his tiny den, when Ferris was announced.

'I thought I'd come round and tell you,' he began, as he

took a cigarette from the case Jack held out. 'That fellow M'Clung's been making more inquiries.'

'What?' Jack asked.

'Well, he had asked Mac and me what we were doing on the Sunday after Platt left—the *Sunday*, mind you. We told him, of course: not that there was anything special to tell. But we told him what there was.'

'Well? For heaven's sake go ahead.'

'Well, I've just seen Mac and what do you think? M'Clung had gone straight to his house after he left us, and asked if he was there on the Sunday.'

Jack stared.

'Not just straight out like that, you know,' went on Ferris. 'He pretended there was some question about the time Platt left for the boat on Saturday night, and that if he knew what time M'Morris had got home it would help to settle it. He said M'Morris couldn't remember and he wondered if any of them there could help him.'

'What's that to do with Sunday?'

'I'm coming to that. It happened that the maid knew what time he got in, for it was her evening out and he'd turned up just after she had: just at the time he'd said. Then M'Clung slipped in a question about what time he'd gone out on Sunday. He did it casually and they didn't notice anything funny about it. But he made quite sure Mac was there.'

'But what's it all about? What's the man after?'

'There's more in it than that,' Ferris went on. 'When Mac told me that, we both went down to the hotel and had a drink and asked a question or two. And he was there too. He must have gone straight to the hotel from Mac's.'

'What doing?'

'Checking up on our statement. When Platt had had dinner, when Mac and I went in, when we left for Belfast. Everything he could check, he checked.'

'But he'd done that before?'

'Of course he had. That's what Agnew and Quirky said. It was all the same questions he asked over again.' Ferris paused and nodded his head significantly. 'And I expect when I go and see the Alexanders in the morning, I'll hear he was there too.'

Jack stared. 'The Alexanders? What on earth are you talking about now?'

'My alibi,' Ferris returned darkly. 'I spent Sunday afternoon there. He'll have been to check up if that was true.'

'I don't know what you're talking about,' Jack repeated with exasperation.

'Well, you will,' Ferris said with gloom. 'He'll be coming to you next.'

Still Jack did not seem to appreciate what might lie behind M'Clung's questions, but with every sentence of Ferris's Pam's terror grew more overwhelming. This looked like what she had feared from the very beginning! And how could suspicions of that kind be disproved? . . .

'He didn't say he was coming to see Jack?' she asked, speaking with difficulty through her dry lips.

'He did. He's coming to see you both. He was looking for you this afternoon, then when I told him you were away he said he'd be down again tomorrow.'

It was evident to Pam that Ferris understood, if he did not share, her fears. But equally obviously the idea had not occurred to Jack. Should she tell him what was on her mind? Should she warn him, so that the hideous suggestion should not come on him unexpectant and unawares? Or would it be better that it should so come on him? Would not his manner be more convincing in the latter case? She did not know. Horribly worried she said goodnight without unburdening her soul.

And in the morning it was too late. She went early to Hillview, but he had already left for the office. She did not follow him to Lisburn. Perhaps after all, things were better as they were.

For the next hour she waited in a fever of unease and apprehension. She could settle to nothing, and the suspense grew almost unbearable. Indeed it was almost with feelings of relief, that at last she saw the small Ford drive up to the door. M'Clung and a plain-clothes man got out. They were shown into the sitting room. She went down.

Now that she was face to face with the ordeal, Pam's nervousness seemed to a large extent to evaporate. She felt calm and her own mistress. To her astonishment she became satisfied that she would be able to control her manner so as not to suggest to these men that she was otherwise than secure and content.

M'Clung's manner also, whether by his own intention or otherwise, tended to put her at her ease. He was polite, almost friendly, and entirely matter of fact and free from emotion. The plain-clothes man, whom he called Brown, seemed kindly and sheepish rather than aggressive. He looked the indulgent and slightly sat-upon father of a family rather than the stern and implacable policeman. Pam breathed more freely.

'It's the same business that I was down about before, Miss Grey,' M'Clung began. 'There's a new feature come into the case since you gave your statement and I want to ask you one or two more questions. It's about a man named Roberts. Did ever you hear of him?'

A wave of relief filled Pam's mind. What a *fool* she had been!

'I heard from Mr Ferris that you had been down here making inquiries about someone of that name,' she answered calmly. 'I never myself heard of any Mr Roberts.'

'You never heard the name mentioned?'

'Not in connection with anyone here.'

M'Clung seemed disappointed. He continued in a sort of half-hearted way questioning her, as if repeating the questions might make her change her answers. Pam's fears had almost evaporated, and even she had the courage to turn the tables on the sergeant and ask who Roberts was.

'Well, that's just what we're wanting to know,' he returned, it seemed to her, apologetically. 'He's a man we think crossed with Mr Platt and saw him on the boat. If we could find him we might get something more about what happened.'

'But is there any doubt about what happened?' Pam asked, growing bolder still.

'Well,' M'Clung shrugged, 'that Mr Jefferson that was over, he's been to the super with some tale that Platt had stolen that secret of yours and that this man Roberts had murdered him for it. Roberts was staying here at the hotel and he certainly crossed by the same boat. I don't think there's anything in it myself, but Mr Jefferson he's got the super's ear and so we've got to go into the thing again. But don't you, miss, be letting on that I said so.'

'Of course not.' A whole weight of anxiety and dread was lifted from Pam. What a *fool* she had been, she thought again. There was nothing to be frightened about. Nothing!

It was queer about Roberts certainly, but it had nothing to do with her. She turned almost warmly to M'Clung as he went on in his rather singsong voice.

'So those being the orders you'll excuse me if I have to go over your evidence again. I have to report that I've done so in the case of all the witnesses.'

'Of course, sergeant. As I said before, I would be only too glad to help you, only I'm afraid I can't.'

'Thank you, miss. Then I'll begin.'

He was certainly as good as his word. Once again he went into her whole statement and in the most minute detail. Indeed he appeared himself to feel how exasperating and unnecessary it must seem to Pam, as he apologised for his persistence. 'I'm wanting to know if there was anything that suggested the secret might have been stolen,' he explained. 'You might have seen something that would suggest it to me, though you mightn't have thought of it yourself.'

The questions drew on to the Saturday. 'When was the last time you saw Mr Platt?' he asked.

'About midday at Mr Ferris's cottage.'

'Oh, then you weren't in at the steamer in the evening?'

Pam hesitated. 'I didn't see Mr Platt off, if that's what you mean. But I was at the steamer, or rather at the shed door.'

'How was that, Miss Grey?'

'I drove Mr Penrose in.'

'I see. Then Mr Penrose and Mr Platt didn't go in together?'

'No.'

'Two people crossing from here by the same boat on the same night. Friends too. Tell me, why didn't they go together?'

For the first time Pam felt some confusion. 'Well,' she replied, less spontaneously, she could not help feeling, 'I think you know that Mr Penrose and I are engaged. I wanted to see him off myself.'

'I understood that. I think you said you had been engaged for some time?'

'That's correct.'

Slowly M'Clung turned over the pages of his notebook. 'I see,' he said presently, 'you and Mr Penrose went into Belfast to meet Mr Platt. Why shouldn't you have done the same thing about his going away?'

'It's not quite the same thing, I think. Mr Penrose was going away for some days. I wanted to have him to myself at the last.'

'Well, that certainly is different.' The suspicion of a smile hovered round the corners of M'Clung's mouth. Under other circumstances Pam would have been furious with him for it: now she was grateful. 'You didn't happen to see Mr Platt or Mr Ferris or Mr Ferris's car when you were in?'

'I did not.'

'They were in about half-past ten. What time would you have got down to the boat?'

'Not till nearly eleven. Indeed we ran it rather fine.'

'How was that, Miss Grey?'

'The car was punctured. When we went out to start, one of the back wheels was flat.'

'Oh? And what did you do?'

'Mr Penrose changed it.'

'He changed it, did he? At that time of night?' M'Clung looked thoughtful. He glanced at Pam with something of suspicion in his eyes. Apprehension surged back into Pam's mind. The atmosphere suddenly changed. Tension grew.

But M'Clung didn't seem to notice it. With his manner more matter of fact than ever, he went on with his questions.

'Let me see that I've got that straight. When did you go out to the car in the first instance?'

'About a quarter to ten.'

'Then you would have been at the boat shortly after ten. That would have been rather early, wouldn't it?'

'I thought so. But Mr Penrose didn't want me to be out too late. You see, after returning the car to Hillview, I had to walk home.'

'I see. Then you found the wheel punctured and Mr Penrose changed it. And I suppose had to pump the spare one up?'

'He had.'

'And you weren't done till nearly half-past ten?'

'Between quarter and half-past.'

Again M'Clung paused, obviously thinking hard. 'Now here's something I want you to tell me,' he went on presently. 'Mr Penrose wanted you back early. But if he changed the wheel you wouldn't get back till late. Now under these special circumstances, why couldn't he have gone in with Mr Ferris?'

It was a nasty question, but Pam felt equal to it. 'Well, it was rather late then, wasn't it? Mr Ferris might have left.'

'Oh, I see. You mean by the time you had walked to Mr Ferris's cottage, he would probably have left? Is that what you mean?'

Pam nodded with some relief.

'And there was no telephone to the cottage.' He paused, then added quietly, 'You're sure that was the reason?'

213

It was not exactly what Pam had meant to convey. She felt as if she had somehow been trapped into the statement, but now that she had made it, she thought she had better stick to it. 'Well, there was a risk of it, wasn't there?' she answered as lightly as she could.

Once again M'Clung paused. Then he said slowly, 'No, there wasn't any risk of it. You knew that Mr Ferris wasn't starting from his cottage but from the hotel, where he was to go to pick up Mr Platt. You said so before. Why did you not ring up the hotel?'

Pam gasped. This was horrible. This was what she had feared from the beginning, but what she thought she had escaped. But she mustn't betray her fear. 'I'm afraid neither of us thought of that,' she answered shakily.

M'Clung's manner, which had grown more matter-of-fact and bored as the interrogation went on, now changed with disconcerting suddenness, and Pam saw that beneath the respectful easy-going exterior there was hidden quite a different type of man. He stared at her fixedly and said in a much sharper tone:

'Now, Miss Grey, you've done extra well up to the present. I would have staked my life on everything you've said. Now, don't be spoiling it. Forget that last answer and let me have the truth.'

Pam flushed. 'It was the truth,' she declared.

'It may be. But it wasn't the whole truth. Now, what was it? I can see by your manner that there was some other reason, and I'm going to know what it was.'

Pam hesitated. She was honest and truthful by nature, but she would have lied herself black in the face if it would have helped Jack. But would any prevarication help Jack? Now that he suspected something, this man would certainly find it out. She could not rely on Ferris or M'Morris lying for Jack. And Jack himself certainly wouldn't lie. He would tell the whole thing without the slightest hesitation. Would her prevarication not arouse the very suspicions she wanted to avoid? She felt profoundly worried.

Then suddenly she saw a way by which she might tell the truth and still keep Jack out of it.

'It's not a thing I want to talk about,' she said, allowing herself to look embarrassed and distressed, 'but if I must, I suppose I must. I can only ask you not to repeat it.' Again she paused. 'The truth is that Mr Platt had—had got a little too friendly. There was nothing in it, of course, but I didn't like it and I didn't want to see more of him than I could. It was I who insisted in driving Mr Penrose in. That's the whole thing.'

M'Clung seemed about to ask another question, then paused in his turn. Again he turned over the pages of his notebook, apparently comparing two items. Then he put away the notebook and smiled.

'That's too bad, Miss Grey. I can understand you wouldn't be wanting to talk about it, and I withdraw what I said. Now let's see; I think that's about all.' He sat for a moment thinking, then rose to his feet. 'We'll be getting along now, and I'm sorry for giving you all this annoyance.'

It was over! And it hadn't been so bad. Except for that unfortunate question just at the end, the man had learnt nothing that she hadn't already told him. And about that she needn't be upset. Obviously he had thought nothing of it. He hadn't even asked if Jack was aware of her feelings, as she thought he was going to. Instead he had looked up his book. But as there could have been nothing about the affair in his book, she needn't worry because of that. No, she had done well. It was over, and well over.

At the same time she felt physically as if she had been beaten, and so tired that she could scarcely hold up her head. She decided she must do something about it. Actually she did two things, both unprecedented. She mixed herself a stiff tot of brandy, and she went upstairs and lay down on her bed.

Her rest-cure was a success. She fell asleep, waking only at lunch time. Much refreshed, she found herself able to talk naturally to her parents about M'Clung's visit.

But after the meal when she was again alone, her anxiety swelled up once more. She felt she must know whether M'Clung had interviewed Jack, and what he had said. She could not possibly wait till the evening. She decided she would go into Lisburn. She would not go to the office, but she would ring up Jack from a street booth and he would come out and meet her. She would only keep him a minute.

Relieved at the prospect of seeing him so soon, she put on her things and went out to get the bus. But before she reached its stopping place she met Ferris.

'You saw the sergeant?' he asked her in a low tone.

She didn't like his manner, which was vaguely disquieting. 'I did,' she answered. 'He questioned me for an hour and more.'

'What time did he leave?'

'Getting on to eleven.'

Ferris nodded. 'Then he must have come straight,' he remarked.

'What?' Pam asked sharply. 'Was he with you too?'

'He was so.' Ferris paused, seeming a little embarrassed.

216

He looked doubtfully at Pam, then went on, still in a low voice. 'What did you tell him about Jack's row with Platt for? Wouldn't it have been wiser to have said nothing about that?'

Pam stared. 'I never told him about it.'

'You what?' It was now Ferris's turn to stare. 'Well, he knew all about it and he said you told him.'

'Fred: I never did!' Her voice sharpened as once again panic seized her. 'Tell me.'

'Good Lord! The dirty hound! He got it out of me by a trick. I say, Pam, I'm so sorry. But I didn't know.' His voice took on a supplicating tone.

Pam almost danced with impatience. 'Oh, what does it matter?' she hissed. 'Tell me! What happened?'

'He came and he talked, as confidential as you please. He said he was wanting to know a bit more about the unpleasantness between Jack and Platt on the Saturday morning. He said you'd mentioned it, but that you'd seemed to feel the thing, and so he hadn't wanted to keep on at you about it. If I would let him know further details, he said he wouldn't have to trouble you again.'

'And what did you say?' Pam's mouth had gone dry.

'I said it was nothing. Platt had got a little fresh with you, and Jack didn't like it, that was all. I said there was no harm done.'

'And was he satisfied with that?'

Ferris looked really upset. 'Well, he was not,' he admitted. 'He said he'd understood from you it was much more serious than that. Then he began—you know the way he has—taking each item of the thing and asking questions about it till all's no more. What exactly had Platt done? Had he taken you in his arms? Had he kissed you? and I don't know what all. Then, where was Jack at this time? Did he see it? What did he do? Then he said he'd understood from you that Jack had gone for Platt and that there had been a fight. Had there or had there not? Well, what could I say? I told him there was no fight at all, but that Jack had struck Platt once. Then I told him Platt had apologised and the thing had blown over.'

'But I never told him a single word of all that.'

Ferris shrugged. 'I'm afraid I see it now,' he admitted, 'now when it's too late. The dirty dog was just guessing and bluffing and I, like the mug I am, didn't see what he was up to. I see now what was on his mind because of the questions he asked me first: I couldn't make out what he was after at the time. He wanted to know hadn't we all dined with the Penroses on Friday evening, and if Jack and Platt were friendly then. I said they were, which was the truth. I didn't know what was coming, you see?'

'Oh, go on!'

'Then he wanted to know what had happened when we left the house after dinner. I said Mac and I had run Platt to the hotel and had a drink with him before separating. By that, he got that Jack and Platt hadn't met again that night. He had it in his book that we'd all been at the cottage on Saturday morning and also that you and Jack hadn't seen Platt after that meeting. So he must have guessed the trouble took place then, because there wasn't any other time it could have. But Pam, you must have told him *something* to make him start wondering?'

'He asked me why Jack and Platt hadn't gone to the steamer together. I put it on myself. I told him Platt had been a little affectionate and that I was just as glad not to go in with him. I never brought in Jack at all.'

'He must have guessed Jack knew or Jack would have wanted to go in together. You see, he's just put two and two together and pretended you told him, and so got confirmation out of me. I'm sorry, Pam, but it'll not do any harm.'

'Oh, Fred, are you sure?'

'I am so. Certain sure.'

'It has never occurred to Jack that there might be— danger.'

'No, nor to anybody else either, except yourself. It wouldn't have occurred to me, only I saw what was in your mind. Don't you be worrying yourself, Pam. Jack's all right.'

He spoke confidently, and she looked at him with grati- tude. Perhaps he was correct and she was needlessly alarmed. After all no one who knew Jack could possibly suspect him. And then again came that horrible qualm. He was known to be passionate. His temper was very short: a quick flare-up and over in a moment. Anyone who didn't know him really well might doubt. Why even she . . . Her cheeks burned as she recalled her thoughts. She knew better now, but others . . .

The bus came up and she took her place. At Lisburn she rang up Jack. And then was dispelled one awful fear which in spite of herself had fought its way into her mind. His voice answered her as normally and unemotionally as ever.

Five minutes later they had entered a café and called for tea. It was early in the afternoon and the place was empty. They could talk without risk of being overheard.

'Oh, Jack, tell me. Was the sergeant with you?'

'He was, curse him. I had an appointment in M'Auley's office and I thought he'd never go. For a whole blessed

219

hour he sat there asking silly questions. I nearly told him what I thought of him.'

'What did he ask about?'

'What didn't he ask about?' Jack grew indignant. 'Every darned thing: things that he'd been told about six times already. A fat lot of good it must have done him.'

'Did he mention the row with Platt?'

'That too. Though how the hell he knew about it beats me.'

'What did he say?'

Jack grinned suddenly. 'He asked me if Platt was stunned when I knocked him down. I told him a fellow with a skin as thick as his would take something more than a blow from me to knock him out.'

Pam shivered. 'Jack, you didn't?' she exclaimed. Was Jack an absolute utter fool, or had he shown the highest form of wisdom? She didn't know, but she remained terrified. 'What did he say?' she went on tremulously.

'He said he understood the fellow had apologised and that the matter was closed, and was this so?'

'Yes?'

'I told him it was so.'

'Well, and what then?' Sometimes she felt she would like to shake Jack. Getting information from him was like squeezing blood out of a stone.

'Well, that was all. He put up the usual story about being obliged for my help and all that guff, and then he cleared out.'

'And did he seem satisfied?'

'Of course he seemed satisfied. Why wouldn't he? When is that blessed girl going to bring the tea?'

It was all right. A little shakily Pam reassured herself.

And Jack had been wise. Whether he had intended it or not—she rather imagined not—he had as a matter of fact said just the right things. He couldn't have done better. Yes, it was all right. Relief stole into her mind.

And that relief continued to grow as day after day passed and the police made no further sign. So far as she was concerned it had been a false alarm. She had worried herself needlessly. As it happened so often before under other circumstances, she had allowed her imagination to run away with her. She was always suffering from things that didn't happen. It should be a lesson to her.

Gradually her thoughts turned from the subject to the brighter one of her approaching marriage. Jack had taken the house at Knockmore on a two years' lease, and she had spent many thrilling hours there over the question of carpets, curtains and wallpapers. Furniture also was a subject of endless delight and its disposition gave rise to the most entrancing problems. In these Jack was even less use than she anticipated, but this perhaps was just as well, for in this house, this marvellous house, this house which was to be really her own, she was going to have everything her own way. But she wanted him to admire her choice, and in this unhappily he became a trifle short also.

'How do you think that chair goes with the carpet?' she would say. 'Isn't it just perfect, as if they were made for one another?' and he would answer heartily, 'Fine! What about a spot of lunch?' However, she told herself, he was made like that and she wouldn't change him for any other living soul on earth.

She was a lucky girl, she told herself again! How incredibly her outlook had changed in the last twelve months! Then, cramped in means as her parents were, she was trying to find an apparently non-existent job, and looking forward to an existence of struggle and privation. Now, about to marry the best man in the whole world, and with a prospect of wealth greater than she could have imagined, her future was assured—as far as anything in this world can be sure. A lucky girl! Incredible was the only word for it.

And then in a moment her entire outlook was changed. That awful, ghastly terror which for so long had been lurking in the recesses of her mind suddenly reappeared, this time as a stark reality.

Early one morning Mr Penrose, white and trembling and looking ten years older, called to see her. He could scarcely speak. But for all that he was able to make his meaning clear. Late on the previous night police officers had arrived and had arrested Jack on a charge of murder.

16

As Pamela Grey Saw It

An icy hand seemed to close round Pam's heart as Mr Penrose told his dreadful news, So it had come: that fearful thing which she had secretly dreaded ever since she had heard of Platt's disappearance! Jack arrested! *Jack!* And for murder! Now that it had happened it seemed incredible: preposterous! How could anyone who knew him doubt his innocence?

Oh, how crookedly things had happened! If only Platt had not lost his head in the cottage on that Saturday morning! If only Jack had appeared a few seconds earlier or later than he did! If only he had not crossed that night, and by the same boat! Everything had occurred in the worst possible way. It was as if Fate was against them.

For a moment Pam could not reply to Mr Penrose. Then she groaned. 'Oh, it's not true! It can't be true! Oh, I've been afraid—so afraid! And then the danger seemed over. And now: it's happened!'

He could but shake his head. She pulled out a chair and made him sit down. He sat motionless with his head bent,

223

as if all the life had drained out of him. She went into the next room and poured him out some brandy.

It revived him. 'Thank you,' he said in more normal tones. 'You must have some yourself.'

'No,' she answered as if in a dream. 'I don't want it.'

'My dear, you must.'

She gave in. The movement and thought for him had helped her. The brandy helped her more. The overwhelming numbing horror seemed to lift. The disaster remained appalling, but it was something human, something that might be met and fought, something that was not necessarily irrevocable.

'Tell me,' she asked softly.

But there was little more to be told than the one devastating fact. Sergeant M'Clung and another man had come. They had asked for Jack. They had said they were sorry, but he would have to go to headquarters with them. They had been as civil and kindly as they could. Jack had gone without a word, except for a brief goodbye. He had not been much upset and had waved to them cheerfully enough.

'He was always plucky,' she murmured.

'Yes, he was always plucky,' he answered, then added with a shake of the head, 'He'll need it all now. My son,' he went on as if unconscious of her presence, 'oh, my son.' He sat gazing forward into nothingness. 'But there,' he seemed to come back to the present, 'I mustn't complain. You're plucky too. You're not complaining. We've got to work for him now. We'll see him through.'

Pam felt as if she were living in an evil dream as she broke the news to her father and mother. They were sympathy and goodness itself, but even so, it proved an ordeal. All the same, the thought and effort helped her. Then she returned with Mr Penrose to Hillview. Mrs Penrose had taken Pam to her heart, and now she clung to her as if to draw strength from the contact.

Gradually the first rude shock wore off and they began to discuss the affair constructively.

'What happens in such cases?' Pam asked 'Tell me.'

'Well,' Mr Penrose answered, 'he will be brought before the magistrates this morning and remanded. That's purely formal. The only thing is,' he hesitated, 'he won't be allowed bail. Then perhaps after some more remands, the magistrates will hear the case. If they think there is a genuine case against him, they will commit him for trial; if not, they will release him then and there. But, my dear,' he paused again, 'we needn't hope for that. He is certain to be committed for trial. And that will be our opportunity.'

'You say this morning he'll be brought before the magistrates? Is there nothing then to be done at once? Nothing to prepare for that?'

'My dear, it's all done: all that we can do. I arranged it last night, after—it happened. I rang up Irwin of Irwin & Magee of Wellington Place, and asked him to act. I am waiting to hear when Jack is to be brought up, and I will go in and attend the court with Irwin.'

'I'll go too,' Pam declared.

'I don't know that—'

'Of course I'll go. What would Jack think if I wasn't there?'

Mr Penrose again demurred, but Pam was adamant and Mrs Penrose took her part. 'It would show Jack she believed in him,' she said.

'Do the others know?' Pam went on; 'Fred Ferris and Mac?'

'I'm afraid everyone knows by now,' Mr Penrose returned sadly.

Further conversation was interrupted by the telephone bell. Mr Penrose hurried to the instrument.

'There's a special court at eleven,' he said. 'We'll have to hurry. Run and tell M'Ilrath, will you, Pam? I told him he'd be wanted, so the car's ready.'

The elderly gardener-chauffeur touched his hat as Pam appeared. Deprecatingly he murmured a few words of sympathy. 'Don't you take on, miss,' he advised. 'There's no one that knows Mr Jack that could believe he did a thing like that.'

The kindliness in his tone comforted her. It was irrational perhaps, but when they started, the weight of her despair had somewhat lightened.

They picked up Mr Irwin at his office and drove on to the court. Irwin was a tall fine-looking man with a bony face, large cheekbones and a square jaw. He obviously meant to be kindly, but his manner was a trifle dry.

'We can do nothing today,' he said after greetings and a somewhat perfunctory murmur of sympathy. 'A remand is a certainty. The thing'll last maybe a couple of minutes— purely formal.'

'That's what I've told Miss Grey,' Penrose answered.

Their prophecies were fulfilled to the letter. The case was called, Jack appeared in the dock, formal evidence of arrest was given followed immediately by a request for a remand. Mr Irwin said he was appearing for the accused but had nothing to say at the moment the remand was granted, Jack vanished, and it was all over.

Pam was thankful in a way that it was so quick. She was able to see that Jack looked normally cheerful and to smile at him as warmly and reassuringly as she could.

'You'll see him, won't you, Mr Irwin?' she said as they left the building. 'Tell him how utterly I believe in him and that I'm coming to see him when I'm allowed. I will be allowed, won't I?'

'Well, we'll see about that later,' Irwin answered without enthusiasm, 'but I'll visit him myself at once and I'll not fail to give him your message.'

'He's not much good at pretty phrases,' Penrose remarked when Irwin had been dropped at his office, 'but he's magnificent at his job: I know no one better.'

'What exactly will he do?'

'I had a chat with him while we were waiting. He'll see Jack this afternoon and have a talk over things. Jack, of course, has met him several times and I know he has a high opinion of him.'

'You didn't think of undertaking the defence yourself, Mr Penrose?'

'No, my dear, I did not. He's too close to me for one thing, but besides Irwin & Magee are better at that sort of work. And of course they'll have any ability that I have at their disposal.'

'The strength of the two firms?'

'I hope so. Then we'll have to get counsel. I'm going to discuss that with Irwin tomorrow, after he's seen Jack. I think Bernard Coates, if he's available, and if Irwin agrees. I certainly think he's the best man we have in Northern Ireland.'

'Just one barrister?'

'Yes, but of course he'll have to have his junior.'

227

A complicated business, a trial! And why, Pam thought, should the defence be left to the friends of the accused? The state is acting against the accused, why shouldn't the state arrange for the trial to be fair? Why should private individuals have to pay huge sums to get justice? Suppose they hadn't the money? Pam thought of the agony of having to put up with perfunctory or second-rate help because one couldn't afford to give one's loved one the best chance for his life. And apparently conviction or acquittal did depend pretty largely on who conducted the case for the defence. At least, so she had often heard. It was all wrong! The facts and the facts only should be the deciding factor; not the clever way in which they were put. Pam thought it was all terribly unfair.

But unhappily her opinion didn't affect the matter one way or another. Jack's friends had to provide his defence, and it was up to them to provide the best that was possible. Well, she was lucky there. Mr Penrose knew the ropes, and there was enough money. Everything would be done.

And done successfully. Of that, of course, there could be no doubt. It was a dreadful business and they would go through a dreadful time before it was over, but as to the final result there could be no doubt whatever. Not for a moment did Pam allow herself to think of anything else. When at intervals the hideous doubt tried to find an entrance to her mind, she banished it with all the resolution she possessed. Simply she dared not think of that other possibility . . . It *couldn't* happen! Nothing so utterly awful could ever take place.

Now for Pam, and indeed for all those who knew and loved Jack Penrose, a terrible period of anxiety and suspense set in. It drew Pam closer to people than ever before. Soon she found her acquaintances divided themselves into two groups. The larger was definitely friendly and tried in all sorts of unobtrusive ways to show her sympathy and kindness. But a few people grew aloof. If she met them they passed without stopping, and if they saw her coming they had business elsewhere.

Among those who seemed most anxious to help were her cousins, Dot and Dash Whiteside. Mrs Penrose had rung them up to tell them the news on the first day, and when Pam got back from court she found them both at her home. The three young women had always been friends, but never till now had Pam realised the goodness that lay behind the other's somewhat bouncing manners. Indeed, so overcome was she by their sympathy that to her own shame she broke down and sobbed openly. But the outbreak proved a relief, and as she bathed her eyes she smiled for the first time since the blow fell.

Ferris and M'Morris were another pair who were tremendously upset by the news. Pam indeed was surprised that they should take it so much to heart. They had always been friendly and she had got on well with both, but she had never really cared for either. She had considered them good business acquaintances, but not exactly friends as she thought of others in her set. But now there could be no doubt of their distress, and she felt drawn to them more than ever before.

On two successive weeks Jack was remanded, and then came the preliminary hearing. This last was a period of unrelieved horror for Pam. She was appalled by the strength of the prosecution's case and disappointed beyond words when Mr Brennan, Coates' junior, rose and said that the defence would be reserved, with its immediate consequence of Jack's committal for trial. Surely, she thought bitterly, Irwin and Coates might have done better than that? They might have put up *some* sort of fight instead of handing over everything to the enemy. Why, they were running away before the battle!

She said something of the kind to Mr Penrose and was relieved to find that he was not greatly depressed by the proceedings. 'Trust Coates,' he advised; 'he knows best. It was all discussed carefully beforehand. In the first place nothing could have prevented Jack being committed for trial, so there was no good trying to do that. In the second, Coates didn't want to give away his line of defence and have the prosecution spending weeks working up arguments against it. He thought it better to spring it on them at the trial when they could only make an improvised reply.'

In this Pam found some comfort, though it seemed to her unhappily like the 'strategic retirements' announced by the commander of a defeated force. However, there it was and nothing could be done about it. She reminded herself that the preliminary hearing must now be forgotten and her attention turned to that vastly more terrible period now only six weeks away—the trial itself. On the trial and on Coates' defence rested not only Jack's whole future, but her own. She could not bring herself to contemplate any other than a successful ending to that awful ordeal, but she knew that if Jack's life were destroyed hers would also be. Without him existence would be insupportable.

There now dawned for Pamela Grey an even more dreadful period than that of the past few weeks. Since the hearing before the magistrates Jack's peril seemed to her infinitely more pressing. She was no longer able to comfort herself by the thought that a conviction was impossible. The case against him was terribly strong, far stronger than she had imagined. Indeed, at moments of maximum depression, she wondered whether it was not quite overwhelming. That he was entirely innocent she *knew*. She would have staked her life on it without the slightest hesitation. But unhappily her beliefs didn't matter. Would the jury believe it? Would she herself believe it if she hadn't known Jack? She didn't know, and sank still lower in her slough of despond.

Pam indeed felt stunned. She did not know what to do. And yet if something were not done there was the fear, there was more than the fear, that her worst forebodings would be realised.

Mr Penrose seemed stunned too. He had aged in these weeks. He had been a fine upstanding man before the trouble arose; elderly, of course, but still vigorous and capable. Now both appearance and manner gave the impression of age. He had grown paler, more fragile looking, more bent, less capable of incisive thought and action. Pam now saw how wise he had been to entrust the defence to other hands.

The remaining members of her immediate circle reacted very much as might have been expected. Her own father and mother were full of sympathy, but owing to Mr Grey's health they were unable to do anything active to assist: not, as she told herself despairingly, that there was anything that they could have done. Mrs Penrose was herself heartbroken, upset not only about her son, but in a lesser degree about her husband also. At the same time her goodness and her understanding were a relief to Pam. Both Ferris and M'Morris were extraordinarily distressed. 'Sure no one that knows anything at all about him could think he'd done a thing like that,' Ferris said indignantly again and again, and M'Morris agreed.

But of all the people who showed their sympathy with Pam, the one whose companionship she found most comforting was Dot Whiteside. Both Dot and Dash and, indeed, the whole Whiteside family had been goodness itself all through, but somehow Dot seemed to understand better and to be more genuinely distressed than the others. Pam found herself slightly surprised, for though she had always liked Dot, she had never been actually fond of her. Now she felt a very genuine attachment growing between herself and the somewhat bouncing young woman.

For some days Pam's inertia lasted and then the very urgency of the danger forced her to action. What, her one cry was, can we do? In vain she was assured that Irwin and Coates were doing all that mortal could: she wanted to act herself. She wanted to feel that things really were on the move: she wanted the relief of personal effort. Importunately she urged first Penrose and then Irwin to let her help.

She had been exhaustively questioned by both Irwin and Coates on her knowledge of the affair, in the hope of bringing out some useful facts. But she did not consider this enough. She urged that all the remaining members of the syndicate should meet counsel, on the chance that from their collective wisdom might come help. And at last, more out of kindliness to her than from faith in the idea, Coates agreed.

But this also proved a disappointment. The meeting was held and the case was discussed from A to Z, unhappily without finding any fact or argument which had not been known before. Pam waylaid Coates as he was leaving and clung on to his arm till he gave her satisfaction. 'Tell me, Mr Coates,' she implored him, 'tell me quite truly and directly what are our chances?'

'Oh, good,' he answered cheerily, but the answer did not sound too convincing in her ears. 'We'll be all right, you'll see. All the same,' he lowered his voice and became more confidential, 'I don't mind telling you that our best defence would be to find the real murderer.'

The excitement of the meeting and these interviews with Irwin and Coates sustained Pam for a few days, but as time continued inexorably to pass and nothing fresh happened, she grew almost frantic. She had begged to be allowed to see Jack, but all concerned had conspired together to prevent her. She could not find out who was to blame for this: there was always a good reason why it could not be done at that particular time. She could not break down this blank wall of opposition and she felt baffled and despairing. But both Mr Penrose and Irwin had conveyed messages backwards and forwards, though neither would take letters, saying they were pledged not to do so. From these messages and their accounts it appeared that Jack was bearing up bravely, that he was optimistic about an acquittal, and that he had no complaint to make of his treatment.

The negotiations about the petrol process were still hanging fire and the affair remained another worry to Pam, a subconscious worry like an aching tooth, forgotten in the daily round. Compared with her real trouble it was of infinitesimal importance, but still it added to her feeling of frustration and hopeless disappointment. On Jefferson's recovery from his accident he had written that he was ready for Ferris to go over to give the complete demonstration and sign the final agreement. But now Ferris had crocked up. Pam did not know exactly what was wrong, but it seemed a kind of food poisoning. However, though he was about again, he could not travel, and once more the business of the syndicate was held up.

So the days went by, endless leaden days while Pam was living through them, and yet passing with appalling haste as inexorably they brought the trial nearer.

At last the fatal morning dawned. Pam had not slept, and as she got up and looked out at the dull sky heavy with rain clouds and listened to the mournful howl of the wind through the trees at the back of the house, she felt her fear grow, as if the very weather had joined in the effort to destroy Jack which was so soon to be made.

But Mr Penrose, when he called for her a little later, proved distinctly encouraging. 'Wait till you hear Coates,' he advised. 'Up till now you have only heard the prosecution. A case always looks badly till the defence have had their innings. Our chances are good,' and during the journey to the court he continued his efforts to cheer her.

Of Pam's immediate associates only Mr Penrose, Ferris, M'Morris, Dot, Dash and old Mr Whiteside were to be present. Pam's father was too infirm to attend, and much as her mother wished to know what was going on, she felt she could scarcely bear the proceedings. Mrs Penrose would not go, as she feared her presence might tend to upset Jack.

They drove the twenty miles through Ballynahinch to the old assize town of Downpatrick. The court, when at last they reached it, was already crowded. But Penrose was known and with respectful salutes he and his party were shown to seats at the solicitors' table. Irwin had arrived, and immediately began whispering to Penrose. 'Coates may be a minute or two late,' Pam heard him say, 'but he'll be here all right.'

The disposition of a court was no mystery to Pam. On different occasions Jack had taken her with him to hear cases on which he had been engaged, and she had a fair idea not only of the structural arrangement of the room, but also of the proceedings which obtained. But the mere fact that it was Jack who had taken her made the present visit all the more distressing.

She had never seen a court so packed. Except for the jury box, every seat was occupied. All round the table were barristers in their wigs and gowns and legal-looking men seated before masses of papers. These were chatting in groups and even laughing! How, Pam wondered sickly, could anyone laugh in such a place? Policemen in uniform stood here and there or walked importantly about. There was a buzz of conversation and a somewhat subdued movement until someone called 'Silence!' Then everyone stood up while the red-robed judge entered and took his place on the bench beneath the Royal Arms.

It was simple, that entry, yet extraordinarily impressive. Pam felt herself overawed by the slight bewigged figure. With the utmost anxiety she searched its face for some indication of the man who lay behind. The expression was stern, and yet she was convinced his disposition was kindly. As she examined the strongly marked features she felt a growing assurance that Jack would get a fair hearing. Abstractedly of course she had known this all along, but it was different to believe it as a result of her own observation.

Directly the judge had taken his place on the bench Jack appeared in the dock. Pam was slightly relieved that her seat was so close beneath the dock that she could only see him by turning and looking up. She wanted him to see her and to feel that she was near to him, but she did not want him to think that she was watching him. After bowing to the judge he glanced quickly round and she caught his eye and smiled warm encouragement.

On the whole she was pleased with his appearance, which, she felt, would make a good impression. He was certainly pale, a good deal paler than usual, but he looked well and not too depressed. He had been careful also with his dress and was well shaved and neatly turned out. How utterly incapable he looked of such a crime! Already she thought she could read approval in the glances of those present.

But she had little time for registering impressions. The business of the court began at once, and she was too much interested to allow her attention to wander.

Without haste, but without delay, the preliminaries were gone through. Jack pleaded 'Not guilty!' in a clear convincing voice, and the jurors were called and sworn and took their places. With the same anxiety as in the case of the judge, Pam scrutinised their faces. There were nine men and three women and they looked what they obviously were, ordinary decent citizens of the middle or lower middle class. The foreman was a portly, good-humoured looking man, rather of the butler type, though less well dressed. Pam put him down as perhaps a small shopkeeper. He, she felt sure, would take the easy or the charitable view. He would probably be for an acquittal, though he might be overruled by his neighbour, a dark man with a thin hatchetty face, gloomy eyes, and a forceful chin. The other men were not in any way remarkable—except two who looked downright stupid—but they all seemed straight and out to do what they thought fair. The women were also of ordinary types, more inclined, Pam felt sure, for mercy than for judgment.

But she had not time to continue her surmisings. Mr Carswell, the Crown Prosecutor, was on his feet and about to make his opening statement. He was a big forceful-looking man with dark impelling eyes and a large blue chin. His reputation was that of a brilliant advocate and a hard fighter, but a clean fighter, fair and not vindictive. Now he got into his stride at once, wasting but little time on introduction and none on rhetoric, but coming speedily to the facts of the case. These he put forward in simple language, speaking quietly and making no attempt to stress his points by action or manner.

Pam with the rest of those present, stiffened into attention.

17

As Pamela Grey Saw It

'My first duty,' said Carswell, when he had finished his short introduction, 'is to tell you why we think this case is one of murder at all. I am well aware that a coroner's inquest was held on the remains of the deceased at which a verdict of suicide was returned, and I must make clear why we have rejected that finding and come to a very different conclusion.

'But before going on to do so, I want to point out that this reversal of opinion contains no criticism whatever either of the coroner or of his jury. I believe, and I am sure that it will be generally admitted, that on the evidence put before them, they could have reached no conclusion other than they did. But since then much fresh evidence has been obtained, and it is upon these new facts that our revised opinion has been founded.

'It is legitimate, however, to point out that even at the time of the inquest, certain difficulties in accepting the theory of suicide did exist. These were four in number.

'First, there was the character of the deceased. Of all

those who knew him and whose testimony was heard, not one believed that he was the kind of man to commit suicide. All agreed that it was not in his nature. Not conclusive, of course, but having some weight when considered with the other facts.

'Second, though the late Reginald Platt was in straitened financial circumstances, he had just carried through a deal which would certainly have increased his resources. Had the deal failed, the motive for suicide would have been much more apparent. But the deal had succeeded and the deceased must have known that his financial affairs would be easier in the future. This knowledge would rule out financial stringency as a motive for suicide.

'The third difficulty was that he had apparently expected to return to Bristol on the Sunday, having written to say so not only to his uncle and employer, but also to his landlady. These letters might no doubt have been sent as a blind, had the deceased intended to disappear and restart life elsewhere, the possibility of which was at that time considered. But a would-be suicide would have no reason for sending them.

'Lastly, all those who had seen the deceased on that Saturday evening of his death bore witness to the fact that he was in good spirits and a perfectly normal frame of mind, so much so that the idea of suicide seemed definitely unlikely to them.

'Now these difficulties were not overlooked by the coroner. He put them very fairly in his address to the jury. But at that time the difficulties in the theory of murder seemed to be even greater. In fact they seemed to be overwhelming. What they were is not of importance to this inquiry and I am not going to mention them except to say that the chief was that no motive for murder could be established.

'But two facts were not known then that are known now. The first is that the difficulties of the suicide theory are so great as virtually to exclude it. The second is that a most powerful motive for the deceased's murder existed, and further, that a person who had that motive in the strongest degree was on board the steamer on that tragic Saturday night. That person is the young man who now stands in the dock, John Wolff Penrose.'

A cold shiver passed over Pam. It was beginning! This was the sort of thing she had been steeling herself to hear unmoved. She knew it must come, but now that it was coming it didn't sound any the less awful for having been foreseen. Oh, that fatal scene in Ferris's cottage on the Saturday morning! If only that hadn't happened! If only Jack had turned up a minute later: twenty seconds later! He would then have seen nothing. He would not have knocked Platt down, and none of this awful trouble would have followed.

But she was missing Carswell's speech.

'Now, to understand what ultimately took place, it will be necessary for us to go back nearly a year. I regret, members of the jury, inflicting all this detail upon you, but unfortunately it is necessary.

'Somewhere about the beginning of the present year a young man named Frederick Ferris made a wonderful chemical discovery. I needn't trouble you with just how it came to be made. Mr Ferris, who is here, and will be called as a witness, will no doubt tell you. He was then a technical assistant to Messrs Currie and M'Master, the analytical chemists of Howard Street. He interested a Mr

Edward M'Morris, a fellow-assistant, who is also here, in his discovery, and both of them saw that if certain improvements could be made in their process, the results might prove extremely profitable.'

Carswell then went on to describe in detail the gradual evolution of the process from the two men's decision to follow up the discovery, to the agreement with Wrenn Jefferson to send a representative to Hillsborough to report on the process. He was a past-master in the art of presenting a thesis. His rich tones, his quiet though assured manner, his simple yet vivid phrases, and his tacit suggestion that his hearers were being privileged in receiving highly confidential information, all made his statement seem utterly convincing. Not only were his Lordship and the jury giving it their undivided attention, but those in the body of the court were obviously intensely interested. For Pam, interested was not the word. She hung on the barrister's phrases as if Jack's fate and her own were dependent on what he should say.

'The representative,' Carswell continued, 'whom Mr Jefferson decided to send across to make the preliminary report was Mr Reginald Platt, the man whom we say that the prisoner murdered. This is the man who disappeared from the *Ulster Sovereign* and upon whose body the inquest at Groomsport was held. However, I'll come to that in due course.

'This Reginald Platt, the deceased, was a nephew by marriage of Mr Jefferson's, the senior partner of the firm, and that gentleman, who is here, will tell the unhappy young man's history. Platt was,' and Carswell went on to tell it himself: the man's birth, his bringing up, his joining the Wrenn Jefferson firm, his life in Bristol, his debts and his circumstances generally. 'This then,' he summarised, 'was the man who crossed to Belfast on Monday night, the 2nd of September last, to report on the petrol scheme.

'But unhappily, Mr Platt was not the type of man who should have been selected for any such purpose. He was in fact unworthy of the confidence which had been placed in him. Mr Platt was present at the preliminary interview between Mr Ferris, the prisoner, and Mr Jefferson. He quite appreciated the enormous fortune that might be involved, and some idea of transferring the balance of it to his own pocket must even then have struck him. Now I shall ask you to consider these dates. On Wednesday the 28th of August, five days before he crossed to Belfast, Mr Jefferson told Platt that he would be sent over. On that same evening Platt wrote to a Mr Mitchell of Surbiton, saying that he was on a really good thing, and could Mitchell see him at his home on the following Sunday afternoon to discuss it? This Mr Mitchell, who also is here and will give evidence, is the head of Messrs Wrenn Jefferson's chief rival firm, a London firm. Mitchell replied to Platt that he would see him, and on Sunday, the 1st September, Platt went from Bristol to Surbiton and had an interview with Mitchell in the latter's private house. At that interview Platt offered the process to Mitchell. Platt's idea was obviously to steal the secret when he was in Ireland, but Mr Mitchell will tell you that he didn't understand this, but believed that Platt had already made a deal for it with Mr Ferris and the prisoner. With the details of the negotiations between Platt and Mitchell you are not concerned. It is neither Platt nor Mitchell who are on trial. It is sufficient to say that an agreement was entered into between the two by which Platt would have supplied the process and Mitchell would have worked it, to their mutual profit.

'That as I have said, was on Sunday, 1st September, and that evening Platt went back to Bristol so as to turn up at the office on Monday morning. On Monday night he crossed to Belfast, going down to Hillsborough on Tuesday evening. From Wednesday to Saturday he carried out his investigations, and in connection with those investigations I must direct your attention to two points.

'The first was that Platt was not shown the method by which the petrol was rendered inert, but only the fact that it was so altered. The apparatus was carefully screened behind metal plates, and the formulæ was locked in Ferris's safe. Mr Ferris will tell you that it would have been impossible for anyone to have learned how the process was carried out without first removing those plates, and seeing the papers from the safe. There were however but few essential papers, only four quarto sheets in all.

'The second point was that Platt spun out his inquiry for four days, Wednesday to Saturday inclusive, whereas according to the evidence you will hear, he could easily have done all that was required in a single day. The reason for this is not far to seek. We say that it was to enable him to obtain an opportunity of stealing the process.

'For that he did steal it is certain. On that last Saturday of his visit he left the cottage, where he had been with the others of the party, shortly after noon, with the ostensible purpose of returning for lunch to the hotel in Hillsborough where he was staying. He did not return there. Instead evidence will be put before you that he went to Lisburn and there sent a telegram to Mitchell in which he said that he had "got the goods" and would hand them over at

Mitchell's house in Surbiton on the following afternoon, Sunday, on certain previously mentioned conditions.'

Though from the preliminary hearing Pam knew pretty well what was coming, it seemed to her that the case was now being put with much more force and completeness than on that first occasion. Carswell had not then been present, and the junior who had taken his place had not had his senior's weight and authority. Now things were going to be more dangerous, more difficult to meet. All depended on Coates, and to Pam, Coates was an unknown quantity.

'Now,' continued Carswell, 'I would ask you to consider the effect this theft would have on the members of the party. They had put in, or Messrs Ferris and M'Morris had put in, an almost heartbreaking amount of work on the scheme. These two had also put in all their money. They had given up their jobs to it at a time when unemployment was terribly severe. They were looking forward to a rich reward of their work. But what about that reward now?

'They must have realised, if they knew of the theft, that their hopes of any advantage from their work were gone. Not only would there be no vast fortune, but there would be no money at all. Moreover they would be left penniless and out of a job, if not in actual debt.

'But you will say, and very properly, that we are not here to consider hypothetical cases as to what Messrs Ferris and M'Morris might or might not have felt had they known of the theft. Whatever they may have known or not known, it is obvious that neither of them killed Reginald Platt, as it has been proved that at the time the man was thrown from the *Ulster Sovereign*, somewhere down Belfast Lough, both gentlemen were at Hillsborough. But I would ask you to consider the effect the news of the theft would have had on the prisoner, if he had learnt of it.

'In the first place there would be in his case, as in that of the two other men, the most profound disappointment at the sudden change in his outlook. There would be the loss of a vast fortune, and I would ask you to bear in mind the fact that for some time the prisoner had been counting on getting this huge sum and making his plans accordingly. That, I say, would in itself affect him very powerfully.

'But in his case there was a second consideration which may have been, and probably was, even more powerful still. He was engaged to be married, as I have said, to Miss Pamela Grey. But, and this is what I ask you to note, an early marriage was dependent on obtaining money from the petrol scheme. Before that was thought of, the engagement had been looked upon as one which might drag on for a very considerable time.

'Imagine the prisoner now on that Saturday night, always supposing that he knew of the theft. His work in connection with the affair was lost, the fortune that he was expecting had disappeared, his marriage must be postponed indefinitely. And there was more in it than that: much more. Miss Grey would be disappointed too. The girl he loved so dearly would suffer as he would himself. And with a man of the character of the prisoner, I submit that, bad as the disaster would be for himself, his anguish at Miss Grey's sufferings would be infinitely greater.

'But all this misery, poverty and disappointment which threatened himself, his fiancée and his friends could easily be prevented. If Platt were only out of the way everything would once again be happy, not only for himself, but for others. A terrible temptation—assuming the accused knew of the theft. And to that point I will come in a moment or two.

'But before I do so just think how extremely easy the murder would have been for the prisoner. The deceased was a small man of rather weak physique, as you will be told in evidence. You can see for yourselves that the prisoner is a powerfully built man. They were both travelling alone on the *Ulster Sovereign*. What could have been easier than for the prisoner to have enticed Platt out on to the deck on that fatal passage, and there to have held a chloroform pad over his mouth till he was rendered insensible, finally throwing the body overboard? Remember that it was a wet night, when the decks would be deserted. And the fact that no chloroform was found in the remains does not in any way invalidate this suggestion. Evidence will be put before you that immersion in water for the time in which Platt's body was immersed, would carry away every trace that might have remained.

'As you must have observed, I am now merely trying to show you that the murder of the deceased by the prisoner would have been possible. Before I state the reasons why we consider him guilty, I must mention one matter which may have had considerable bearing on the affair. I mention this with the utmost regret, as I am aware it must give pain which I would be only too thankful to avoid. The point is this:

'On the Saturday morning an incident occurred at Hillsborough, trifling in itself, but as I said, weighty because of its probable consequences. The party were to meet at Mr Ferris's cottage, and when Miss Grey arrived she found

Messrs Ferris, M'Morris and the deceased already there. The prisoner had not yet arrived. Messrs Ferris and M'Morris had occasion to go to another room, and then Platt had the audacity to seize Miss Grey in his arms and attempt to kiss her. As it happened, just then the prisoner entered. He saw his fiancée struggling to escape from Platt's arms. Very naturally—I do not think any of us can blame him—he rushed forward and with a quick blow knocked Platt down. The others, hearing the scuffle, ran in and got Platt away to another room. There, it is only fair to say, he apologised, and the matter dropped.

'I do not wish, members of the jury, to make too much of this incident, and I do not suggest that it formed the prisoner's motive for the murder. But I do submit that the recollection of that scene some twelve hours earlier would have tended to overcome any physical reluctance he might have had to the actual carrying out of the crime. To that extent it may have been a contributory factor.'

Pam breathed slightly more freely as Carswell reached this conclusion. This was what she had been so much dreading, and now that it was over, it had not been so bad. Indeed she was becoming slightly more reassured as Carswell went on. They hadn't proved, either at the preliminary hearing or here, that Jack had known of the theft of the process. And they never could prove it, because it was false. And if they didn't prove this, the whole of their plausible case fell to the ground. Yes, she thought, things were not looking so badly.

But as Carswell went on, her growing complacency received a rude shock.

'After these somewhat rambling remarks, necessary to give you the required resumé of the case, I must now put before you the reasons why we believe that the prisoner and no other is guilty of this crime.

'And first, why are we sure that the deceased's death was not, after all, suicide?

'There are first the four points already mentioned. These are now strengthened, strengthened overwhelmingly, by the deal with Mitchell. Just consider it. Platt had accomplished what he came over to Ireland to do; he had stolen the process, and he was now taking it to the man who had promised to buy it, at tremendously advantageous terms for Platt. Platt in fact believed that he was about to become an extremely wealthy man, perhaps a millionaire. There is not much suggestion of suicide in this. Still, however, this is a matter of inference rather than direct proof.

'But there is direct proof that the death was not due to suicide. We have seen that Platt had stolen the process and must have left Ireland with a copy of the four sheets of formulæ in his possession. I needn't repeat the proof of that. No other explanation of his wire to Mitchell that he had got the goods is possible. And we may be certain that he was taking the sheets with him. He would never have let them out of his own custody or sent them to Mitchell, as this would have been to surrender his bargaining power and to place himself helpless in his accomplice's hands. But—and here is a point of the first importance—no such papers were found on the body. They must therefore have been removed from it. That, I submit, proves conclusively that the deceased was murdered to obtain those papers and to prevent knowledge of the process from being lost to its rightful possessors.

'But this fact that the papers had been removed from

the body not only proves the death was not suicide, but it also proves something more. It proves beyond doubt or question that the murderer knew of the process and knew of Platt's theft.

'Now let us make a list of all the people who could possibly have had this information. There was Mr Ferris, Mr M'Morris, Miss Grey, Mr Whiteside, Mr Mitchell, the accused and one other whom I will mention directly. The most careful research has failed to reveal any others. These persons themselves have been unable to suggest any others. There are, in point of fact, no others. Let us further see where each of these persons was on the fatal Saturday night and the Sunday following.

'Mr Ferris was at Hillsborough. Mr M'Morris was at Hillsborough. Miss Grey was at Hillsborough. Mr Whiteside was at Carnalea. Mr Mitchell was in Surbiton. But where was the prisoner? The prisoner was on the *Ulster Sovereign* with Reginald Platt.

'Now here I particularly wish to call your attention to another point. The prisoner had, or tried to have, some direct dealings with the deceased after the ship left Belfast. Evidence will be put before you that he asked the purser for the number of Platt's cabin. His own cabin steward will tell you that about eleven-fifteen he saw him coming out of Platt's cabin. Further, this same steward will tell you that some fifteen minutes later, about eleven-thirty, he saw him again. This time he was going into his own cabin, but the point I wish you to notice is that he was wearing a waterproof and that the waterproof was glistening with fresh rain. That is to say, the prisoner was on deck about eleven-thirty. And evidence will be put before you, from the place in which the body was found and the run of the tides, that Platt must have been thrown overboard just about eleven-thirty. What, I shall later ask you to consider, was the prisoner doing on the deck at that hour on that wet night?

'I said there was one other person who might have known something of the affair. This was an acquaintance of Mitchell's who crossed by the same steamer. The police however, have gone carefully into the case of this man, and they are satisfied that he could have had nothing to do with the affair. I mention him merely for completeness and accuracy. At the same time all known information about this man, Herd, is at the disposal of the defence, should they desire to obtain it.'

Pam was by this time experiencing a dreadful revulsion of feeling. Horrible doubts filled her mind. *Had* the secret been stolen? If so, did the others know? Did Ferris? Did M'Morris? She remembered that she had never wholly trusted either of them. Did Jack know? Had Ferris and M'Morris denied their knowledge in order to help Jack now? Oh, ghastly!

Then once again Pam felt ashamed of herself. If Jack had known, he would have said so. Whatever he might or might not do, he would never be party to a deliberate and continuous lie.

'This then,' Carswell continued, 'is the case against the prisoner. Let me summarise it in a word. The deceased had stolen the process and was on his way to sell his booty for a high figure. Therefore he did not commit suicide. Accident was out of the question. Therefore the case is one of murder. The prisoner had an overwhelming motive for his death. Of all those who in part shared that motive, the prisoner alone had the opportunity of carrying out the crime. He could have done so with the greatest ease. He was looking for the deceased on the *Ulster Sovereign*, and was on the deck in the rain at the estimated time of the crime. Moreover, no one else is known or can be suggested who could possibly have been guilty.

'Admittedly the prisoner was not seen to commit the crime, nor can the fact that he knew that Platt had stolen the process be established by direct proof. But in a murder case I need not remind you that direct proof of the accused's guilt is seldom available. Here as in other cases you have to weigh the evidence, and upon that evidence come to a conclusion. If you consider that there is no reasonable doubt that the prisoner committed the crime, you will have no option but to bring in a verdict of guilty. On the other hand, if you feel that, tried by the ordinary standards of everyday life, there is a real and reasonable doubt of his guilt, you will of course bring in a verdict of not guilty. I will now call my witnesses.'

Carswell sat down, and his junior, Mr Adair, immediately rose and called 'Frederick Ferris.' Sundry policemen echoed the cry and Ferris stepped into the witness box and was sworn.

Led sympathetically by Adair, Ferris described his discovery and the gradual working out of the process, first in Belfast and then at the cottage at Hillsborough. He told of the entry of Jack, Pam and Mr Whiteside into the affair and of the negotiations with Wrenn Jefferson, of the visit of Platt and of his seeing him to the boat on the Saturday night. Very unwillingly he told of the row between Jack and Platt, and stressed the fact that Platt had apologised, that Pam had accepted the apology, and that the affair had blown over immediately. Ferris was an important witness,

251

as he was able to testify to almost the whole of the facts to be established, and his examination lasted till the court adjourned for lunch.

Pam contrived to flash another smile of encouragement to Jack before he disappeared from the dock, though she felt she wanted for herself all the encouragement she could get. Once out of the building she eagerly plied Irwin and Coates with questions. How did they think things were going? Was it worse than they had feared? What were their hopes? She was sorry to make a nuisance of herself, but she must know.

'It's only what we expected,' Coates returned. 'We know Carswell's a good man. But wait till our turn comes. Keep up your heart: Penrose'll be all right.'

In spite of the assurance Pam was quite unable to banish her despondency. At lunch she could not eat, though she was thankful for the coffee which came after it.

Back in court, Ferris returned to the witness box and Coates rose to deliver the first blow for the defence. He, like Carswell, had the knack of insinuating to the jury that he was giving them secret and quite invaluable information for themselves alone, which would place them in a privileged position above all other persons. The suggestion tended to produce a sympathetic hearing, and Coates used his advantage to the full.

He began in a quiet friendly way by repeating certain of the questions which had already been asked by Adair. Then gently he slid on to new ground.

'Tell the jury, Mr Ferris, just what precautions were adopted to prevent a possible theft of the process?'

Ferris had already given the answer broadly, but now he was pressed into details. He described more fully the metal screens covering the converter pole pieces and swore that Platt had never been allowed an opportunity of removing them. There were only two copies of the formulae in existence, one of which was in the strong room of his, witness's, bank, and the other was locked in his safe. He declared that during the critical period he had taken out neither. No one else, moreover, could have obtained them, as the bank would have required his personal application before giving up the copy they held; and as for his own copy, he had not even opened the safe during Platt's visit. Coates then turned to the question of the witness's keys, and Ferris swore he had not allowed them out of his possession while Platt was in Ireland. It would have been impossible, he declared, for Platt to have obtained possession of them, either to use directly or to copy. 'Besides,' he concluded, 'wasn't I in the house myself during all Platt's free time, and wouldn't I have heard him if he had tried to get in?'

'Then,' went on Coates still in his quiet friendly voice, 'if all that is true, how do you explain the fact that the process was stolen?'

'I can't explain it at all,' Ferris returned emphatically, 'and what's more, I don't believe it ever was stolen.'

Coates shook his head as if mildly shocked. 'I'm afraid, Mr Ferris, we can't listen to that. I am not asking for your beliefs, though if your beliefs are founded on definite facts, you may tell us the facts.'

'Well,' said Ferris, 'I can do that easy enough. I don't believe it was stolen, for the simple reason that it couldn't have been. Neither Platt nor anybody else could have got at it.'

Coates now changed his tactics. He tried to break Ferris

down on the point, suggesting all kinds of ways in which Platt might have burgled the cottage. But Ferris only grew more and more dogmatic. He pointed out the defect in each of Coates' suggestions, and repeated his declaration that the thing just couldn't have been done. It was not till afterwards that Pam learnt that the whole scene of question and answer had been rehearsed beforehand.

The remainder of the cross-examination was more perfunctory. Ferris admitted that he knew little about Platt and therefore could not speak with any certainty as to whether he was or was not depressed on the fatal Saturday evening. A few points of this kind were brought out, but Pam thought that none of them were important. And Adair in his re-examination seemed to her only to repeat his former questions.

M'Morris was the next witness, but he had not much to add to Ferris's statement, and except for obtaining corroboration, neither counsel took much trouble with him.

Then came Mr Whiteside's turn. He told of his entry into the affair, again doing little more than corroborating what Ferris had already said. Brennan cross-examined in both these cases.

Jefferson was examined as to Platt's career and mission to Ireland. Once more his evidence largely paralleled Ferris's, but Coates cross-examined him in considerable detail about the deceased's position in Bristol. He brought out strongly his straits for money, and the serious position in which he found himself immediately prior to his visit to Ireland.

'Did you notice any abnormality in the deceased's manner about the time of, or prior to, the visit of Mr Ferris and the prisoner to Bristol?' Coates went on.

'No, I don't know that I did.'

'Do you mean by that that his manner was just as usual?'

'Yes, I think so.'

'Yes, Mr Jefferson, but are you sure? Was it normal or was it not normal?'

'It was normal.'

'Did you know at that time of his critical financial position?'

'No, not till afterwards.'

'And there was nothing in his manner that suggested he was undergoing this mental strain?'

'No, I noticed nothing.'

Coates nodded and paused as if to underline the statement to the jury.

'Now another question. Did you inform the deceased that he would make some money out of this petrol business?'

'No, I did not.'

'So that he didn't know that he'd get anything out of it?'

'He would have guessed it.'

'Now, not your opinions, please. You discussed the affair with him and you said nothing to let him suppose he'd get a penny?'

'No, not directly.'

'Did you do so indirectly?'

Jefferson hesitated. 'No, I assumed he would know it himself.'

'Neither directly, nor indirectly did you give him the slightest hint. Thank you, Mr Jefferson, that's all.'

Mitchell was then called. He made a very poor figure in the box. His evidence was in accordance with Carswell's statement, but it did not carry conviction. Brennan, it seemed to Pam, was perfunctory in his cross-examination and did not obtain any useful admissions. Mitchell seemed extraordinarily apprehensive, and his relief, when he was told he could stand down, was little short of abject.

But though his statement carried no conviction, it did not for that reason help Jack's cause. Rather indeed it had the opposite effect. Mitchell's object was so clearly to show he did not know, and could not have known, that the process was stolen, that it amounted to a tacit admission that he had been perfectly well aware of the fact. After listening to Mitchell hesitating and stammering in the box, no doubt could possibly remain that he knew that Platt had gone over to steal it, that Platt had stolen it, and that he himself had intended to become the receiver of the stolen goods.

Pam's own examination proved less trying than she had anticipated. Carswell dealt with her gently and sympathetically. He simply asked her for a plain statement of the Saturday morning episode. She gave it and almost at once he thanked her and sat down.

Coates himself cross-examined and with equal gentleness. When the episode was over, had Platt apologised? Quite. Had she then expressed a desire that the affair should be forgotten? She had. Had further conversation and negotiation then taken place with Platt, just as if nothing had happened? Quite so. Would he be correct in suggesting that before they left the cottage the affair was virtually as if it had never been? He would—quite.

'Now tell me, Miss Grey,' Coates went on, 'did you drive the prisoner in to the boat?'

'I did.'

'During that drive was there any further conversation

about the episode? I don't want you to repeat it, but was there any?'

'There was.'

'Did you make any request of the prisoner?'

'I did.'

'What was the nature of that request?'

'I asked him to see Mr Platt on board and have a drink to show there was no ill will.'

'You asked him to see Mr Platt on board and to have a drink to show there was no ill will. Quite so. Did he agree to do so?'

'He did.'

'Did he give you a definite promise?'

'He did.'

Coates sat down and Carswell rose once more. Again he was polite and friendly. He asked but few questions and only one of them Pam found a little awkward.

'You said just now that when you left the cottage that Saturday morning the affair between the prisoner and Platt was virtually as if it had never been? That is correct?'

'It is.'

'Then if so, why were you so anxious for a fresh reconciliation on the boat?'

Pam hesitated. 'It wasn't to be a fresh reconciliation,' she declared. 'It was simply a sort of confirmation of what had happened already.'

'Did the prisoner agree to look up the deceased upon your first request, or had you to ask him more than once?'

'As soon as he realised I was in earnest he agreed without further requests.'

'Not quite an answer to my question, Miss Grey. How

many times did you ask him before he realised you were in earnest?'

'Oh, I don't know. A couple of times, perhaps three.'

'Two or three times. Quite. He wasn't in fact very willing to do what you asked?'

'I think he was.'

'Come now, Miss Grey, if he had been willing wouldn't he have done it at the first time of asking?'

'He didn't think it was necessary, but he was quite willing.'

'And you don't think his hesitation was due to the former reconciliation not having been complete?'

'Of course not.'

Carswell paused for a moment as if uncertain whether to press his point, then suddenly he nodded and sat down.

With relief Pam returned to her seat. It had been bad, but not so bad as it easily might have been.

Several minor witnesses were then called. Mr M'Bratney and Thompson, the purser and cabin steward on the *Ulster Sovereign*, respectively, gave the testimony which might have been expected from them. M'Gonigle, the master of the Groomsport smack, told of the recovery of the body and Dr M'Gowan described its condition. Dr Anderson gave general medical evidence. Sergeant M'Clung explained certain of his activities. A representative from the bank confirmed Ferris's statement about the packet deposited in their strong room. Post office representatives proved the telegraph and telephone messages. One or two other persons were called to give more or less technical evidence on certain points, but Pam did not think their testimony either important or interesting.

When the last witness for the prosecution had been

examined, a discussion took place as to whether the court should adjourn. Finally the judge decided that though it was rather early it would be better not to divide the defence. Jack therefore disappeared from the dock, his Lordship left by his private door and the proceedings were over for the day.

Pam was luckier than she had been on the preceding night. She was more exhausted than she realised and she fell asleep directly her head touched the pillow and did not wake in the morning till Mrs Grey knocked at the door. Somehow on this next morning things did not look so black as on the day before and Pam was ready to face the court with less apprehension. For one thing she knew the worst. The dreadful fear of the unknown was over. And today she would listen to the arguments on Jack's behalf instead of against him. For another, the morning was fine and bright and unconsciously her spirits reacted to the sunshine. Happier than she had hoped to be, Pam climbed into the car with Mr Penrose to face the second day of the hearing.

18

As Pamela Grey Saw It

Soon after they had taken their places in court the proceedings opened and Coates immediately rose to make his opening speech for the defence.

Pam listened if possible with even more breathless attention than she had to Carswell on the previous morning. Of the two, she thought Coates the more dominant personality. She was delighted with the way in which he spoke. Moderately, and yet with compelling force he made his statements, his voice rising and falling musically in harmony with his phrase. As he developed his thesis Pam had a swift revulsion of feeling. Quickly she saw that her fears had been groundless and that Jack was manifestly innocent. So clear did this become that she speedily became satisfied that no one could hold the contrary view.

'I am not going to take up much of your time, members of the jury,' began Coates, 'for all that I have to say can be put in a few words. There is fortunately no dispute as to the majority of the facts, though certain special allegations have been made by the prosecution which we strenuously deny. These I will put before you in due course, and now without further introduction I will proceed with the case for the defence.

'Only one point I wish to mention at present, the remainder I will deal with after calling my witnesses. That point is the personality of the young man who is here on trial for his life. I ask you to consider that before he goes into the box—for I am going to call him—so that you may obtain your own impressions from his demeanour. John Wolff Penrose was born,' and Coates went on to sketch rapidly Jack's life history. 'Like the rest of us,' he continued, 'Penrose developed a character, which through his actions has become familiar to those among whom he lived. There is surprising agreement as to the nature of that character, and you will hear witnesses who have known him for many years giving their experience of him. They will tell you that he is a quite estimable hard-working young fellow of kindly and generous disposition, and a general favourite among his acquaintances. They will tell you that he is a trifle blunt in manner, rather hot-tempered and inclined to act without proper thought, but that his hot temper cools quickly and leaves no bad feeling behind. Moreover they will tell you that he has proved himself uniformly straightforward, honest and truthful, and that he is universally trusted and respected.

'This, members of the jury, is the man whom the prosecution say committed this abominable murder. And why do they say he did it? As the result of a sudden wave of hot temper? Nothing of the kind. They say it was a premeditated crime, a murder carefully thought out beforehand and carried through coldly and without passion. And for what? For money! I ask you to bear this vital fact in mind during the remainder of the case, and particularly when you hear the prisoner tell his own story of what took place. Watch him, I beg of you, and consider his demeanour; and then ask yourselves is it in the character of this young man really to commit such a cold-blooded and devilish deed? I have little doubt you will find yourselves forced to the conclusion that the very suggestion of such a thing is absurd.

'But though the prisoner's character and demeanour may suggest his innocence, I admit in the fullest way that they will not prove it. It might be argued that under the stress of possible wealth his character became warped and changed, like that of a doctor in a certain well known play. This is a question for you to decide. I submit that his known character and demeanour have a considerable weight, but I am not depending on these to prove his innocence. For that, when I have called my witnesses, I will put before you definite facts.

'My defence in a word will be,' and here Coates drew himself up and a ring came into his voice, 'that the case for the prosecution is an edifice of pure hypothesis, unproven and unsupported by the facts, and that it entirely fails to connect the prisoner with any crime whatever. I will suggest that the prisoner never even saw the deceased on the *Ulster Sovereign*: that not only did he not murder him, but that he had no motive to do so; that the secret process was not stolen; and finally that no murder was committed at all, the deceased having committed suicide.'

As Coates sat down a little buzz of movement and whispering broke out over the court. This was certainly an unexpected and dramatic defence! Pam was quivering with excitement. Suddenly she saw that Coates was right. She felt utterly convinced. *Of course* that was what had happened! The coroner's jury had made no mistake. Suicide was the simple and obvious and completely satisfying explanation of the whole affair. How had the prosecution ever come to doubt it? In delighted imagination she began to see Jack acquitted and leaving the court with her before many hours were over. She felt—

But Brennan, was on his feet. 'Dr Garrett Maxwell,' he called, and after the usual repetitions from policemen, a tall athletic-looking young man strode with easy loose-limbed movements into the box and was sworn.

'You are the principal of the Cliftonmore College, Dr Maxwell?'

'I am.'

'Was the accused a pupil at your school?'

'He was,' and the witness gave the dates, recounted Jack's scholastic achievements, and said that he had borne a high character in the school and had been liked and trusted by masters and boys alike.

A professor from Queen's University then gave similar evidence and he in his turn was followed by Mr Penrose, who told about Jack entering his office and what he had done there. None of these witnesses were cross-examined.

The next witness was Robert Herd. His demeanour in the box to some extent resembled that of Mitchell's. He was obviously acutely apprehensive and his relief when he stood down was just as great as the other's. But unlike Mitchell he gave the impression of speaking the truth. The prosecution did not indeed waste much time on him.

To Brennan he admitted that he had been instructed by Mitchell to spy upon Platt and had come to Ireland for that purpose. While in Ireland he had spied on him as well as he was able. He had received a telephone call from

Mitchell that Platt was returning on the Saturday night and that he was able to shadow him on the way back. He had asked for Platt's cabin just to make sure that the man was on the boat, but he had not gone to the cabin, nor had he seen him on board.

Coates then called his star witness: 'John Wolff Penrose!' Jack left the dock, and accompanied by a warder walked to the box and was sworn. Pam clenched her hands. Now was coming the most crucial period of all. Jack's evidence, she felt sure, would affect the issue more profoundly than anything else in the whole hearing. Well, his appearance was in his favour at all events! How splendid he looked! So upright, so true, so honest, so—she hesitated for a word—so *sterling*! How could anyone who saw him believe that he was guilty? And his replies were so convincing, so straightforward, so direct, and given with just the proper amount of courteous deference and without the slightest suggestion of servility. Pam was delighted. So far nothing could be better.

In the nature of the case Jack's examination could not bring out much that was new. He generally confirmed the evidence which had already been given as to his own career and of the petrol discovery. Without the slightest attempt to water down the facts he told of the trouble with Platt on the Saturday morning, admitting that at the moment he was mad with anger, but saying that when he found Pam wished the affair to be forgotten he had agreed to put it out of his mind. He confirmed Pam's evidence that she had asked him to have a drink with Platt on board, and said it was with that object he had inquired for his cabin. He had gone to the cabin, but Platt was not there, and he had therefore looked in the dining saloon, smoke room and lounge. Not seeing him, he had assumed he must be on deck and had gone once round the decks. He estimated that his search had occupied him from about eleven-fifteen to eleven-thirty as the steward had stated. He described the remainder of his journey to England, and swore positively he had neither known at the time that the secret had been stolen nor had he suspected it since; that he was entirely ignorant of the murder, and that he had never even seen Platt on the boat.

It was then Carswell's turn. He did not trouble much with Jack's career and the petrol affair, but concentrated on the two points so obviously vital to the prosecution: whether Jack had known of the theft, and whether he had seen Platt on the *Ulster Sovereign*. With the utmost persistence and ingenuity he tried to break down Jack's denials or to trap him into some damaging admission. For Pam it was a dreadful half-hour, even more so than for Jack himself, to judge from the latter's expression. But to her overwhelming relief Jack stood firm, unmoved and unshaken. He did not know whether the process had or had not been stolen, all he knew was that the idea of such a thing had never entered his mind. He had never had any reason to suspect it, either now or at any other time, and he never had suspected it. With regard to Platt's death, he knew nothing about it whatever. He had no idea whether it was murder or suicide, but he was certain that he had not killed Platt himself, nor had he seen him on board the boat. He had not known of the man's disappearance until he had seen it in the paper in London.

Carswell suddenly gave up the effort and sat down, probably realising that his persistence was simply damaging his own case. Pam felt that it was a triumph for Jack.

Then came the final step in the conduct of the defence Coates stood up and said that the prisoner was his last witness and that he would now very briefly put before the jury the case for the defence.

He began with a short reference to the importance of the matter upon which they were to give judgment, referring to the valuable 'young life' which was at stake. If Jack were a murderer he would be well out of the way, but if he were innocent it would be an appalling catastrophe if he were not acquitted. He needn't dilate on the gravity of the issue. The matter was not one which concerned the young man and his friends alone; the whole system of justice of the country was equally on trial. He could only say that he was thankful it was in such safe hands, as he knew the members of the jury would give the case every consideration before coming to a decision.

Coates then repeated a good deal of what he had said in his opening remarks about Jack's known character and his appearance and demeanour in the box. Was this young man, he asked, the jurors' idea of a murderer? Particularly a cold-blooded calculating murderer, not committing a crime in the heat of passion, but with premeditation and with the object of gain? He enlarged on the fact that even the great and universally recognised ability of his learned friend had been wholly unable to shake the witness's testimony. 'I submit,' he declared, 'that only one thing could have enabled him to stand such a test: that he had the truth behind him.

'Now,' Coates went on, 'you must have realised that the case for the prosecution depends on one point and on one point alone: Was the process stolen or was it not? If it was not stolen, the only motive put up for the murder disappears. It might have been argued that the prisoner met the deceased on the deck of the *Ulster Sovereign* and that the anger he had felt with him that morning over the episode in the Hillsborough cottage revived and that for that reason he killed him. But he is not accused of this. Not even the prosecution have dared to stand for such an absurdity. No, according to the prosecution, the motive he had, and the only motive he could have had, was to regain the secret which had been stolen, and so save money for himself and his friends.

'Therefore it follows that if the secret was not stolen, no motive for the murder existed, and the case against the prisoner breaks down. Now, was the secret stolen? Let us consider the precautions designed against theft and how they were carried out.'

Coates then summarised the evidence which had been given on this point: the screens on the converter poles, the locking of the copies of the formulæ in the bank and in Ferris's safe respectively, the care that Platt should not be left alone in the cottage, Ferris's precautions about keeping his keys in his own possession, the fact that Ferris and M'Morris alone knew the secret: Coates stressed the importance and efficacy of each. 'Against such a system,' he declared, 'a thief would be helpless. How could a theft have been carried out? The prosecution have not told us and I challenge them to do so. I submit with respect that no theft such as they allege could have or did take place.

'And this view is supported by what is to my mind an overwhelming and unanswerable piece of evidence. Mr Ferris went into that box and swore that no such theft had actually taken place. I put it to you, members of the jury, would such a theft have been possible unknown to

Mr Ferris? He was in the cottage—he was living in it. He was there, he has told us, at all times when the deceased was free from the observation of some member of the group. He himself told you that a theft would have been impossible without his knowledge. And if you should say, Mr Ferris may have been mistaken, then I answer that you yourselves have heard the conditions and you yourselves can judge how likely such a mistake would be. If on the other hand you suggest that Mr Ferris was lying, I would reply that apart from his manner and appearance in the box, which was that of a perfectly honest man, he had no reason to lie? Why should he? To assume that he did so would make him a party to the theft, which would be equivalent to a householder going into partnership with a burglar for the theft of his own property. But if Mr Ferris was neither mistaken nor lying, his statement is true. I definitely submit that there is no evidence whatever that a theft took place, while there is evidence, and that of the strongest kind, that it did not.

'But you will say, and justly, that the prosecution would never have put up this idea of the theft without good reason. I agree. Well, they have told us their reasons. Let us examine them.

'The prosecution found their idea of a theft on a telegram which the deceased sent to Mitchell, in which he said: "I have got the goods." The "goods," they say, did not represent some article of Irish production, perhaps difficult to obtain in England and which Mitchell might have commissioned the deceased to obtain for him. It is not for the defence to suggest what such an article might have been. Alcohol that has not paid duty is not unknown in the country, as you are aware. I do not say it was alcohol. I suggest it was something peculiarly Irish which the deceased had undertaken to try to obtain. But the prosecution say: "No, the 'goods' represented the secret." And therefore, they add, "the secret was stolen."

'Now, what do they found that opinion on: that opinion that the "goods" represented the secret. They found it on the evidence of Mitchell, and on that alone. Now, you have seen Mitchell in the box. You have witnessed his demeanour and listened to his statement.' Coates paused dramatically, then added in his quietest tones: 'Need I say more? Would anyone hang a dog on the evidence of this man? Would anyone who had seen him in the box believe a word he said on any subject? Yet it is upon the evidence of this witness that you are being asked to condemn the prisoner.'

For the first time since the defence opened Pam felt a little dissatisfied. This last point did not seem so convincing as the others. Coates however apparently recognised the weakness and quickly dealt with it.

'But this after all is a minor point. Suppose if you like that Mitchell was speaking the truth, and that Platt had performed a miracle and stolen the secret in spite of the precautions taken to prevent it. Suppose again, if you like, that Platt was murdered. Does this incriminate the accused?

'The answer here is surely obvious. Of course it does nothing of the kind. The prisoner was not the only passenger of the *Ulster Sovereign* who was interested in Platt and who knew of the secret. Do not forget Mr Herd. He knew, as I say, of the secret. If Platt had stolen it, he almost certainly knew that also. By his own admission he had come to Ireland for the express purpose of spying on the deceased. He crossed by that boat because the deceased was doing so, ostensibly to continue to keep him under observation. Why should he not have been the murderer? If it would have been possible for the prisoner to have murdered Platt unnoticed, it would have been equally possible for Herd.

'Now, I'm very far indeed from saying that Herd committed the murder. I don't suggest it for a moment. But what I do say is that the evidence against Herd is as strong as that against the prisoner. It therefore won't do for the prosecution to select the prisoner and declare that he is the guilty man. They must bring some evidence to prove it, and until they do so the doubt as to which of the two might be guilty remains. And I respectfully submit, as long as such a doubt remains, it is your duty to give the prisoner the benefit of it.'

For some time Coates continued driving home his point, then he turned to another.

'The prosecution have attempted to make capital from the fact that the prisoner went to the deceased's cabin about eleven-fifteen, and was seen about eleven-thirty wearing a damp waterproof. I ask you not to allow your-selves to be swayed by this. The prisoner has never denied that he looked for Platt on board. From the first he admitted it. And he has given an explanation of his conduct. Miss Grey has sworn that she specially asked him to see the deceased, so as to make it absolutely clear that no ill feeling remained as a result of the unfortunate little incident of that morning. The prisoner has sworn that his action was taken with the object of carrying out Miss Grey's wishes. I put it to you, what more utterly complete and satisfying explanation could anyone desire?

'Now may I ask you for a moment to rid your minds of all the difficulties and complexities which we have been considering, and which arise inevitably from the theory put forward by the prosecution, and examine what we hold is the simple and obvious explanation of the whole affair. And that is, as I have already said, that no murder was committed and that the deceased committed suicide by throwing himself overboard on that fatal Saturday night.

'Let us begin by examining the objections the prosecution have put up to the suicide theory. First, they adduce the fact that Mr Ferris and others said that the deceased was in a normal frame of mind on the night of his death. But against that I would remind you that the deceased was a man who hid his feelings. His own uncle and employer, who knew him a good deal better than Mr Ferris, has told you that he noticed no difference in Platt's manner at a time when Platt must have been extremely depressed on account of his financial difficulties. I put it to you that this fact that Platt could and did hide his feelings, robs Mr Ferris's evidence on this matter of any weight whatever.

'The prosecution have further argued that the deceased could not have committed suicide because he was then bearing the stolen secret to Mitchell, and for that secret he was about to be paid an enormous sum of money. I have given you reasons for believing he was doing nothing of the kind. However, suppose he were, and suppose he were to be paid this enormous sum—grant everything that the prosecution claims—is that any reason why he should not have committed suicide? Of course it is not. You know as well as I that suicide is caused, not by a man's outward circumstances, but by his inward physical and mental condition. How many persons, otherwise in perfectly normal circumstances, have committed suicide during the depression caused by taking certain drugs? Case after case is on record. Suppose the deceased were a bad traveller. Suppose he had taken a dose of one of these drugs as a sleeping draught. Is that an absurd supposition? Of course it is not: it is a thing which is done every day. And if he had done so, is it absurd to assume that it produced on him a fit of suicidal depression similar to that which these drugs have produced on other people? Again of course it is not. I do not say the deceased did take such a drug. To say what took place is not the business of the defence. But I do say that he might have taken it, and that if he had, it would account for his death. And with the utmost respect I submit that unless proof is put forward that this did not happen, you must admit the possibility. And if you admit the possibility, you admit doubt of the prisoner's guilt and once again you must give him the benefit of it.

'Lastly, I wish to put before you the final reason why we believe that the deceased died through suicide and not murder. To this I beg your very earnest attention, as to me it is quite conclusive. It is this—there was no mark on the body. Let me remind you of the significance of this.

'The medical evidence is that death occurred from drowning and that there were no bruises or signs that physical force of any kind had been used. Now just consider the absolute impossibility of murder having been committed under these circumstances. Picture them. The murderer lures his victim to a lonely part of the deck, then according to the suggestion of the prosecution, he holds a chloroformed pad over his mouth till he becomes unconscious, when he throws him overboard. But chloroform does not act instantaneously. What, I ask you, was Platt doing during its application? Waiting quietly and silently till the drug took effect? Members of the jury, the very idea is absurd.

The victim of course would have struggled, and struggled desperately. And if he had struggled there would have been some mark on the body. And of course he would have cried out. He would have screamed at the top of his voice. There are officers on deck. It was a calm night. He could not fail to have been heard. From this it follows that he neither struggled nor screamed. Therefore he went over voluntarily. That is, he committed suicide.'

Coates paused, but only for a moment. 'Let me in a word recapitulate and I have done. I say the prisoner is innocent of the crime of which he is accused for the following reasons: First, he is an upright and generous though passionate man: he is not the type who could have committed a crime of this premeditated and sordid kind. Second, his demeanour in the box made it impossible to believe him capable of sustaining a long and complicated lie. Third, the sole motive suggested by the prosecution hinged on the theft of the process. The precautions that were taken to safeguard this secret and Mr Ferris's direct evidence make it impossible to believe in the theft, thus leaving the prisoner without a motive. Fourth, there is no reason why the deceased should not have committed suicide, particularly if he had taken a drug to help him to sleep on the journey. Fifth, the carrying out of the murder as suggested by the prosecution is a physical impossibility— it simply could not have been done.

'When you consider these matters I feel absolutely satis-fied that you will come to the conclusion that there is no case to justify you in sending this man to his death. With complete confidence I leave his fate in your hands.'

As Coates sat down Pam was filled with eager delight. That had done it! The speech was unanswerable. In the face of those arguments they would simply have to release Jack. A few hours more and he would be back with them at Hillsborough. Oh, it would almost be worth all the previous misery for the inexpressible delight of that moment!

How clever Coates was! How simple, how obvious, how telling his speech had been! She had thought over the case more perhaps than anyone else, and she had never seen those overwhelming arguments which Coates had produced. They could never thank him enough. He had saved two lives, Jack's and hers. She would never forget it.

But Carswell was now about to begin his final speech for the Crown. She must listen.

It was now, counsel said, his duty to restate where necessary the case for the prosecution. He began by paying a tribute to his learned friend's speech, a masterpiece for which he might be allowed to express his admiration. At the same time he was bound to say that if it had been a little less imaginative, it would have been a lot more convincing. That was not a criticism of his learned friend—it was a criticism of his case. No man could have done more, but even the leader for the defence could not alter the facts. And it was upon the facts only that the case must be judged.

This delivered in a quiet voice with that air of omniscience which refused to admit the possibility of another opinion, came to Pam like a douche of cold water. Then it was not over. There was more to be said. Oh, if the proceedings could have stopped there and then! All her old fears swept back in a flood as she set herself to listen.

Carswell continued by making a short summary of the case he had already put up. 'The defence,' he went on, 'has raised certain objections to that case. Let us now examine these objections and see how far they are justified.

'The first was that the prisoner was not the type of man to have committed the crime of which he is accused. Now while I don't admit that there is anything in the nature of a criminal type in connection with the crime of murder, it is not necessary to argue the point. Because please notice the contradiction in the argument of the defence. This argument was that while for the love of a girl the prisoner might have committed murder, he would not have done so for money. A motive of passion might have moved him to the crime, but not a cold-blooded endeavour to obtain wealth. My learned friend actually admitted as much. But what my learned friend did not point out to you was that the motive the prosecution suggested was not that of obtaining money. We say the motive was a motive of passion. He committed the crime for the love of a girl. It was to avoid the postponement of his marriage and the resultant unhappiness both to himself and Miss Grey—but particularly to Miss Grey. Money of course—but only as a means to an end. The real motive was the kind of motive which *would* have actuated the prisoner, according to the direct statement of my learned friend.

'And as to his demeanour in the box, you as men and women of the world know very well demeanour is so misleading that no reliance whatever can be placed upon it.

'The next point made by the defence was that the motive for the crime hinged on the theft of the process, that this theft had not taken place, and that there was therefore no motive. Now in reply to that I would remind you that the fact that there was an arrangement between the deceased and Mitchell whereby the deceased was to obtain the process and hand it over to Mitchell for a consideration has been established beyond possibility of doubt. Mitchell

275

has admitted it. The fact that the deceased sent a telegram containing the words "Got the goods" and saying he would hand them over to Mitchell has been proved. The fact that this meant that the deceased had obtained the process and was taking it over to Mitchell has been admitted by Mitchell himself. This the defence don't deny, but they have tried to throw doubt on Mitchell's evidence.

'Now I ask you, is there the slightest chance of these statements of Mitchell's being false? They might, and may, lead to a prosecution for conspiracy to defraud; which Mitchell knows very well. Do you suppose that he would have given that evidence if he could possibly have avoided it? He must have known he was making a case for his own possible imprisonment. If any other explanation could have been put on the facts, don't you think he would have given it? No, it was because there was no other that he made the admissions he did.

'Mr Ferris's statements about the difficulty of stealing the process I fear must be taken with some reservations. He was the guardian of the secret. Is it likely he would minimise the precautions he took? Would it be human nature to do so? Without suggesting any dishonesty on his part, there is no doubt that Mr Ferris would put forward the best case he could for his own watchfulness.

'And it has to be remembered that the deceased was an extremely able and ingenious man. Mr Ferris met his match: that was all. I accept his statement that he believed the theft was impossible, but I suggest he underestimated his opponent's ability.

'Then with regard to my learned friend's rather brilliant suggestion of the deceased having committed suicide through the depression following a sleeping draught, I have only to remind you that he did not bring forward the slightest iota of proof for such a theory. The deceased would not have *begun* the use of such a drug on this perfectly calm night. If he had taken such a thing, it would be because it was his habit. Such a habit would certainly be known. Besides, such drugs are not easy to obtain. No doctor was brought forward who had ordered it. No chemist who had supplied it. No acquaintance who had heard the deceased speak of his habit. No, I'm afraid the making of such a suggestion was a counsel of despair, only put forward because of the absence of any real case.

'Further, you must not minimise the fact that the prisoner visited the deceased's cabin about eleven-fifteen. And particularly you must not minimise the fact that he was on deck—on this cold wet night—at about the very time the murder was committed. What was he doing there? Would it take him a quarter of an hour to look for the deceased? The fact that Miss Grey wished a reconciliation to be made—and I think we must believe she did so—in no way proves the prisoner's innocence. It might have been the very thing the accused wanted—a reason for his suspicious actions. We have no evidence indeed that in formulating her wishes Miss Grey was not responding to skilful suggestion by the prisoner. I do not say so, but I repeat that Miss Grey's request is no proof of his innocence.

'Lastly I come to the point about the difficulty of committing the murder. Once again I submit that a powerful man like the prisoner might well have got behind a small and weak man like the deceased, put a chloroformed pad over his mouth and simply held it there till the victim was unconscious. Of course the victim would have struggled, but held from behind in a powerful grip, his struggles would have been ineffective. He would have hit out, but he would have hit the air and no marks would ensue. No, our common sense will tell us that such a thing is perfectly feasible, and again I suggest that my learned friend put his argument forward as a counsel of despair.

'In conclusion may I remind you of what of course you know perfectly well, and that is that the prosecution is actuated by no ill will towards the prisoner! If he were proved innocent of this crime I, for one, would be only too pleased. But my duty, and with all respect I may say your duty also, is towards the community as well as towards this young man. I think that you have now before you all the evidence to enable you to come to a decision on this extremely grave matter, and I do not wish to say one word in an attempt to influence you beyond the bounds of what is my duty and is strictly fair.'

A brief summary, a briefer peroration, and Carswell was done. And then, following with relentless swiftness, came the final stage in the presentation of the case, the judge's summing up.

Sitting there beneath the Royal Arms, the slight red-robed figure began to speak, quietly and conversationally, and yet so clearly that every word could be heard all over the court. The jury had had both sides of the case presented with great fairness and skill. It was now their duty to weigh the evidence they had listened to, and to reach a decision as to the innocence or guilt of the prisoner. In doing so they must banish from their minds anything they had heard of the case outside that court, and found their judgment on the evidence which had been given, and on that alone. They must not allow themselves to be swayed by any feelings of sympathy for or against the prisoner.

Their duty was to the public and to their country as well as to him, and the result of their verdict was not their responsibility. He was sure they would perform their duty to the very best of their ability. A few more preliminary remarks and his Lordship turned to the evidence.

'With regard to the great proportion of the facts,' he said, 'there is no difference of opinion. Let me briefly review these facts,' and he went on to sketch once again Ferris's discovery, its development, the formation of the syndicate, Platt's visit, his disappearance, and the discovery of the body. It was a clear and concise but exhaustive summary of what had taken place during those eventful months. To Pam, though she listened so as not to miss a syllable, it was intensely trying. She felt when he began that she simply couldn't bear to hear the whole story over again, and as the thin incisive voice went on it was only with a strong effort that she forced herself to remain calm.

His Lordship then turned to the evidence of Jack's character. 'I am sorry to tell you that you must not allow this to weigh heavily with you,' he pointed out. 'Many people, perhaps I may even say most people, go straight because they have never been tempted to do otherwise. Few can say what they would do under strong temptation, and because the prisoner has borne a good character up to now, it is unhappily no reason why he should be innocent of this particular crime. I do not say that you are to banish this evidence of character entirely from your minds, but I must warn you against placing too great a weight upon it.'

Some further remarks and the judge came to the main pillar of the defence—the theft or otherwise of the process. 'Now here you have for the first time direct conflict of evidence. Did Platt steal the process or did he not? I agree with learned counsel that upon your conclusion on this point will depend to a very large degree the verdict which you will bring in. And I confess that the point is difficult and the evidence confusing. On the one hand a very strong case has been made by the prosecution that it was stolen,' and his Lordship went on to analyse the possibilities as to the meaning of Platt's wire 'Got the goods'. 'Counsel for the defence tried to argue that the word "goods" need not necessarily have referred to the process, and you will have to decide how far he was correct in that. But I must point out that counsel for the defence was unable not only to make any very convincing suggestion as to what else it might have referred to, but still less to bring any evidence to support his suggestion. Further, had that word "goods" applied to anything else, it is difficult to understand why Mitchell did not say so. In admitting it referred to the process, Mitchell was undoubtedly giving evidence which he knew might land him in prison. The evidence therefore is very strong that Platt did steal the process.

'On the other hand rigorous precautions against the theft were undoubtedly taken. You have heard Mr Ferris on the point and there is no reason to doubt the truth of his evidence. These precautions were,' and his Lordship described them in detail. 'It has been suggested that Mr Ferris, being responsible for the safety of the secret, has now put the best face on these precautions. I have here to point out to you that certain of them—notably the never leaving the deceased alone in the cottage—do not depend on Mr Ferris's statement alone, but have been confirmed by other witnesses.

'You will have to decide what actually happened, founding your opinion on the evidence, which you will weigh and interpret on the same common sense principles on which you conduct the affairs of your own daily life. Did Platt steal the process, being, as counsel put it, one too many for Mr Ferris? Or if not, how do you explain the phrase "Got the goods" and the admissions of Mr Mitchell?'

As Pam listened her heart sank lower and lower. It was fair—she could not complain of it in that way—but it was devastating. It was terribly against Jack and its very moderation made it the more deadly. That it contained some dreadful flaw she was sure, but she could not see just where. She glanced at Coates, but his thoughts were inscrutable. He was leaning back gazing up at one of the windows, his face entirely devoid of expression.

Inexorably the quiet voice went on. One point of the evidence after another was taken up, dissected, left with a clear-cut issue for the jury, laid aside. Sometimes the direction seemed to sway in Jack's favour, but more usually against him. Though he did not say it in so many words, it was obviously his Lordship's opinion that a case for murder, as against suicide, had been established. And he also indicated his belief that murder on the deck of the *Ulster Sovereign* would have been perfectly possible. On one point indeed he came into the open against the defence. He suggested that little attention should be paid to Coates' argument that the evidence equally incriminated Herd.

Despairingly, Pam realised that the summing up was dead against Jack. As she looked at the faces of the jurors her heart turned to stone. It was going to happen: this ghastly thing which she had feared, yet which she had thought too awful to be possible. She was going to lose Jack . . .

Numbed from horror she was only partly conscious of what was happening, how the judge finished his summing up, how the jury left the court, and how Jack disappeared from the dock. Irwin asked her to come and wait outside, but she shook her head. She couldn't risk a delay of seconds in knowing Jack's fate and her own.

Pam had already learnt that time could crawl, but never till now had she realised how appallingly slowly it could go. The minutes seemed hours, the hours, weeks. She grew cold and stiff and cramped. She seemed to be only partially existing, only partially conscious of her surroundings, fully awake only to her enormous capacity for suffering.

And if the waiting seemed like that to her, what, she thought, must it be for Jack? Jack! Was this the end? Could anything so awful really happen? Oh, if the jury would come back, so that she might know!

But when after two hours and twenty minutes they did return, it was only to turn terror into despair. A glance at their faces was enough. Irwin tried to get her out of the court, but she took no notice of him. Half-conscious, she heard the question put, the answer given, and through the roaring of waterfalls, the awful words from the judge.

Then there was a sudden stir.

It was over.

19

As Pamela Grey Saw It

The days of waiting before the trial had been terrible enough for Pam, but now there settled down upon her a crushing weight of black despair. Jack's life—was over. She would see him again once, for half an hour, in the presence of warders: and that was all. After that she would never see him again.

She could scarcely bear to think of him, there—where he was. Oh, if what had happened could be undone! Oh, to have him with her again! For him to be once more free! And if that could not be, if he were really going to die, she would die too. She could not live alone.

At times she would feel herself in the grip of a hideous nightmare. Then with a sensation of cold sickness she would realise it was no nightmare. It was real. Jack *was* going to die. Nothing that she could do—nothing that any of them could do—would make the slightest difference.

Of course there would be an appeal. Coates was sure it could be wangled, though the judge had been so careful and accurate in his charge that the usual plea of a misdirection of the jury could scarcely be advanced. But she could see that Coates was not too sanguine as to the result. He put the best face on things before her, but she feared that in his heart of hearts he had little hope.

When she reached Hillsborough after the trial Pam felt that her life was over; that never again could she concern herself with the trivialities of everyday existence; that this dreadful blow had shattered her entire world. It was therefore with a slight feeling of bewilderment that she found everything going on as before. She went to bed, she got up, she slept, she ate: she was forced in spite of herself to take part in her usual minor activities. True, part of her seemed to have gone numb and she moved and acted as if in some kind of evil dream. Yet she did move and act, and to her surprise this movement and action grew more and more normal. By the end of a week her life was outwardly much as it had been before the catastrophe.

Now instead of dreading the coming trial, she was looking forward with a sickening anxiety to the appeal, which thanks to Coates' exertions had been allowed. In spite of her reason, hope refused to die in Pam's mind. Everything was not yet over. There was still one tiny chance. In living on that hope she grew still more normal.

Then occurred an incident which she was to remember as the episode of M'Morris' pencil, an entirely trifling incident in itself, and yet one which had an unexpected sequel.

One morning some ten days after the trial she found she had to do some small commissions in Hillsborough and went to her room to get her hat. Among other things she wanted to match some wool, and at first she couldn't find the colour pattern. As she was looking for it in an old shoe box which contained all kinds of odds and ends, she came on the pencil.

She looked at it in some surprise, wondering for the moment how it had got there. That it was M'Morris's she was sure, because it was the only one of its kind she had ever seen. Not only could she identify it from its make and colour, but also because the clip was broken off and the india-rubber holder was slightly flattened, and she had noticed that his had just these small defects. Then she remembered. Dot Whiteside had asked her if she knew whose it was, saying she had found it on their drive. Obviously M'Morris had dropped it on one of his visits. Pam had forgotten to return it, then the trouble about Platt and Jack had put everything else out of her head. She put the pencil on her dressing table, intending to take it over to the cottage the first time she was in that direction.

In the shoe box she also found her wool sample and in due course set off for the village. There the first persons she met were Ferris and M'Morris. Both had been very much upset by the verdict; indeed M'Morris seemed to be definitely ill, as if the shock had drugged him. But both tried to remain as cheerful as they could. The three chatted for a moment and then Pam mentioned the pencil. 'Oh, yes,' M'Morris answered, 'I lost it somewhere: my beautiful American pencil that takes the four-inch leads. It cost me one-and-six and it's the best pencil I ever had. Where did you say you found it?'

'I didn't find it,' Pam explained. 'It was Dot Whiteside. She found it on the drive at their place. You must have dropped it when you were down. When did you lose it?'

M'Morris shook his head. 'Haven't the faintest,' he declared.

'Dot'll know when she found it. I'll ask her next time I see her.' Then staring at M'Morris, she added: 'What's the matter, Mac? Are you not well?'

M'Morris had gone deadly pale. He pressed both hands to his heart, staggered across to a shop windowsill, and sat heavily down on the ledge. Ferris sprang to his help, and supporting him, saved the glass.

Ferris shook his head at Pam. 'It's his heart,' he whispered. 'He gets these turns once in a while. It'll pass. But they'd frighten you while they last.' Ferris was also looking grave and scared.

Pam was shocked. She hadn't previously seen an attack. 'Oh,' she cried, 'what should we do? Better bring him into the shop. Mrs Getgood will give him some water.'

'No,' M'Morris said faintly, 'don't trouble. I'm all right. It's passing. Just let me stay quiet a moment.'

'He'll be all right directly,' Ferris repeated. 'He's had these turns many a time. They've never lasted.'

'What about your car? He could never walk home.'

'He could so. But he won't have to. The car's there down the street. We'll wait here a moment and then go on down.'

'You'll do nothing of the kind,' Pam declared. 'I'll go for the car. You wait here.'

She hurried down the street to where she saw the car standing and drove it up to the two men. M'Morris was still pale, but he said he was better and he was able without assistance to walk across the footpath to the car.

'I'm better,' he repeated when they had both got in. 'Sorry for scaring you, Pam, but when these attacks come on I just can't do anything. I get the wind up and think I'm going out. Then they pass over and I feel all right.'

'Have you asked the doctor about them?'

'I have that. I have some drops he gave me. But they're never there when I want them.'

'You should carry them in your pocket.'

'I know I should. Perhaps some day I will.' Ferris slipped in his gear, but M'Morris stopped him with a gesture. 'By the way, Pam,' he went on, 'you promised me that book your father's got. You remember, a book about ships. Has he finished it? Could I have it, do you think?'

Pam had forgotten about the book. But now she remembered she had promised it some time earlier.

'Of course,' she said. 'I'll take it over first time I'm going.'

'No, I wouldn't have you do that. I'll come for it. Then you can give me the pencil at the same time. What about now? If you're going back now we could give you a lift.'

'No, I'm sorry. I've got to see Mrs Stokes about some things for the mater.'

M'Morris hesitated. 'Well, I'll be passing your place after lunch and I'll call. If you're out, leave them for me, will you?'

'Right.'

'Don't forget, like an angel. I'm out of a book and that would suit me well.' He waved his hand as Ferris let in his clutch and the car glided slowly away.

For once Pam's thoughts were turned off Jack. As she passed from shop to shop executing her commissions, it was of M'Morris that she was thinking. She had not known anything about these attacks. How brave he had been, having this really terrifying skeleton in his cupboard and never complaining about it! Anything connected with the heart was so ghastly. However, the attacks couldn't be very frequent or she would have been bound to know about them.

But nothing, not even the presumably serious affection

of M'Morris, could keep her thoughts long from Jack. Soon they were circling in their familiar orbit . . .

She finished her business in the little town and returned home. There she found distraction awaiting her—such distraction as she could still obtain. The small 'Loughside' car was at the door and Dot Whiteside was talking to her mother. Dot waved her arm as Pam appeared.

'I've come to carry you off for the afternoon,' she exclaimed. 'Dash has gone to Newcastle to see the Arnolds, and the house is too ghastly with only me. I can't face lunch alone with the pater. You'll come?'

'I'd love to,' Pam answered, though thinking that in her present state of mind her society wouldn't do much to cheer things up. However, Dot was a good sort and it would be a relief to talk things over with her.

'Then come right on now. I've been waiting for you for hours and I've got to call at Robinson & Cleaver's on the way through Belfast. A message for daddy.'

'I'll not be a minute changing.'

'Change my eye. I can't wait any longer. There'll be only daddy to shock anyway.'

'All right,' Pam agreed. Somehow since this trouble had started, she agreed with most things. Nothing seemed worth while fighting for. If Dot wanted to start, let her start. It didn't matter to Pam what she wore. Nothing mattered— but the one thing, and nothing that she could do would affect that.

Suddenly she remembered about the book for M'Morris. 'Dash!' she muttered, 'I've forgotten something.'

'She's in Newcastle,' Dot replied sweetly. 'What have you forgotten?'

'Nothing, really: only a book for Mac. I say, Dot, he's

just had the most horrible attack I ever saw. It scared me absolutely stiff. I thought he was going out altogether,' and she related the incident.

Dot was suitably impressed, then as they got into the city traffic she grew silent and gave her attention to the wheel. She was a good driver, much steadier and more careful than anyone knowing only her flighty manner would have believed possible. In fact, as Pam was now coming to see, that flighty manner was merely on the surface, and beneath it was a truly sterling character.

They passed through Belfast, reached Carnalea, lunched, and retired to Dot's sanctum for a chat, all without incident. Settled down there before the fire it was not long till the talk turned to the coming appeal.

'It'll be no good,' Pam declared heart-brokenly. 'I can see that Coates doesn't hope for anything.'

'You mustn't say that,' Dot answered. 'How can you know?'

'I know from his manner. It appears that only that the authorities were willing under the circumstances to close their eyes to a wangle, we couldn't have had an appeal at all.'

'Does he say so?'

'Not in so many words. But I know that's what he thinks.'

'I'm sure you're wrong, Pam. There's a tremendously strong feeling for Jack all through the Province.'

Pam shook her head despondently. 'A lot of good that'll be! And there's nothing that any of us can do. That's one of the worst parts of it—for oneself, I mean. Not that oneself matters, of course.'

'Of course it matters. It would worry Jack dreadfully if he knew you felt like that.'

'What I mean is, it seems wicked even to think about oneself at all when Jack is—where he is. It's Jack that matters. Nothing else seems worth even discussing.'

Dot nodded. 'Well, you've nothing to reproach yourself with at any rate. No one could have done more than you did. Dad was just speaking about those two, Irwin and Coates. He was saying they were the best couple to be had in the country.'

'I know. And they've been very decent as far as that goes. They had that meeting of us all, you remember, and I believe it was just to please me. They neither of them believed anything would come of it. And of course nothing did. Do you know what Coates said to me afterwards? I've thought it so absolutely true and so utterly unattainable. "The best defence," he said, "would be to find the real murderer." We can see now how right he was.'

'I suppose there must be a real murderer? I thought Coates made a strong case for suicide at the trial.'

'I don't think he really believed in it.' Pam made a little gesture of despair. 'Oh, Dot, what's going to happen? I get just sick when I think of it. We're in a trap, Jack and I. Caught, and we can't escape. And all we can do is just to wait for it to close. I get crazy almost: I think sometimes I'm going mad. Here are these few days—do you realise it's—it's only a fortnight now? The only days we've got: and what are we doing with them? Nothing! There's nothing we can do. But he's innocent and there *must* be something,' her voice rose into a sob, 'if only we could find it.'

'Poor old Pam. I know just how you feel.'

They talked on and on. It was a relief to pour out her distresses and Pam felt eased, though a little ashamed of herself. But Dot was such a good sort she wouldn't mind.

'Poor old Pam,' she repeated. 'I understand.' She leant forward and meditatively stirred the fire. 'Do you know,' she went on presently, 'I've been thinking a good deal lately about that English police officer who was over: French, I think you said his name was. You liked him?'

'I didn't like him or dislike him,' Pam returned. 'I only saw him the once, when he came over to inquire about Platt at the beginning. But I certainly did take to him. He seemed fair and kindly. Why?'

'I wondered if he would help.'

'Help? How? I don't follow?'

'Well, he's been into the case, hasn't he? But it's not his own case. He's got no personal interest in a conviction. I wondered if he would tell anything that might help.'

Pam looked at her cousin with a new interest. 'I don't even follow yet,' she declared.

'Well, those police discuss things pretty thoroughly before they act, at least I've heard so. Perhaps he might know some flaw in the case that hasn't been mentioned, or perhaps there's some alternative explanation that could be worked up. It's a pretty thin chance, I admit, but there might be a chance. What do you think?'

'But how could we find out? Suppose he had some doubt in his mind, he'd never say so.'

'You don't know. He might.'

Pam was growing more excited. 'Then what do you suggest? How could we find out?'

'I thought perhaps you might go over and ask him.'

'Oh,' Pam breathed a long breath.

'I wouldn't suggest it if there was anything else,' Dot went on. 'It's a counsel of despair, I know. But it might be worth trying.'

Again Pam breathed deeply. 'I'll go,' she declared excitedly. 'I'll go at once. I don't hope for anything, but perhaps there is just a chance. I'll try it. Oh, Dot, suppose something did come of it!'

Pam's mood was suddenly changed. The prospect of action, however unprofitable it might prove, transformed her. She was once again the old good-humoured cheerful Pam. She sprang to her feet.

'I'll go over tonight,' she declared. 'I'll see him tomorrow. He can't eat me. He can only refuse me.'

'Suppose he isn't there.'

Pam was not to be damped. 'Then I'll wait till he comes.'

Dot smiled. 'Sit down, Pam, and don't be such a goat,' she advised. 'Hadn't you better write over first and make an appointment?'

Pam slowly sat down. 'No,' she returned after a moment's thought. 'He might refuse or try to put me off. If I was actually at the place, having crossed from Ireland to see him, he could hardly refuse to speak to me. No, I'll go without telling him and chance it.'

'I think you're right really,' Dot admitted. 'But I expect your people won't be pleased.'

'Why not? They'd be glad if anything could be done, no matter what.'

'Oh, yes, I dare say. But they'll tell you this could do no good, and that you'd much better let it alone.'

'Not they. And if they do, it can't be helped. I'm going.'

'Would a spot of cash be helpful?

'No, old thing. I've got enough.' Pam smiled gratefully, then stood up again. 'But I must go. I'd better catch the bus at half-past.'

'You'll sit down and have your tea like a civilised mortal and then I'll drive you home.'

'You will not. I won't have you coming all that way again.'

They squabbled amiably, then Pam gave in. Though her reason told her she was embarking on a wild-goose chase, she refused to listen to it. It was something to be done—for Jack. As long as there was the millionth of a chance that something might come of it, she would try. What would she feel like all the rest of her life if she had allowed one tiniest possibility to remain untested? No, the question of not going simply did not arise. But she would take advantage of this offer of Dot's to drive her home to do better still. She would get her to wait while she changed and then drive her to the L.M.S. Station—it would not be much out of her way home. Then she would cross by Larne and Stranraer and be in London early in the morning instead of not till nearly midday, as would be the case if she chose the Liverpool route. The train left about half-past six and there would just be time.

At home she found that M'Morris had called for the book and had seemed a good deal annoyed that it had not been left for him. Though Pam thought this a little cool, she would probably have looked it up for him had she had time. But it was only by hurrying as quickly as she could that she was able to change and pack and get back to Belfast in time to catch the train.

His call, however, reminded her of the pencil and during the drive to the station she mentioned the matter to Dot. 'Mac was wondering when and where he lost it,' she said. 'Tell me about finding it.'

'I told you when I gave it to you,' Dot returned 'I found

it on the Sunday morning and gave it to you that afternoon: the Sunday after that Friday, you know,' she hesitated, 'when Platt was with us. You remember, that was the Sunday the Smiths were coming, but they cried off at the last minute.'

'I thought so,' Pam agreed. 'Did you say you found it on the drive?'

'Yes, just inside the gate at the road. Mac must have dropped it when he was down on the Friday.'

'That'll be it. Not that it matters, but Mac asked out of curiosity.' There was silence and then Pam went on. 'Oh, Dot, you've just given me new life. I'll be scared stiff going to see French, but if anything comes of it, won't it be a thousand times worth it?'

'Don't build on it too much,' Dot returned, 'and remember that if nothing comes of it things are no worse than before.'

'I know all that,' Pam agreed. 'But something's going to come of it. I feel it in my bones.'

As the train started Dot thrust a small package into Pam's hand. 'Sweets for the child,' she explained, stepping quickly back. 'Best of good luck!'

When she had settled down in her corner Pam opened the package. It contained ten one-pound notes. A scrap of paper bore the legend. 'In case you are lost in the wilds of London.'

Pam's eyes were moist as she tucked the money away in her bag.

20

As Pamela Grey Saw It

It was calm though cold at Larne and Pam, as far as her anxieties would allow her, enjoyed the crossing. Except while having supper, she paced the deck during the entire two hours of the passage, taking a slightly curving line connected by a mathematical formula of extreme complexity with the easy roll of the ship. She had the entire promenade deck to herself, her fellow passengers preferring the light and warmth of the saloon. But she was glad to be alone. Her mind was full of the coming interview, and she prayed with painful intensity that out of it some good would come.

The exercise in the open air had made her drowsy and when she entered the train at Stranraer she climbed at once into her berth and switched off her light. But now when she had the opportunity to sleep, she found she could not do so. She was too much excited. A journey to London in itself was such an unusual experience that she could scarcely remain wholly unmoved. Then her situation was stimulating. Instead of her fixed bed in the silence of Hillsborough, here was this gently swaying berth, and the mutter of the wheels on the rail joints, slow and faint as the train mounted the incline out of Stranraer. There seemed something of destiny in that steady rhythmic tapping, as if each recurrence meant a period passed and gone beyond recall, and a new period entered on inexorably and without conscious choice. For a time Pam relaxed herself to mere sensation, then once again her thoughts went back to her journey's end.

She wondered what Scotland Yard was like and what you did when you got there. She remembered having been told that it was somewhere on the Embankment and that if you once got in, you wouldn't be allowed out again unless you produced some kind of pass. But French, if he were there and would see her, would arrange all that.

But would he see her? Now that she was definitely committed to the enterprise, it began to appear much more formidable. Instead of good, might she not be doing harm? Might she be prejudicing the appeal? All this business was so strange and unfamiliar to her. She felt now that she had been precipitate. She should have waited to consult Irwin.

However, right or wrong, she had burnt her boats. She would not now flinch or draw back. She would see French and throw herself on his honour not to take advantage of any mistake she might have made. She felt she could trust him so far.

Her thoughts passed back to the whole succession of incidents which had led up to the dreadful position in which she and the others found themselves. The first suggestion through Jack that they should throw in their lot with Fred and Mac, the lunch at the hotel, the visit to Carnalea and Mr Whiteside's decision to finance the research. Then those long weeks of work in the cottage with their splendid result, the negotiations with Wrenn Jefferson, and the coming of Platt. She lived through again that thrilling week, with its tragic ending. She saw as if it were being re-enacted before her eyes the unhappy scene in the cottage on that Saturday morning. Platt taking her in his arms, Jack's unexpected entry, the blow, Platt's fall. Vividly her mind portrayed the room with its overturned table and—

Suddenly she ceased her dream. Something had flashed into her mind: nothing of any importance, and yet strange enough in its way. She remembered now that on the floor beside the upturned table had lain Mac's pencil: the pencil Dot had found on the 'Loughside' drive.

There must be some mistake, she thought. If the pencil were in the cottage on Saturday, Mac couldn't have lost it on the previous afternoon when they had their fishing excursion. Dot must have made a mistake. Or she herself.

She forced her mind back to that unhappy scene, Platt seated on the floor nursing his jaw, the upturned work-table, Ferris's notebook, the broken test tubes, and the pencil. Yes, she clearly recalled the pencil with its broken clip and the flattening of the bright part which carried the piece of india-rubber at the top. It was all stamped like a photograph on her mind and she remembered wondering who had tramped on it. Dot must have mistaken the date.

But Dot had seemed as sure as she was herself. She had been able to connect the find with the Smiths' proposed call and that fixed the date. Pam remembered when she went down that Sunday afternoon being told about the Smiths and how their visit had fallen through.

All the same there must be a mistake about the date. It must have been on some subsequent Sunday that Dot had found it.

Then Pam remembered that it was not. It was on that very Sunday, the Sunday after that horrible Saturday. She switched on her light and took from her bag the small engagement book she carried, which after use remained as a short and scrappy diary. She turned the leaves. Yes, she was right. That was the only Sunday she had been to Carnalea since the affair. And she was certain she had got the pencil on a Sunday, because of the story of the Smiths. Besides, neither Fred nor Mac was exactly *persona grata* at 'Loughside'. They would never have been asked down without her or Jack. And had not Dot said the Friday was their last visit?

What did it mean? If the pencil were in the cottage on the Saturday morning and at Carnalea on the Sunday, how had it got there? Pam's brain reeled.

At last she came to the conclusion that she herself must have been mistaken about the Saturday morning. She had seen the pencil on the floor, but at some other time. Admittedly this was not her recollection, but memory plays queer tricks and this must be a case in point. Yes, that must be it.

But she was far from satisfied, and again and again as the train rushed on through the night she wondered how the error had arisen.

Then suddenly an extremely disconcerting thought occurred to her. That illness of M'Morris! She had been astonished to learn that he had had a serious heart affection and that though they had been associated so closely all those months she had not even heard of it till then. It had indeed seemed almost incredible, but of course it hadn't occurred to her to doubt its reality. But now she wasn't so sure.

298

She recalled the details of the little incident. They had met and talked in the Hillsborough street. M'Morris had been perfectly normal. She had mentioned the pencil. He had still been perfectly normal. Then he had asked where it had been found. She had said on the 'Loughside' drive, and added that she would ask Dot when. It was then that M'Morris got the attack.

Was there, Pam asked herself, any connection? Now she remembered, what she had noticed at the time but had not seriously considered, that M'Morris had looked frightened. Scared to death in fact. She had put this down in her mind to fear of the disease, but was it? Was it rather the finding of the pencil which had so upset him?

The idea seemed absurd, and yet she was by no means satisfied. Ferris had also looked frightened. Here again she had taken it as due to the attack, but was this necessarily so?

As Pam lay turning this over in her mind a further point struck her. If M'Morris were really ill and frightened because of his illness, it was strange that he should have thought of the book on ships. There was nothing urgent about the book. It had been promised in a general sort of way, but Pam and M'Morris had met several times since and he had not mentioned it. But now it occurred to Pam that not only was the book mentioned, but it had been coupled with the pencil. M'Morris would call for the book and would get the pencil at the same time. Why, Pam now remembered, he had even proposed going home with Pam then and there to get them. Was it the pencil he had really wanted?

And then there was the visit he had paid while she had been at 'Loughside'. He had called for the book—or had he? Again, was it the pencil he had really wanted?

With a revulsion of feeling Pam told herself that her ideas were absurd. But she could not banish them from her mind. If she were right and the finding of the pencil was important to M'Morris, why should this be so? Why should he mind where or when it was found?

To Pam it seemed as if there was here some mystery, some dark and horrible mystery, if the possibility of its coming to light had so greatly upset M'Morris. What should she do about it? What could she do?

She could tell French. But should she? After all, though she did not personally care for M'Morris, he had been very decent to her all through. No, she didn't think she should tell French.

She continued worrying over the affair, but at last drowsiness began to set in, and presently she dropped off to sleep. Once or twice during the night she was awakened by the train stopping and, peeping out of her window, saw interminable grey platforms with a few tired-looking people carrying bags and with children dragging on behind. Then the platforms would begin to glide away and the wheels would once again set up their muffled rhythm.

She had decided that she must neglect no precaution to be at her best at the coming interview, so on reaching town about half-past seven, she went to an hotel and had a long slow bath and a leisurely breakfast. A map at the hotel showed her where Scotland Yard was, and she took the Tube from Euston to Charing Cross, and walked from there along the Embankment. Big Ben was just striking ten as she turned into the gates.

At first she couldn't find the door at which to apply. There were several entrances on the part of the roadway which passed between the gates and no one to ask. At length a policeman came out of the building and rather timidly she explained what she wanted.

'Chief Inspector French, miss?' he repeated. 'I don't know whether he's in, but I'll find someone who can tell you. Come this way, please.'

He seemed kindly and Pam's heart warmed slightly. They crossed the road and passed through a large door. A policeman was guarding it. Pam's policeman spoke to the other, who nodded.

'Yes, miss, he's in. Have you an appointment with him?'

'No, I'm afraid I haven't,' Pam confessed, 'but I'm sure he'll see me. Tell him, please, that it's Miss Grey from Hillsborough in Northern Ireland.'

She was asked to sit down. There seemed to be a lot of people passing in and out, and she tried to divert her thoughts by speculating on their possible business. Then a constable asked her if she would please follow him.

They went up four flights of stairs and along corridors painted a dull green above dark varnished wainscotting. The constable knocked at a door and threw it open.

It led into a smallish room painted in the same shade of green and with a window looking out over the Thames. It was furnished like an office with somewhat ancient dark wood furniture. At a table in the middle of the room French was sitting. He got up as Pam entered and advanced with outstretched hand.

'How do you do, Miss Grey?' he greeted her with grave politeness. 'I didn't expect to see you here. But you're cold. Won't you come over to the fire. I'm afraid it's not very good.' As he spoke he carried over the one tolerably comfortable chair and stirred the fire into a blaze.

'Thank you,' said Pam. 'I don't know if I've done something dreadful in coming over to see you, but I just couldn't help it.'

'You don't mean that you've come over from Ireland just to see me, do you?' he returned, smiling.

'Yes, I have. I've just arrived this morning.'

French shook his head. 'Now I'm sorry you did that,' he declared, 'for the simple reason that I'm going over myself to Northern Ireland tomorrow night—on a week's holidays. If you had written or rung up I could have seen you there and saved you the journey.'

'I was afraid you might put me off if you knew I was coming,' Pam confessed, 'and I felt I must see you. I hope it wasn't very wrong?'

'I don't know what you're going to tell me, so I don't know whether it is very dreadful or not,' French said, smiling again. 'But I'm glad to see you and if I can help you in any way I shall only be too pleased.'

She thanked him once more, really gratefully this time. 'You say that because you think I'm bringing you some information,' she went on, 'but I'm afraid you won't be so pleased when you know what it is I really want—some information from you instead.'

'I don't know what information I have that might be of use to you,' he answered, 'but I shall certainly do what I can.'

'You are very kind,' she said with relief. 'It's about Jack, Jack Penrose, you know. You perhaps don't remember that we're engaged. He's innocent of this awful charge. I *know* it. I'm as certain of it as that I'm alive. And so is everyone who knows him. He simply is not capable of such a thing. He *couldn't* have done it.'

302

'I was sorry to hear how matters had developed over there,' French declared, and then waited for more.

'I know, we all know, he's innocent,' she went on, 'but the trouble is that we can't prove it. The case against him looks bad, I know it looks dreadfully bad. But it's all circumstantial; in spite of the verdict there's nothing actually to prove he did it; there's nothing really to connect him with it. So Mr Irwin says, at all events. That's the solicitor who's acting for him. But all the same there's a real danger that the appeal may be dismissed;' she paused in deep emotion, then recovered herself, 'because we can't suggest anyone else who could have done it. And someone must have.'

French looked troubled. 'But how can I help you, Miss Grey? The case is not in my hands. It's being conducted entirely by the Northern Ireland authorities. What exactly is in your mind?'

'Only that you know the case—you have gone into it, haven't you?'

'To a certain extent, yes.'

'Then some other theory may have struck you. If you could give me only the slightest hint of another possibility, it's all I would ask. Just something the defence could work on. If we could only establish a possible alternative, Mr Irwin thinks it would be enough. I'm not asking you anything unfair?'

'You're certainly not asking me anything unfair,' French returned, 'but I'm afraid you're asking me something impossible. I must tell you that looking at the affair abstractly and without considering the characters of those concerned, I did think that the most probable solution was that some member of the group at Hillsborough, or someone

303

connected with them, had removed Platt to prevent the profits of the secret being lost. You see I'm being quite straight with you.'

'Yes, that's what I want, and I'm grateful. I think if you put me off with mere phrases I'd go mad. But we wondered if it mightn't have been that someone else knew that Mr Platt had the secret—if he really had—and stole it from him for his own purposes? I mean, to sell to still another firm.'

French shrugged. 'That was considered: I may tell you that much. But no other person could be found who might have done so.'

'Mr Irwin was wondering about that Mr Herd?'

'That was gone into carefully. Herd was able to prove an alibi.' French paused, then glancing at the woebegone face, went on: 'Tell me, why didn't you go to the Belfast authorities instead of coming over here?'

Pam hesitated. 'I was afraid they wouldn't listen to me,' she admitted. 'I could hardly expect it. I would be asking them to prove their own case wrong.'

'You are mistaken there, I'm sure,' French said kindly. 'If you could bring any evidence to bear on the case they would be only too glad to hear it. You mustn't think they want to do anything that's not fair.'

'Oh, no, I didn't mean that,' Pam declared earnestly.

Had she? Well, it didn't matter. What was now beginning to worry her was the question of M'Morris's pencil. The interview was coming to an end and she hadn't mentioned it. Should she? Could she do it as it were unofficially?

But French suddenly solved her problem. 'I think, Miss Grey,' he said gravely, 'you have got something more on your mind. Now I don't want to force a confidence, but if you like to tell me everything, I shall be pleased to listen. Of course you must understand that it cannot be confidential. If you have anything to say that should be told to the proper authorities, I should have to pass it on.'

'Thank you for being so straight with me,' Pam answered. 'I hesitated for two reasons. First, there's probably nothing in what I have to say, and second, it seems to be insinuating against a good friend of my own without sufficient reason.'

French leant back in his chair. 'If that's all, go ahead. If there's nothing in your story, no harm is done. If there is, probably it should be known.'

Pam, feeling dreadfully mean, but not knowing what else she could do, told the tale. She did not stress any part of it, but on the other hand she did not gloss over the details. French listened carefully, but without displaying any special interest.

'You evidently think that M'Morris must have been down there on some business connected with the case?'

'Well, doesn't it look so?'

He shook his head. 'I'm afraid you must not build too much on that,' he declared. 'Those sort of things are often capable of a very simple explanation. For instance, I don't want to make insinuations against your friend, but are there any pretty girls in the household?'

Pam started. This was something she hadn't thought of. And French was right. The parlourmaid, Bessie, looked quite charming. Could this be it? Mac? And Bessie?

It might well be true. To her Mac had always been scrupulously correct, but all the same she had thought he might be that sort of man. And Bessie certainly looked that sort of girl. This would account for the whole thing.

Pam didn't know what she had been expecting, except

305

in some vague way that this matter of the pencil might be connected with the case and might help Jack. But just how she had never been able to visualise. Now, however, even that vague possibility was gone. If there had been anything in her idea, French, with his great experience, would have seen it at once. He had indeed suggested a far more probable explanation immediately on hearing the circumstances.

But he was speaking again. 'I'll tell you what you might do,' he was saying. 'Send me the pencil to the L.M.S. Station Hotel in Belfast. There might be some mark on it that would tell me something. Just send it along and say nothing to anyone about it. Not, I may tell you straight, that I think there's any chance of its being useful.'

Pamela sighed. This meant nothing less than the final collapse of her hopes. She had been buoyed up by the excitement of the visit, but now this stimulus was dying down. A feeling of utter despair was taking its place. Her reason had told her that she must not count on getting help from French, but with that fatal weakness of human nature she had believed what she had wanted to believe, and based all her hopes on the interview. It was in vain that she now assured herself that in a way her failure didn't matter, that things were no worse than before. But she knew they were worse. The last line of defence, the very last, had failed her. She had come to French because there was literally no one else left to whom she could apply.

She knew she could not continue to occupy his time, but she was loath to leave. He had been very kind, but he was not going to help her. Could not, she was sure: she believed he would if he were able. Despairingly she asked her last question.

'And is there nothing that you can suggest that we, that

Mr Irwin, might do? No line that he might investigate? "It," once again she all but broke down, but saved herself with a great effort, "it means everything—my life as well as his."

French shook his head. 'I'm really very sorry, Miss Grey. I should be only too glad to help you if I could. The matter is not in my hands. And apart from that I am not able to suggest an alternative case for your solicitor to work up.'

She got up reluctantly. 'And if you think of anything will you let me know?'

French rose also. 'Yes, I think I can promise you that,' he assured her. 'But please don't build on anything of the kind. I'm afraid it is only fair to say that such a thing is unlikely in the extreme.'

She held out her hand. 'I have to thank you very much for seeing me,' she said, turning away.

'When I'm over in Northern Ireland,' he said as he shook hands, 'I shall keep in touch with the case, and as I said, if anything does occur to me I shall not fail to let you know. But again, nothing could be less likely.'

So that was that! Pam left the Yard as if in a dream. Automatically she passed round the corner opposite the Houses of Parliament. She felt utterly done. Every muscle in her body ached with weariness. She stumbled forward, not knowing where she was going. They were going to lose the appeal. Jack was going to die. And she would die too. She couldn't live without him.

Suddenly she felt she just couldn't go another step. There was a tea shop just beside her. With an effort she pushed open the door, went in, and ordered tea.

The hot stimulant revived her. The dreadful numbing

weariness passed and her outlook grew more sane. She began to wonder what she should do.

Go home, she thought. She had in a sort of mild secondary way looked forward to the visit to town, a treat which seldom came her way. But now she hated London. All she wanted was to get out of it. She wanted someone she knew: someone to speak to: someone to whom she could tell what had happened and who would understand.

In a somewhat more normal frame of mind she returned to Euston, wired to Liverpool for a berth, and sat down to wait for the train. She sat without moving, looking straight before her, scarcely conscious of the passing of time. Jack . . . he would have to die . . . And she . . . she would die too . . . What would there be to live for?

Looking like a ghost she reached home at breakfast time on the following morning. After one glance Mrs Grey hurried her to bed and sent for the doctor. He came, gave her a draught and said she was not to be disturbed. She slept like a log all that day and most of the night.

Next day she sent the pencil to French at the Station Hotel. But as occasionally happens under similar circumstances, she had scarcely posted the packet when she would have given a great deal to recall it. For not more than a few minutes later she received a shock, a shock which filled her with a distress not far removed from remorse in its intensity.

Just after she left the post office she met M'Morris wheeling the push-bicycle he used when no car was available.

'Hallo, Pam,' he greeted her. 'You've been over in London? So have I. Queer we should have both gone at the same time and both unexpectedly.'

Pam felt horribly mean as she answered him. He seemed so friendly and she had just been striking him behind his back. She thought she ought to tell him what she had done, but she just couldn't.

He chatted on, talking about the funeral he had attended and praising her enterprise in seeing French. 'Going home?' he asked presently.

'Yes.'

'Then wait a second for me and I'll go so far with you. I just want a two-way switch for my wireless. Come and help me choose it.'

She would have preferred to escape, but her feeling of having acted badly towards him made her agree.

The radio shop was close by and they entered and M'Morris called for his switch. But he didn't seem to be able to make the shopkeeper understand the type he required.

'Look here,' he explained, 'it's like this. Show me a scrap of paper.'

The man pushed forward a block and M'Morris began to sketch rapidly. 'Like that,' he went on, passing over the drawing.

'Oh, aye, I know the kind you mean,' the man answered. 'We've had them, but we haven't them now. But I could maybe get you one.'

It was then that Pam received her shock. She was not much interested in the switch, but she suddenly noticed something else which made her eyes grow round with astonishment.

'Mac,' she exclaimed tensely, 'your pencil! Where did you get it?'

In his hand he held the green American pencil with the missing clip and bent top—the one she had seen lying on the floor in the cottage on that horrible Saturday morning: the one, she would have sworn, had her eyes not told her to the contrary, that she had just posted to French.

'Ah,' he said, 'it well becomes you to talk about pencils. You wouldn't think of giving me back my own property, I suppose? What have you done with the one your friend found?'

Pam continued to stare. 'But that one,' she persisted urgently, 'where did you get it?'

'Where did I get it? Why, where I got the other one, of course: in Belfast, in Montgomery's of Donegall Place. I liked it so much that I went back and got a couple more. I lost one, here's the second, and you,' he pointed an accusing finger—'you've got the third. And I'd like to know when you're going to return it.'

'But they're both damaged at the top?'

'I know they are. It's the one thing that's poor about them. The tin holder for the rubber is too weak. It bent in each case and the clip fell off.'

Pam felt overwhelmed. What had she done? Oh, *what* a mistake she had made! That was the result of meddling in other people's concerns and being evil-minded! All that mountain of suspicion she had built up during a sleepless night—and founded on nothing! The pencil now in M'Morris's hand was the one she had seen on the floor in the cottage on that Saturday morning. The pencil Dot had found was another one altogether, dropped on some previous occasion. And it didn't follow that it had been dropped by M'Morris. He had lost one of his three, and someone might have picked it up and dropped it at Carnalea. In fact—Pam was at last beginning to use her brains on the matter—the one that Dot picked up might never have belonged to M'Morris. If Montgomery was selling them, there were probably dozens in the country. Oh, how foolish she had been! How criminally foolish!

She reminded herself that it was the damaged top that had really led her astray. But she should have known better. If the top was a weak feature, there might be many with damaged tops. She must at all events repair her error as soon as possible. She must ring up French and tell him to forget what she had told him. And she must do it at once.

She felt she could not bear any more of M'Morris at the moment, so she excused herself on the ground that she had forgotten a call on the doctor's wife. M'Morris, nodding amiably, rode off.

Pam was so anxious to keep her conversation with French a secret that she took a bus into Lisburn and spoke from there. She was in luck. French had just come in. A little breathlessly she explained what had occurred. French asked a question or two, then replied reassuringly.

'You've posted the package, have you? Very well, I'll keep it safely for you. And I understand that your state-ment was made in error. All right, Miss Grey, I've not repeated it to anyone, so no harm's been done. I wish you good luck.'

For the moment and about the matter immediately in hand Pam felt mightily relieved. But with regard to the larger issue there remained in her heart a ghastly gnawing fear, a fear she could not crush down. With the apathy of despair she settled down to face the few dreadful days that still remained before the appeal.

21

As Chief Inspector French Saw It

Though Pam had been bitterly disappointed with her Scotland Yard interview, she had underestimated its effect upon French. The chief inspector was indeed more impressed with her visit than he would have cared to admit. Long experience had made him an almost uncannily accurate judge of character, and he had found himself forced to believe not only in Pam's complete honesty, but also in the genuineness of her belief in Jack's innocence. And he saw moreover that she was by no means a fool. If then she was so convinced of the young man's innocence, was not this in itself an argument for reconsidering with care, even at this late hour, the evidence against him?

This argument might not have weighed so much with French had it not been for another quite different circumstance. He had listened to that story of the pencil with extraordinary interest, almost with excitement. Of course he had not allowed Pam to think so. It would have been cruel to do or say anything which might raise her hopes. But he felt he must get hold of that pencil, and that he must very seriously consider whether he should not reopen the affair with the Northern Ireland authorities.

For that episode did certainly seem to support a theory which had on different occasions passed through his mind. When he had thought of it, it had seemed so fantastic that he had dismissed it as absurd. But now would he be justified in not speaking? Dare he risk the possibility of a miscarriage of justice?

The affair was not his business. He had been mixed up with the case only to a very limited extent. The Liverpool police had opened it, but it had then passed into the hands of the men of Belfast. He was out of it. He had done what he had been asked, and, he was glad to think, he had done it well. But he was in no way responsible for its later developments.

But was he not? Was it not as a result of his interference that Jack Penrose had been arrested? Was it not he who had suggested that the criminal might be one of the Hillsborough group, acting to retain their source of wealth. He hadn't been compelled to write the letter to Belfast setting up that theory. He had done it to help on the case: if the truth must be told, to show his own superior acumen. If that advice had led the Belfast men into error, was not he to blame?

He turned back to his work, but he could not entirely banish the question. At intervals Pam's face of despair floated up before his mind's eye. Presently he saw that for his own peace of mind he would have to do something. He was crossing the next evening to Belfast. He would postpone his journey to Portrush and have another word with Rainey. His new theory might not be true—it was certainly unlikely enough—but he would put it up and then he would have done everything he could to avoid a possible mistake. He phoned across asking for an interview.

Owing to the hitch about his holidays, he had now been granted a week's leave, and he had decided to spend it at the sea: at real sea, as he explained, suggesting that that along the South Coast was but an imitation and a sham. He was going to where great waves thundered in from the open Atlantic: first to Portrush and then to Donegal. He hoped that he might see a really wild gale for once in his life. Someone had described to him the joy of standing on the headland at Dhu Varren at Portrush and watching from end on the huge rollers passing inshore across the West Bay, unhurried, inexorable, relentless as fate; great ridges with tumbling foaming crests, separated by valleys marbled in white and green and a hundred or more feet in width. He wanted to see their stately and unending procession for himself. He felt the sight would be thrilling. But he wasn't heroic and he didn't wish to be on them. He agreed with his wife, who accompanied him, that the shore was the best place from which to make his observations.

To his relief no emergency arose on the following day to cause the postponement of the trip, and that night the travellers crossed from Liverpool to Belfast and went to the Station Hotel for breakfast. French's first act was to inquire for letters, and he experienced a feeling of sharp disappointment on finding the pencil had not arrived. If it did not come by the next post, he decided he would go down to Hillsborough to get it.

There was, however, a letter from police headquarters. M'Clung wrote to say he was sorry, but Rainey was on sick leave and he himself was due at an inquest

314

that forenoon. It would almost certainly be finished by lunch time, and if French would come to headquarters after lunch, he would be happy to meet him.

French was disappointed, as this would still further postpone his journey to Portrush. However, the morning was not lost. He hired a car and drove with Mrs French up *via* the Horseshoe to the back of the Cave Hill, and from there walked across the summit to M'Artt's Fort, a pinnacle on the front precipitous face. The day was clear, and they enjoyed a magnificent view. Immediately below them the ground stretched down to the Bellevue Gardens and Belfast Castle, in the grounds of which, in some of those green leafy patches far below, he and Rainey had fought for their lives with Mallace and Teer and Joss on that frightful night of rain and wind which saw the final act of the Sir John Magill case. To the right lay the city, a huge dark eruption spreading over the green of the surrounding country, with the dome of the City Hall and the great gantries of the shipyards standing out high above the general level. Opposite and stretching away to the left was the Lough. On the near shore was the dark square tower of Carrickfergus Castle, while at the other side were Holywood and Grey Point, with the Parliament Building showing grey against the rolling tree-clad hills of County Down. A dozen miles or more beyond the city there was water, and again beyond that there was land: Strangford Lough and the Ards Peninsula. French had been told that on a particularly clear day it was possible to see further sea and still further land beyond the Peninsula: part of the Irish Sea and the Isle of Man. But today it was not clear enough for this. Seaward, however, there was a faint smudge on the horizon, that stretch of Wigtownshire from Corsewall Point to the

Mull of Galloway, so much of which he had been over in that same Magill case.

They had just returned to the hotel when French was called to the telephone to speak to Pam. For a moment he found her statement disconcerting, then he saw that it was one which he should have expected. The great thing was that the pencil had been posted to him. Lest nothing should come of the matter, however, Pam must be allowed to think it ended.

Lunch over, French presented himself at police headquarters where M'Clung greeted him with polite evidences of pleasure. 'I'm sorry you'll not can see the super,' he went on. 'He's bad with the lumbago this week and more.'

'I really wanted to see you,' French returned diplomatically, 'but I'm sorry to hear Mr Rainey is ill. A horrible thing, lumbago.'

The disease and its remedies adequately discussed, French turned to business. 'I'm afraid you won't be pleased when you hear what I've called about,' he went on. 'In fact, if you tell me to mind my own business, I won't be offended. But as a matter of fact it's about this Hillsborough case. Did you know that I'd seen Miss Grey?'

'I did not.'

'Well, I saw her. She was in London and she looked in at the Yard. She didn't want anything special: was evidently trying to find out if I thought the young man guilty or innocent.'

'If she'd 'a' wanted anything from the police she could have come here.'

'She didn't do that, I think, because she didn't get much encouragement from her own solicitor, and I suppose she thought she'd get less from you. I'm afraid she didn't get much from me either. But that's not what I want to talk to you about. When she was chatting she dropped a remark which interested me a lot. She didn't herself see in the least what it might involve. But as a matter of fact it fitted in with something I'd been thinking. Of course I said nothing except that the case was in you people's hands and that I had nothing to do with it.'

'And what was the remark, sir?'

'I'll tell you in a moment. Now, M'Clung, you and I are old friends, and though we're nothing to each other officially, I'd like to say something to you that may perhaps annoy you.'

'Sure, Mr French, sir, you couldn't do that. What is it you want to say?'

'This.' French leaned forward and spoke more confidentially. 'As man to man, are you satisfied that Jack Penrose is guilty?'

M'Clung's face changed. That he didn't like the question was obvious, but so was his desire to be polite to French. He hesitated.

'That's a nasty question,' he said at last, 'and me arresting him for the job.'

'I know,' said French. 'If you weren't as straight as I know you to be, I shouldn't have asked it.'

M'Clung grinned. 'You're not leaving me much chance to tell you a fairy story and that's a fact,' he declared. 'You know the evidence yourself, and you'll agree it's pretty conclusive.'

'I certainly do,' French admitted. 'But drop the evidence for a moment and look at it from the point of view of character. Is Penrose the man to commit that sort of crime?'

M'Clung moved uneasily. 'Well, Mr French, if you will have the truth,' he said after a pause, 'I don't pay so much attention to that side of it myself. I've seen that many mistakes made about thinking what a person might do or what they mightn't do . . . I'd rather have evidence and that's a fact.'

'Put it this way,' said French. 'You have evidence that Penrose committed this murder, and that ends the thing for you. And quite right too: I'm not criticising it. But suppose you had equally convincing evidence that some-one else might be guilty: Would you not then weigh up their characters?'

'Yes, sir. But there isn't any other evidence.'

'I'm not so sure of that.'

M'Clung stared. His appearance was so expressive a query that French could have laughed. He did not speak and French continued.

'This is what I've learned. A certain pencil of a particular make has come to light. It belongs to M'Morris. On the Saturday morning of the row between Penrose and Platt that pencil was in the cottage at Hillsborough. On the Sunday following—the next day—it was found by Miss Whiteside on their drive at Carnalea.'

M'Clung continued to stare. 'And you mean, sir?'

French made a sharp gesture. 'Well, what do you take out of it yourself? The question of how the pencil got from one place to the other suggests itself. How would you answer it?'

Obviously M'Clung did not grasp what was in French's mind. He was puzzled, but unimpressed. 'Maybe there were two,' he suggested.

'Oh, no, there weren't. This pencil was a metal one and its top was bent. It was the same pencil.'

'Is it sure, sir, that it was where you say? And on those two days?'

'Quite sure.'

M'Clung paused. He looked doubtfully at French.

'Well?' said French.

'If so be that these facts are all correct and that M'Morris didn't lend the pencil to anyone, I suppose you mean he'd been down at the Whiteside himself.'

'Ah, now you're talking.'

'But why shouldn't he be?'

'The pencil was seen in the cottage before twelve on the Saturday. Now, consider what M'Morris was doing between that hour and Sunday morning when the pencil was found.'

M'Clung took some papers out of a drawer and turned them over. 'Saturday,' he repeated. 'He was at the cottage with the others till between twelve and one. Then he went home for lunch and returned to the cottage immediately after. Then he and Ferris drove in Ferris's car to the hotel in Hillsborough and picked up Platt. They drove round the Mourne Mountains through Rostrevor and Newcastle. They left Platt back at the hotel and M'Morris went home for dinner. Then they went back to the hotel, had a drink with Platt and left in Ferris's car. They drove to the cottage so that Ferris could give Platt an address. Then Ferris and Platt went on into Belfast and M'Morris went home. He was at home all night and stayed at home on Sunday morning.' He glanced at French. 'I don't know what you get out of that, sir?'

French grinned. 'I get that your facts are incorrect,' he declared.

'All checked up: right through.'

'No,' said French. 'You had no check on the middle of the night.'

M'Clung stared and looked more interested. 'By the hokey, that's a fact! And do you think he went down to Carnalea?'

'How else would the pencil get there?'

M'Clung suddenly looked incredibly sly. 'Yon wee servant girl?' he suggested as one man of experience to another.

'Perhaps,' said French; 'and perhaps not.'

For a moment there was silence, as M'Clung stared with a puzzled expression. Then a dawning wonder grew slowly into amazement, and he almost whispered, 'You're not meaning—?'

'I am,' said French grimly. 'I see you've tumbled to what's in my mind.' Briefly he sketched his idea. 'Now I'm not saying anything's proved. But I say: Here's a doubt, and for our own peace of mind we ought to go into it.'

'But it couldn't be,' M'Clung persisted, speaking like a man in a dream. 'All that evidence—and him sentenced—'

'We'll have to see if it can be broken down. One or two simple tests would show us. I can't, of course, do anything. But you could. What about making them?'

As M'Clung grasped the full significance of French's new theory, he grew more and more upset. What he was being asked to do was nothing more or less than to nullify the work of several anxious weeks, and not only to prove himself in the wrong, but to show that he had made one of the most serious mistakes possible to a police officer.

Moreover the ignominy and disgrace he would suffer would not be confined to himself. Rainey would come in for a major share, and the Royal Ulster Constabulary as a whole would not escape. What future would he, M'Clung, have in his profession, if he so completely stultified himself and antagonised his superiors? He would be done: completely and utterly done. He might resign from the force, if some excuse wasn't found for kicking him out. And what other job could he turn to at his time of life. Besides it was not himself alone. He must think of his wife and family.

French, watching him with profound sympathy, could not but follow his thoughts. The dilemma was a dreadful one for the sergeant, but his knowledge of the man told French that the issue was not in doubt. He leant forward.

'I know just how you feel,' he said, 'but believe me, when the immediate thing has passed, your people will be only too thankful to you for keeping them from hanging an innocent man.'

'Maybe,' M'Clung admitted gloomily. 'But it'll not even be me that'll do it.'

'Of course it'll be you,' said French more sharply. 'Do you think I haven't enough of this sort of thing in England without wanting to start it over here? And remember I'm on holiday. No, if there should be any credit in it, it's yours and yours only. Besides it's only a test of the new evidence that I suggest.'

As French had foreseen, M'Clung agreed without argument to do all in his power to clear up the new situation. It was not his own prospects which weighed with him in the end. Though he would never have admitted it, it was that he, like French, could not bear to think of a miscarriage of justice.

'Well,' he said presently, 'I'll start and make some inquiries.'

'Good,' French nodded. 'May I make a preliminary suggestion?'

'I'd thank you for anything you can tell me.'

'Very well: put a man or two on to go over all the shops in Belfast which might have sold those American pencils. Begin with Montgomery's in Donegall Place. See whether you can find if M'Morris tried to buy a pencil of the kind three days ago. I better describe the pencil in more detail. I haven't seen it yet myself, but I'll do the best I can.'

M'Clung was now showing almost as much surprise as before. 'I will say, Mr French, you've got me beat,' he declared. 'I don't know what you're after, and that's a fact.'

'Never mind for the moment,' French urged. 'You do as I ask, if you will. Ring me up at the hotel if you get a result, and I'll come back and talk about it.'

M'Clung, obviously worried, agreed. 'I don't think you'll regret it,' French assured him as he took his leave.

By that evening's post French received the pencil and early next morning he took it to police headquarters and handed it over to M'Clung. 'Keep it safe,' he adjured the sergeant. 'It may prove worth a lot more than its weight in gold.'

'I will so,' M'Clung agreed. 'I was just going to ring you up, Mr French. We've got something on that line you mentioned last night.'

'Good man. What is it?'

'I don't know how you got on to it, but you were right enough all the same. M'Morris has been all over Belfast trying to get a pencil like that one of yours. We got five shops that a man like him tried in, on that afternoon you said.'

'But he didn't get it?'

'He did not. It was a trial order Montgomery had stocked and they hadn't repeated it.'

'But he wanted it so badly that he crossed to London that night, and he got it there.'

'Do you tell me?'

'It looks like it. I'll send the pencil and a photograph of M'Morris over to our people tonight and see if they can find the sale.'

'You have me beat there, Mr French. What's it about anyway?'

'Of course I have. That's because I didn't tell you the whole story. As a matter of fact I was afraid if I did you mightn't make the inquiries I wanted. When Miss Grey got back from London she found M'Morris had what looked like the pencil Miss Whiteside had found and given to her, and which at my request she had sent to me. So she asked him about it. He said he had two and that this was the second. Don't you see the point?'

M'Clung nodded his head several times. 'I see it right enough. It would about knock the bottom out of your bit of proof.'

'That's the idea, and quite a good one too. But if we can prove he bought the pencil immediately he learnt about the other being found, it'll knock the bottom out of his.'

'Would Miss Grey be able to identify the pencil she saw in the cottage?'

'I don't know. He had crushed the top of the second one to confuse her. I'm going to suggest that later on you put both before her and see if she can pick the right one.'

'Aye, that would be the thing to do.' M'Clung paused as if considering the immensity of the vista opening out before him. 'I declare to goodness, Mr French,' he summarised his views, 'but this beats all.'

Whereupon the two men went into committee of ways and means on the speediest way of proving or disproving the new theory which French had put forward.

22

As Chief Inspector French Saw It

That night French and his wife went down to Portrush by the six-fifteen train. He was satisfied that M'Clung would deal with his new idea in an entirely adequate way. The sergeant had promised to keep him posted as to his progress, and French in a quite private and unofficial way was to help with sympathy and advice.

For two days he heard nothing, but on the morning of the third there was a long letter from M'Clung. It was headed '*Reginald Platt, deceased*', and marked '*Private and Confidential*'. It read:

'DEAR SIR—As agreed at our interview I put in hand certain inquiries relative to the new theory of the crime put up by your good self, in three instances with useful results.

'*M'Morris's visit to England*. I went personally to Hillsborough to interview M'Morris. I found him with Ferris in the latter's cottage. To account for my visit I had brought a note of some points of their evidence at the trial, and I discussed these with them, saying they would come up at the appeal. Then I worked the conversation round to M'Morris's visit to England, and got out of him that he had gone to Windsor to the funeral of an uncle. I did not ask the address of the uncle as I did not want to put him on his guard, and so turned the talk on to the difference between Irish and English funerals.

'I then got an urgent inquiry made to the Windsor police. They informed me that there was no funeral in or near Windsor during the two days M'Morris was away. I have no doubt that when he is asked his uncle's address it will give us all the proof we need that he went to no funeral.

'Car to "Loughside." I put some men on to visit every house alongside the road from the station at Carnalea to the sea, also with good results. At Ivanhoe, a house a short distance from the sea, a servant girl, by name Mary M'Gaw, stated that about 3.30 on a Sunday morning about the date in question she had heard a car coming up from the sea. She had not been able to sleep and she remembered it was a Sunday morning because she had been thinking that she would not need to get up as early as usual. She had noticed the car because, though there was an occasional car passed down going home at that hour of the night, there were very few started up from the shore so late. She remembered wondering if there had been a dance at any of the houses lower down, because she had not heard of any. Then when there were no more cars passed, she knew it was not a dance and wondered if maybe someone was ill. She had a friend living down

there who had had a baby two days before and she wondered if it was maybe her, but afterwards she found it was not. She said it sounded like a small car with a rattley engine. We found the date of the child's birth and it was two days before the night of Platt's murder, so that fixed the passing of the car for the night of the murder. A house-to-house call at all the houses on the seaside of where this girl is living showed that no car had arrived at or left any of them at that hour anywhere near the date in question.

'This would work in all right because Ferris's car is small and has a rattley engine. Further, it would coast quietly down the hill and the girl would not likely have heard it arriving. Up the hill it would have to work and she would have heard it.

'Penrose's Flat Tyre. I had an interview with Penrose and asked him about his tyre being flat on the evening of the crime. He said he couldn't tell what had punctured it, for he hadn't seen any nail in the tyre. When I asked him if he thought it might have been done maliciously he got very excited and said he had not thought of it, but it would explain what had puzzled him many a time. From his manner and all he said I thought it was as likely as not that it was done on purpose. The man who mended the tyre said there was a hole like from a nail, but there was no nail there.

'All this makes your theory look likely enough, and only for the difficulty at the boat I would be ready for an arrest. But I don't see how the evidence at the boat is to be got over.—Yours faithfully,

'ADAM M'CLUNG.'

French proved a somewhat silent companion that morning, as with Mrs French he took the tram out to Dunluce, explored the ruins of the castle on its isolated and once impregnable rock, and then walked back to Portrush beneath the magnificent chalk headlands of the White Rocks and along the firm clean sand of the East Strand. It was a bright day and the thin winter sunshine drew out the colours everywhere; the dead green of the bent on the dunes, the yellow of the sand, the ultramarine of the sea with its fringe of brilliant white, the dark brown of the Skerries and the hard straight line of the northern horizon against the pale blue of the sky. French felt he should have enjoyed every inch of the scene and every minute of the time. But he couldn't. Pamela Grey's despairing face came up between him and the landscape. He knew that for his own peace of mind he must do something more about her trouble. But what that something should be was not so obvious. Then he thought he saw his way and rang up M'Clung.

'If you like,' he suggested, 'I'll run up to Belfast this afternoon and we'll go down together to the Liverpool boat and have another look round.'

M'Clung was enthusiastic. 'I'll meet you at the train,' he said joyfully, 'and we could have a bit of dinner before we go over.'

He was there smiling on the platform when French arrived. 'I'm glad you came up, Mr French,' he greeted him. 'I believe you're right about this thing and that we've been diddled about what happened on the boat, but I'm blessed if I can see how.'

French was hungry and he refused to talk shop till after their meal. Then as they sat smoking, he returned to the subject.

'Now let's see just what we want to do. I think I'd better state my theory again and you note the points that have to be gone into.'

'I'll do that, Mr French. I've been thinking of little else for the last three days, but I only get the more puzzled.'

'Very well: we'll try again. I admit my ideas are not proven, but here they are for what they're worth.

'Platt cames over with the intention of stealing the process to sell to Mitchell, and he succeeds—he does steal it. Doubtless he means to disappear, starting life again elsewhere. Ferris or M'Morris or both get wise to the theft—probably on the Saturday morning. You remember, Miss Grey said both of them seemed worried. They see that if Platt gets away with the secret all their work and hopes are gone. And nothing will meet the case—nothing but the one thing. Only if Platt is dead will they feel safe. Why? Because he now has the thing in his head. They decide to kill him.'

M'Clung nodded.

'Very well. They keep in touch with Platt that day to prevent him from giving them the slip. They spend the morning, afternoon and evening with him, though they leave him alone for lunch and dinner, when doubtless they think he will be at the hotel and out of mischief. About nine they leave the hotel with him to take him to the steamer.

'On their own statement they drive to the cottage instead of straight into Belfast. There I suggest the murder takes place. They begin by rendering Platt insensible. Probably Platt is sitting beside Ferris and when Ferris stops, M'Morris from behind puts a chloroformed pad round his face while Ferris prevents him from struggling. Jammed up in a small car it could be quite easily done. I suggest that they then lift him into the cottage and put him with his face in a basin of water till he drowns. That's the first stage of the affair.'

Again M'Clung nodded.

'Next,' went on French, 'they arrange their alibi. They strip the body and Ferris puts on the clothes, having used some make-up lotion to make his swarthy face pale like Platt's. Ferris then starts off for Belfast while M'Morris rides his push-bicycle home. Afterwards M'Morris says he has walked, so that the time will work in correctly and give him his alibi.

'In the meantime Ferris, made up as Platt and with Platt's tickets, now drives as quickly as he can into Belfast. He reaches the quay and parks his car. Then as Platt he goes aboard. He is shown his cabin and pretends to be going to bed. Actually he slips ashore, picks up the car and drives home.'

'Ah, but that's just what he couldn't have done, sir. The passengers are too well checked.'

'That's the point we're going to look into presently. Leave it for the moment and suppose he manages it.'

'Right, Mr French.'

'After waiting till the house is quiet, M'Morris slips out silently and goes back to the cottage. There Ferris presently joins him from Belfast. They redress the body in its own clothes, putting in the pocket the rail ticket, now punched by the steamer purser, as well as the berth ticket which Ferris had got aboard. Then they put the body into the car, run down to Carnalea, take out the Whitesides' boat, which we saw could be untied by anybody, row out to the track of the steamer, throw the body into the sea and return to Hillsborough.'

'It could be,' M'Clung admitted.

'But,' French continued, 'here they strike their first bit of bad luck. In lifting the body out of the car at the gate of the drive M'Morris's pencil—of which the clip has been broken off—is worked up out of his pocket. When he starts with Ferris to carry the body to the boat it falls out. Miss Whiteside finds it; and the whole affair comes out.'

Once again M'Clung nodded.

'Now for one or two bits of confirmatory evidence. First, we have the pencil: its being found down there and M'Morris's efforts to replace it. Second, we have the car. On that Sunday morning a rattley car is heard coming up the road from the Whitesides', and you have proved that this car was not coming from any of the houses in the area. Third, we have the difficulty of committing the murder on board, which is admitted on all hands, but which only this theory meets. And lastly, we have the evidence of the car puncture. Just consider this puncture for a moment.

'On Saturday morning when Ferris and M'Morris have worked out their plan, they get a horrid shock. They learn that Penrose is crossing by the same boat as Platt. If Penrose sees Ferris on board, the game will be up. They cannot urge him to change his plans, as this might afterwards seem suspicious, so they work out a scheme to safeguard themselves. They hear the arrangement that Miss Grey is going to drive Penrose in, and they decide to make use of that. One or other slips up to the Penrose yard and drives a nail or a bradawl into the car tyre, withdrawing it again. This delays Penrose and Ferris completes his stunt at the boat before he arrives. Probably they intended Penrose to miss the boat altogether, and it must have been a dreadful blow to them when he was arrested for the murder.'

'To my way of thinking, Mr French, all that's as sound as you could wish. If it wasn't for the evidence we got from those steamer people that no one who went on board could have got ashore again unbeknownst, I'd be thinking of an arrest.'

'Well, it's getting on to eight o'clock. Let's go down to the steamer and have a look round.'

'I don't believe he went down the gangway,' French declared, when a few minutes later they were aboard the boat. 'The checks, as you said, are too complete. We must concentrate on looking for other ways of getting ashore.'

M'Clung agreed, but his manner indicated that there were none.

French did not reply. A phrase from one of the Sherlock Holmes stories was running in his mind, though he wasn't sure of its exact wording. 'Eliminate the impossible and the result, however unlikely, must be the truth.' Something of this kind seemed the motto for their present search.

'Eliminate the impossible.' That, they had agreed, meant, eliminate the gangways. There were two, one for the first class and one for the third. What other means were there of getting ashore?

So far as French could see, only three, and two of these he felt he might dismiss without further consideration. There were the mooring ropes. Could a man pass down one of these from ship to quay? He thought not. Physically it might be possible, but there were two serious difficulties in the way. These ropes were at the bow and stern where passengers were prohibited, and with the loading of the cargo fore and aft anyone going towards them would certainly be challenged. The second difficulty was still greater. There were a number of people about the wharf, as well as aboard the steamers berthing above and below the *Ulster Sovereign*. It would be strange indeed if an attempt to pass down the rope should not be seen. And if Ferris tried it and were seen, his guilt of the murder would be established. Passage along the mooring ropes need not be considered.

Secondly, there was the river itself. Could Ferris have dropped into the river and have swum ashore? When French looked down the towering side of the ship he felt it would be utterly impossible. A man would want a rope to slip down, else he would make such a splash that he would be heard. Besides even if he reached the water in safety, French did not believe he could ever get out. A boat was out of the question; no boatman could have been trusted with such knowledge. And there was no place along the wharf nearby where he could have landed. Besides, if he were dripping wet he could not have regained his car unobserved. No, jumping into the water was equally out of the question.

There remained the third method; by means of one of the gangways from the fore and aft well decks used by the freight porters. But here observation was just as keen and complete as at the passenger gangways. No unauthorised person would be allowed to cross unchallenged.

French stood with M'Clung at the rail looking down into the gaping cavern of the after hold. Cargo was coming aboard and he watched it automatically while puzzling his brains over his problem. Boxes and bales, roped together in slings, were swinging in from circling derricks and being raised and lowered to the whine of the electric winches. Men below were storing, men ashore bringing forward, men on deck level operating the winches and passing to and fro on various jobs. It would have been quite impossible for Ferris to have gone ashore here unobserved.

But would it? Suddenly a fresh idea shot into French's mind and he stood rigid, thinking it over. Yes, he believed there was a way in which it might have been managed. Given any kind of reasonable luck, he felt increasingly certain it could have been done. Excitement began to grow in his mind. If this new idea were correct, and if he could prove it, the case would be well on to completion.

'Look here, M'Clung,' he said; 'see this ladder? It reaches down from here to the well deck below. What's to prevent you or me or Ferris or anyone else from climbing down and walking ashore over those planks?'

M'Clung grinned. 'If you really want to know, sir, I'll try it and then you'll see.'

'You think you'd be stopped?'

'I'm certain sure.'

'Well, so am I—if you went down looking as you do now. But suppose,' French glanced round and sank his voice, 'suppose you were to leave off those clothes and put on a sailor's or a steward's or a greaser's? What about it then?'

M'Clung looked at French with an expression which turned rapidly from surprise to admiration. 'By the hokey, Mr French, I believe you're on to it this time and no mistake. Ferris could have got the clothes and changed in his cabin. He'd have had to carry a bundle of Platt's clothes that he'd worn coming aboard, but that wouldn't have mattered. He could have covered them with his overcoat while passing through the alleyways, and on deck—perhaps behind a boat—have taken off the coat and have put it in the parcel with the clothes. Yes, sir, I believe you've got it!'

A number of experiments soon demonstrated the

feasibility of French's suggestion. Six tests on different ships with different stevedores showed that passengers in their ordinary clothes were instantly stopped when they attempted to use the cargo gangways. But when these same persons were made up as greasers they were allowed to pass unchallenged. Indeed, in four cases out of the six it turned out that they had gone ashore entirely unnoticed.

At a conference at police headquarters, at which French was present through a hearty invitation from Rainey—whose lumbago was better—it was agreed that on general grounds the theory of the guilt of Ferris and M'Morris was at least as likely as that of Penrose; that from the point of view of character it was more likely; and that while there was no specific piece of evidence directly connecting Penrose with the crime, that of the pencil did definitely suggest the guilt of M'Morris. On the whole it followed that the new theory was the more likely of the two. It was therefore decided that the appeal must be put back for a day or two.

It was at this point that French suggested a simple test of the whole affair. 'It may not work,' he admitted. 'But if it doesn't, you're no worse off, whereas if it does, your entire case is proved,' and he went on to describe his idea.

Rainey was enthusiastic and as a result the test was made. James Thompson, the cabin steward of the *Ulster Sovereign*, was invited to police headquarters and placed behind a screen in M'Clung's room, a tiny hole enabling him to see what went on in the room while himself remaining invisible. At the same time Ferris was asked to call, on the pretence of a fresh point having cropped up about his evidence. Some half-dozen young men, as like Ferris as could be found, were also collected.

Thompson having been placed in position, the half-dozen other young men were brought in one by one, and prearranged mythical business was discussed with each. Then at last Ferris was called, while the police officers grew tense. But their anxiety was quickly removed. Thompson gave the required sign! It seemed that he had noticed—and forgotten—the curious length of Ferris's earlobes, and seeing them again recalled the man to his mind.

This evidence that Ferris had masqueraded as Platt on board the *Ulster Sovereign* was considered proof of the new theory, and Ferris was immediately arrested. M'Clung then went down to Hillsborough and brought in M'Morris. At the same time a hint was given to Jack and Pam to expect a happy end to the appeal.

Research on definite lines for definite ends was now possible and further information began rapidly to come in. Three facts in particular were learnt, which with the evidence already held made the conviction of the newly accused a foregone conclusion.

The first was that at some time in the comparatively recent past someone had entered or left M'Morris's bedroom by the window. The window gave on a balcony supported from the ground on moulded pillars. One of these pillars revealed numerous scrapes, such as could only have been caused by the shoes of a climbing man.

The second piece of evidence was more convincing, indeed it was this which finally clinched the case against the two men, leaving no doubt that the murder had been premeditated and carried out in cold blood with the object of preserving the expected fortune. When Ferris's safe was opened and the four sheets of chemical formulæ—the secret of the process—were examined, all four were found to bear Platt's fingerprints. How French congratulated himself that though he had not foreseen that anything could come of it, his devotion to routine had made him photograph the impressions he had found on Platt's ink bottle! Now there could no longer be any doubt of the theft and of the motive for the crime.

The third matter unearthed by M'Clung's researches was suggestive rather than in the nature of direct proof. On Ferris's key ring were two keys for which no use could be found. One was like a Yale doorkey, the other was smaller, that perhaps of a box or chest. A considerable search ensued, and was at last crowned with success. The large key was that of the entrance door of Messrs Currie & M'Master, the analytical chemists of Howard Street, the former employers of both men, and the small one that of a cupboard containing poisons and drugs not easily obtainable by the public. Before giving his keys up on leaving, Ferris had evidently taken the precaution to supply himself with duplicates, in the event of his requiring for his own purposes any of the firm's property.

An inquiry from the staff of the chemists revealed the further interesting fact that about the date of the murder some chloroform was missed. It was not a large quantity, and after an investigation by the heads of the department the conclusion was reached that a mistake had been made as to the quantity previously existing. Now, however, it became pretty obvious not only where it had gone, but also that French's suggestion as to the method of the murder was broadly correct.

After arrest Ferris still tried to brazen things out. But M'Morris went completely to pieces. As soon as he heard the evidence against him he broke down, confessed his part in the affair—which he said had been forced on him by Ferris—and offered to turn King's Evidence against his former friend; an offer which, it may be mentioned, was not accepted.

But he said enough, when added to what the authorities already knew, to enable a pretty complete history of the crime to be built up. The points thus established were as follows.

On the afternoon of the first day of Platt's inquiry, the Wednesday, Ferris happened to come suddenly into the room where the visitor was working. He observed that Platt was trying to see behind the pole piece screens by means of a tiny mirror fixed to a pencil. Ferris pretended to have noticed nothing, but the incident showed him Platt's character and what he and his friends might have to face. He therefore took the precaution of never again leaving Platt alone with the apparatus.

But he took, too, further precautions. That night he removed the screens from his pole pieces and inserted a tiny piece of hair between each screen and its base. Over the edges of the sheets of formulæ in his safe he laid a longer hair. These hairs would unfailingly indicate if either were tampered with.

The last precaution was of a grimmer kind. That night he and M'Morris discussed the situation and decided that under no circumstances would they allow Platt to rob them of the rewards of their work. They would do all they could to preserve their secret by fair means, but if Platt outwitted them there would be only one result—he would die. It was Ferris's keen brain that worked out the scheme to be adopted under these unhappy circumstances, a scheme which was to be put in operation on whatever night Platt proposed to leave Ireland.

After this, however, all seemed to go well and though the two men had made all necessary preparations, they were congratulating themselves that their dreadful plan would prove unnecessary. But on Saturday morning Ferris discovered that he had been duped. He woke that morning much later than usual, feeling sleepy and heavy and with a bad taste in his mouth. His suspicious mind instantly leaped to the idea of a drug, and when he considered the incidents of the previous night he felt sure that such had indeed been administered.

The party on returning from the fishing expedition to Carnalea had dined at the Penroses', after which he and M'Morris had driven Platt to his hotel. Platt had invited them in for a drink. They had not particularly wanted to go, but he had insisted on the ground that it was his last night. Now Ferris remembered that Platt had told the waiter to leave the drinks on the side table and had himself mixed them. To slip a drug into his, Ferris's, glass would have been child's play.

Directly this idea occurred to Ferris he hurried downstairs and removed the screens from his apparatus and opened his safe. It was as he had feared. All the tell-tale hairs had disappeared.

He saw at a glance what Platt had done. Seizing some opportunity—possibly on the first day when he was not being closely watched—he had doubtless snatched the key from the large lock of the front door and taken an impression. Having made a new key, he climbed on that Friday night out of his room at the hotel—it, like M'Morris's, gave on a balcony and as in M'Morris's case, shoe scrapes were afterwards found on one of the columns—entered the cottage knowing Ferris would be asleep, and removed the screens. Then he must have taken Ferris's keys from beneath his pillow and opened the safe, copying the formulæ. He replaced the keys and left all as he had found it—except the hairs.

It was later on that same Saturday morning that the conspirators learnt that Jack Penrose was crossing that night by Liverpool, a fact which bid fair to wreck the whole of their scheme. They immediately saw that at all costs Jack must be kept off the ship, if possible altogether, but in any case till Ferris had completed his impersonation. Here again it was Ferris's keen brain which evolved the means. He would go as early as possible to the *Ulster Sovereign*, and by puncturing a wheel of Jack's car would keep him late. Thus he himself would have left the boat before Jack arrived—if Jack did arrive—whether Jack changed the wheel or ordered a taxi. The puncturing was done by M'Morris who slipped up to the Penroses' garage while the family was at dinner.

The actual murder was accomplished almost exactly as French had suspected. On leaving the hotel, ostensibly for the steamer, they had driven to the cottage, Platt being told that Ferris had forgotten some letters for the post. In the car Platt was rendered insensible. A chloroform pad was applied by M'Morris from behind, while Ferris held the man's arms. The chloroform had been obtained as a precautionary measure from Messrs Currie & M'Master's laboratory in the middle of the Thursday night.

When Platt's pockets were searched, the copy of the formulæ was found. Ferris had been certain that he would not have posted this vital paper to his confederate, lest the confederate, having obtained the secret, should refuse to pay for it. Having kept his knowledge to himself, Platt's murder would adequately safeguard the party.

The insensible man was drowned in the cottage, the impersonation on the *Ulster Sovereign* was carried out, and the body was disposed of, all as French had guessed. Ferris saw that for his own sake he must deny the theft, so as to avoid the suggestion that he had a motive for the murder. He was tempted to back up the suggestion of suicide by saying that Platt had been deeply depressed during the drive to the boat, but he saw that if he were contradicted by the hotel staff this might become suspicious. He thought in fact it would be safer to pretend that the affair was a mystery to him, than to try to explain it.

The conspirators' second shock came when Pam mentioned the pencil. M'Morris remembered clearly that Pam had seen it on the floor on the Saturday morning, as she had remarked to him on it. He believed that it would only be a question of time till she remembered the episode, when a question would immediately arise which might lead to their undoing. So upset had M'Morris been that he had at first thought of murdering Pam. Then the idea of replacing the pencil had occurred to him.

At the subsequent assizes both Ferris and M'Morris were found guilty. Before the end both men confessed their guilt, swearing that if Jack's appeal had failed, they would have told the truth.

Then one wholly unexpected and disconcerting fact came to light. When Ferris's formulæ was at last examined by Jefferson's technical staff, it was found to be incomplete. Ferris had held back one essential and the sustained and almost frenzied work of all concerned failed to reveal it.

This, whatever it was, had died with the inventor, and the so-called process was now absolutely valueless. Whether this was Ferris's final revenge on society, or whether—as a good many people now began to think—there never had been any process, and the whole thing was a clever fraud designed to be sold for cash, no one ever knew. Pam, at first intensely disappointed, soon grew reconciled to the loss, particularly as in her heart of hearts she believed real happiness was more likely to be achieved in comparatively humble circumstances.

M'Clung, instead of being censured for his *volte-face*, was highly complimented on what he had done, and when sheepishly he muttered that only for French he would never have discovered his mistake, a letter of warm thanks was sent to French.

French later had another visit at the Yard from Pam, this time with Jack in attendance, and he had to admit to himself that the sight of their happiness fully recompensed him for all the trouble he had taken. He had frequently been assured that virtue was its own reward, but this was the first time he had thought the arrangement equitable.

By the same author

Inspector French's Greatest Case

At the offices of the Hatton Garden diamond merchant *Duke & Peabody*, the body of old Mr Gething is discovered beside a now-empty safe. With multiple suspects, the robbery and murder is clearly the work of a master criminal, and requires a master detective to solve it. Meticulous as ever, Inspector Joseph French of Scotland Yard embarks on an investigation that takes him from the streets of London to Holland, France and Spain, and finally to a ship bound for South America . . .

'Because he is so austerely realistic, Freeman Wills Croft is deservedly a first favourite with all who want a real puzzle.'
                                        TIMES LITERARY SUPPLEMENT

By the same author

Inspector French and the Cheyne Mystery

When young Maxwell Cheyne discovers that a series of mishaps are the result of unwelcome attention from a dangerous gang of criminals, he teams up with a young woman who is determined to help him outwit them. But when she disappears, he finally decides to go to Scotland Yard for help. Concerned by the developing situation, Inspector Joseph French takes charge of the investigation and applies his trademark methods to track down the kidnappers and thwart their intentions . . .

'*Freeman Wills Crofts is among the few muscular writers of detective fiction. He has never let me down.*'
DAILY EXPRESS